SHADOWLIGHT

With an Introduction by Colin Wilson

Shadowlight is a vast and thoughtful reverie on the life of the little-known German Expressionist poet, Gottfried Benn. An army doctor in Brussels during the First World War, Benn was responsible for treating a syphilis epidemic amongst both soldiers and prostitutes, the occupiers and the occupied. Daily contact with the ravages of war and disease and an over-familiarity with death caused Benn to despair, resulting in a profound cynicism, to which he gave voice in an outburst of Expressionist writings.

Benn's experiences made him a solitary and often indifferent man whose personal life was as cold and unrelenting as the times. In vivid contrast come moments of understanding in *Shadowlight*, of identification – at the execution of the nurse Edith Cavell in 1915, with a prostitute in inter-war Berlin and with his estranged daughter in Hamburg in 1936.

In Brussels Benn wrote his most realistic and moral work, *Home Front*, a short play dealing with a corrupt military govern-ment. Seen as a protest against war it made him popular with Berlin liberals. But when, in 1933, Klaus Mann wrote to Benn begging him to declare his position *vis-à-vis* the Nazis, Benn replied, "What is here at stake is not forms of government but a new vision of the birth of man – perhaps an old, perhaps the last grand concept of the white race, probably one of the grandest realisations of the cosmic spirit itself . . . I personally declare for the new state, because it is my people whose trail is being blazed here. Who am I to exclude myself?" Goebbels published this letter widely and Benn was thereafter counted amongst the leading Nazi literati.

But Benn was soon to become disenchanted with Nazism and in 1936 he himself became a victim of Nazi persecution,

after his early "immoral" work was discovered. He was denounced and his writing banned.

During the Second World War he wrote secretly, completely disillusioned with the regime and the people he had defended so passionately, while continuing as a military doctor.

Two volumes of Benn's poetry and three of his prose were published in 1949. For the next six years, until his death, he ranked with the most prolific, and most controversial German writers. The de-nazification of Germany began but Benn's status was always unclear. However his writings struck great chords of sympathy with thousands of readers. *Double Life*, his political autobiography published in 1950, in which he defended his error, spoke for many Germans, the double life was his and theirs.

Though he had vowed never again to make personal appearances, by 1951 Benn was back on university platforms, giving lectures, receiving prizes, being fêted at conferences.

Shadowlight is a magnificent exploration of the question of conscience, loyalty, duty, friendship and love in time of war.

Pierre Mertens was born in Brussels in 1939. Having travelled extensively he now lives and teaches in Brussels. He has written several novels and collections of short stories and Shadowlight *is the first to be translated into English. It won the Prix Médicis in 1987, and in 1996 Mertens won the Prix Jean Monnet de littérature européenne for* Une paix royale.

SHADOWLIGHT

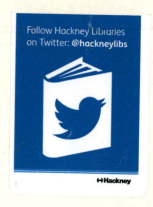

SHADOWLIGHT

Pierre Mertens

Translated by Edmund Jephcott

PETER HALBAN
LONDON

FIRST PUBLISHED IN GREAT BRITAIN BY
PETER HALBAN PUBLISHERS LTD
42 South Molton Street
London W1Y 1HB
1997

British Library Cataloguing-in-Publication Data

A catalogue record for this book is available from the British Library.

ISBN 1 870015 50 9
Copyright © Editions du Seuil, 1987
First published under the title Les éblouissements
Translation copyright © Edmund Jephcott, 1997

Pierre Mertens and Edmund Jephcott have asserted their rights
under the Copyright, Designs and Patents Acts, 1988 to be identified
as the author and translator respectively of this work.

The Publishers gratefully acknowledge permission from
Faber & Faber, Ltd. to quote from *The Waste Land* by T. S. Eliot
and from DACS for the cover illustration An die Schonheit by Otto Dix
(1922), Von der Heydt-Museum, Wuppertal. © DACS 1997.

Cover design by Hilary Turner

Typeset by Computape (Pickering) Ltd, North Yorkshire
Printed in Great Britain by
WBC Print, Bridgend

Acknowledgements

This book is based on a number of episodes in the life of Gottfried Benn as described by his German or French biographers and in his correspondence with his family and friends.

But only the novelist's imagination is responsible for the essential meaning of the book. It is a reverie circling around a particular destiny. Intuitions and hypotheses. A "controlled skid" of the kind all fiction is entitled to.

Quotations from the works of Gottfried Benn that appear in this novel are always indicated by quotation marks. They are taken where possible from existing translations, or have been rendered from the German by the translator.

The same has been done with quotations from Else Lasker–Schüler.

I wish to thank all those who have allowed me to finish this exploration.

My particular gratitude is due to the Deutscher Akademischer Austauschdienst which invited me to spend a year in Berlin, so permitting me to complete a task which rendered such a stay indispensable. I shall not forget the welcome I received from the representative of the Berliner Künstlerprogramm, Joachim Sartorius.

More especially, I am also indebted to: Ilse Kaul, the poet's last companion, and Nele Soerensen, his daughter, whose confidences were precious to me; Professor Michael Nerlich (and his wife Évelyne Sinnassamy) who allowed me to conduct a writing workshop at the Technische Universität from which Benn was never absent; to Barbara Schild and Françoise Wuilmart, whose translations of unpublished texts

Acknowledgements

into French sent us in new directions; to Dr Paul Chailly and Professors Georges Achten and Antoine Dhem, who guided us through the sometimes tortuous maze of legal medicine and venereology.

Introduction

This remarkable *tour de force* belongs to the same tradition as Joyce's *Ulysses*, Musil's *Man Without Qualities* and Broch's *Death of Virgil*. It is a vast reverie – the author's own description – on the life of the disturbing German poet Gottfried Benn. And since most English readers know little or nothing about Benn, it is clearly the duty of the writer of this introduction to provide them with the basic information which will enable them to understand what Pierre Mertens is trying to accomplish.

Benn, who died in 1956, is still regarded by many as a Nazi, although his poem "Monologue" (in which Nazis are described as "coxcombs of a clown"), and half a dozen anti-Hitler poems, make that claim absurd. Like the French novelist Céline (another "authoritarian nihilist"), he was a doctor, and his work has a certain grim and ironic quality that is the result of spending a life among corpses.

> "Fragments.
> Refuse of the soul,
> Coagulations of blood of the twentieth century."

But Céline is uniformly savage, while Benn is full of flashes of beauty, *"verwandelbare Wolken eines Glucks"* (which Michael Hamburger translates "mutable clouds of a happiness"). Like all true poets, he transcends his own philosophy of pessimism. This explains his fame in post-Second World War Germany. And this is the paradox that Mertens attempts to capture in this powerful novel.

Benn was born in a country parsonage not far from Berlin in 1886, and in his autobiography *Double Life*, he describes the simple country childhood where he spent much of the year barefoot, and mixed just as happily with peasant lads as with children of the nobility – the kind of background that formed the basis of his brief flirtation with Nazism. In deference to his father he studied theology for two years before entering a military academy to become an army surgeon, and served with a regiment that had won renown during the Franco-Prussian war, in which Nietzsche had also served as a medical orderly.

Nietzsche had also been sickened by the sight of mutilated corpses, but had experienced a strange revelation one evening as his old cavalry regiment rode past him. As he saw these men, "riding to battle, perhaps to death", he experienced a surge of sheer exultation that led him to write: "The will to war is greater than the will to peace." But Benn experienced no such revelation, and his first half-dozen poems, written in the course of a single hour in 1912, are all grim and nauseating observations of the dead in the morgue – for example, of a girl found dead among the reeds, and in whose diaphragm cavity Benn discovered a nest of young rats.

In the same year, Benn left the army, and during the next two years worked "freelance" as a pathologist and a ship's doctor in the Mediterranean. His work, with its grim naturalism, became fashionable among the Berlin literati. Then, in 1914, he went back into the army and entered Belgium with the occupying German forces; he became director of an army jail and – as a specialist in venereal diseases – was in charge of Brussels' prostitutes. And the bizarre, Céline-like quality of his life there produced an outburst of expressionistic work that seemed to celebrate the disintegration of the human personality and of human values. A play called *Home Front* portrays the army with annihilistic bitterness reminiscent of Buchner's *Woyzeck*.

It was unlikely that such a man could ever make a recovery from despair; Benn never did – but at least, he produced some magnificent poetry out of his nihilism. Moreover, some of the rhymed poems of the twenties – his earlier poems had been in "free verse" – are as exquisite as some of the great romantic poems of the nineteenth century.

But nihilism made him cruel. His first wife had died after an operation in 1922; his daughter was handed over to foster-parents. An actress with whom he lived threw herself out of a window. Benn told the wife of the composer Hindemith, "Never forget that the human mind originated as a killer." Yet his savagery was seen as a protest against war and bureaucracy, and he became something of a darling of the Berlin liberals, who wrongly assumed that he must be a Leftist.

Their mistake became apparent only in 1933, after Hitler had come to power. Benn had failed to resign from the Prussian Academy of Arts, thus lending tacit support to the Nazis, and Thomas Mann's son Klaus – who was later to commit suicide – wrote to Benn as "an ardent and faithful admirer", asking him to make his position clear. Benn did so in a letter "to the literary emigrants" that is usually cited as Exhibit A in literary indictments of Benn. What he said, very forcefully, was that he did not share Mann's view that Nazism was barbarism. It is quickly made clear that Benn disliked liberals as much as he disliked Communists, and that he did not regard Nationalism as a dirty word. He speaks of the "great movements of history", and evokes the rise of Gothic architecture in the twelfth century. "Do you think that was *discussed*" – the implication being that Mann and his liberal friends are all windbags. Does Mann not realise, he asks, that what is happening in Germany is "the emergence of a new biological type, a mutation of history a people's wish to breed itself". He compares Napoleon and Hitler, "two great minds". Napoleon was the individual genius whose will drove his armies to conquer Europe. But Hitler is a "magical coincidence of individual and generality", one of the "great men of the world's historic course". For the basic problem is to "breed a stronger race".

Dr Goebbels was understandably delighted with Benn's

"open letter" and made sure that it was widely published in the German press. It looked as if Benn had landed himself a comfortable position as one of the leading Nazi literati. Indeed, he became "Acting Leader" of the poetry section of the Academy, wrote essays on the "people", and achieved a Kipling-like popularity with a poem called *"Dennoch die Schwerter halten"* – "to hold the swords in spite of ...", which has something in common with Pound's "Sestina: Altaforte" with its refrain: "I have no life save when the swords clash." It is, in fact, a kind of mystical Nietzscheanism rather than Nazism, but the two admittedly are easily confused.

This official approval was not to last. By 1934 Benn was likening Nazism to an amateur theatre that keeps on announcing *Faust* when its actors are only capable of "Hussar Fever". Like Spengler, he had recognised that Hitler was a *"Heldentenor"* – the heroic tenor who plays the lead in operas – rather than a *"Helden"* (hero). Benn was an intellectual aristocrat, and he was revolted by the stupidity and boorishness of the Nazi élite. And as those views leaked out, Benn suddenly became *non grata* with the Nazis. His Berlin job application was turned down and he moved to Hanover – the equivalent of banishment to the provinces.

The Nazis went on to denounce his earlier work as filthy and immoral. That might seem unfair, but there is more than an element of truth in it. Benn *was* an "immoralist", a nihilist, a prophet of disintegration, and the Communists were right to acknowledge him as a fellow spirit. The Nazis hoped for a magnificent, Wagnerian future, and for a short time Benn hoped with them. But he obviously had no active role to play in such a future. In 1938, his writings were banned by the Nazis.

Then came the war, and it was back into the army. Ironically, it was in Landsberg – where Hitler had written *Mein Kampf* – that he experienced one of the happiest periods of his life, living with a young wife who had succeeded in becoming an army typist, and writing at leisure.

The war ended; Benn sent his wife to a remote village while he stayed in Berlin and worked for the Red Army, who were indifferent to his politics. He sent a maid to collect his wife, but the girl was intercepted by the Russians and raped. His wife committed suicide before he saw her again.

When the Allies came to Berlin, there was talk of "denazifying" Benn, but he seemed to have no desire to be rehabilitated. If he had died at this time, his life would seem an anti-climactic failure, like Céline's. Fortunately, he was to live for another decade, and to achieve the kind of fame that, under different circumstances, might have led to a Nobel Prize. He married again; his works were translated into many foreign languages, and – as we discover at the beginning of this novel – he was asked to play the lion at literary conferences. His autobiography *Double Life*, a kind of apology for his flirtation with Nazism, became a bestseller in Germany, for millions of people had shared the idealism that had dazzled him in 1933. When he died, at the age of 70, the controversies "faded in the solemn chorus of eulogies" – as E. B. Ashton expressed it in his Introduction to the British edition of Benn's selected writings. This volume, *Primal Vision* (1961) was my own introduction to the work of Gottfried Benn, and the present introduction is heavily indebted to Ashton's fine essay. My own fascination with Benn enables me to understand the obsession that led Pierre Mertens to try to capture the paradoxes of his amazing life in *Shadowlight*. Mertens has soaked himself in German culture, and it is undoubtedly necessary to be German to fully appreciate the combination of erudition and artistic subtlety that characterise this novel. But it is possible for us all to understand the early "morgue" nihilism, the anti-sentimentalism that led him to initially sympathise with the Nazis and the sheer irony of his later recognition of the magnitude of his error. *Shadowlight* is not an easy novel to read, but those who become absorbed in it, as I did, will find themselves sharing Mertens' "magnificent obsession".

Colin Wilson

By this, and this only, we have existed
Which is not to be found in our obituaries.

T. S. Eliot, *The Waste Land*

To the children of those who have erred

Knokke-Le Zoute,
Belgium, 1952

The Sea

Prologue to a dénouement

After a war. An end of season. A restored casino at the seaside. An international reunion of poets.

Among them, the German poet. Very German.

Something is lacking. Something has yet to happen.

But what?

The German poet's death, perhaps?

"We must resign ourselves, and from time to time look at the sea ... "

These words, which conclude one of his last prose pieces, come into his mind as he leaves the festival hall.

As if Dr Benn were in a hurry to take refuge in words, his own words. Once again, he is more or less pleased and displeased with himself. Yet he has given his hosts in Knokke-Le Zoute, this Friday, 12 September 1952, the same talk that he has been repeating, with slight nuances and variations, for the last forty years.

"It is not intellectual movements that interest me ... or even the art of poetry. It is the poem alone, which a lyric 'I' insists on producing." Such is the position he has taken up, while on the same rostrum a Belgian minister of education, a popular poet from Africa and a South American man of letters have expressed their faith in universal culture. "I am in a difficult position," he began by saying. But his audience may have misunderstood the reason for the difficulty. Of course, it was partly because he had to speak French, when he had expected to use his own tongue. I must be the only exotic trouvère in this place, he thought. The Moroccan and the Senegalese, even the Ecuadorian and the little Japanese lady, are all fluent in the language of Victor Hugo. Even when seeking the French for his cautionary opening remark: *Ich befinde mich in einer schwierigen Lage*, which was far from improvised, he had conveyed his perplexity to the interpreter. Was it better to say: "I am in a difficult position", or "I find myself in a delicate situation"? Who, among the unknown audience whose looks he paused a moment to decipher – looks that express sometimes

3

curiosity and often indifference – could be aware that his discomfort came from further off, from deep within himself? Just as it was in Brussels, he thought. Brussels in 1915, when I was a medical officer. Alone in the heart of a foreign city, where, to make things worse, I represented the invader. All the same, I was sometimes inexplicably happy there. Even the hostility on the faces I met in the street could take nothing from the joy of being outside my own life, where I could better attend to the words that expressed my alienation, my absence ... Today in Knokke, where I am treated as a friend, where people look at me well-meaningly or just blankly, what message can I convey that will not seem disappointing?

The German poet then set about explaining his lack of a moral mission, why he felt no more called upon to improve mankind than to endorse the high aspirations of youth. "The lyric 'I' wears no such wigs ... "

Without intending to, he might have appeared provocative. But he had not shrunk from offering his audience once again, barely warmed through, the same old dish he had been serving up since he went into poetry, not as one goes into religion, but as others have themselves committed to an asylum: to live out their madness, not to be cured of it. As if the age had not capsized in the meantime, as if the very nature of history had not changed. Two total wars had devastated the world, two wars in which he, to say the least, had been not a little implicated. Was there not something indecent in asserting that all these catastrophes had been survived by an "I" which expressed nothing but "plasticity, intoxication, exuberance, wit, *élan*" – even if that "I" addressed only the void from which it had been plucked, and expected nothing in return?

Such were the questions that occupied him as he stood in the blue-green light that filtered through the glass walls, seeming to hesitate before descending the monumental staircase. For he could see through the partly open doors of a gaming room black-suited men and elegant women from another age, bending over a roulette wheel and ivory dice. A rather bright idea, wasn't it, to organise an international festival of "half a century of poetry" in a casino? Poets of all countries, the war is over. Place your bets. No more bids.

On one of the façade walls, neither history nor the weather had quite been able to obliterate a poster advertising a long-past song recital by Richard Tauber; nor was it hidden by the one announcing a forthcoming appearance of Marlene Dietrich. Different times, different German voices. Though the flags of all the nations invited to the Poetry Biennale at Knokke-Le Zoute flapped in the wind above the peristyle, their rings tinkling against their poles in what might well be taken as a derisive welcome, a piece of quite planetary sarcasm, none of this could unduly trouble a bard born sixty-six years before on the plain of Westpriegnitz, and who, in his way, had taken fifty years of poetry upon himself – poetry which was not without a sarcasm of its own. Must we not ford that river of shade and brightness, in mourning for our transparency?

"What is there left for us to kneel before?" he asked.

Of course, he had taken the precaution of declaring, without false modesty, that he represented only himself. But that made no difference: had he not been given an implicit pledge, if not an order, by a whole generation? Necessarily implicit, being posthumous. They were all dead, the Trakls, Heyms, Stadlers, Werfels, Lasker-Schülers. Only he was left – he'd just have to be enough – to voice the rousing injunction bequeathed by Nietzsche on all those shades, the proclamation that art was the last metaphysical activity of which Europe would henceforth be capable. Over the smoking debris of the ideologies, straddling the decomposing corpse of Utopia, the spirit would dance alone, on its own account, like a star above an abyss. Intent only on weaving its own choreography. And probably none of this would affect the fate of the species, or yield a compensatory increase in soul. Such would be his weakness – and his greatness.

"What will you tell them, then?" his wife had asked, the day he left for the Belgian shore. "I'll save it as a surprise for myself," he answered, indulging in one of those sallies he was fond of, since they always contained a secret truth. And he was not entirely insincere in hoping to switch his talk at the last minute for one that would take him by surprise. But was he not condemned to repeat himself?

What would he have thought at that time, this German poet of the leaden years, if he could have foreseen that twenty or thirty years after his death some young thinkers who probably had not even read him, or would have disowned him outright if they had, were to make his unbelieving word their own. That was a surprise he was not to save up for himself – it would fall to his unwitting heirs. So it is with the glory, and the disfavour, of this world.

For the present, Gottfried Benn was not thinking about posterity – he had trouble enough getting back to his hotel while the wind sweeping over the embankment assailed his corpulent person.

> *Frisch weht der Wind*
> *Der Heimat zu.*
> *Mein irisch Kind,*
> *Wo weilest du?*

These lines from *Tristan* – which modern poet had quoted them? he wondered. Which poet of his generation? My generation ... My generation ... I talk about it so glibly. When am I going to let the dead bury their dead, now they are no longer there to answer me, to refute me, perhaps? Peace to their mingled ashes. How much longer am I to preen myself as the sole, miraculous survivor amongst countless shipwrecked? Perhaps even their gravedigger ... Someone had to hold the necrological torch. Georg Heym, drowned in 1912 for contemplating himself in the mirror of a frozen pond. Dead, most of all, for having sensed the coming cataclysm, for having foretold in a few imperishable lines the nightmare that was descending on the world. Georg Trakl, dead two years later at Cracow, for trying to draw a curtain of cocaine between himself and "the broken eyes, the black mouths" of the soldiers who had died beside him at the dawn of the war. The same year, 1914, Ernst Stadler blown to pieces here, on Flemish soil, by an English shell – Stadler who had made his own the motto of Angelus Silesius: "O man, become essential". Another prophet: "To the sea, to the shipwreck," he had written. Then August Stramm, killed in 1915 on the Russian front. In 1918 Wedekind disappeared, having had little time to savour the peace. Then it was Klabund's turn, obliterated at Davos in 1928 by the illness that the hero of the *Magic Mountain* had escaped in the same place. Funeral oration by the master of ceremonies, Gottfried Benn.

> "How scanty, alas,
> are the full heart's beats."

Soon afterwards, the death of Stefan George, rejected by those Germans who owed him most. (Another homage by Gottfried Benn – now a graduate in obsequies – was planned, but prevented at the last moment by the Nazis.)

Then came another war which rendered these crepuscular stylistic exercises redundant for a time, even when someone died a natural death. In 1942, for example, Carl Sternheim disappeared in Brussels, the very town where Gottfried Benn had met him in 1914, a war earlier. The final house-moving for a man who had never stopped changing his residence, the length and breadth of Europe, as one changes one's clothes, because one does not feel comfortable in any of them. He believed in nuances at a time when they had been outlawed. And he had struck a blow against metaphor in a world possessed by the demon of analogy for fear of looking truth in the face. He believed courage a private virtue. He was thought to be subject to fits of madness. The same was said of Else Lasker-Schüler, whose life ended in penury in 1945, on Palestinian soil. (After fleeing the regime to which Gottfried Benn, her ex-

and ephemeral lover, had proclaimed his brief but compromising allegiance.) May the peace of evening descend upon the Mount of Olives.

But sometimes the war struck from a distance, or after a delay. In 1942, the suicide of Stefan Zweig, orphaned of all the values in which he had believed. In 1948, the suicide of Klaus Mann, a victim of the same malady.

Dr Benn shivered. He stopped in his tracks. He was offering too much purchase to the wind. But one cannot always walk sideways on. He thought it time to close this family album with its bronze-heavy cover. He might as well hang it round his neck, to sink the better on Judgement Day. He had surely forgotten some of them on the way, those contemporaries of his who had made Germany, and whom Germany had unmade. No more orations for any of them. No poetry biennale for Miss Lasker-Schüler ... My generation – my generation, mumbled Gottfried Benn. Happy are those who have one. Happy and unhappy are those who survive it. But courage to him who now rides on the shoulders of the dead, now carries them on his. He would not drink their blood to the lees. He would be content to present the following statistics: two-thirds of the German poets he had loved – or betrayed – had died in the two wars. Two-thirds of these two-thirds had been killed in the First World War. And of these two-thirds, two-thirds again had already stopped living in 1914. So that the "half-century of poetry" that he had to report on here had been more than half consumed by 1915 ... That was how he would have to put it. With that prickly crudity. In any case, didn't the poems by him that had been translated for the occasion date from 1910, 1912 at the latest?

I must be, in every sense, untranslatable, he thought. And who really reads me in my own country? All the same, just as you talk to no one when you address everyone, you can speak a universal language when you share it with no more than thirty people in the entire world ...

In the name of everyone he has said almost nothing. But in a sense he has indeed talked of everyone ... In his own name he has told the truth, and also lied. By omission. For the past forty years has embodied all the contradictions of his time, his country. Why he? Why did they elect him, why did he choose himself? A prophet gone astray. A disowned renegade. A blinded visionary. All this is so heavy to bear, for so long – although one has hardly told anyone anything; one hardly confides even in those who are closest. He is enmeshed in a tangle of paradoxes. One moment he wants to run away, the next to take full responsibility. He has never succeeded in doing entirely one or entirely the other. A squall constricts his heart. He suffocates. He turns to left and right as if calling for help. On one side, the tenebrous, fuliginous horizon under the grandiose turbulence of the clouds. On the other, bouquets of marram grass, buckthorn, blue thistles caked in dust on top of grey dunes, between the hotels Thalassa, Stella Maris and Isola Bella, the villas Mon Rêve, Ça m'suffit, or Nitchevo ... Further on, it looks as if the sea itself has sculpted the façades of these empty palaces, so that they resemble old steamers stranded on the esplanade. Keep going. It's nothing. He should have armed himself with a cane to fence with the wind. He'll do without. He'll walk on along the sea front white with rain, harassed by gannets with their pale cries, gulls with their witches' laughter. It would be wrong to make too much of it: he has merely given a routine lecture, at the end of the summer of '52, in a small seaside town which announces a last beach competition, organised by a chocolate firm, and a campaign for the prevention of infantile paralysis. In the avenues leading off the promenade slumber villas with would-be English names: Victory, Gaby, New Style. There is not one aircraft deep in the sky that does not hum a peaceful tune – an end of season. Peace is a resort out of season. This lecture that causes him a lingering regret – he surely isn't going to rewrite it here, facing the sea? (Will he not add a codicil to this testament?) It was probably as good as the Senegalese poet's, or the Ecuadorian's. Don't poets have to find some pretext for their meetings, if in fact they need to meet? So they give talks, bad talks, which are the opposite of poetry. That's how the game is played. It even cements their solidarity. This evening they will go together by coach to see a *son et lumière* display at Bruges-la-morte, like children on a school outing. Bruges from which one day, miraculously, the sea receded ...

Once the poets had gone home, back to their respective countries, the casino, lit by a seven-ton chandelier created in Murano, would advertise *Violettes impériales* with Rudi Iri-goyen, a recital by the Étienne sisters and, soon, *Tovaritch*, as part of the Christmas festivities. When summer came, a beauty queen would be chosen here. And in September 1953, no poets would return, as they were offered a platform only every other year. Meanwhile, what had he, Gottfried Benn, to complain about? Hadn't he been introduced this morning as the equal of Valéry, Lorca, Mayakovsky? As the heir of Rilke?

Rilke ... He too had written lines on those who leave us too early. And then, one day, he had said: "Who talks of victory? To endure is all." However, it sometimes seemed to his "heir" that the poetry of the man with an androgynous first name had grown somehow flaccid in apostrophising "his Lord" again and again – while at the same time reverting to rhyme ... Whereas God is so much present – if negatively – in the poem that he no longer needs to be invoked.

> *Frisch weht der Wind*
> *Der Heimat zu.*
> *Mein irisch Kind*
> *wo weilest du?*

the walker muttered again. It was Eliot, he remembered. Eliot, in *The Waste Land*, had quoted the German lines. These, and also: *Öd' und leer das Meer*. They were the words of the look-out announcing to Tristan that no sail was in sight, that the sea was empty.

He stops, once again. He is feeling better. As he does every time some lines by another poet have passed through him, like an electric current with a resistance he can verify. As he does each time a poet attaches lines from yesterday to those inspired by his today. Eliot had quoted *Tristan*, and then had said: "I had not thought death had undone so many." And then: "These fragments I have shored against my ruins."

Those who proclaim the immortality of poetry aloud, in their official speeches, should be more careful of what they say: it has been expiring for the last two thousand years. Those who speak of men passing the torch of the word to each other should think again: they are addressing pyromaniacs who have put to the torch the ancestral wooden party talk. That pungent scent of eternity their activity gives off was really a smell of burning ... He, Gottfried Benn, was born in May 1886, at the very moment Rimbaud's *Illuminations* came out. How was he not to believe, without shame or misplaced pride, that a baton had been passed?

Wasn't that the implicit conclusion to the abortive debate they had had that morning, at the casino?

But hadn't they taken some short cuts to arrive at this happy outcome so promptly?

His life had resembled nothing less than an "irresistible rise" – with good reason. But what did his audience know of the man they had invited to fête – not to judge? He came from far off, this prodigal old man. Was he therefore amnesic? It was rather that he had too much memory – too many contradictory memories – and no longer knew what use to make of them. This hadn't started just today. It was a curious malady that prevented him both from preparing his own defence and from really hoping for an amnesty from others. He was like someone coming out of a nightmare who does not know which world to wake into, having far too many to choose from.

In his timetable there was a gap, in which almost twenty years had vanished like a single hour – but an hour that could not be annulled by the lapse of time. Now, this autumn day in 1952, beside the sea, he could still hear its echo like the murmur in a shell. He should perhaps have been thankful that his past had been veiled in courteous silence. Curiously, he was not a man to be wholly glad of that. Of course, he would not have liked it any better if the past had been mentioned. But it was only when no one asked him for an explanation that he felt called upon to produce one, however slight it might be. One can get over anything except – try as one may – the mutilation of one's destiny. He had simply gone in search of a habitable form, to wed it with words, make it his couch. He abominated History: the only time he had thought he could attach himself to its movement it had closed on him like a trap. The time it took to get out of it – and to expiate – he had spent trying to comprehend the hidden face of what had happened to him. He had hardly talked about it, even to intimate friends. All that mattered to him was the secret meaning of his going astray, and that interested only him: the obscure chain of causes and effects, the accidental or necessary conjunction of circumstances, the play of forces, the particular collection of states of the soul that fell prey to the state of the world. The storm had passed. The tempest of Expression had moved away. The bloody curtain of History had fallen again. What sound and fury. Blackness and terror. Night and horror. And error. Compared to what really happened, he thought, our youthful salvoes were fired at cobwebs. We were crying wolf in a fog. We did not know that dawn would rise purple on a desert where the mind could only move in a state of hallucination. We opened our eyes as stupefied children who have set light to the mansion while playing with matches.

Fifteen years of silence, of shadowlife. And then, in his own country, his words began to circulate again. A young generation which wanted to call forth a new Germany, purified by her losses, discovered in him not a photograph of what had happened but something like its negative. His fame crossed borders. Here he was, being invited to the very country to which he had first come, four decades earlier, in the uniform of the occupying empire ... And now he was being compared to Saint-John Perse, Pasternak, Ezra Pound. To what did he owe this forbearance, when he had not even had to lodge a plea for pardon? He imagined himself a spy who had infiltrated the ranks of those who had once put a price on his head. Wasn't it all for the best? he wondered. It was not without irony. Nor without melancholy. And that arose not only from the ambiguous mixture of euphoria and vexation that always came over him when he talked of his work. *Post verbum animal triste.*

He raised his head and turned towards the sea.

The fishing boats bobbing on the horizon, pursued by a swarm of gulls brilliantly lit by a momentary break in the clouds: it all seemed as magnificently improbable as the Amazons trotting heraldic animals along the water's edge. Suddenly, the walker found himself perusing images of an absolved, an exorcised world. After all, it was the last week of summer, 1952: a new war had broken out, but it was in the Far East, while yesterday's alliances broke and the strategists' chessboard was overturned, one craze always chasing the last from the memories of men. The beach at Knokke could not be blamed for failing to hold up a mirror to that. In this part of the world husbands and fathers no longer went to the front, they had just gone into town to keep track of their businesses. Only women and children were left on the shore. A few men too, here and there; but they were only fishermen, or poets ...

The German poet might have been cheered by this, or at least moved. But repentance is a flighty muse who picks her hour and can take you by surprise. Suddenly, the representative of German lyric poetry at Knokke felt wounds, suspicions reawakening. He was in danger of leaving here less innocent than he came. So he expected nothing more of life than to be purged of whatever it was that ailed him. He would finish his journey still unripe. In the end, he thought, I have shown just a single virtue: I have lasted.

At last, he is back at the hotel. He leaves a message at reception for his friend Walter Lennig. Would he call for him early in the afternoon? The poet will go without lunch. The emotions of the morning – a sort of voluptuous regret – have cost him his appetite. As he goes up to his room he indulges in his favourite pastime: if he were not now here, where would he be, what would he be doing somewhere else? For, since having realised that in a single life one can live at least two – even, or especially, if one does not want to – he has wondered about the ramifications of other lives that might have unfolded elsewhere.

In Berlin, in his consulting room on the Bozener Strasse, he would be getting ready for his afternoon patients: men and women humiliated by their malady, whose compassionate master he would be for an hour. Ilse, his wife, would come in at the end of the consultation to sit opposite him like an extra patient, one who had not made an appointment. But she would reverse the roles, questioning him on his state of health and handing out advice on how to spend the evening ... Or he might have left on the spur of the moment for Copenhagen, feeling a sudden irrepressible desire to see his daughter who has lived there for thirty years. But he might just as easily never have had a daughter, never even have married the woman who had given her to him at the dawn of the Great War, and left him a widower soon after ... So true was it that everything – absolutely everything – might have been different. Only the poems, he thought, would hardly have changed ... so strongly did it seem to him that in a quite different set of circumstances the same paraphrase of the world would have issued from his pen.

He had not stayed in Berlin with Ilse, he had not gone to Denmark to visit Nele, he had come to Knokke-Le Zoute, preceded by the notoriety of that handful of verses that no other biography would have exempted him from writing. That was what, in different words, he had tried to express that morning. That was what one never says, doubtless from modesty: for fear of revealing the monster each artist harbours within him. The monster that no contingency could distract from its few immutable snatches. But if he had not let it be heard, why had he made the trip? In Berlin or Copenhagen this silence about oneself, in oneself, would have been less heavy ...

He runs himself a bath. Not that this has been recommended to him. The excess of ablutions does him no good, in view of the eczema that has always covered his body. Water, to quench the burning, if only for an instant. But the fire rekindles, hotter still. He laughs, thinking: one metaphor to drown another, and excite it all the more. What good has it done me to become a dermatologist? Covered in this leprosy, isolated in my own leper colony. But doctors are notoriously incapable of curing themselves, just as philosophers' precepts do little to console them and priests are often bad at praying for themselves. And then, skin diseases only appear to be on the surface: they come from the depths, and go back there. Their scales contaminate those who make their own misfortune.

Naked, he is flayed. He has lost his hands, his feet, the top of his head: flames lick the ends of his arms, his legs, his cranium; his limbs consume themselves. He is caught in a burning bush, a bed of nettles. He cannot tell where the itching starts or stops, it's all one. What he wants to scratch is outside him. He'd like to scratch his shadow till it bleeds. He has the feeling that he is expiating something more than himself. (Hence the interest, which the allergy incites instead of abating it, that he has had since he was a young man, the taste for everything pertaining to the flesh. Is it even pity – this attention he pays to people's skin, to everything that impairs its grain, that chafes the bark of the human tree?)

You think of Marat. You like to imagine that the Jacobin inflicted his illness on himself to avoid having to absolve himself from being born. Then, only the knife of some magnanimous lover of justice could cure him. Did not Charlotte Corday stab the Friend of the People only to put an end to his suffering?

You have heard, moreover, that the man in the turban was not responsible for all the crimes which History, that character

assassin, has laid at his door. Only reformers have crimes
ascribed to them. It should be said that before shedding blood
he had practised illicitly as a healer. In the end, the charlatan
merely reverted to type. The bungler had himself soaked in
vinegar. He might as well have called a vet. You can't catch
flies with spirits of salt. For my part, thinks Dr Benn, I should
have treated him with Alibour water, or zinc oxide and
ichthyol. That always works ... He recalls that, in the painting
by David, the Jacobin Führer appeared to rest in peace, freed at
last. He died in battle, pen in hand. Such ardours: pathetic.
Such martyrdom: ludicrous.

But we know the scourge to be congenital. That's not its
least injustice: the fathers' sins are the skin irritations of the
children. The poet recalls that "eczema" was the first word his
daughter could utter. So each New Year's Day he sends Nele a
card with what seems a prosaic message: "Success in all you
undertake and, above all, no eczema." If this distant father were
able to pray, he would pray for that: that at least the pruritus he
suffers from may die with him.

He stands up in the bath. His body fumes. The bathroom
mirror is misted over. He picks up the blue towel emblazoned
with the arms of the Hôtel du Roi Albert. He decides not to
dress at once. To kill time, he reads the list of participants at the
Biennale. Alphabetic chance has decreed that *Allemagne* will
head the list, and that his name, with its *B*, will be the first to
be called ... Moreover, the Germans are there in force. Rudolf
Hagelstange, Hans-Egon Holthusen, Wilhelm Lehmann are
among them. And of course, Walter Lennig.

His gaze falls on the name of Alexander Lernet-Holenia,
who is representing Austria. He did not notice him in the hall
this morning. A year ago, the historian had called upon the
poet Benn to emerge from his Nietzschean solitude and renew
his dialogue with the German nation that past events had
interrupted. All who speak monologues are destined to fail, his
Austrian correspondent had warned. The addressee declined

the invitation. He would like to explain to this man that just because everything had chosen to shatter within him, it did not mean he had failed. That one might even attain a kind of goal at the end of, and at the cost of, a monologue without hope. But could one buttonhole someone to talk about that in the corridor of a casino, or at a closed reception at the Hôtel des Ambassadeurs?

Poets had come from all directions. From "Free Catalonia", now residing in Brussels or Indre-et-Loire. The Luxemburg delegate lived in Belgium and the Senegalese in Paris, rue de la Grande-Truanderie. One by the name of Bonaparte originated from Haiti. And a certain Bayle came from Morocco . . .

Most of the names were unknown to him. That is what war does: it separates you not so much from your enemies as from your friends. All the same, he knew that some of his contemporaries were still alive. Some were mentioned in a recent edition of *Merkur* sent to him by an admirer. He had been overjoyed to find disciples or heirs but even more so to realise that after what had happened in Europe a voice had been disinterred, rescued from the rubble.

But here in Knokke one was immersed in a cosmopolitan horde. Were there still so many poets alive in the world, he wondered, without intended black humour. Had not two planetary conflicts been able to exterminate them?

Once more, weariness bloats him like an oedema. It is one of those fits of boundless fatigue that, since childhood, have magnetised his brain and drawn him towards the centre of the earth. He has always had to outwit them, negotiate with them, gradually make the infirmity a defence. To turn this languid Fury into a sister. And on more than one occasion she has protected him.

He thinks back to the welcoming cocktail party the day before, at the casino. How weighed down he had felt amid his distinguished *confrères*, his voluble *consoeurs*. A rhinoceros that has strayed into a ballet. It was the doctor in him that their distinction and worldly aplomb had not deceived. Job conditioning: by the time they left the reception there was not one whose malady he had not diagnosed, the invisible worm that gnawed and would one day have the better of them. He could X-ray the body that most adroitly concealed the secret lesion. In each face he deciphered the hidden woe. He could not have sworn that all those gathered there had a rightful claim to the title of poet – but all were hatching, deep in their eyes, the egg of their death. Was it because those who play with words plunge more unarmed into the world's affray? Was not poetry, on the best estimate, symptom and diagnosis intertwined? Suddenly, there were too many poets around him. Much as he might assert that one could only talk to artists, that there were words that could only be exchanged with them – passwords which alone can penetrate the defences of those to be seduced – all too soon came the moment when one wanted to get away – especially when the words were running their errands most nimbly, drawing from another the unwonted avowal like a blissful sob – yes, it was especially then that one had to take one's leave. They drained you, those people who resorted, like you, to a certain babble whose syntax was drawn from that outmoded attribute, the soul. They sucked your blood. Nothing was to be gained by coming together to probe too many shared stigmata.

On the bed, from which he has not removed the counterpane, the portly poet has stretched himself out. Winded as if he has run an obstacle race against his shadow. He has shut his eyes. He applies to his temple the trumpet of the universe. The earpiece of a telephone which the eternal has forgotten to hang up at the end of a conversation with someone else. In the hollow of his ear, the sea is telling him things that would make you blush.

He feels as if he has worn himself out contending with everything at once. That has been his way. Now he is motion-less. Becalmed, but in the eye of the maelstrom. He doesn't expect to slip through the net again. He is in the place of death, living an inverse nativity. Bloated body, lissom dreams. He lets the poem's violent peace sink down into him, so that he can feel the shock that comes from everywhere and nowhere. So that the drugged bliss will last a moment more. Like a rabbit punch from God, an electric shock from the void.

> "The creatures in which pearls are made are closed.
> In their repose they only know the sea."

He wakes with a start. There is foam on his lips. A nightmare, the details of which elude him now. He immediately turns to the window, his eyes seeking the ocean, as if superstitious, as if his salvation depended on it. Ah, that supreme cliché! The marine horizon, the last emergency exit for those who have read all the books and are aware that the flesh is more dead than alive. Those silhouettes scattered on the beach, do they know what drowning they have escaped? For their own good, one hopes they may remain in ignorance ...

The watcher remembers being the child of a countryside that blazed in summer, and in winter was engulfed in torpor. It smelt of leather, iron and milk. Even the work in the fields was performed in the dun, insipid odour of a bad dream. Eternity, back there in Neumark, had the taste of sleep.

When he entered the cities' jungle – to borrow the phrase of a poet people were fond of contrasting to him – he had to placate its monsters. A new Orpheus, he knew that it was there above all that "the Muses exult and wail". They have husky voices and a taste for blood.

This is the man who is learning to look at the sea. Who lends ear to its *basso ostinato*. But, like a watermark, his whole life is passing in front of it and being reconciled. Images map on images.

> "O to be our primeval ancestors ...
> The bay's soft curve. The dark forest dreams.
> The stars, like heavy snowball flowers.
> The panthers leaping softly through the trees.
> All is the shore. Eternally calls the sea."

He has arrived. No one will go further. Here the Self ends, the world starts. What he sees draws from him more than love: respect. Nothing in the world could distract him from this soft brushing of silk, this dull churning of lead.

For example, he will not look at that woman who is walking away along the dike, who has caught his eye with her braided hair, her pinched sea-horse's waist ... She is not jealous, Ilse, his wife, but to know his eyes were pursuing the silhouette of another would have given her heart a furtive stab.

He has followed in the wake of a good number of women in his life. Mentally, he has fallen in step with many more. Among those he has known: some of his patients, and often, whores. Then, an element of pity was mingled with vice. Poverty is an irresistible courtesan. If she has once been kindly received, she is apt to settle in. She's there among the furniture, as if for ever.

But why think of such things when facing the sea? Because the sea is cruel and generous. Because in thinking of all the women he has known he does not forget the one who joined him at the end of a war, on the threshold of his old age. Those who have shared his life, he has not often reminded of his love. Not out of modesty. But because poverty, when you have known it, and pity, when you have felt it, finally fill all space. They are the most talkative rivals. They don't oust the loved one, but gag the lover. He ought now to dedicate an epithalamium to Ilse, in which his own wretchedness or that of the world would appear only negatively, in which love alone would be invoked with its murmur of long waves, its patience of ebbing tides. It would happen like this: he would simply have to place his blank page on the lectern of the sea. Framed in the window, against this "early-medieval sky", as his friend Carl Sternheim used to say, when he lived here so many years ago.

Thinking of Ilse, his wife, the poet remembers how they would sometimes amuse themselves like children, at the end of the day, when their respective consultations were over, by placing their foreheads together until their two eyes had merged for each other into a single, vast, cyclopean eye.

The time to think about that is darkest night. Like the negative of a photo that would never be developed.

Just when you expected it least, he is suddenly in buoyant mood. Those close to him know that these playful whims are just a reprieve. He who dislikes travel suddenly wants to find out everything about the place where he happens to be. Anything can take his fancy. "Did you know," he asks Walter Lennig, "that you can eat *boules der Berlin* outside the patisseries? What might they be, do you think? Balls of saveloy filled with fresh cream? I can recommend the little bifid rolls they serve with your morning coffee. They have a cleft like a baby's bottom, and names of firearms. They call them *pistolets* or pistols." He pauses a moment to watch the Lorelei on the hotel balcony, scattering crumbs which the birds intercept before they have touched the ground. Who was it, the poet wonders, they called the Generous Hand? A goddess, a courtesan? He is amused to hear "Eternally" from *Limelight* coming from the doorway of a brasserie. "Do you realise, Walter," he asks delightedly, "that yesterday I heard someone humming the theme of *Pêcheurs de Capri* at this very spot. Just think of the competition we get from all this tuneful rubbish all over the world. In Berlin this summer we heard nothing else. Didn't someone say that everything finishes with songs? They ought to consider exactly what those words mean. We are suffocating in scented cotton wool. Hell is no more than a sweet box. We forget that those boiled sweets that are handed out on baptism days imitate the colours of the human corpse." He seems to be brooding again, the German poet – taking things far too seriously. But in him it's another form of high spirits, veering towards ferocity. Entering a tavern, he hears a singer claim that *son coeur est un vi-o-lon*. Why not, after all? Who is he to argue with such a claim?

Is he to be put out by a trifle like that? Why does he always have to fight against the attacks of a rampant melancholy?

Hasn't life suddenly become much easier for him? *Petite fleur de pa-, petite fleur de pa-, petite fleur de pa-pi-llon.*

Didn't everything work out for him just when he had stopped hoping? Shouldn't he feel at least some gratitude? Perhaps he still has some years of belated happiness, of unexpected fame. *A girl was swinging on a swing on a Sunday afternoon.* He imagines Ilse throwing crusts to the gulls on the Bayerischer Platz. He sees her sculpting little effigies in dough, lending her the gestures of an enchantress. He watches her arranging gladioli in a vase of clouded glass. From now on life will be like that, beautiful and a little unclear. *Cherry-trees pink and apple-trees white ... The little stagecoach dancing on the pretty roads of France.* Of *enfance?* Of *trance?* Above all, refuse to understand the words of these inane lyrics. Let everything go back to being incomprehensible; be unintelligible to yourself, as you were in Brussels in 1916, when you lost yourself entirely, a daytime sleepwalker, in the rue de Terre-Neuve, the rues de Nuit-et-Jour, Chair-et-Pain, Notre-Dame-aux-Neiges. Borne by a current of the incommunicable. When the light begins to vaporise it goes opaque. You are dazzled: you know everything and see nothing, and the voice which risks telling of this stammers, mumbles and yells, trembles and grows strident. So let us not miss any chance to be happy. If we can throw bridges across from ourselves to the world, from the present to the past, from one thing, no matter which, to no matter which other, isn't that always a triumph? A joy? Or at least an amusement? "Did you know," he goes on to ask his friend, "that when Engels rejoined Marx in exile, here or a bit further along, in Ostend, then Brussels, he took up horse riding? To Karl's delight, Friedrich was fond of imitating the neighing of a horse. You wouldn't have believed those two fellows could put on an act like that, I dare say. People turned round to look at them in the street, taking them for a couple of drunks. How could they have suspected those two were concocting the *German Ideology,* planning to found an international proletarian party, that they were going to shake the world? But in the meantime – on the

Ostend promenade not far from the racecourse built by
Leopold II, King of both Belgians and negroes and hence a
double colonialist – Friedrich Engels would pretend to amble
along, tossing his head, while Karl Marx belaboured him with
the whip ... We always oversimplify famous men. Or we
don't simplify them enough, it depends. Sometimes we balk at
their contradictions, sometimes we forget their coherence.
Engels, a shrewd accountant, didn't only meditate on global
economics; he remembered to keep a daily record of his and
Marx's joint incomes and outgoings. In a sense, he was
practising. A well-ordered budget begins at home. We know
this because paper table-cloths have been found on which are
traces of the figures they wrote while eating at a restaurant.
That's precious information, Walter! We ought to know everything about philosophers', poets' and scholars' relation to
money. That relation, like the one to the flesh of our fellow
creatures – is often where the die is cast. (My patients, the
whores of the Schöneberg quarter, know something about
that.) By the way, did I tell you that on average my poetry
earned me a total of four-and-a-half marks a month in royalties
– including the translations, of course? And since venereology
hardly keeps a man's head above water now that we have
penicillin, you can understand why I'm always hard up. Ezra
Pound – you know, the American bard I have had the honour
of being compared to here, who seems to have had a much
harder time of it than I have – wrote somewhere that between
1914 and 1915 he earned approximately forty-two pounds, and
was not a little proud of it. One can understand that. Believe
me, all the Orpheuses in the entire world ought to be obliged
to present their balance sheets. It would certainly be edifying.
Of course, some commentators would be surprised to hear we
had such mundane preoccupations. But we don't hide our
faces. Everything's a contract, from the treatment of the human
body as a negotiable commodity (slavery, transportation, prostitution, marriage) to the legalised bequest of our precious
remains. We should keep an account of all our expenses apart

from money. We don't need to waste our polemics on people who shut their eyes to such matters. Other-worldliness has never been my strong point. Please note that there is nothing shameful or unmentionable in this. All the operations can be cited without shame: we are born, we give, we receive, we recoup, we lose, we win, we buy, we sell, we barter, we sell off cheap, we use, we abuse, we embezzle, we traffic, we commit fraud, we make out an invoice for everything pertaining to life and death, we are dealers in nothing, we buy the wind, we sell our souls, we lose our shadows: and the only laws which govern all these ups and downs, all this coming and going, are those of the market, of that you can be sure. Engels, in his little daily sums, wanted at least to work out what the revolution was costing him. It was all quite legitimate, part of the game . . . "

It's not often that you see him excited like this, carried away by the pleasure of talking. His listener is doubly disconcerted, first by the unwonted loquacity, then by the anecdotes he claims to know. Marx and Engels! No one would have suspected him of such reading. Rightly, no doubt: he cannot have read a line of either of them. But he had heard about the equestrian episode at Ostend. Where did he get his information from? He always knew a little more or less than expected. His interests and preoccupations, like the gaps in his knowledge, were all the more disconcerting because he was making no attempt to surprise. He gave so little away that when he emerged from his mutism he was liable to give only the baldest facts. But he gave them by the yard, in fine disorder. Proceeding backwards, along the flanks, tracking down the hidden infancy of things. He searched so little, he who found so much. Everything was grist to his elegy's mill. To him the world was a radio set which he endlessly switched from programme to programme, seeking the singular, enigmatic phrase which things in their polyphony formulated unawares: Friedrich Engels striding along the seafront, his own worries about money; the trite words of a foreign song, an advertising slogan: he ruminated on all this with broody minuteness, but with unfailing curiosity and even amusement. And in this way, unbeknown, his insect's eye captured whole the anecdote of the real. It was an activity both funereal and blithe. One way of being contemporary. Weak spirits might argue that it lacked tenderness. So be it: there is a virile nostalgia which does not feel obliged to state its name.

He drags his friend Walter off on a tram excursion along the shore. An adventure in itself! "Do not speak to the driver", say the notices on the backs of the polished seats. "Do not lean out" is written on the window ledges. These "diktats" seem especially meant for visiting Germans. The poet looks for the adverts that will tell him where he is. He remembers having baptised one of his heroes Karandash because of a make of pencil he had seen in Brussels in 1915. What is more, the Russian word was transcribed in phonetic spelling on the adverts: Caran d'Ache. "I only learned later," he tells his friend, "that was a pseudonym adopted by a caricaturist who had served with the rank of corporal in the French army at the end of the nineteenth century, a man of proverbial eccentricities and charm. Among other things, he had a liking for disguise and hoaxes. After the Panama Scandal he had a chequebook printed in facsimile, enriched with his personal commentary. I knew nothing of all that. Only when I found out did I realise that it fitted my character like a glove. He is a sort of metaphysical crook who never has what it takes to do business with the universe. In his dealings with others he issues drafts, obtains extensions, signs blank cheques. His putative father, in a sense, did nothing else. You see, Walter, how chance accounts for many things. There are no coincidences: our intuitions shore up our works as blindness, alas, sometimes damaging our lives. If only we poets could see just as clearly as our poems! But they always have to go on ahead of us while we walk crablike in their wake, their shadow. Tell me, Walter, can you see me telling this bad news at the casino tomorrow? But have a look, rather, at that advert up there, urging us to consume a lot of salt: a chick pursued by a little boy with a salt-cellar. Think about the slogan: 'See how it runs!' Or that other one, more austere and direct: Banque d'outre-mer – Crédit mutuel – 'Life is a struggle. Take out a life annuity today.'"

The neighbourhood tram skirts elaborate fountains and façades tiled like bathrooms. "Les heures claires". "Cosy Corner". "Mélancolie des chats". The German poet is surprised not to see on the beach the wicker armchairs which afford such pleasant siestas on the Baltic shore. Soon he grows silent, gloomy. He has noticed that between the deserted golf courses and the tennis courts drained of colour, the cottages and little farmhouses with their roofs of false thatch, everywhere traces of combat are beginning to emerge. Among the dunes blockhouses still open their grey shark's jaws. Seeing a disused amusement park, a ruined mill, instantly you sense bombers diving vertically from the sky ... Soon, each side of the rails miraculously intact, you can imagine nothing except bombardments, infantry charges, disembarkations. The reef jutting up far off at the rim of the waves, could it be a buoy, or a live mine? And then, that child pushed in a wheelchair by a governess along the Zeebrugge front – is he a victim of polio or war? And here am I, thinks the poet, almost telling my hosts about my joy at seeing this country again, as if I were renewing a love affair of my youth. Did it not occur to me that I was coming here not as a visitor but as a pilgrim, after a long exile? That would have gone down well, beyond doubt. *Blancheur Persil*, he reads above the head of the passenger opposite: She thought her washing was white. Obsessed with cleaning, the people here. They have good reason. What we brought here will take a long time to bleach out.

"Walter, look at that memorial ... "

"To the dead of '14–'18?" asks Walter.

"No, they've put up one memorial to the dead of both wars. That must have cut the cost ... Or perhaps they built it twice as high ... "

To remember two wars, both against the same enemy, he thinks, is much like commemorating all wars ... When Walter asked me, with a hint of hope, if it was for the '14-'18 war, I thought: for mine ... As if the one of '39 was not mine too. At least I didn't fight it here.

"You'd think it was built yesterday, wouldn't you?" says Walter.

"What was?"

"The monument. It's still quite fresh."

"But it was yesterday, Walter. Those two wars happened later than yesterday. We have just seen both of them finish together. We're living the aftermath of two wars."

And supposing he had come to Knokke only to see Brussels again?

When the invitation first reached him, all he said to Walter was: "I'll show you the town where everything started for me ... " He even decided to go there before the opening of the Biennale de Poésie. "That way," he joked, "if I find what I'm looking for, I can skip the conference. I won't have any more declarations to make." What was he seeking, then? He did not say. And his travelling companion did not force the issue. He suspected it was more than a matter of brushing up some old impressions or testing his memory.

For thirty-five years the poet had believed he would not again set foot in this town. But each time one of his friends or a member of his family went to Brussels he overwhelmed them with information and advice that often turned out to be anachronistic. He recommended them to walk past the little theatre in the rue de la Loi which backed on to the Parc Royal; at the beginning of his stay he had lived close by. Were there still orchids in the hothouses of the palace where Leopold II and Cléo de Mérode had spun out love's sweet dream? Would they remember to bring him back some pralines and scented toilet soap? They should not fail to see the Musée de Tervuren, which bristled with African masks filched from the colonial population. Masks as far as you could see ... Perhaps it was while looking at them that he had learned to see. However, like the sun they could only be looked at for an instant. But when you turned away it was as if your sight had been restored. Everything reeled: the world the masks surveyed fell away beneath your feet. The masks saw rightly: the world was a void into which you were plunging head first. And the Café de la Toison d'Or, was it still there? Above all, don't forget the soap! Of course, that was at the time of the blockade, when there was nothing to be had in Berlin. But after the blockade was lifted, when life began again and the display windows of Wertheim or the Kaufhaus des Westens filled with provisions and luxury goods, the doctor went on living as if Berlin were stifling in its insularity. Berlin, the divided city that Nefertiti overlooked with her single eye as if a stray bullet from the bombardment had carried off the other. Under her gaze too reality began to tremble. By the way, do stay at the Hôtel Métropole: a singer, famous at the time, had a room there where I would meet her between the recitals she gave to raise the spirits of the wounded in the military hospitals. Me, go back to Brussels? Out of the question! What I lived there, he thought, was without precedent and was to remain without sequel.

As soon as he arrived, he started walking. He went unerringly from one point in the city to another, as if he had left it the day before and were finding it intact. No, he thought, everything has changed, of course it has. But I seem to be adapting instantaneously to the destruction of the city I knew. As if I understood its logic. As if I had foreseen it or imagined it at a distance. What I learned here was precisely that: that everything trembles under our gaze, nothing stands really upright, everything is caught in the toils of self-destruction. At best we are mere spectators of the abysses yawning between all things. We are permanently in mourning for a cohesion that falters at each moment beneath our feet.

His friend Walter commented that the doctor was an excellent guide who never lost his bearings. "It's because in Berlin we have learned to move about in a phantom city," replied the poet. Who would believe, he thought, that I am merely walking with the proverbial assurance of the blind?

"The curious thing, Walter, is that they all detested this city. Can you imagine it? Whatever did they expect it to be like?"

"Who?" asks Walter. "Who expected what?"

"The poets," replies the doctor. "All the poets who came to live here before me. None of them really liked it. Baudelaire hated Brussels, heaped abuse on it. Hugo and Nerval hid their tawdry love affairs here, cut themselves to shreds on their mistresses. Verlaine and Rimbaud preferred to make it the scene of a melodramatic incident . . . This, as you see, is a town that can make you laugh, or suffer . . . But adopt it, feel at home here? I was enslaved by it – do you want to know why? Because I was at the edge of a crumbling world. I doubted everything I saw. And I was right. The town did all this for me. I crossed it, it passed through me. I was really at the edge of the world. Where my own existence started. I had to choose between being nothing but this little addendum, this postscript – and being nothing."

"Incidentally, Walter, would you like to see it again with me?" asks the doctor.

"See what again, Gottfried?"

"The hotel where I lived at that time, in the rue Saint-Bernard, if it still exists."

The building had survived. The covered balcony, now over-hanging a grocer's shop, had been preserved. Had he identified the house correctly? Hadn't it been buried under one of those bombardments whose traces the doctor thought he could see everywhere? No matter: he now stood on its doorstep like someone who is about to produce a bunch of keys from his pocket and simply step back inside after thirty-five years' absence. He looked happy. This house, or rather the town around this house, must surely have witnessed some event that had influenced his life for ever after. Something – this was all he could tell Walter – that had helped him keep his balance later, in his most difficult hours: something like a certainty wrung from uncertainty itself.

"It was in this house, Walter, that I finally learned to write."

"But it can't have been, Gottfried," his companion objects.

"Why not?" asks the doctor.

"It started earlier, in Berlin," Walter states emphatically.

"What do you know about that?" asks the doctor, somewhat surprised by such unwonted aplomb.

"It was at the morgue, Gottfried, before the war, when there was already a lot of dying, but before the wars – that's when you learned to write. You've told me so often enough, over the years! You read the secret of the gods in human entrails," Walter adds – poets' friends always being somewhat prone to the emphatic – "as pagan priests claimed to read the future of cities in the entrails of sacrificial beasts ... "

"Let's leave the gods where they are," grumbles the doctor, "and the livestock won't be molested. In the human viscera I managed to decipher two or three secrets about human beings themselves, that's all – two or three of their paltriest mysteries. But all the rest, Walter – I had to come here to find it, understand it, on the first floor of this house, in this street, in the heart of this city, in the midst of these people who hated us, the Germans, and whose language I didn't understand ... After colliding with the words I kept walking into the foreigners. And there was such a silence in me, Walter, such a prodigal, raging silence I was afraid people would notice. I didn't know where to hide myself with it ... Finding myself stranded here, having to go on that punitive expedition against my own vacuity – that was my chance, Walter, the big chance of my little life. How can I explain it to you? Perhaps I'll come back to it later. On the other hand, it probably isn't right to come back to the scene of an inexplicable happiness any more than to the scene of a crime. Incomprehensible. Even slightly scandalous. After all, I'm not an idler, Walter. I'm not given to solitary walks or sentimental journeys to Italy. I don't need to move about, to be somewhere else: *it* has always happened where I was at the time!"

He certainly had an odd way of being a vagabond, his friend was to think later; as were those who loved him, and those who did not. Having gone to Knokke to read a talk more like a will about some German poets whose names meant nothing to anyone any more, here he was holding forth ecstatically about the advertisement hoardings in Brussels in 1952, which had replaced the ones he had known long before. Then: L'autopiano, reproducing twenty thousand repertory works on cylinders. Now: His Master's Voice, long-playing records. (But not afraid to keep as their trade-mark a gramophone with a trumpet speaker, immortalised by a music-loving fox terrier.) Then: Five o'clock tea in the refreshments room. Now: Milk-and-Snack Bar. He started spelling them out: Lavécire: that makes *lave et cire* – it waxes as it washes! Sapoli: *ça polit* – it polishes! *Ça va seul* ... It goes by itself – all on its own. How true, how well put! For reasons that only concerned him, these slogans made him as happy as a child. "You see, Walter? Such is the alphabet of the modern city. Whiteness, hygiene, polish ... To be cleansed of one's sins, and go by oneself: quite a programme, isn't it?"

The poet wanted to perform a pious duty. "Carl," he said, "Carl Sternheim, one of us, who was here at the same time as I was, is buried at Ixelles. Not far, it seems, from Général Boulanger. He would have appreciated that ... "

After a lot of wrong turnings the two visitors at last came upon a grey sandstone grave at the edge of a line of chestnut trees, with a slab bearing a modest dog-rose carved in an oval medallion of white marble. The caretaker they questioned told them the grave had been moved several times. Like the man himself, Gottfried Benn remarked. Even when he was alive he could not stay put.

That eagerness to find a grave in a strange city, Walter thought later – wasn't it really his own grave that Gottfried had come here to find and meditate upon?

But he wasn't thinking about death then. No more his than his friend's, whose epitaph lay in his shadow. The last summer sun warmed his neck and back. He was striving finally to understand what had happened to him here thirty-six years before. Only someone who had lived in Brussels, he thought, someone who, in thirty-six years' time would walk and lose himself in the streets of Berlin in search of the places where I had lived, if they had not all been razed in the interval, might have an inkling of the hidden meaning of this magical, happy accident. I would be long dead. He in his turn would attain the state of absolute exile. He would know nothing for certain any more. He would suddenly be bereft of all the reference-points, the mental images that brought him here. Then his ordeal would begin. He would have to learn everything anew. So much on the alert that tears of fatigue and joy would spring from his eyes. Without blinking he would have to sound the abyss that he found yawning beneath him, suddenly not knowing whether it was in him or outside. The disarray into which he was plunged, as I was, would henceforth be his treasure, as it was mine. He would know at last that he is to himself like an unknown person who cannot speak to him in his own language. To understand himself from now on he would have to invent a code, to communicate like a Robinson Crusoe with this Man Friday. It would be like harbouring a great love without yet knowing if it would be returned . . .

And about all this, if he is like me, he will not say much. Delirious joy, unlike great pain, can be mute. That man would be totally absorbed in his epic: the epic of his dereliction.

It was, he thought, like having been struck by a dark illumination. My catastrophe and my eureka! I had just had some very sombre news about the state of things. But at the same time a secret had been revealed to me: the secret of their dislocation. I was, in the fullest sense, dazzled. I was suffering from a loss of perception through an excess of perception. No, I was not exulting about being the only one who could see in a world of the blind: rather the opposite. I was just going blind slightly before the rest ... The malady had struck me first, that's all. I knew it was the start of the contagion, that I was merely inaugurating the sickness that all would share with me in times to come. The frightening secret: that reality may not exist, nothing may have happened up to now. Of us and the rest of the world, one always tells the truth and the other always lies, but which? Ladies and gentlemen, I'll tell you: the king who, in each of us, thinks he is ruling over the world, is dead: long live the king! We have only to slip into an empty suit of armour. Gone, the subject who was inside us. Only the form is left. To be sure, the news will cause a big stir later on, but for now it's better not to spread it. Who would take us seriously? We ought to make the best of the disaster. See it as our only hope, our sole accomplishment.

Thus the poet ruminated, in a kind of drunkenness. With such thoughts rambling grandly through his mind, he walked somewhat unsteadily along the rue Vilain XIIII, or tottered back up the rue de l'Aurore. And here at the Ixelles cemetery, after so many years had passed, he discovered that the incongruous message he had to deliver was still premature. When the world had twice been put to the sword and the torch, was it the time to announce the arrival of a gentle apocalypse, which would ruin the ultimate certainties hidden in the recesses of our souls? What the poet still did not dare ask himself, moreover, was why the truths he had discovered here had been of no help at all to him when the nightmare had become reality? Worse: they may have helped to lead him further astray. Hang the revelations! "Of course," he felt obliged to say to Walter to justify his long silence, "like everyone else I thought the war would last merely a few weeks. The golden age still lingered on ... "

He had only given himself up so readily to his delirium in these streets because peace had seemed imminent. My nightmares, he thought, were not an end but a beginning. The nightmares of a child who had known only the infancy of our century. Or of an old man who had fallen asleep long after, on its ruins. A story I might have told myself to make myself afraid.

"You're right, Walter," he said. "It's very uncommon, my way of travelling ... "

This was true, literally. He had moved about as little as possible. He remembered going to see the Monts Maudits. Buying some old furniture in antique shops in Paris and Avignon. Listening to the sound of the wind in a Swiss valley. Leaving his daughter with her children one day on a Danish beach, going to sit a little way off because he felt so weary. Strange father, singular explorer. In New York he had heard Caruso at the Metropolitan, and seen him playing patience in his box during the interval, to calm his nerves. On board a Hapag freighter that was taking him to America, he had listened to the idle confidences of a shopkeeper. Anchored off Hoboken, the ship had been put in quarantine. That only happens to me, thought the poet, as is only right and proper: if the truth comes out, we'll never get off the ship ...   He thought of a whole immobilised Sunday on the Hudson River. Again, the unreality. One ought not to move about. Already the human race was scattering itself into space ...   But, in Brussels, he had seen palms sprout within an hour between the paving stones of the rue du Midi, and camels cross the desert of the Marché Sainte-Catherine. The place smelt of saffron and cinnamon. You had to look out for the tigers who would leap over the rue du Lombard in a single bound. For the length of a season, which was like an extra life one had received as a gift by mistake, Brussels was a luxuriant jungle and a sumptuous Ahaggar. The grace was not dispensed solely by the cocaine he sometimes snuffed before embarking on the Boulevard Botanique or the rue Neuve, to absorb the bizarre life of the city from the reverse side, and outface its perils ...

He returned home. From now on he was a part of the city

where the plot that changed the face of the world was being hatched. Whatever happened there, he thought, he was not to leave it again. He moved from the Passauerstrasse to the Belle-Alliance-Platz.

"Walter?"

"Yes, Gottfried?"

"I'd like to go back to Berlin."

He would have liked to add: For ever.

Nevertheless, he came to Knokke and delivered the talk he had prepared. An old talk he had already given elsewhere. A talk as old and tired as he was. Which no one would remember. In the next room, they were playing blackjack and baccarat.

Later, someone would ask: "Are you sure the German poet really came? Wasn't his address read by someone else?"

In fact, he did not stay till the end of the conference. He discreetly took leave of his hosts, passing his visiting card to each. He wouldn't even go on the coach trip that took the members of the congress to Damme, the home of *Till Eulenspiegel* and Nele, his eternal and faithful fiancée – so he told Walter.

"I was so fond of the stone couple they made at Ixelles, not far from the avenue Louise ..."

All the same, he had not shown any inclination to revisit it while at Brussels; but one day in Knokke, while he was taking a few steps down the neighbouring avenues, he came across another monument dedicated to the Flemish Don Quixote and his Dulcinante. He noted that it had just been unveiled. Though scarcely surprised by this epiphany, he took much pleasure in it. There are no coincidences, he thought, only meetings, conjunctions, some of which we miss. It is always thus.

The day before he left he wanted to go down on to the beach, just once, with his friends Walter Lennig, Wilhelm

Lehmann, Hans-Egon Holthusen and Alexander Lernet-Holenia. They noticed how difficult he was finding it to walk. The wind had blown a handful of sand into his eyes, and a dog dashing between his legs had almost knocked him over. Here on the beach, when he was not expecting it, he felt the brush of death. There was no fear in him. Just the apprehension that he might be interrupted *just when he was beginning to understand* ... He – who claimed to have lived a "double life", to have been a spiritual bigamist who had married his age twice over – did not judge a third existence too many to be truly embraced. To disappear would be nothing; but for the machine that created images to stop, for that ultimate intuition, that might at last be the truth, to petrify – that he found unbearable. I'm so slow ... Already, so soon and for ever, it was too late. A shame, really. His companions watched his heavy silhouette: a fallen king deported to an island for the rest of his days. He might have looked like a mandarin bowed down with wisdom, though with a touch of perversity. But he embodied less than that, and much more. He was that block of congealed despair sweating and melting in the mild autumn sun. A parcel of perturbation. A twitching of the void. The knot of a noose that was choking the light. A bone tossed to History, that bitch, for her to try her teeth on.

Turning his back on the horizon, he saw the waves reflected in the hotel windows far off on the esplanade. They looked like photographs. The splendour gripped his heart, and he wondered why he had not bathed his eyes more often in the milk of the world.

"Dear friends," he said, "did you realise I have never really looked at the sea?"

Berlin, 1906

The Dead Bodies

This is where childhood ends, thinks the student. In front of this rigid body with its parchment skin, that the pathologist is about to open. This is where the father-son conflict is resolved, the student also thinks, as he meets the pathologist's gaze. A gaze made enigmatic by the antiseptic mask. All of childhood comes to an end in this amphitheatre, with its filtered light pouring through the skylight on to the blue granite table. And everything begins under the gaze of the pathologist – who has supplanted the father. Today the scalpel artist is to operate, but soon the student, dressed like him in a rubber apron, booted, gloved and masked, will take his place and cut up his first dead person. In a few days, not more. It will almost be summer. It will be hot like today. Picking up his shining implements the young operator will feel the blood drain from his cheeks, his forehead, the back of his neck. The moment he first touches the body that has been assigned to him, the blood will rush back and squeeze his temples like a crown. It will be as simple as making love for the first time. The student finds himself thinking that he will look handsome for the occasion. That he may never again look so handsome as the day he dismembered his first corpse. That it will be very difficult to talk of it afterwards. Because, of course, it too will have to be translated into words. That may be the main reason why he has come here, to the Moabit Hospital in the heart of old Berlin, why he has left behind step by step the little village in Neumark, close to the Polish border, where on summer days like this you used to cut reed flutes if you were not spending hours at the top of a cherry tree. Then the *Gymnasium* in Frankfurt-on-Oder, where you were ashamed of your rustic manners and garb and struggled to do and say nothing that would arouse the contempt of the scions of *Junkers*. You had to learn to be parsimonious with your words, prodigal with your silence. Finally, the theology faculty where your father had entered you against your will, in Marburg, where the whole city was the university. You grew to like poetry all the more in a place where it seemed dissected, autopsied. You began to dream, with a vehemence that was only inflamed by the study of those on whom you were supposed to model your thought, who dreamed seldom. So you decide to switch to medicine, to rejoin the sick and the dead as one returns to one's true family. Your father gives in. You arrive in Berlin, whose citizens claim to dislike it but cannot leave, held by a bitterness that has all the symptoms of a degrading passion. You'll be an inhabitant of this city whose poisons try your nerves. This city that is sometimes hideous, always enchanting. You'll be a doctor to the poor. One who lays hands on the bodies of men. The humiliated bodies of the living, and those abandoned to death. You'll be the poet who reveals for all to see what others hide or keep to themselves. Others before you have described the *Leichenhaus*, the morgue. Lachrymose elegies. When the public should have heard the bitter, grating laugh of one who has been flayed. That's why you have come here, step by step. To take that risk.

"In Berlin, in weather like this," says the pathologist in a somewhat tired voice, "we have no trouble getting supplies. The morgues are bursting with anonymous stiffs. We don't even have to steal the left-overs from executions. However, let's see if this young man has any revelations to share with us . . . "

For the man the operator is measuring with a folding ruler for the purposes of the autopsy must, indeed, have been quite young. Measuring him up isn't easy: at the moment of death he seems to have sat up in bed, got into a defensive posture with balled fists, squaring up to death like a boxer . . . "It's often like this," the anatomy instructor remarks. "This is the position in

which rigidity first comes over the body when it is hardly
dead."

But the scalpel has suddenly set to work. "It's a mistaken
idea, gentlemen, and a poor method, to drag things out. The
over-cautious operator wears away the tissue and loses sight of
the separate layers ... " Already there is a Y-shaped incision in
the thorax, from the clavicles to the sternum, from the chest to
the pubis. After opening a buttonhole at the level of the
epigastrium, the operator parts the lips of the incision, running
along the grating of ribs. They are cut with secateurs, like dry
twigs. Fat floods from the gutters. "Our man was obese,"
declares the anatomist. "You're not going to like the fat ones,
gentlemen. They make things awkward for us. They seem to
want to hide the secret of their demise ... Fat retains water,
clogs the blood. Especially in summer; that's when the worms
come up, head for the orifices, even get under the facial
skin ... "

That's the first ungracious thing we've heard him say about
the dead, thinks the student. He does't like fat ones, and
decides that we – assuming we intend to become pathologists
or autopsists like him, of course – won't like them either. All
the same, he generally takes good care not to disparage the
dead – as if it might reflect badly on his own job to suggest he
wasn't on good terms with them. Normally, he's more inclined
to sing their praises ... But the fat ones offend him. It would
be so much better without them. They spoil his fun.

I didn't hate my father so much as his voice, he muses. It was
so loud. Everywhere he talked as loudly as if he were in
church. Hard to believe that God wasn't speaking through him,
out of his mouth. The verbal avalanche that descended on his
parishioners each Sunday was not a question posed to God, or
an exegesis of his thought, an earthly paraphrase of the divine
text, though you might first have thought Pastor Gustav Benn,

addressing his Lord, was holding a dialogue with an Equal. No, he was merely letting words from Above pass through him, he was content to conduct that current. With him suspended in his pulpit as if in the nacelle of an airship between heaven and earth, I got used to contemplating him only from below. And the One on high who spoke through my father – I didn't hear about his death until I arrived in Berlin, while reading a preface by the philosopher Nietzsche written in 1886, the year I was born. Was my father completely out of touch, lending his voice to a star that had already gone out? True, my father never read anything apart from the Bible, and never listened to music. He had only been to the theatre once in his life, to see a play by Wildenbruch with jingoistic, quasi-socialist pretensions that he dinned into us afterwards. So, of course, the pastor had not heard about Nietzsche and his prefaces to *The Gay Science* and *Beyond Good and Evil* ... In any case, where did Nietzsche get his information from? Was it so certain, after all, that the Immortal One's decease was on record? Which forensic expert in eternal affairs had put a mirror of timeless truth to the divine lips, to make sure it did not go misty? Was he credible, this philosopher who, having spread the good news about God's death in such wildly triumphant tones, could not get over it himself and soon succumbed to madness? Yes, he had had to come to Berlin to find this out, after leaving behind, step by step, Mansfeld, Sellin, Frankfurt-on-Oder and Marburg – to Berlin that Nietzsche disliked, seeing petrified, labyrinthine vice in every German city ... Whereas to the young medical student from the village in Neumark the city appeared magnificently glaucous and slimy straight away, enfolding him with a female, maternal hospitality. Here, without doubt, he was going to be able to start living, and to find out who he was. Was this Friedrich Nietzsche afraid of his shadow, lost in the shadows of the city, despite his iconoclastic fervour to know the truth? No. He had merely discovered that he was "entirely body and nothing besides". To which Zarathustra would add that he had had a successful fishing trip: "He had not caught a

man, but a corpse." But why think of Nietzsche here, in front
of this unknown body that the anatomist has just opened and
unfolded; why think of Nietzsche where childhood has just
ended? Perhaps because the philosopher believed throughout
his life that his own father had died of a softening of the brain,
which, after all, was no more or less proven than the Death of
God ... Now as to my father, thought the student, I probably
hated him less than his voice, which was so loud. It was the
voice of someone incapable of error, who would never have
permitted himself the slightest meanness. It's because of him,
his ringing voice, that I've smothered my own, let it sink to the
depths of my being. That's why I've finally adopted this
monochord tone. This pale, soft monotone suits what I'll have
to say, the piercing doubt, the heavy uncertainty, the dismay in
face of things. You don't shout words which are already a
shout before they are born.

The anatomist severs the cartilage with bone forceps. He
disconnects the joints, the clavicles, with a surgical knife.
Looking down into the abdominal cavity, the students see
floating organs like exotically coloured plums of every shape.
Once again, the voyeur might be amazed at the magnificence
of what he sees, which tames and censors its horror. Nothing
could equal the sculptural perfection of this machine, the
multicoloured profusion of its interlocking parts, the precision
of their contours. Each of us unwittingly harbours such a
cornucopia! But has to die before it sees daylight. The anatomist pauses a moment in his work. He is bathed in sweat. But
he probably also wants to let his students contemplate the
terrible splendour of this human landscape no eye could ever
exhaust or have enough of, this script it seeks in vain to
decipher, this net it tries to scan ... His glasses have misted up,
no doubt from emotion. Everyone holds his breath. You catch
yourself miming the body's hieratic solemnity. For a further
moment nothing will disturb the topography of the open
corpse. Then will come the dismantling, the bloody, didactic

pillage. Putrefaction will do the rest. For a few seconds, for the space of a mirage, this intestate carcass, this utter orphan, has appeared like a sovereign. The decency of this flesh which, folded back, no longer seems naked. The bluish brilliance of its noble structures. The torrential silence of these viscera exhumed like a miniature of a buried city. Feast your eyes on a masterpiece more ephemeral than a chalk drawing done by a child on a pavement in Alt-Moabit. You wish it could last for ever. You want the spectacle of death to console you for death itself. But it will not last. It's not only in life that beauty is fleeting.

In Paris some years before, Xavier Bichat had declared: "life is a set of functions which together resist death", and this neat aphorism had raced through all the lecture-theatres in Europe like fire along a gunpowder trail. As if all one could assert about a living being was that he wasn't dead! Life would never be more than the exception which confirmed the rule of death. Life was there, on the world's stage, but nowhere did it reveal its own principle. You come into the world, the professor of physiology had said, introducing his second-term course, and at once you start to disintegrate. No sooner are you born than your funeral starts to roll . . .

To show their approval the students had drummed on their desks with their knuckles or the tips of their pencils.

All the same, the pastor's son wondered, couldn't you counter Bichat's dictum, like all such grand assertions, with its opposite: that death gathers together the forces that resist life? (All it involves being the abdication of a piece of protoplasm.) A resistance usually rewarded by success . . . There was so much more death than life! And that was probably only the start. He thought of Leonardo da Vinci, his nocturnal trysts with the corpses he skinned, boned and resected at Santa Maria Nuova in Florence, to extract the secrets they had not yet confided to anyone. He now understood why da Vinci always spoke of them as horrible, and never quite mastered the nausea they aroused. It must have been less a revulsion of the living body in face of the dead one, than the mind's aversion to a task that was literally desperate. Did not the heart that he now knew contained no vital principle turn out to be a muscle like any other? Even in Leonardo's day death was winning. Having come to anatomy by way of art, the painter must have returned to art richer in knowledge and poorer in illusions. What he left behind him on the dissecting table, soiled with fat and animal lymph, was a certain idea of the Infinite that he had cherished throughout his life. One more dead body . . .

There won't be any more summer holidays. You won't go back to Sellin in midsummer. Ruth, the elder sister you love dearly, who wrote poetry before you started writing it yourself, is a house surgeon at Göppingen. You will not mount the carts at harvest time again. You will not make hay, go bird's-nesting, drink in the odour of washing hung out in the orchard. You will no longer, for the benefit of your younger brothers and your sister Edith, call things by their names, trees, plants and beasts, stars, the phenomena of nature. Lilac, acacia, black alder, dandelion, goldfinch, brown owl, jackdaw, shrew, weasel, Morning Star, Betelgeuse. No longer will you describe the fate of birds in winter. You will tell no more stories and fables, neither the one about "the uncle who walked about in the forest after losing his skin", nor the one about the black knight who made the empress dance all night at the coronation feast in Frankfurt and who, when challenged to take off his mask, turned out to be the hangman of Bergen; but the emperor, not wanting to spoil the festivities, knighted him on the spot. No, you will tell no more of those tall stories, since grace is never bestowed except in books, and the men who have lost their skin can only have had it removed on the dissecting table. Never again will you share your store of nuts and mint biscuits in the torrid gloom of the barn. You won't celebrate Easter in Brandenburg style by beating yourself with green twigs. You will no longer be secretly amazed to see your mother ageing, thickening, growing less and less like the portrait you found of her one day in an album, her hands resting on the back of an armchair and clasping a fan. The photo showed her with all her astonished ardour for life – although, of course, she had not yet become engaged to your father, who may not even have entered her life. You'll never again hear her sing: "The bright air shines with the church bells' chimes", with a trace of a French-Swiss accent. You will not hear the dear foreign voice evoking the mountain peaks where the sunbeams never grow tired. No, there will be no holidays this year in a countryside burnt and anaesthetised by summer, holidays in which you die of boredom and which you afterwards find enchanting. Nostalgia starts to blurt helplessly. The memories you have gathered: reed flute, haycart, mint biscuits, take on a touching banality. You'll not meet your old friends this summer, sons of the country nobility who come home from Baden, Düsseldorf or Munich where they may have met cabaret singers or dancers. You won't need to feel ashamed this time, or hide your chagrin. You've chosen medicine, and Berlin. You'll never be the same again. Your father has given way. Putting all his faith in the ordinances of an inscrutable God, the pastor must have seen medicine as an almost superfluous activity, as arrogant as it was frivolous. But now you have to do with the sick and the dead, you are cut off by them from the rest of the world, and even from your origins. At the end of the summer you'll do some army service, work as a military doctor to pay for your study. Haven't the army and medicine a lot in common? Next year perhaps, when summer comes, you may go on a visit to Sellin, see how much more of her youth your father has stolen from your mother. You won't even be able to talk to her about what really matters: that you're rubbing shoulders with dead people every day, seeing them from close to, that you've also touched some women, but that even they are not always enough to restore your taste for life.

The anatomist withdraws the contents of the rib-cage with forceps, pulling out the cardio-pulmonary system. The hardest part of the drudgery. Is that because it involves the sacred organs? It's also the heart, thinks the student, that has the worst smell. But perhaps he's just getting ideas. Squinting, the scalpel virtuoso swabs the blood which is already coagulating at the bottom of the cavity, like tepid chocolate. He takes up the sponge to go in search of the kidney, the aorta. He extracts the small and large intestines, severs the guts, tying them with a cord knotted by an assistant beside him. "As you see," he announces, "I am severing the mesentery where it joins the intestine; I then introduce the buttoned arm of the enterotome into the lumen of the organ, and finally I cut along the edge of the mesentery. Note, gentlemen, the routine I follow: I extract the spleen, assess its volume, its colour, its consistency, ask the lab assistant to weigh it ... " The inventory continues: removal of the liver, stomach, duodenum and pancreas. Placing the entrails on the autopsy table. Assessing their volume, weight, colour, consistency.

The gloved hands plunge deeper into the chest whose lid he has forced, to seize the pirate's treasure, these human gems with their sheen of sapphire and rubies. But the onlooker's eyes hardly have time to widen, to revel. The anatomist blows hot and cold, he enjoys spoiling his own effects just when fascination is reaching its height. (Later, puncturing the bladder, he remarks: "Note, gentlemen, how the dirty fellow is not afraid to piss into his own body. Will you behave better, I wonder, when the time comes?") Thus, if the operator neglects the alimentary bolus, if he leaves his assistant to cut the tissues and membranes into slices, if, above all, he gives scant attention to the glaireous mass of lungs and defers exploring the pleurae and examining the pleural fluid, if he disdains the ramifications of the bronchi, everyone thinks it is just a trick, that the master is building up to a *coup de théâtre*, merely delaying the climax ... He's not likely to waste any of the materials put at his disposal by the abandoned body ... Already the throat is gaping; having perforated the floor of the mouth, he unfurls the tongue at the end of the forceps. He withdraws the thyroid. Examines the mucus in the larynx and trachea. "Observe, gentlemen, that he did not bite his tongue while dying. Please note the presence of bronchial mucus ... But let us now turn to the essence of the matter. Death can be defined as, above all, the abolition of the intellect – although, I repeat, two-thirds of the cerebral mass consists of mute zones. Let us turn, then, to the summit of the edifice ... Normally, as you know, we start from here. If I've made an exception, it was, no doubt, to let the young man keep an eye on what we are doing with his remains for as long as possible ... " The students feel obliged to laugh. The one among them who originates from Sellin wonders if such a joke does not contain a certain modicum of contempt.

The scalp, parted from the bone from one mastoid to the other, folds forward over the face, blinding the dead eyes a second time, and back over the nape. The bone of the skull can be seen: splinters fly in all directions, there's a smell of burning. The dura mater is incised with the point of a pair of scissors, revealing an opaline chamber full of almost black blood: a Grail. The gloved fingers are inserted under the frontal lobes. Deftly, the operator's hands receive, like a donation, the brain and cerebellum. "See for yourselves, gentlemen. A *purée*, a marmalade that's started to froth. Incidentally, you'll have noticed a pulmonary oedema bursting just now ... Drugs, gentlemen, of course. The laboratory will tell us later what a journey of discovery he's been on. Our client, we'll call him Ulrich for convenience, will have just had time to taste a moment of inebriation, euphoric dizziness, then sink into a delirium that we may hope, for his sake, was at least of an erotic nature. Then he must have felt a deathly cold. Was racked by nausea till he gave up the ghost. The whole thing didn't last more than a few hours. I'll raise the poor knight's vizor: look at his lips, eaten away with acid. *Exit* Ulrich. *Sic transit gloria mundi. Taceant colloquia effugiat risus hic locus est ubi mors gaudet succurrere vitae* – All words fail, all laughter falls silent,

this is the place where death is fond of paying his visit to life."
The students in the first row signal their approval by tapping
the edge of the bier with their pencils. For if the anatomist,
somewhat carried away by his apparent monopoly of the truth,
now tries to extract every last ounce of it from Ulrich, his
departed slave, turning to the lab assistant to invite him to cut
the bulb of the cerebellum first frontally, then transversely – the
spectators know full well that these are merely the concluding
formalities of a ritual. If, with an artist's whim, he inscribes a
few last scalpel slashes into the fat of arms and thighs, they are
no more than embellishment. It's just not easy to separate
yourself from a man you have dismembered. You could go on
for ever: you are compelled to keep breaking the corpse's
silence. All the same, you have to hand him over to the
morgue attendants who will render in bulk unto Caesar the
things that are Ulrich's, put his organs or what is left of them
back into the body's cavity, add two or three balls of screwed
up newspaper and sawdust to fill the gaps, then sew him up
with big catgut stitches. It doesn't really matter how you wrap
the body in its natural shroud, since no one is going to reclaim
it.

Just as he is about to leave the lecture hall, the student from
Sellin takes a last look at Ulrich's hair: it might be that of a
monstrous lifesize doll. Shutting his eyes for a moment, he
recovers the clear, dazzling image of the body at the moment
of being opened, so carefully fashioned, as if in marble, that it
looked like a fake. A superb imitation of life. He reflects that,
contrary to all the rules of hygiene, it would be better not to
wash one's hands on leaving such a place.

You're the product of a scientific century, the little peasant
from the banks of the Oder tells himself: you couldn't change
that even if you wanted to. Whatever you may say, that's the
only argument you've got to brandish in the face of your
father's fanatical God, apart from the philistinism of people who
have nothing but apish Darwinian beliefs to oppose him with.

Take your stand on the natural sciences – and you are made all the more aware of the inanity of practically everything we call nature! How narrow the mind's room to manoeuvre has become. It's because it alone perceives the world as it is – an abattoir, an isolation wing for plague victims, a nightmare from which you don't often wake – that it has to fall back on its own resources, to put itself in quarantine in the midst of the world. Hide in the whale's belly to escape the whale. And keep your log-book up to date in the eye of the storm. Formulate a *credo* in the rigorous language of a science that is called upon mainly to survey nothingness. Leave the trouble of believing in progress to squeamish hedonists. The only progress is that made by capital. Take up the natural sciences to keep your eye on man; never let him out of your sight, for he is murderous and pitiable. That's enough to take up all your time. Espouse the world, so that you can the more passionately commit adultery against it. And then, of course, because there's no smoke without fire and no medicine without art, just as there's no art without medicine, take note of the fact that the record of experience opens and closes with a cry.

The moment he first arrived at Berlin's Stettin station, the city took him by the throat. I'm coming home, he caught himself mumbling. Since then the stones had not loosened their grip. It was like the start of a dialogue with them, a dialogue that was threatened in constant interruption by all the emotions at once. Nothing had summoned the little peasant from Sellin here except an irresistible movement. Maybe a fear that might be heightened by love, or vice versa. He had come to try out the city, like someone undergoing an initiation rite.

He was struck by how many people talked to themselves in the streets. But wasn't the city itself soliloquising all the time? It seemed to him that in Berlin you never talked of anything except Berlin; the city could only paraphrase itself. It was an immense solipsism. A Gorgon, barely able to shake off a heavy sleep. What vehemence might a real awakening unleash? She wasn't, never would be, venerable. On the contrary, she seemed terribly juvenile. She could lay claim to just enough history to launch herself into a surfeit of adventures. She asked only to go to the dogs. Her miseries could not dampen her spirits. But the joy you saw on certain faces had something wild about it. There were fangs glistening in the darkness. She was ripe for every betrayal. Starting with the betrayal of the dead by the living. Even the streets he had walked down a hundred times at night were unrecognisable by day.

The little peasant from Sellin knew he was going to be alone here. But alone as you can feel in the midst of promiscuity. Alone as when you rub up against people and cling to things which you have lost so utterly it makes you dizzy.

He felt he was the same age as this city. That he was Berlin's absolute contemporary.

He was not afraid. Not even of losing the few illusions he still nourished. Nor of going to the very end of the bitterness he felt in the face of life.

The soot of Stettin. The black façades of Kreuzberg. The sharp, cutting cornices, imported campaniles, borrowed mouldings, columns, cupolas, domes and pinnacles of Charlottenburg, the frontons, glazed tiles, obelisks, spires, lightning conductors, caryatids, cherubs and atlantes of the Tiergarten. The emphatic statues of the Siegesallee. The flowery balconies at Moabit. The allotments with Tyrolian chalets and plaster dwarfs. Kitchen gardens with turnips, gherkins, celery. The faded trees of Unter den Linden. Grey willows on the bank of the Havel. Jingling cabs. Clashing trams. The Café Adlon. The Bristol Tavern. The Restaurant Kempinski. Drinking songs in the dives off the Schumannstrasse. Public dances at Treptow. A dawn dinner *chez* Tony Grünfeld. Schiller at the Lessing Theatre. Büchner at the Schiller Theatre. Richard Strauss, conducted by Felix Weingartner, at the Opera, Mahler conducted by Nikisch at the Philharmonic. Yaks and zebus at the Zoological Garden. Birds of prey of all wingspans. An insect pavilion. A little lodge for ferocious beasts. The feeding of the giant tortoises. River chameleons. Golden carp of the China seas. The Ethnographic Museum in Prinz-Albrecht-Strasse. The Schliemann Collection. First floor, room three, the itinerary of Cook's first voyages, masks from the Bismarck Archipelago. Submerged Polynesia whose enigma survives.

The bluish glow of the gaslights. The Saturday evening billiards game. Mushroom-picking on Sundays, in the Grunewald forest. The reading of *Vorwärts* all week for those who, like the pastor of Sellin, still think you can change the world. Hikers' associations. Gymnasts' corporations. *Feldgrau* frock-coats and jackets, satin top-hats, boaters, Panama hats, pointed helmets, short-peaked caps, top-boots, gaiters, hobnailed boots. Pumiced craniums, blue chins, moustaches like claws, monocles. Plaits, flaxen tresses, peroxided hair, short skirts. At the fair there are women with beards and men with breasts. Cripples, people with one arm. Truncated women, stumps of men. Silent films rocked by the languor of the pianola. Sellers of bootlaces – to hang yourself, or matches – to set light to the city. Amateur astronomers – for the joy of discovery. Knife-sharpeners – for the pleasure of killing.

In the gloom of drawing rooms fragrant with wax polish, the Gothic furniture with lion's feet cut out with a jigsaw, the polished chests. In other places there is no more than a table to prop your elbows on, and your hunger-heavy head on your knuckles. Rancid bacon, bran bread, beetroot jam. *Gott mit uns.* At the back of the knackers' yard, day and night, runs the vermilion blood of pigs and heifers. In the streets, in early morning, the scent of sausage mixed with stale cigar. In summer, jasmine and vomit in the shade of the blossoming hedges. Shit under the limes. But they claim that in a short time Berlin will be linked via Stettin with Hamburg and the ocean. Imagine! They'll rediscover the south seas.

Then, there are the women. Why is the city so full of them? At all events, you're going to have to make them love you.

Whatever sense one attaches to those words: love, women …
It won't be easy. But you won't get out of it. The woman
appears in the life of the man just as surely as the last sleep. Life
without a woman is like death without euphemisms. The time
is not long past when the pastor's son, walking at nightfall in
the Brandenburg countryside, as if to hide his thoughts in a
propitious darkness, imagined himself the only little boy who
desired the flesh of girls. And he is still surprised sometimes to
think that he shares that pang, that alarm, with the species.
When he came to make love, he felt himself losing his age. He
discovered this: that you became a child again each time you
"became a man".

The pastor's wife stands facing a swing-mirror. One strap of
her bodice has slipped down her left arm, baring the shoulder
blade. She doesn't know she is being watched. She's unaware
that her eldest son is in the room. It's too late for him to show
himself. Confusion overcomes him. Not for surprising his
mother in her intimacy. But for discovering that her back is so
beautiful and that she certainly does not know it. He ought to
tell her, so that she shows it more often – and because his father
doesn't know it either: he never talks of it. The little boy is
filled with melancholy at having within reach a mother, a
woman so ignorant of her beauty. Of the peace this beauty
gives to the one who looks upon it.

The child's gaze moves to the mirror, to see the reflection
which the body hides. The uncovered breast, with the Cyclopean eye of the teat, seems no less chaste, no less splendid, than
the winged shoulder of creamy white that supports it. The gaze
with which he will from now on look on the bodies of women
opens in Gottfried – that gaze touched with emotion, more
respectful than he would ever admit to himself, but a little
desperate.

For some time his mother is the only woman at Sellin who
merits looking at. Another time she is immersed, drowned, in a
black dress. She's in mourning, no doubt. Not for anyone in

particular. Another time again, she walks bent forward – as if dragging a load – her hands flat against her thighs. Her eyes tried by the light, wide with a secret torment, a groundless sorrow. Unless it's sorrow at having a body entirely taken up by the laborious duty of existing. Gottfried would like his father to be conscripted as an army chaplain.

He would also like to possess all women, to avenge this one who is so irremediably bowed by life, and in a hurry to be bowed further.

The city was teeming with women one might have loved. Also, women for sale. Sometimes they were the same. The man who claims to love women but is not also attracted to the women for sale does not know of what he speaks. He's like someone talking a language he hardly knows.

Was the whore a woman like others? And was any woman other than a whore? Such were the grave questions which, as early as 1906, agitated the drinkers of beer – whom women frightened. True, this debate hardly troubled the pastor's son from Sellin. But like everyone else he had read Otto Weininger's *Sex and Character.* "Oh, give a less ghastly face to vice, so that I can practise it without fear!" All the same, it was a bit simple to divide women into mothers and courtesans, even if the author didn't necessarily see them as opposites. For where the precocious, suicidal Viennese genius hit the mark was in maintaining that women, unlike men, had no fear of adopting this twofold nature. It was enough, indeed, "to say the word double to make a male heart beat faster". Apart from that, how much did it matter whether Weininger was right or wrong? Wittgenstein had observed that even if one said "no" to the book in its entirety, it would proclaim a truth no less important for that. It was in its enormous error that lay its greatness, so he concluded. At all events, thought the crafty peasant from Sellin: mother or whore, provided I can attract one or the other it's not my business which she is – for me, that's not even a question that exists . . . And he saw more deeply than that. If women were not afraid of their shadow, most men were alarmed by their feminine double. (Oh, let each side have its way. Even that is hardly enough!)

Let us start, therefore, thought the young man, by getting admitted to the society of whores, even if its tenderness is fake. There, at least, the easy women do not stand out from the others ... And in fact, how many cute bourgeoises are more provocative than either! So much so that you approached the blank-faced creatures who patrolled the Friedrichstrasse – even the ones with the gaudiest make-up and the most mascara-laden eyelids – with caution, even deference. And you were right. In one case out of two you picked the wrong one, but when you chose right it was the void-haunted eyes that hooked you, even their most negligent glance stabbing you in the soul. That was what took your breath away, made you happy, and gave you a touch of nausea.

But if the girl turned down the student's unhealthy demands or just his paltry means, leaving him to watch her retreat along a muddy pavement with a regret that went beyond humiliation, his chagrin could easily turn to genuine sorrow. Then he'd go and buy an obscene postcard, though the least obscene possible, so that he could, once back in his room, vent on her his grief at not having had even the chance to despair of the flesh.

You might as well fall back on those who cost nothing, he decided. That was the way: he would go and cruise the Arcadia, the Café Riche, or the lobby of the Métropole. Since he was not frightened by death but actually found it interesting, he'd be a seducer. "Bloom not too soon, bloom only, flowers, for me." Not without a certain bitter satisfaction, he noted from his own case that poverty does not always make men better.

"What really interests me," the anatomist confides in an unguarded moment, "is the skeleton. What a construction – what an edifice! You'll see, gentlemen, that the future of our profession is tied to it. It will give the people of tomorrow more information about themselves than all the flesh in the world. Doesn't the Bible say that our sins are inscribed in our bones? Nothing could be more true. At the Charity Hospital I saw them bring in, on the same day, a young dragoon and an old pauper woman. Both had had their legs broken, his by a fall from a horse, hers by being knocked over by a dog in the street. You may not believe it, gentlemen, but she recovered much more quickly than he did. There was no explanation – except that the man was a debauchee. Vice had eaten away the columns which supported him, his femurs were as porous as chalk. Think of the atrophy, the disorganisation of the bones that the pox causes. Yet our cavalier wasn't even syphilitic. As for the old woman, she'd led an exemplary life. She was rewarded by a swift recovery. We don't always have to wait for the afterlife to get our deserts ... Those of you who might be inclined to smile about this will remember, one day, that I warned you. All the upheavals of our lives are engraved deep in our bodily husk, leave their deposits in our bones. What do our forgiveness and forgetfulness really matter, gentlemen: our bodies forget nothing. Alive or dead, they speak. They're a catalogue we consult. When I open a man like a book I can reconstruct his whole history. Were the ancients so wide of the mark when they read their future in their entrails? That, gentlemen, is why anyone who cannot stand the sight of a gaping body, who can't meet the divine stare that comes to him out of that body, who can't overcome his disgust at the sight – that person, in my view, should abandon the idea of being a doctor, even a doctor of souls, since, nowadays, such things exist ... Would anyone expect to be a deep-sea captain if they suffered from sea-sickness?" But, the student wonders, does the future corpse realise it is going to yield up all its humble secrets, its intimate miseries, to a man in white with flesh-coloured rubber gloves? What he has sought and found in vice and orgies, wasn't it a scattering of his own substance that would throw his pursuers off the track? And why is a body only recognised, identified, once it has passed from life into death?

The Dead Bodies

The anatomist suddenly seems a formidable figure endowed with excessive powers. The idea crosses the student's mind that if you have once had a dead body at your disposal like this, you have, in a sense, profaned them all. In other ages the anatomist and the surgeon were treated as untouchables since, like the executioner, these explorers of entrails had to do, *inter faeces et urinas*, with blood.

"The most worrying thing," one demonstrator told him, "is when something unexpected happens. You don't find what you're looking for ... the dissection goes on for ever. You want to pee, and you can't let go of the rudder while the body's being shipwrecked ... Now you can think of nothing except emptying your bladder ... If you let yourself have your own way you would piss in the corpse's face. Once, when I was working on one, I thought he smelt burnt. Believe it or not: it made me hungry. I don't know what I wouldn't have given to drop my instruments and get myself a nice greasy fry-up."

Now, the master wants him to hold the implements that shine in their cases, taking the pedagogical opportunity to name them as they pass from hand to hand: scalpel, lancet, retractor, rachitome, hammer, saw, probe, xyster ... "Take care not to cut yourself, Mr Benn, and if it happens, stop work at once and clean the wound."

Lying on the granite table, the body in its nudity has recovered all its decorum. Of course, he's been given an embalmed one. A natural death, as far as there are any. The anatomist keeps the dubious or executed stiffs to himself. The Punch and Judy show, as his assistants call it: drownings, poisonings, stranglings, rapes.

More than fifteen litres of formaldehyde have filled out the corpse, giving it back some colour, erasing its features. "If you had to dissect your own grandmother you wouldn't even recognise her," the anatomist is fond of saying with great delicacy. The student is glad he has not been allocated a woman. Or a hunchback, or one with an arm missing. Either out of superstition or for technical reasons, the students are afraid of disabled corpses: incomplete, mutilated, they put the analyst off his stroke. The student from Sellin has hardly glanced at Günther – let's call him that for simplicity, says the anatomist – but it has been enough to confirm what he has noticed every time: that all dead people look like aged children. Huge babies covered in hair and endowed with enormous sexual parts.

Wasn't this the grinning, spiteful face of a senile old man? You are going to have to feel, through the gloves, the excessive softness and coldness of flesh. Just as you'll be struck by how icy the little remaining blood seems. And then, once the man is incised from the collar-bone to the perineum – the clavicles, the abdominal wall, the blind sun of the navel, the gullet of the pelvis – you'll be startled, yet again, by the profusion of organs, the multitude of tissues, the complexity of the structure. *De humani corporis fabrica*, said Vesalius with a kind of pride – the pride of belonging to the species that stood out by this super-abundance of forms, volumes, colours. Beauty where you would least expect to find it, and where finding it is scandalous. All that in a body ...

"You are tired, Mr Benn?" asks the anatomist. Not at all, thinks the student. At least, not more than usual. In any case, that's the least of my concerns. Just let us collect our thoughts in face of the palette of bright colours and semi-tones, of ramifying branches and geological reliefs that this man, this Günther, carried about inside him without knowing it. We'll know nothing else about him. Incision of the cranium passing through the vertex. Insert the lever. Breach. Sever the nerves at the base of the bulb. Drain the cerebro-spinal fluid. Excise the brain.

The student understands why it is important to remove oneself as soon as possible from the gaze of the person one is dissecting, even if his eyes are closed. It spares you the ecstatic expression which the old engravers, Casserius, Estienne, Valverde, Paré, showed on the faces of anatomical models when they were being bled. The student from Sellin raises his head for a moment; the dirty light which the skylight casts on the operating area reassures him. It isolates him, as in an aquarium, from the world in which no one could imagine a corpse being treated as he is busy treating it. He recalls that in the prints depicting the vanity of worldly pleasures and the anatomical drawings of former times, the engraver took care to show eviscerated bodies and skeletons in the foreground of smiling landscapes dotted with clumps of trees and neatly marked out with cippi or fortifications. Were they trying to domesticate horror? They only made it more palpable. The student thinks of his father, the pastor of Sellin. He sees his worried brow. As if weighed down by an obstinacy devoid of an object. He recalls the course on the history of modern philosophy given by Hermann Cohen at Marburg. Caught between his father, who did not discuss God, the neo-Kantians who were only too happy to underline the impossibility of proving His existence, and Nietzsche who danced on His grave, he, the little Sellin peasant, had felt very alone. It had not seemed so important to him to discuss God's existence as to stress the enigmatic way He manifested Himself, the opacity of His presence in the world. Gottfried was still a child then, but Kant, Nietzsche, Weininger appeared to him to be heroically uttering puerile nonsense – measured against the infernal complexity of life. At the same time, however, he had seemed to hear all the secrets of the universe resounding in a single couplet of a syrupy song ground out on a barrel organ in a backyard off the Leipziger Strasse.

Remove the ribcage, take out the organs that maintain life. Move to the thorax, which is marbled with blood. Rupture the fibrous adhesions which join the pleurae. Sever the diaphragm on each side from the broken pericardium. Open the aorta from the bifurcation to the arch. See the arch dilate. Don't confuse the cavities in the cardiac muscle. Of course, this is where it happened. The operator straightens himself, as if the better to admire the marquetry of the visceral landscape that spreads before him. The violet tints of the heart. The virgin forest harboured by this carcass ... He remembers a photo of himself taken in 1896, when he was ten, that his mother had pinned to the wallpaper of his bedroom. It showed him on the edge of a swimming pool, his arms crossed on his bare body, to shield it from view or to protect it from the cold. He was frowning. He can't have realised the picture was being taken. Another showed him with his hands closed around a bunch of flowers. As delicate as a girl. And then, in a third, he is already made to look manly in the school uniform: the cap, the trouser legs halfway down his calves, the elastic-sided boots. Each time, he saw himself a bit uglier. Old for his age. Eyes always somewhat averted. On the first floor of the Ethnographic Museum in Prinz-Albrecht Strasse, there were some enormous maps on which forgotten archipelagos emerged from cobalt seas. To resist the feeling of infinity inspired by the ocean's vastness, the natives had raised colossal statues made of a material whose source remained a puzzle. These effigies surveyed the horizon with ineffable arrogance. After that no one knew what to invent to appease the nameless fear.

Penis in the flaccid state. The wrinkled, violet pouches of the scrotum. In death, all parts are intimate. No relief more noble than the others. You are a voyeur everywhere. Rectum, ureter and bladder, prostate, seminal vesicles: what a fine *mélange* of ordure and imaginings these entrails contain. We are so trifling a thing and, at the same time, so immense ... For even here, around these detumescent organs, isn't there still some hint of transcendence prowling? Dr Kant, show yourself now, fine prince! Come on. Let's cut the spermatic cord, sever the roots of the member on the pubic arch. We're only doing it to be exhaustive, to hone our gestures to the finest point. The Sellin student recalls the lithograph in which a subject whose penis has been severed remains in a pensive pose ... In New Guinea the Papuans collected the skulls of their enemies, which they stuffed with clay. The natives of the Marquesas believed that the power of the adversary could be transferred like an inoculation from the vanquished to the victor, and they only ate him with this in view. Who could swear they were not right? But on the first floor of the Ethnographic Museum in Prinz-Albrecht Strasse, in room three, you could gaze on a galley so imposing that its makers must have been too weak to haul it to the sea, so that their race was doomed to extinction. Peoples could disappear: you had to realise that. Happy the ones who could at least leave behind a sign on the shore. So it was not always enough to ingest the body of your enemy, if you wanted to survive. Now there was something for doctors to get excited about!

Before resuming work the Sellin student reflected that other dissectors after him – particularly if like him they were poets – would be interested in what was being hatched in the secret depths of the oceans. Was not the melancholy of the blood relayed by our nostalgia for warm seas? You navigate the sounds and reaches of the body too. To finish off, examine the rachis of Günther. A lab assistant turns the cavernous man on to his stomach, places a block under his throat and another under his abdomen. At this point Günther abandons all hope of appearing sublime. No question of Wagnerian cadences now: it's Günther, not Siegfried, who is being killed, and he is slit from nape to sacrum and coccyx without further consideration for his feelings. This isn't the body of Caesar – the one in which Antistius counted twenty-three wounds, only one of them mortal. At any rate, a few ritual slashes in the arms and thighs, a final laceration of the stiff, but only by way of a signature, a flourish. For the cause of death has long been obvious: ruptured aneurism. It would be a totally explainable, commonplace death, but for the youth of the subject ... Yet again, the operator thinks almost bitterly, there is no mystery.

Whatever made him mix up Polynesia and Professor Kant with all this? With the politics of these remains? Perhaps because of the fragility of civilisations, which is far greater than that of men, despite the monstrous unreality of the statues raised by the Papuans on the shore of their island to ward off the unknown, perhaps the infinite. As for the philosopher of Königsberg, the Sellin peasant suddenly remembered that after the earthquake which ravaged Lisbon that thinker had written on the advantages of seismic disturbances – such was his belief in the perfection of our world as it is. Which led him quite naturally to condemn suicide as immoral. Finally, hadn't this punctual walker, so regular in his outings that the citizens of his town set their clocks when he passed, had he not, just once in his life, lost track of time: when reading Rousseau, who "taught him respect for men"? Even better, thought the medical student, to learn to venerate them by opening them up from larynx to anus, just to know exactly what one is talking about. At Königsberg God, whom pure reason has placed in doubt, is given a second chance by practical reason. Eternity turned down to a glimmer. Immortality reduced to the finest filigree – an invisible net for a faint-hearted trapeze trickster. So that Kant, the incurable pietist, only appeared to have closed the era of smug optimism, had only half emerged from its "dogmatic slumber", its domestic vigil. The incorrigible idealist flung rotten bridges across the abysses his own thought had dug. Kant never questioned himself: he just went from one reversal of an idea to another. A terrorist giving lessons to tyrants. A celibate vaunting the morose joys of marriage. Siding with the dull, conjugal woman against the adventuress avid for knowledge and semen. In short, resignation as to the ultimate ends and faith in the wisdom of nations. Beauty as the recognition of the established order. The orderly user of time and dietician of the soul. Immanuel Kant had never had to cut open the rind of a man. Who knows whether the sight of this logic arrested on the point of decomposition might not have made his splendid system dizzy, given it a limp? And who knows whether an investigation of Kant's remains might not have brought to light some debauch of the mind, some timid orgy, some sad Bacchanal – imprinted in the structure of his bones? Luckily, there had later been Nietzsche, who wanted to be the Don Juan of knowledge, "that agreeable form of perdition". It was all over with categorical imperatives, boiled to a pulp with Prussian sauce, which really conveyed only a bottomless incapacity for doubt. All in all, better to laugh to yourself in the street. Embrace a martyred carthorse. Choose to die in summer, at the stroke of midday. Die the play-actor rather than the pontiff: your carcass won't be any more difficult to inventorise. "All in me is a lie, but when I break, that break is true."

The anatomist does not offer his congratulations to his pupil – nor is it his habit to do so. But for the Sellin student it is enough to have his fellow-students grouping themselves around their master – the master today being the one who has officiated, himself – to make him feel the obscure fraternity of those who search together. At this moment he is sure that the most blinkered suburban quack knows more about men than the imperial thinker who will never know that you can only combat death with your hands. Taking off his rubber gloves and putting away his instruments under the murky skylight of the lecture theatre in Alt-Moabit, he remembers that he only wanted to become a doctor because he felt afflicted by a gloomy detachment from the reality of things. "Woe to him who harbours deserts in his breast," the philosopher dear to his heart had written in his *Dionysian Dithyrambs*. "The desert is a hunger that disinters the dead."

A wash-tub is steaming in a backyard off the Potsdammerstrasse. Two tarts hard up for clients dance together to keep warm in a deserted music-hall in the heart of the afternoon. The chimney-sweep passes with a tin hat on. A dressmaker's dummy has been pushed out on to the pavement. The barrelorgan grinds out the "Radetzky March" next to a cold brazier. You would have thought winter had arrived. The city hasn't learned how to pitch its voice. When its voice breaks, that's when you hear Berlin singing.

Berlin, 1906

In his mind's eye the medical student sees the pastor's house, its covered verandah, the fruit trees stretching their branches further and further, as if they wanted to clutch at the windows. The echo of an axe at work deep in the forest. A clatter of buckets in the yard. The washing hanging on the line clapped like a sail in the middle of the garden. In the midst of the world's desert. The sun made the sheets blue, reflected in them as if in window panes. It was in another time, probably 1896 when the pupil came home for a few days' holiday from the grammar school in Frankfurt-on-Oder where he was a boarder.

He soon tired of these excursions, of which he expected too much. He sees himself walking in the stunned countryside, arms dangling, with nothing to carry or to hold on to.

He sees himself, finally, head bowed in lamplight. Harnessed to his work-table: the ultimate handrail against the abyss, the last resort.

At that time he thought he loved life. But he had a presentiment that, heaven knows why, the project of life was going to be difficult to put into practice.

Later, he is given a drowned man for autopsy. Bluish face. Cyanosed lips. Saponified flesh. Early stage of gaseous putrefaction. Emphysema. Alveolar fissures. Dilution of the blood. Dilation of right ventricle. Liquid matter and vegetable debris in the respiratory tract, stomach and duodenum. Retraction of the penis. Maceration of the skin of the extremities. Mutilation probably caused by contact with a barge.

The sequence of operations. The gassy sputtering of a lung subsiding on the table. The tumefied garland of bowels. The spongy liver of a cirrhotic squeaking under the knife. The peritoneum has split. Puncture of a tumour with a trocar.

Some days it's the stale smell of blood that is most intolerable. But the scalpel tirelessly furrows the abandoned bodies. Without hope of ever attaining a final mastery. It must always be re-done, undone. Just when one is launched on the trail of apoplexy, meningitis, infarction, metastasis. All these blotches and blemishes, everywhere: vascular, purple, brown, cicatricial. You're in death's wake. Reeling in the thread of its causes.

Once he had to dissect a woman. Fine scissors severing a vulva, last visitors to a vagina. Ecchymosis of the tubes and ovaries. Erosion of the uterus. Placentary debris. Discovery of an egg . . .

It was that day that the scent of death seemed most acrid and you thought that from then on it would follow you every-where. You imagined the dead woman's entrails were about to start boiling.

Then there was a hanged man, a fairly old corpse. The face had melted; he looked like a ghost in his shroud.

Of course, you also see live people operated on. Bodies that are perforated to keep them alive. Later, you're even in charge of several confinements. But the screams of the mother, the first cries of a sticky baby, how can you believe they don't signify more suffering, that they counterbalance the deaths of the others?

"Don't worry," the anatomist declared with a kindly smile, "you never get used to it. No danger that your sensibilities will ever be blunted. Whatever we do, it will always be too much for us. That's how it is. Living is walking on a high wire. Science just gives us a balancing bar. And if we happen to have known or just met in life the person we are opening up, it makes no difference, or hardly any. It's always a dismantled person. One pities them all, you know. Pities the species. One's always alone in face of that. And a prey to personal feelings. There are some days when, for some reason, it's harder than others. Are you thinking of continuing along this road, Mr Benn? Not decided yet? It would be a pity if you were tempted by other adventures: you have a gift, you know. You operate with a lot of foresight . . . "

How can I be lucid, when I am beginning to doubt the reality of everything?

And supposing the only reality were the one being skinned on the operating block? The medical student forces himself to think that he has been granted the privilege of working at an academy which has produced Virchow, Helmholtz, Leyden, Behring, whose spirits still reign between these walls. And he is living in a great epoch. He recalls that this year, in 1906, Wassermann has produced the reaction that will allow the diagnosis of syphilis. He is not far from giving way to enthusiasm at the thought that, thanks to Schwann, the cellular structure of animal organisms has been established. He himself, the young medical student, has discovered, the first time he bent over the lens of a microscope, that the real, apprehended on an infinitesimal scale, is adorned with new forms and undreamed-of colours. But then, how can you fail to suspect, sometimes, that these are just so many mirages?

He would like to be ten again, or even younger, when to delouse him, his mother washed his hair with paraffin. After that, he thought his face would shine in the dark like a storm-lamp.

He recalls that he sometimes crouched at the end of the entrance hall of the vicarage. He would spend long moments watching the light that frosted the polished wood stairs. He knows now what was so moving about Sellin: it was a place of luxurious poverty.

From where he crouched, he could see his father sitting on his bed in his room, reading the social-democrat newspaper to which he subscribed, or the *Imperial Messenger*, the *Journal of the Cross*: columns of inert, defunct words.

Sometimes his mother would say to him: "No one here knows anything about the country I come from. I could tell you some things about it ... "

But she soon gave up. She must have thought it wasn't worth it. Her modesty had no limits.

At Frankfurt-on-Oder the young man from Sellin had learned the price of things. A mark was a mark: a whole fortune. Sometimes he did not even have the price of a meal at the students' mensa.

During his lessons in religion or geography, he sometimes caught sight of his reflection in a window the sun turned into a mirror. He thought: that is the face of a man who will later spend his time writing poetry.

At Mohrin, where the pastor had just been transferred, in 1910, the young man was photographed on the bank of the Oder: he had never been, and would never be again, as handsome as in that photo. It's because I was just starting to write, he thought. Later, the same work was to make him uglier.

He was already studying at Marburg when he decided to send a few poems anonymously to the *Review of the Novel* which had its office in Berlin-Lichterfelde. After some time, the verdict dropped like the blade of a guillotine: "Idea worthy of interest. Language somewhat harsh. Weak expression."

Expression. That's it – expression . . .

He analyses a reproduction of Matthias Grünewald's *Altarpiece*. He notes the suffering, even decomposing body of the Saviour. The Virgin's almost ecstatic swoon. The evangelist broken with grief. Mary Magdalene, whose resplendent attire slightly heightens her lamentation. Her joined hands are twisted as by rheumatism; suffering ruins her siren face. The lamb pisses blood into the chalice. And then St Anthony, the hero of this dolorous saga, is delivered up to the demons. He looks as if he is experiencing an attack of *delirium tremens*. A commentary suggests that this "sacred fire", which charred and tore off the limbs of the sick in the Middle Ages, is more likely to have been convulsive or gangrenous ergotism. And maybe syphilis, already? But is it his patients who are assailing the saint in a crisis of their illness, or rather his own fever which is summoning them in an hallucination? The master's brush did not make this clear. The exegetist wonders if the artist hadn't given his own features to St John. Unless it was to St Sebastian – or even St Paul? And then, of course ... Christ as well! And why not Mary? And was Grünewald to recognise himself even in the puniest of the imps?

And yet no one could be further from naturalism. What a lesson. That's how to go about it. There was nothing here but a reproduction of anecdotes. Nothing but expressiveness.

Expression. Expression – that's it!

These Prometheuses with their livers eaten away from the inside, or these hetaerae with their Ophelian tresses – before they are dumped on the dissecting table with the registration number burnt on their foreheads in case they lose the identification labels attached to their big toes, one ought to pay them some unhoped-for, some heart-rending homage. Show how their whole life is crystallised in the last image they have left behind beyond all nudity. No word of commentary. Any paraphrase would be an indecency. Poems that would be nothing but blocks of pity petrified like lava.

The Sellin peasant has had from early on an unhappy love for the language of Luther, a language still so young that you could bend it to your will without even having to subdue it.

Remember Nietzsche riding to hounds in pursuit of style. Hurling his megalomaniac halloo over the baying pack. Having already said practically everything that was still left to be said, because he had bagged the reality of the modern world like game, cast it at our feet, torn to pieces ...

One should not forget the lesson of an unknown poet named Stefan George: he saw that there were only bodies, nothing else. That only bodies do not lie. The body is a god, an unhappy god, plighted to catastrophes.

The Dead Bodies

All lessons were worth taking: those you could get from the young Rilke, or from Detlev von Liliencron, to whom in a fervent moment you sent a postcard while on an excursion to Rüdesheim. Even the ones to be learned from Vesper's *Harvest of the German Lyric*, published this same year, 1906.

A few more years, and you will be a doctor. You will have submitted a dissertation on "The incidence of diabetes mellitus in the army". In the meantime you will have received a prize for your research on "The aetiology of pubertal epilepsy". (You will be able to choose between a medal or a sum of two hundred marks. You choose the money. You'll be able to pay your debts at last. Even the cuir-bouilli case with which you first arrived in Berlin had to be bought on credit.)

A few more years, the same years, and you will not have become a psychiatrist, although, at the Charity Hospital, you are always tempted to link the body to the soul. You are only too ready to believe that myths are really just objects we have been collecting for several thousand years. But you shy away from using that kind of jargon in your diagnoses. You want to find the psyche somewhere else. And then, most important of all, you are so steeped in melancholy that hearing about the sadness of others leaves you voiceless, your throat dry, your eyes red as if from insomnia. You're incapable of treating one case after another, analysing them, sounding the abyss that threatens to engulf you yourself at every moment. You can write about all that – an essay, above all poems – but live through it again? Out of the question!

A few more years, still the same ones, and you will have been pronounced unfit for active military service: a congenital condition, something rather nebulous that came to light after a horse-ride lasting a whole day. You won't ride a horse again. You will be in no doubt that your path and the army's will cross some other time.

And during those same years your mother will have died at Mohrin, of breast cancer. It is Dr Benn she will call to her bedside. But he will be unable either to relieve her pain with morphine injections or to ease her passage towards death. Pastor Gustav Benn takes too good care that no earthly suffering is abridged, since it is the will of God and a spring-board to resurrection. The young doctor will return to the capital with a baggage of hatred and sorrow that will accompany him for almost his whole life. The bitter taste of blood in the mouth: will you never escape it? Your mother will not have seen her son's first collection of poems come out. But that is perhaps as well: what would she have thought of all that human death on display, she who was so close to life, the life of animals and plants? Who knows if he did not delay publication when he saw that same death bearing down on his mother, proving him right and her wrong?

For those same years he'll have as his mistress a woman seventeen years older than himself, though she will keep the fact to herself, another mother, in a way, a Jewess, extravagant and beautiful, with enormous eyes. They'll meet at the Café des Westens, where the great plots of art nouveau are hatched, Else Lasker-Schüler being its presiding goddess. It is Gottfried's poems that will guide him to her. Poems lead to women, and women to more poems, so it seems. Else captivated the men who still had souls at that time; she played the doll, covered herself with fake jewels, made herself look like a Christmas tree. A thirst for life that was equalled only by her unfitness for existence. And then, between them, that avalanche of poetry that will bring them to such understanding of each other will also conspire to separate them. Else will later leave for Palestine, slightly bowed, like a gambler who has lost her fortune in a single night. In another life she must have been a she-cat so wild that it was mistaken for a panther – or so trigger-happy hunters would say.

So it is in those years, by the end of those years, little by little and yet all at once, step by step and in a single bound, that you will become a poet.

The Dead Bodies

A cycle of six poems composed in the course of a single
nightfall, after leaving a dissection class at Alt-Moabit. Written
in the space of an hour – and leaving the author himself
dismayed.

But thinking back on it "in tranquillity", he wondered if he
hadn't taken years creating them. If they had not been elabo-
rated in spite of him, fomented in twilit inner depths as in a
buzzing hive.

From the first autopsy he had seen, up to that evening in his
room in north-west Berlin when the cry had unsealed his lips:
it was like the vision of the dead themselves. The shock-wave
produced by his first corpse had travelled in him until he was
sure the language to translate it was there. It was through
seeing, and seeing truly, that he had fallen into a kind of trance.
Through all these years the medical student had not grown
used to the horror. Far from exhausting itself in him, it had
chosen him as the place to formulate itself. It was like a sickness
that had had to incubate and had suddenly broken its silence.
For a long time, no doubt to elude his terror, to harden
himself, he had posed himself problems of aesthetic theory. To
express such things, he decreed, you had to abandon the words
of medicine ... Even the words of poetry ... You had to
make poetry with everything it normally excluded. And then,
suddenly, it had been necessary to note only one thing: that our
dead were speechless. We knew them even less than we knew
the people of Polynesia. We would simply have to give them
back their speech, even if we had not yet found it for ourselves;
so you went looking for it, at the same time as you gave it to
them. The dead were going to speak through you. (Yes – you
were in a position to give what, an hour before, you had not
even had for yourself.) Oh, it was no longer a technical
problem, this time! It would be like letting the city too express
itself through its intermediary: Berlin, from which so many of
its inhabitants averted their eyes, as if embarrassed by its
indecency. (They would look somewhere else, pretending they
had seen nothing ... And, indeed, they really had perceived

nothing.) A poetry which transcribes this meeting, this tête-à-tête between a living and a dead person, just the two, as in a private funeral. As if they were alone in the world. Love poems, then, though the reader would be unable to make them out.

The beer delivery man found with an aster wedged between his teeth. The drowned woman who had gathered a nest of rats inside her under the water. The prostitute whose gold filling had been filched by the undertaker's assistant. The girl with her throat cut open, reposing like a fiancée on the blissful shore of first love. And then, the man and the woman coupled by death on the dissecting table. What cancer left behind of what, for someone, had once been landscape and allurement. And the child delivered from a womb eaten away by disease. And again, women in childbirth and those having their wombs scraped, uttering the same cry that attends on birth and death. Such poetry was so unexpected that people would see in it a hideous sarcasm, a provocation, a profession of utter cynicism. It was nothing other than an invincible disgust before creation, and pity for the creatures.

Henceforth write nothing, Nietzsche had said, but that which drives those bustlers to despair. And how untimely you had proved yourself, how true to Nietzsche's vow. The Berlin morgue was not on the agenda! You were not, would never be one of those poets of whom Nietzsche, again, said that they reminded him of chastely neighing stallions. That was the commitment you had made: your verse would never console anyone. You would not be convenient. You would demoralise polite society!

For it was a strange song the corpses sang. And you were starting to sing it in a round. No one was obliged to listen to the duet. We beg your pardon; we weren't even trying to shock you ... How could you know that the same people who were tossing the world to the vermin had such delicate nerves?

Much later, the poet was to amuse himself by checking off

some of the events which marked the year 1886, when he was born. Among others: "The visits Turgenev paid every day to the Viardot sisters, when they were staying in Baden-Baden. It was decided to Germanise 1088 words of *Faust*. The thirteenth edition of the *Brockhaus Dictionary of Conversation* came out. Tolstoy's *Power of Darkness* flopped, and Flaubert's *Salammbô* was a financial disaster. On the other hand, Schneider (Creusot), Krupp and Putiloff increased their capital by one hundred per cent."

He was to recall that in the pastoral home at Sellin there was a tiled stove manufactured by Tobias Christoph Feilner. The irons for the washing were made of cast iron. On Sundays biscuits were served on plates of openwork porcelain. His sister Edith played with a Kruse doll.

Throughout his childhood his mother had said to him repeatedly: "I could tell you some stories about the country I come from, what used to go on there ... " But she never told him anything. The revelations were always postponed.

And now it was too late.

Brussels, 1916

The Ecstasy

The soldier who conquers a town sometimes finds himself stranded in it like a beached whale. He is no longer in his element. He has to discover a new way of breathing.

Before being an enemy town, it is a foreign town. It's not just that a different language is spoken there. The town is itself an unknown language – that will have to be learned.

In Brussels, Officer Benn had from the first a feeling of unreality. His status as a military doctor – that double agent of warfare who has one foot in life and the other in death – heightened the sense of disorientation, dizziness.

Two years earlier, Belgium had claimed that the Imperial Army was violating its neutrality. The Kaiser retorted that it had prostituted that neutrality by proffering favours to Germany's enemies. But however that may have been, the Germans should have been more careful of that original neutrality; did it not suggest that, even victorious, they might be trapped in it, drugged, immobilised?

Had not the uhlans taken the whole of Europe by storm by promising their wives they would be back by the end of the summer at the latest? As for the Belgians, would it not be enough to send the Düsseldorf firemen against them?

The medical officer recalled the fall of Antwerp, which had waited in vain for English reinforcements, and that Joffre had doubtless never intended to help. It was to be the only engagement in which he was involved. At the end of August, a

Zeppelin had dropped a dozen bombs on the port. But the stronghold held out until the autumn. On 7 October the River Schelde was itself on fire. But two days later the besieging army found itself in possession of a city which its defenders had evacuated, absconding to Holland.

The victor was reduced to marching through deserted avenues where the buildings had been preventively destroyed by the vanquished, to reduce the spoils. The petrol storage tanks had also been set ablaze, to prevent the Germans from using the fuel to set the city alight in frustration. The medical officer was struck to see that a number of big cats had been killed and the snakes poisoned at the zoo ... (Was it really there, and for what feat of arms, that he had won the Iron Cross, Second Class?)

As they left for the war, some poets and painters that he met again in Brussels had liked to think that at least it would broaden their horizons ... On both sides there was no lack of wits who would have been much put out to miss the "excursion". And many of them had been sorely tempted to confuse the emotions that sometimes swelled their hearts with a full-blooded initiation into warfare. They felt a tenderness that they believed disinterested. A solemnity to which even the most practically-minded succumbed, surprising themselves by its ineffable vibrations. Against the background of History even a certain spinelessness found itself gifted with sublime utterance. The military doctor recalled the arrogance of those who, at Antwerp, felt only relief at not having to fight. The same who, safely back in their barracks in the evening, talked loudest about the women of whom, in reality, they were also afraid.

That, moreover, is the battle-front that will keep him busy in Brussels – him, the expert on venereal ballistics!

Four years earlier, he had published some poems in which he diagnosed the state of health of words. In which he listened to their ailments, and revived certain words that poetry had let wither. In this way he restored to them more than their meanings: a sort of organic life in which not only the mind was involved. The poet, too, is a doctor, who masks the symptoms of words, sometimes cures the cancer devouring them. For words are driven by a single haste – to gallop towards the nothingness from which they have been hauled. Only the poet grants them a remission. Except when they are under his pen they are asleep on their feet, tottering, letting themselves die over a low gas. To have his first words presented to him by the dead, perhaps after he had forced their doors, was to come quickly to the point. Especially when the language which brought death to life economised on the sensitive palpitations, reproducing only the deafening decomposition of corpses. All the sufferings of life condensed in an ultimate cacophony.

The critics yelp with fright, splutter with disgust. A first misunderstanding. Success for the wrong reasons: the public throng to the Galerie Paul Cassirer to listen to the author of *Morgue*.

He also meets some genuine readers. One evening he seduces a female admirer, at the Romanisches Café, or the Café des Westens. But she is so terribly close to him, Else Lasker-Schüler, that they can't both breathe the same air for long. Suddenly there is too much of this reduplicated poetry and tragedy. It saturates. The words of each jar on the other. When they are both poets, lovers inflict wounds on each other that are unlike any others. It is a confirmation of melancholy. He wants to escape. However, they all emerge from the shadows at the same moment, the poets who tell of the horrors of man-eating cities, naked wretchedness, the twilight of the West. They publish in *Der Sturm* or *Die Aktion*. They recite at the Neopathetisches Cabaret. Even when they do not know each other, an incestuous fraternity links the poets and painters of a generation suddenly requisitioned by History. Things are accelerating. In Gottfried Benn a doctor specialising in gonorrhoea and hard and soft chancres collaborates with a poet who, from the outset, has gone banco with the death-cards of the Tarot.

Time for him to meet an actress called Edith, whose stage name is Eva, to marry her, conceive a child, and then a crank at Sarajevo shoots a pistol which mobilises several nations, none of which, if they are to be believed, wanted war. We announced an apocalypse, sometimes vociferously, thinks the young husband. And it's happening. We're going to die or grow old. We've hardly uttered a word and History already wants to take it back, or drown it with its own expectorations.

It was not in Brussels that he started to lose that sense of reality which he believed he prized so highly as a man of science. It happened little by little after he moved to Berlin and began to have dealings with the sick, the dead. He has already given up the idea of being a psychiatrist: he could not endure what he saw crawling in the human mind. He would have wept with boredom. Poetry was neurosis enough. He preferred to apply himself to the degradations of the skin.

Since he arrived in Belgium, at Beverlo, and has had to treat the illness which contractually links the invaders with the women for whom the invasion has meant an employment boom, that old science of reality seems to have abandoned him. But he has no regrets for the amputated limb . . .

At this moment, he is listening to the confessions of young recruits whose exploits in the beds of wanton women made them as cocksure in the canteen last night as they are now crestfallen, confronted by the evidence of stigmata they still try to deny. He reassures them as best he can. He explains that since the beginning of the war scientists have invented new remedies, and that in a short time everyone will recover, provided he is treated in time. Those listening to him are children, a bit cowardly or hypocritical, and terrorised. They suddenly remember the warnings they were given at school, which merely inspired smutty witticisms. They remember seeing daguerreotypes and plates on which the scourge was endowed with volumes and hues that made it seem somewhat unlikely. They shiver. They already see their flesh putrefying, their bones crumbling like chalk, their tendons corroding and snapping, their cartilages melting. Soon their noses will drop into their bowls just as they are dipping in their spoons. Their eyes will dissolve as if attacked by acid. A harsh cry will escape their mouths, stretched and torn open like a Caesarean section, a death rattle smothered by pus ... The medical officer listens to them stammering their horror. Underneath it, he discerns a latent wretchedness. Soon he hears nothing but this refrain the soldiers hum without realising it, which is the truth of that time. Taking care of them means first of all taking their hands to assure them they have not got leprosy, they won't fall to pieces by tomorrow; they have more chance of being maimed by the cannon on the Yser than by the microbe they harbour ... A fatuous smile lights up their faces. They do not realise how terribly true that is.

It only remains to extract from them the name of the one who has contaminated them, the woman who, somewhere in a barrack hut, an attic, a shop back-room, if not in the mire of a path or lane, has turned with her lifted skirt and parted thighs into a little machine for making "damaged" flesh, for distilling putrid blood, fetid vapours. The sickness prowls like a bacillus around the juvenile cannon fodder. The medical officer's task is to keep these brats as healthy as he can so that they can later be sucked into the sludge of the battlefield, where their death, no doubt, will be the more worthy ... He suspects that some infect themselves in the hope of being sent home, or kept away from the front for a long time. Others try to hide the chancre for fear they will be given no more leave. Others again refuse to denounce the harlot who has marked them. They would think themselves informers. If panicked, they would name someone else. As for the girls, he could swear that they see it as their patriotic duty in these garrison towns to transmit to the enemy the virulent message they carry. It is war conducted by other means! Are they at least decorated when they come back from such missions? In the old days, didn't these putrid women cause more havoc than grapeshot or cold steel? Thus everyone forms a certain idea of honour, which gets blurred by the proximity of danger.

The medical officer registers one more couplet of the song sung by the recruits' chorus. They could never bawl loudly enough in the guard-room, never had words crude enough or epithets depraved enough to season the stories of their de-bauches.

But their listener no longer allows himself to judge. Once again, though only too sure he has heard properly, he doubts the veracity of the situation itself. That half-closed eye – as if against the smoke from a cigarette that was a permanent extension of his right forefinger – picks up everything, but selects as it goes along, perhaps rejecting more images than it retains. That drowsy attention, that is sometimes unconfirmed by any sign for long intervals. It can be disconcerting to the speaker. The interrogator seems to be dozing. Then you realise he has missed nothing. You might think him indifferent or absent-minded. But who knows if he is not crushed, on the contrary, by an excess of attention? By the work which seems, in him, to be carried on midway between the intelligence and the sensibility.

Syphilis: puncture the veins with a needle sterilised in a flame. Blennorrhagia: remove a drop of the purulent secretion or the suspect serosity on a clean blade. In women, insert the speculum, wash the neck of the uterus.

In the evening, before sinking into a sleep infested with nightmares that only slightly outdid what he experienced while awake, he would peruse monographs on recent research into the diagnosis and treatment of syphilis and blennorrhagia, on the bacteriological and microscopic level. *War and the Sexual Diseases* by Professor Albert Reiffer, that had just been published in Stuttgart. He also went back to the classic works of Neisser, on experimental syphilis, and Hoffmann, on the inoculation of rhesus monkeys with Treponema. But wasn't it, again, a fiction that fascinated him in all this? A legend of conquistadors at work in the laboratories?

Finally, as they were advancing on Brussels, he would read this or that scene from Goethe's *Egmont,* to find out how the conquering country's greatest writer had looked on the country conquered. It was the story of a man who thought he was mastering his own destiny when he was merely bewitched by it, as one can be by the song of the Lorelei. A man, or men in general? When he wrote this play, what doubt could still have been plaguing a writer who had steered his own bark so skilfully clear of the reefs? Would he have still chosen that theme when he was covered in honours? At least it was a work that had a more "realistic" ring than the *reconquista* of the venereal peril!

In the heart of the capital he first sets up house in a patrician dwelling near the Palais de la Nation and the Parc Royal, that its owners have abandoned in disarray to flee towards Sedan with half their furniture and even the hangings from the salon. But what does it matter? Doesn't he risk being sent back home as soon as he has arrived?

Sitting on a tin trunk, the medical officer smokes a cigarette while casting amused glances into the empty rooms. He wonders what pictures could have adorned the reception rooms: seascapes, idylls or still-lifes? In their place there are rectangles on the wallpaper that the sun has not yet discoloured. In the antechamber a wall mirror surmounts an empty space, orphaned of the mahogany chest which must have been carried off in the exodus. The warrant officer wonders if he ought not to set up his study at the back, in the bedroom, and move the bedroom here. He smiles. Though only "visiting" and not even having the means to furnish a single room completely, he is already laying plans like some whimsical lord of the manor. In any case, won't the city be responsible for heating and lighting the residence?

The new tenant gives no more thought to this fact than to

any other infringements of the laws and customs of war that may have been committed by the army whose uniform he wears. Is not his life here unfolding with a complete disdain for logic? The war itself does not revolt him. It does not fill him with shame. At most, it moves him as a phenomenon that leaves a trail of churning devastation across the flesh of men. Only this obscene spectacle of illness and death at work holds his attention. That is how this man is made: he almost never takes an ideological view of a situation. Political abstraction is abhorrent to him. He stays too near the bodies to think of raising his head, looking beyond, conceptualising. He does not feel threatened by this myopia, or suspect he ought to be more mistrustful of his own standpoint. In any case, he hasn't eyes enough to reflect all the suffering bodies ...

The expedition is taking longer than anticipated; it is bogged down in the north of the country, along a river bank. It is taking a long time to open up access to the sea. From now on it seems to be held up at the rear for an eternity.

The medical adjutant has moved house; he now occupies a town residence with eleven rooms in the *quartier Louise*, purloined from its émigré owner. He lives alone, with his orderly. Here, he does not lack a pipe rack, silver cutlery or even a bonbonnière, which happens to contain cocaine snuff. He'll never be as rich again. He would not give this kingdom for a horse. He rules over a desert. But is there none other than the artificial paradise? Will he not be able to "bloom once more before our ruin"?

The occupant wakes with a dry throat. The thirst of the pagan god that nothing can slake. He remembers the girl bought for the night – a night that seemed interminable – who must be asleep in another room, on the second floor. Unless she has left without asking for the balance. Or with a silver table set. He remembers the woman wrapping herself around him like a carnivorous plant, like algae, a net with liquid meshes, he remembers her pungent mouth. He remembers the woman, then forgets her – forgets her entirely – then remembers her again, remembers she had the sweetness of putrefaction. Again, he knows nothing of her, nor how much he has paid her. Was she a whore, or did she become one tonight? In stretching out time, the drug has suggested a different memory in which women who give themselves for money are no longer prostitutes, in which soldiers attend to quite different matters than war, in which one is rejuvenated with age and colours change their sound, even their meanings. Afterwards: these little pools of icy sperm. Later still: only her scent, persistent as a pain. There, on the first floor of 1, rue Saint-Bernard.

He ought to have gone back to Antwerp, he reflects. Seen the city again, in the aftermath of its capture. Had it resumed a form of life? Could you hear the tugs calling again in the fairway?

The officer remembers his orderly. The young man must still be asleep in his room, on the first floor. Next time, he'll have to send him the girl, so that she finishes the night beside him. Then he reflects that it's just that kind of contact that he is supposed to be forbidding the troops, to eradicate the epidemic at the heart of this foreign town that is ravaging the occupying army. He smiles. Another way, he muses, of not losing sight of the body ... So as not to break the thread of the unavowable story which History is writing in secret, with a trembling hand – the story it hides beneath the other that it avows.

Usually, he takes the liberty of wandering the streets in civilian dress. But he does not always intend to take advantage of this opportunity. Even if he sets no store by wearing uniform, he does not want to go incognito, to assume any other anonymity than that which is itself such scant justification for his presence in this town. In any case, adopting one or the other changes nothing; the *Baedeker* this singular tourist parades in its mica sheath gives him away to the passers-by. If a woman gives him an eager smile as he walks up the Avenue Louise towards the Bois de la Cambre, or if a citizen flaunting a rosette or cockade as big as a saucer and in the national colours, in contempt of the military government's regulations, spits ostentatiously as he passes, he knows that both the invitation and the insult are addressed to him only as the invader. If he turns into the Avenue de Flore or the Chemin des Cavaliers, he may well pass a street urchin who puts out his tongue at him and holds his nose before running off towards the gully or the skating rink you find at the end of the avenues ... The adjutant of the Imperial Army would not make himself so ridiculous as to give chase to the offender. True, people are arraigned before the military court for less than that. These subversive attitudes interest him, he registers them as one fact among others. They feed his solitude: he gorges himself on them. They sharpen his vigilance: he practises maintaining the watchfulness that has its value in any situation. Beneath it all, he enjoys an unbounded liberty. Of course, it is not without risks. Everything puts him to the test; that is what he wants. He does not understand the languages spoken here and learns as little as possible of them. For the use he will make of words from now on, it matters that he should know only those of his own tongue.

Day after day around the rue Saint-Bernard, he paces the perimeters of concentric circles. Methodically exploring his surroundings, he moves out a little further each day, radiating in the direction of the Abbaye de la Cambre or the Fort Jaco, or the Place Malibran, or La Jonction. This progression might appear timorous. In fact, he is taking care not to rush his fences. His method resembles the delicate approach work of some amorous strategy. He likes streets, squares, quarters to be for a time no more than names: the only foreign words he assimilates willingly. Rue Hydraulique. Rue du Pépin. Rue des Six-Jeunes-Hommes. Place des Martyrs. Port de l'Allée-Verte. Rue Villa-Hermosa. Rue de la Vierge-Noire. Montagne des Larmes. Rue d'une Personne. Impasse de l'Asile ... Then he studies the vegetal ornamentation of the façades and monuments he passes on his walks, listening to their polyphony. There are so many styles mingled here, in such an eclectic frenzy, that in the transition from the rue Saint-Bernard to the Avenue Louise you pass from the French neo-Renaissance to neo-Gothic while being brushed by phantoms of the Italian Renaissance. Going the other way you come across a Babylonian Palace of Justice with borrowings from Rome, Byzantium and Nineveh as well. Sometimes this proliferation has burgeoned from the simple joy of creation; sometimes it has given way to a drunken megalomania. You would think a party of art nouveau architects had hacked their way with machetes through this urban jungle. Here and there glass, steel and cast iron articulate the stony discourse like punctuation marks.

Sometimes the visitor is won over by the exuberance of this debauch of invention. He reflects that he ought to attempt such asymmetries in words too, similar dissonances; ride his vitality to the point of feverish exhaustion.

His eye lingers on the heavy denticulated cornices, the bow-windows with their fluted lintels, the glazed brick of the façades ... Something Wilhelminian in him continues to protest at so much anarchy. The little Neumark peasant has not succumbed to the bombast and the affected flourishes of Berlin to give in without some slight resistance to the disorderly charm of a town that you are not sure whether to call large or small, a town which might well be falling into ruins as it is being built. You sense that its *élan* has been broken, and that it's not only the war that has, for a time, suspended its expansion. Leaving behind a flamboyant sketch that may never be worked out in detail.

One day, while he is wandering among the vestiges of the World Fair between the Avenue des Nations and the Solbosch plain, devastated by a kind of premonitory fire in 1910, the visitor finds confirmed once more the feeling that has sometimes come over him since he arrived in Brussels of Europe's end. Here at the fair's site, the seismic shocks have demolished only a children's village. But is it not symbolic that the pavilions of certain great powers have been spared, including Germany's, surmounted by a Wagnerian eagle? Isn't there a rumour going about that Kaiser Wilhelm, fresh from his inaugural reception, himself plotted the fire? As he passes, the visitor has a thought for the wild animals roasted in the Luna-Park enclosure.

Would the Belgians be likely to believe the prophesies of pythonesses? Not long ago some very serious astronomers predicted that Halley's comet would land here, causing the planet to burst like a ripe pomegranate. Brussels had already believed itself to be melting under the effects of a pale radiation. Then for a time it went back to its old pursuits. It invited Mme Sarah Bernhardt to recite in one breath *Phèdre* and *Dame aux Camélias*. These performances closely followed *Elektra* and *Salomé*, then the *Ring*, at the Théâtre de la Monnaie, with Schutzbach and Lohse heading the cast. Just time for the population to get used to the Germans' language and dreams of grandeur. Posters announcing the *Rhinegold* for 4 May 1914 and the *Twilight of the Gods* for the 9th have not yet been completely torn from the Morris pillars on the Boulevard Anspach. But a few discreet notices state that the theatre is closing. Just as others mention the closure of the aquarium at 525, Avenue Louise and of the museum of pisciculture. What has been done with the fish, the macropods, the axolotls, the visitor wonders? Have they been returned to their respective oceans while the nations of the Alliance and the *Entente* resolve their differences?

Now, the visitor surveys a small lake that seems to have been drawn with a compass, in the middle of a forest, surrounding an island straight from a fairytale. He sees an elegant carriage gliding away beyond the lawns. Another time he lingers under the glass vault of the Passage du Nord; he is amazed at the clearings that appear everywhere in the city, on the outskirts and even in the centre. He would like to give himself up to this light, entrust himself to its transparency. Suddenly, the war is so far off: it is always so near and so far simultaneously. Like God.

The visitor, the occupier, wonders why he is beginning to feel, for better or worse, in harmony with this place where he has landed in spite of himself, cast up by the storm ... No doubt he has opened himself to his solitude for so long that he has grown tired of seeing it remain a mere metaphor. It was time to give it its full weight and solidity, to set it no more limits. Was it not conceivable that out of so much fullness and so much emptiness, out of the void that yawned in him and the profusion of horrors carried along by the time, out of the nothingness into which the war plunged and the plenitude of horror gathering within him – so that the cataclysm ripening in his conscience seemed like a harbinger of global disaster – yes, was it unthinkable that from all that might be born something as tragic, as harrowing, as torn asunder and as pure as God? In a situation like this, having an experience like this, is one not to draw from it a lesson that will last a lifetime?

German writers sometimes meet for an aperitif on the terrace of the Bon Marché, or for five o'clock tea on the roof of the Old England. They believe it gives them a better understanding of the city to view it from above.

"The occupying forces have set the Brussels' clocks by Berlin time."

"That doesn't make the Belgians get up an hour earlier," Otto Flake remarks.

"The best course for them," says Flechtheim, "is not to wind up their watches. That way they don't have to choose."

"For my brother Siegfried they've stopped for good," Benn mentions; already, no one expects him to be the life and soul of the party.

"As they have for a lot of German poets," says Wedderkopp. "Lichtenstein and Lotz, killed in France. August Stramm, on the Russian front ... "

"The most unjust death of all must be Stadler's. He taught

the French poets and got himself killed in Flanders, fighting France!"

"I've heard it said," says Carl Sternheim, "that a few days before he died he was able to exchange ideas with Charles Péguy, who was fighting in the trench opposite."

"Must be just a story," declares Carl Einstein with a shrug. "Things like that only happen in anthology prefaces."

"A nice story, though," says Wedderkopp. "Worth remembering ... "

"Nonsense!" says Benn.

"I beg your pardon?"

"Stuff and nonsense! Let's stop sounding so humanitarian, so downright amorous, about the war! It is what it is. Each of us has resigned himself to it and will fight it in his own way. But at least spare us the stories of noble gestures and splendid epitaphs."

"Gottfried's right," Carl Sternheim agrees. "When it's over, the war is going to glory in having shed poets' blood, instead of being besmirched by it. It will claim the sacrifice was justified since poets gave their lives for it."

Stadler is the poet who was closest to me, Benn muses. When my first poems came out, he was almost the only one who did not see them as a piece of macabre bravado. He realised that compassion can be the opposite of mawkishness. That may have saved me. And I didn't even know him. "Ephemeral," he liked to repeat. It was his favourite epithet. He stood by it in the end. He had plumbed all the depths, but it never made him blasé.

"Does anyone know how Trakl died?" asks Flechtheim.

"Came to grief in the battle of Grodek, didn't he?" asks Wedderkopp.

Hausenstein replies: "That's the official version. He went mad in a Cracow asylum."

Trakl, thinks Benn, who became a pharmacist to have access to drugs. Trakl who talked in his poems of those who died before they had lived. Those who were only "half born".

Those who would never be born. Trakl who had announced his imminent flight to Borneo. And who, when he died, seemed to turn back and rush towards his own birth.

"Of us all," says Flake, "Stadler was the one who understood the people here best, who loved this city most ... "

"Now I am that one," Carl Sternheim interrupts him. "This place has everything I could want. I could spend my life here!"

It was the most generous tribute the inveterate nomad could have paid to a town. The more so as he had been treated as a spy when the Germans invaded. He was almost lynched, his property confiscated.

"Why did Germany have to come out here to join me?" He jokes. "I was getting on so well without her!"

"What is it you see in this country?" asks Flechtheim.

"Van Gogh lived here," he replies. "Can you imagine the painter of the *Potato Eaters* discovering the plain of the Yser as it is now? The wide world across the sea starts at Antwerp. At Bruges the Middle Ages begin."

"At Brussels Europe ends," Flechtheim puts in ironically.

"Brussels," Sternheim retorts, "is at the centre of a web with London, Paris, Amsterdam and Cologne at its edges ... "

"And here's our dear spider!" jokes Wedderkopp patting him on the shoulder.

"In any case," says Carl Sternheim, "I invite you all to visit the Central Africa museum at Tervuren ... " And he launches into his favourite reflections on Negro art appearing in all its savage purity, its false barbarism, while the declining West is busy losing all sense of its own values ...

Carl and I made our débuts together, Benn recalls sadly, that evening when we gave a public reading of poems which, without our realising it, prefigured the war. And now we are here, as if our artistic adventure were already behind us. War brings us together so that we can grow communally old.

"You should read the writers who work here," Einstein assures them. "At least, some of them. Clément Pansaers, who is always one aesthetic revolution ahead of all the other revolutionaries. You meet him at the Compas, or the Diable au Corps. And then René Verboom, who wears mourning for himself, at the velodrome, or the cafés around the Porte de Namur. Jean de Boschère has unfortunately left Brussels for London, where he's joined Eliot, Pound and the Imagists. Don't be surprised if he moves on. He says he suffers from 'home terror'."

Is it because he has stopped believing in Europe that Carl Einstein keeps himself so well informed about what is happening here?

"And here I was thinking Brussels was empty," Gottfried Benn remarks. "I mean, deserted by its poets, if not by poetry."

"Please note," Wedderkopp intervenes, "there are more German poets writing about Brussels now than native Belgians!"

"Perhaps it will always be like that," Otto Flake remarks. "This place produces insular poets who are scattered by the wind from the Ardennes to the sea without meeting any obstacles ... "

Benn says nothing more. He feels slightly frustrated in the company of these upper-middle-class people who are just as much at ease in the Place Royale or the rue Neuve as they would be at the same hour in a café on the Kurfürstendamm or the Savignyplatz. When the armistice arrived most would go straight into the diplomatic service.

"Did you know that our dear Thomas Mann got off the train here just a few days ago, to attend the première of his *Fiorenza*?" asks Otto Flake.

Yes, at least Gottfried Benn knew that. The Mann family fascinates him. It's not a name, it's a patent, a certificate of truth. Even when they contradict each other Thomas and Heinrich, the fraternal foes, both seem to be in the right. They were born like that. And then Nietzsche passed through both of them, as he also irradiated Carl Einstein and Gottfried Benn. The depositories of the same legacy recognise each other, even if jealously. They may even appreciate one another.

"You can bet we knew," Hausenstein grumbles. "Most of us were there!"

But Flake, as if he had not heard, Flake whom Nietzsche frightens and who has little taste for the author of *Death in Venice*, is not to be done out of the story he has all ready to serve: "Luncheon given by our dear Governor, a full complement of officers all sporting the Iron Cross, First Class, and giving our good Thomas the 'Dear Comrade in Arms' treatment. A bit much, wasn't it?"

"Yes, we know, Otto. We were there ... " Hausenstein insists, patiently.

"And just imagine, the soldiery were instructed to attend the performance. What the devil's your common trooper going to make of something like that? If the Manns get into the habit of coming to Brussels, we'll never be at home!"

Gottfried Benn abhors this kind of gossip. The wit is wasted on him. But there is a diversion. All ears are pricked at the sound of gunfire rolling in distant Flanders.

"It sounds like a gigantic sewing-machine," says Otto Flake dreamily.

"Who would have thought the Belgian king would hang on to the Yser like that?" asks Wedderkopp.

"Clausewitz," Einstein replies. "He must have read Clausewitz. Hegel as well. He wants to give us more than we bargained for. It appears he goes riding every morning to keep up appearances. Gallops along the beach with his aide-de-camp chasing after him on a bicycle, out of breath ... "

"It's more likely to be Elizabeth – the Queen," Sternheim declares.

"Who chases after her husband on a bicycle?" asks Wedderkopp in surprise.

"No: she must have read Hegel," Sternheim tells him. "She's not a princess of Bavaria for nothing, you know ... "

"Shall we talk about poets instead?" Benn suggests.

Is that the only thing that can arouse him today? Has he no interest in crowned heads and the great ones of this world?

"All right, let's talk about French poets," Hausenstein proposes. "As we know, they often passed this way. Nerval in pursuit of Jenny Colon, deploring the fact that the city was only bathed by a paltry stream ... Victor Hugo, when he fled France, stayed at an hotel on the Grand-Place and installed Juliette Drouet nearby, in the Galerie du Prince. Baudelaire also stayed near here, at the Hôtel du Grand Miroir. And then Verlaine emptied his revolver at Rimbaud just a few steps further on. One has to say that nothing is very far from anything else here."

"It wasn't only the French," Wedderkopp mumbles. "Charlotte Brontë pined for her tutor between the Montagne de la Cour and the Villa Hermosa ... "

"And don't forget our own Karl Marx," says Otto Flake. "Not much of an economist, it seems, but quite a good poet in his way."

"All the same, it's funny they all came here," says Flechtheim.

"To this rotten dump? It certainly is surprising. The backside of the civilised world," Einstein pronounces. "Leaving aside the Musée Colonial, of course. What the barbarians stole from the Negroes."

"No doubt they came here," Benn muses, "but they were just passing through. None of them stayed long." He feels a bit like the orphan of these great poets in transit.

"We shouldn't forget," Carl Sternheim goes on, "that Brussels has welcomed outcasts only to get rid of them in short order. Sent them away more wretched than they came."

"This city even managed to make an idiot of Baudelaire, one of the geniuses of his day," Hausenstein reminds them.

"Baudelaire only poured scorn on Brussels," says Carl Einstein, "because France had scorned him, and he found France again here. And what was even worse ... "

"Yes, but if you take Hugo," Otto Flake objects, "he didn't play the fool here. He paid the tarts to let him measure the diameter of their 'mouth of darkness'. Never had enough of it.

Made it a subject of comparative research. Juliette, who kept the accounts, would note down expenses like: P. five francs, P. four francs fifty. Later she claimed the P. stood for Poor wretch, inviting people to admire her lover's generosity. We can be pretty sure Hugo got something in return for his alms!"

Gottfried Benn feels a certain uneasiness. He doesn't like hearing men of letters expatiating on prostitutes when they may not even have approached them themselves. He knows what darkness talks through that second mouth that money kisses. He understands how Victor Hugo never tired of it. That maw is an Amazonia. He thinks the author of *Choses Vues* must have explored it as much in Paris as in Brussels, Jersey or Guernsey. Why should the female aperture be more unfathomable here than elsewhere? And then, they talk of Hugo ... One would like to know how Marx, for example, stood in relation to all this. Did he have other fish to fry? What did anyone know about Marx's nights of insomnia, his nocturnal prowls along the rue de la Limite, the rue du Cirque or the rue du Marché? No one asks whether the author of *Das Kapital* frequented whores. No doubt he did not have time. Or it went against his revolutionary principles. I'll wager that if he did go with one of them, his thought would have been the richer for it! The military doctor thinks of de Quincey, who rescued a prostitute of fifteen from penury and madness. He tries to tell the others about it ...

"Exactly!" Otto Flake promptly interrupts him. And claims to have picked one up a few days before who can't have been any older. What is more, she turned out to be a lesbian. She had the breasts and hips of a mature woman. How young must she have been when she passed the "awkward age"?

"Now you, of course, doctor," he insinuates, turning to Benn, "you're called on in the course of duty to pay much closer attention to that world of beauty than we are ... "

Much closer, indeed, the military doctor reflects. But so close that he could hardly say anything about it. Then he thinks of the city that harbours the creatures they are talking about, the city they are overlooking from a café terrace in the middle of a war, as if they were just as absent from these walls as from the war. He thinks that in this place he has arrived at the end of the world, and that he would like to go to the end of himself. But out of politeness he tries to answer Otto Flake.

"I should like to stay here for some time," he confides, "see it all from close quarters, as you say ... "

"I don't doubt it, doctor!" the other exclaims.

And the military doctor wonders why they all burst out in knowing laughter.

Of the city, to be sure, he mainly sees the hospitals, the prisons, the brothels. Could it be that he likes it the better for catching it in the act? Anyone who is susceptible to the magic of the theatre prefers backstage to front of house.

He has no very clear idea where his professional competence begins or ends. Sometimes the officer in him oversteps the limits of the doctor, even contradicts him. He has to requisition hospital beds for German soldiers returning wounded, mutilated or sick from the front on the Yperlée. Help keep the clinics supplied with sugar, cod-liver oil, lint. Seize bicycle tyres, pneumatic and solid, to meet the needs of the ambulances. Sanction the redirection of food supplies. He also has to make sure that incapacitated soldiers return their weapons to the commandant based at the grenadiers' barracks. Many of the unfortunate men are afraid to part with them and try to hide them. Others claim excessive quantities of saddles, bridles and harnesses, which they sell. He also has to ensure that men restored to health immediately report to the barracks in the rue des Petits-Carmes. He has surprised malingerers in the quarantine station who scrambled back under their blankets fully dressed, with their boots on. He reported them. He has heard that similar cheating was happening on the Belgian side. Fake paupers were getting themselves admitted to the central refectory. People stealing meat from the out-patients' kitchen were having to be body-searched. Everything is being stolen, scraps of bacon, animal fat, bundles of sausage skins, dog-food, floor-cloths.

Another time he has to have a train crammed with bodies from the Yser opened up to confirm the deaths. Collect the enrolment badges and the service records. Supervise the return of the bodies to the families. The objects left behind by the dead are sent to Headquarters, rue de la Loi.

The Governor-General requires an identity certificate to be issued for each case admitted to the clinics in the capital and the provincial sanatoria. A special list is made of those "foreign to the local conflict" – who are neither Belgian, German nor Austro-Hungarian. The adjutant records the name of a Romanian jeweller, a Moroccan domestic servant, a bronzer from Perugia, a musician from Ivanovo, a nurse from Providence, Rhode Island, a hotel thief called Salomon Rosenblatt (without nationality), a piano tuner from Bratislava ... What had they been looking for in Brussels, these Constantinescus, Mahjoubs, Vassilievs, Sparacos and Kastanidises? Did they have time to see the war bearing down on them? Leaving aside the possibility of espionage – never ruled out *a priori* by the military government – it is the imbecility of chance that immediately strikes the reader of this catalogue of outsiders.

Sometimes the military doctor has to listen to the grievances of the Belgian authorities, at the clinic in the Avenue Molière where he gives consultations. The aggrieved are often women of the nobility, doing charitable work. They complain that the German officials posted at the door have been found in an inebriated state while on duty, or have been smoking in the corridors. He for his part deplores the lack of courtesy shown to the German nurses. For a moment the parties size each other up, each wondering how far a refusal to give way will take them, and when the open expression of hatred will come. The medical adjutant can't help admiring somewhat these slightly haughty aristocratic ladies with their withering gaze. He feels the plebeian in him awakening, becoming obstreperous. However, he suggests: "We representatives of the Medical

Association will always agree in the end ... " This familiar touch may mask a wish to be conciliatory. They break it off there. A pity. The dialogue had hardly begun. Perhaps the medical adjutant only believes in exchanging words when any understanding seems impossible?

He grows weary of putting his hand to everything. He is surprised that the military hierarchy is not more concerned about the proper distribution of duties. He asks to be relieved of certain paramedical chores, claiming to be a doctor of wounds, not frauds. He wants to deal with bodies, not red tape. Those in high places readily understand. They even take him to task for excessive zeal, for overstepping his limits. He agrees they are probably only half wrong.

All the same, he is asked to help the occupying authorities draw up an order setting up a vice squad for Greater Brussels.

"It has come to our notice, Doctor, that you have a facility with words. So let us have a little sample of your talent."

He was not pleased to see the poet called upon to set in motion the wheels of the law. He was still more repelled to find the doctor in him shadowed by a lawyer. But he gave way. One can be a rebel against the general order of things and still believe in the legitimacy of a demand made by an army at war.

He returns to his quarters through little streets still lit by gas, the street-lamp glass having been painted blue. Everywhere the shutters are closed, the curtains drawn, the blinds pulled down. The lampshades in hotel foyers have been draped with black cloth. The planes patrolling the sky look down on a city swallowed up in darkness. It is not without significance that the curfew conceals the war even as it emphasises it. The stroller wonders where the danger could come from in this abyss of darkness.

For some time he has been imagining a person who is staying, like him, in an occupied town. Who, like him, is plagued by doubt about the reality of things, a reality he would like to capture, encompass like a nebula. Who, like him, wants to throw a bridge between the world's discourse and his own silence. To become himself this bridge. He was going to tell of the comings and goings of this double, this *alter ego*, describe his cortical moods. But this would only seemingly be a novel. An autobiography? Certainly, but one written at the deepest level, the level where, in others, words fail to cross certain interior thresholds.

In recent years he has had so many adventures – which weren't adventures in the normal sense of the word – that he could not tell them all. First, he arrived in the metropolis where the history of the world risks being played out. He has consorted with corpses and has not been deaf to the siren calls of their disillusion. He has opened some bodies and tended others. He has even found time to read Nietzsche, a victim of the illness in which he, Dr Benn, has become a specialist – carried off in a fit of euphoria beyond the wars and peace of the spirit. Then he loved a woman who believed, like him, that words needed to be turned back against the perverted meanings they were given. He separated from this woman, fearing that together they would become a kind of pleonasm. He married another woman, and a war immediately swept them apart. And now an analogous separation had set him down in the margin of the world. This did not add up to a story. It was the beginning of a confession, of the kind that is wrung from you *in extremis*.

Telling about himself, he would like to write the opposite of a novel of apprenticeship, since what he has learned about his relationship to the universe has to be relearned over and over again. His novel is not novelistic, his story not historical. But he dreams of a fragment of story detached from literature as a meteorite is split from a star. A cloud of unprosaic prose through which he would move in utter freedom. Then the character whose father he would supposedly be, who would resemble him, like two peas in a pod, and that he could equally well call Constantinescu, Sparaco or Rosenblatt, would dissolve at the same moment as he appeared, through the effect of style. He might be called the "Vassiliev Syndrome", or the "Rosen-blatt Complex", or the "Constantinescu Effect" ... Coming down the Chaussée de Charleroi the stroller reflects that he is reduced to secreting a pure form – that would flare for only a moment like a cinder buried in ash. Thus the poet would take up arms against the world, and make his peace with it.

The officer finds his orderly smoking one of his cigars on the balcony of the hotel at 1, rue Saint-Bernard.

As a punishment, Gottfried makes Max translate the Belgian newspapers which are coming out clandestinely and are circu-lated as propaganda.

Max is of Alsatian stock and obeys his master with suspicious alacrity. Benn suspects his valet of taking a malicious pleasure in mouthing with impunity the insults the bulletins heap on the occupying army. Bloodthirsty Huns ... cruel ogres ... preda-tory hussars ... infamous starvers ... Teutonic rabble. Boches devoid of honour ... Curiously, the listener does not become inured to the harangue, especially when Max is unable to suppress a laugh. "Begging your pardon, Doctor, but they're not letting us off lightly!" (Doctor, he calls his superior, since the officer, without giving reasons, has forbidden any allusion to his rank in private.)

La Libre Belgique and *La Flandre Libérale* do not even need to quote Caesar, Tacitus or Velleius Paterculus to prove that even in the old days the Germans deserved nothing but opprobrium and contempt. Closer to us, Kant espoused the impiety of the modern world, Nietzsche played at exterminating angels and Hegelian philosophy engendered nothing less than Prussian imperialism ...

The officer is not amused to see German thinkers having to shoulder responsibility for real events. If he asks Max to go on reading, it is to find out from the mouth of the enemy those few bits of useful information that the imperial command takes good care to conceal from its diligent servants. That, for example, stray birds from the Palace of Justice have been mistaken for spy pigeons by the general staff, information which, unfortunately, is too ludicrous not to be true. Another Zeppelin, upset by a storm, has landed on a herd of cows, from which it proved very difficult to disentangle. At Lovenjoul the uhlans have rigged themselves up in wasp-waisted corsets and combinations borrowed from some inhabitants whose doors they had forced, then paraded in the streets bellowing obscenities.

Gottfried feels his cheeks begin to burn. He recognises only too well the soldiery who, at Beverlo and Malines, had made him retch with disgust.

Finally, a film director has come specially from Berlin to record the "arrival" of the pointed helmets in the Belgian capital "to the acclaim of the civilian population massed on the pavements" – a population clearly made up of extras. Would this fallacious documentary deceive those people within the Empire's frontiers who believed with Liebknecht and his associates that Germany had embarked on an unpopular adventure? Who, back home, would credit this masquerade of fraternisation? Who in Berlin would imagine we had been welcomed with open arms? The adjutant asks his orderly to leave off reading for today.

"Shan't I even give you the list of atrocities and misdeeds our troops are supposed to have committed?" asks Max.

"Are they still as bad?"

"They don't seem to get any better, Doctor. A priest has had his nose and ears cut off, some nuns have been abused and become pregnant – a girl has been violated before her father's eyes. There's something about some mock executions, and several hostages being detained. Here, a cow is cut up on a piano, there German doctors drink the wine of wounded people entrusted to them ... "

"Max, you say people have actually done this or that. You don't put the assertions in the conditional. You surely don't believe them?"

"Oh, I'm sure they're exaggerating, Doctor. But as they say in French, you only lend to the rich, there's no smoke without fire ... "

"Max, just remember what we Germans were taught when we were mobilised. That of all the nations we were to fight the Belgians were the most ferocious ... What didn't they tell us! That we would come up against snipers metamorphosed into drunken, fanatical Apaches. That Belgian girls gouged wounded people's eyes out and sawed off their legs, and that their mothers would offer us cigarettes loaded with gunpowder, when they were not pouring boiling oil on us as we passed. Belgium was the Middle Ages! You had to watch out for bakers: as soon as you turned your back they would hit you over the head and throw you into the oven. We should not trust well-water, which had been poisoned. This war is being fought among other things with communiqués which cry to heaven for vengeance or swear that the blood of the victims will be visited on the heads of the guilty. While the *Kölnische Zeitung* denounces the Russians and the sadism of our adversaries, *L'Âme Belge* is spreading the rumour that our soldiers will cut off children's hands so that they can't turn their guns against them later. No better way of predicting that the war will go on for ever ... On both sides, tall stories are being deliberately put out. The bigger the lie, the more chance it has of being believed ... "

"It says here," Max goes on, "that we're forcing people condemned to death to dig their own graves before being shot. You don't want me to read the headline: 'The Belgians know how to die'?"

"Why – have there been more executions?"

"One condemned woman had transported five kilos of dynamite in her bodice. Another was an assistant in a large store. She passed information."

The officer does not comment. No doubt his orderly takes a certain delight in mentioning this turn of events. He is not unaware that his master has for some time been somewhat parsimonious in his confidences on such matters.

"They were playing a fatal game," says Gottfried, after a silence. "They must have known what they were doing. They would probably not have wanted any other death. They do indeed 'know how to die'."

"Because we 'know how' to kill them," the orderly adds.

"That may be the price for our winning the war," says the officer curtly. "The only reason there is for this war – perhaps the only excuse for it – is that we really want to win it ... "

How else can an officer talk to his orderly, the military doctor asks himself, suddenly overcome with gloom.

"And then there's more talk of gas," Max remarks, apparently deciding not to let the matter drop. "A new gas that can be used to smoke out the enemy trenches. Never been done before. Do you want the details, Doctor?"

"We'll find out more about what is really happening from the lungs of the victims than from enemy newspapers. The French are also using gas against us. And then the wind can change and send their own fumes back to asphyxiate them. I know a fair amount about that."

Could he be afraid of the truth, this time? Or is it simply making him despair? Despair makes you a fatalist. He has never believed strongly enough in the legitimacy of the German aggression against half of Europe to believe that that half was going to accept it graciously. He suddenly can't stand any more of this dialogue of sententious drunkards that his servant has insidiously drawn him into. And while, to cut it short, he goes back to reading the German translation of *Till Eulenspiegel* he has brought with him, it does not occur to him that De Coster's novel celebrates the civic virtues of a free people preyed upon by the sinister Spanish invader ... He reads it as if it were pure imagination. He gives way to the fable's charm because he is himself in love with Nele, the eternal fiancée of the subversive dissident, she who so naturally, spontaneously, is in love with humanity ...

"Is that a good book, Doctor?" the orderly enquires with

concern in his voice. "I ask because I've heard that book prices have gone through the roof since we arrived here."

Strange, thinks the officer, that the high price of books should trouble my orderly, who would never dream of opening one.

But the question comes back into his mind the same evening, when, in his day-lit room, he sinks his heavy brow between the breasts of a tart picked up by Max in the rue de la Vanne or the rue des Chevaliers. He finds himself caught in a vicious circle between two mirages caused by a pinch of cocaine: this terrible time when a book costs almost as much as an hour of oblivion spent in the arms of a courtesan ... but also this absurd time when the amnesia you experience beside a woman about whom you have time to find out nothing costs more than the finest book ...

Those who are now said to be "damaged", i.e. syphilitic, are proliferating. Neither the sanitary inspections, nor the prophy-lactic advice, nor the suppression of soliciting, nor the surveil-lance of brothels, nor the distribution of condoms to the troops, nor the precautions taken at the time of diagnosis, nor the instruction of doctors in therapeutic morality, have been able to check or even slow down the spread of the disease. The proximity of danger exacerbates the desires of men hardly out of childhood, who fear nothing more than going to their deaths without having tasted pleasure, if only for one more time, in the belly of a whore-mother.

It has been decided to quarantine syphilis cases in the Dailly barracks. The local population is up in arms, with some reason, to find the city burdened with the lamentable consequences of the occupants' debauches.

The military doctor rereads the history of the scourge since its alleged importation into Europe on board the caravels of Christopher Columbus, up to the isolation of the pathological agent, pale Treponema, on 2 or 3 March 1905, the exact date being disputed.

Schaudinn had driven it out of hiding in the serosity on

mucous slides taken from a prostitute under observation by Hoffmann. (In passing, the reader regrets the ungrateful omission of the name of this devoted collaborator. Could not professional secrecy have made an exception on such an occasion?)

He follows the stages of a discovery no less exciting than that of America itself, from where the disease is supposed to have come. The research carried out here in Brussels by Bordet, whom a different final consonant would have ironically predestined for the work. The reaction achieved by Wassermann, with its irrefutable diagnostic implications, and bearing his name. Finally, Ehrlich's invention of a remedy, practically on the eve of the pistol shot in Sarajevo, which permits an abortive cure. From now on patients will no longer be rubbed only with mercury or, as in the old days, with sarsaparilla, tincture of guaiacum or calomel. They will soon be treated with bismuth, and salvarsan, a compound of arsenic. Two or three years ago the soldiers who came here to flounder in the mud of Flanders, assuming they got out, might never have fully recovered from the microbe they took home with their kit. This war, at least, is in the process of being won . . .

Carried away by his enthusiasm, the military doctor recalls the inoculation experiments attempted so far. Those of Neisser in Batavia, on the simian species – then on children when there was a shortage of animals. Those of Hoffmann on the lower monkeys. Finger's and Landsteiner's experiments with baboons. Siegel's with rabbits. Mulzer's and Uhlenhut's with guinea-pigs and goats. Finally, those of Steiner and Siemens on general paralytics. Truly, few mammals had escaped this consecration. Cats, dogs, rats, foxes, horses, sheep, pigs and llamas had all made their contribution.

Gottfried has long marvelled at the audacity of Anonymous of the Palatinate, who inoculated blind people – naturally unaware of what was going on – with the products of scrapings from secondary infections, causing an irreproachable chancre to burgeon in many of them . . . An anonymous doctor treating blind people: what a symbol! Didn't the history of science often give rise to such images?

Before closing his reference works the military doctor wants to see what sort of a face these laboratory pioneers put on their discoveries. His left hand slipped into his waistcoat, Anonymous adopts a Napoleonic pose. Schaudinn's beard and handlebar moustache elicit a smile. There is something touching about Neisser's goatee beard and goggles. As for Ehrlich, he looks the reader straight in the eye, over his glasses. He has a worried look. He is uncertain about the future. He is not wrong.

Leave at last, time to go and kiss his wife and daughter at Hellerau. When the baby was born, a few months before, he was unable to get hold of an authorisation to attend the baptism. And that complicated everything, because of the name he wanted to give the child.

"Names matter," he tells his wife, holding her round the waist as they go down the staircase leading to the Brühl Terrace.

They have come to Dresden for the day. No doubt he felt the need to be back with his family, but also to see a German city again.

"A city on a river, at last," he says. "No river waters Brussels ... This will be our honeymoon, since the war has denied us the one we should have had, at Epidavros, Paestum, how do I know where? Borneo, perhaps. Yes, names matter," he repeats. "Who knows if I didn't marry you because of yours?"

"Edith?" she asks. "What do you mean? You never talked about it ... "

"Eva," he replies.

"Oh, Eva! That was my stage name. It doesn't count."

"It's the stage name of the first woman who was ever given a role!" he jokes.

He looks at his wife, then her reflection in the Elbe. Is he really in love with her? Sometimes he's no longer sure. But how could he not love her? She falls on the landscape like a shaft of light. She's so vivacious – why then did she join her fate to mine? She certainly does not know me. She has not had time to.

"Why were you so keen on calling your daughter Nele?" asks Edith.

"Because of the statue ... do you remember it?"

Yes, she remembers the effigy of a pair of lovers they could see from their hotel window the first time she had come out to join her husband, at the beginning of the war.

"As I remember her, she looked very gentle and very modest. Is it because of that?"

He laughs.

"Yes, probably because of that: because of all the blind love of men she carries in her, which holds her up in all the catastrophes, epidemics, wars she passes through. She's so devoted to *Till Eulenspiegel* that it splashes all around her. At the end, she believes him dead, and for some moments, from being a fiancée, she becomes a widow. But he wakes up and drags her off towards another destiny. We do not know, says the author, where Till sang his last song. It's more than a feeling she has for him. It's like a gift she has from nature. When you have such a gift, you must be invulnerable."

Edith says nothing, and looks at her husband curiously.

"You don't believe me?" asks Gottfried.

"Yes, of course I do. But, coming from you words like that are so unexpected. Did you look at her this morning, in her cot? We've called her Nele, the wretched little creature." It had not been easy to get it accepted by the registry office.

They cross the Carola Bridge. Edith takes small steps, like a convalescent. She is worried about Andreas, her son, whom Gottfried has adopted.

"He always looks so threatened," she says. "Every morning, when he opens his eyes, he seems to be unsure whether to live or stop living ... "

"It's the times that are crushing children's spirits," says Gott-fried. "When it's over they will really start breathing again."

"It can't be," says Edith. "Look at our little daughter. How she eats, how she fills her lungs! A true little Brünnhilde!"

"All the same, she'll just be passionately gentle," Gottfried insists. "That unshakeable gentleness will take her through the wars."

"Do you think there will be others?"

"Yes, of course. Unless this one lasts for ever."

Edith is downcast.

"But it will never spread as far as here," he says. He looks at the reflection of the city trembling in the Elbe currents. "Dresden will always be preserved: they never attack art centres, you know that."

"What about Louvain?" Edith asks. "Wasn't that an art centre? You wrote to me yourself in one of your letters that our soldiers had set it on fire ... "

"That's true. It seems those oafs even destroyed a velum edition of Andreas Vesalius's *De corporis humani fabrica*. Respect has gone down the drain. Nothing will ever happen to Dresden – no one would build rococo palaces if they thought they might be destroyed one day. Rococo is the supreme image we have of our immortality. A frivolous immortality ... "

This whiff of cynicism does not disconcert Edith Osterloh. She is more familiar with it than the sentiments her husband expressed earlier.

"Do you know what is happening in Berlin?" she asks. "People are demonstrating more and more openly for peace. Even though the left-wing pacifists have been told to march under the flag, or else they've been locked up. They're saying the main enemy is in our own country ... "

"And people are starting to believe," says Gottfried, "that if we haven't won the war by now it's because we might equally well lose it. The French think the same thing and no one is wrong, since no one can really win it now. I should not have become a dermatologist. I should have been a thanatologist: that way you never lack work. But am I depressing you again ... Eva?"

"Yes. And why do you keep calling me that?"

"That's how it is," he says. "It's only for today. Just for one walk by the Elbe, in a war ... I'd like to tell you ... "

He has stopped. He'd like to tell her why he has the habit of censoring his feelings for those who are dearest to him, why he has no words to express them. It is a weakness, he knows. He cannot change it. If he did find words, he would seem to be making fun of what he meant. How could Edith know of the secret exaltation they sometimes make him feel, she who is so alive, Nele who is so busily getting ready to live and Andreas who still hesitates to survive? But if he did find those words, he could only say that they are for him like a lost paradise on earth. But that they probably wouldn't save him from his personal hell. And that he probably does not want to be saved. That is the most fervent homage he could express. So isn't it better to keep quiet?

"Gottfried ... "

"Yes."

"Do you want to ask me something?"

"No, nothing ... That's to say, yes. Next time, you'll come to see me in Brussels, won't you?"

"At the little hotel facing the monument of Till and Nele, by the ponds?"

"No, this time you'll stay under my roof. I am allowed to receive you there, after all. Anyway, last time I walked by the ponds they had been drained. That cretinous governor von Bissing, who sees plots everywhere, thought some terrorists had hidden weapons under the shadows of the water lilies and the bellies of the ducks ... By the way, before we leave Dresden, what about going to the Zoological and Ethnographic Museum? They've got stuffed birds with their nests and eggs. And then some artefacts from the Indies, Java and Polynesia. From Polynesia, Eva."

"You're a doctor, aren't you?" the traveller asks.

It's a superfluous question, just a way of getting into conversation, since Medical Adjutant Benn, travelling in civilian clothes, has identified the function of the man opposite him by his ash-grey uniform, his long greatcoat and his round cap.

The other gives an affirmative nod.

"Destination?"

"Dixmude. And if you also want to know where I am coming from, I'll tell you: Königsberg – you know, the home town of Kant, where Napoleon left such pleasant memories ... Imagine the faces those two would pull if they had to fight each other in the polders today, or just argue philosophically!"

"You're right," the traveller agrees. "There'd never be an end to it."

He would like to add that if Beethoven had to compose his Emperor Concerto now, he would be no less embarrassed. Perhaps a "Hymn to Mud" might be more appropriate. But he keeps the joke to himself. The man on the bench opposite looks on edge. Almost out of control. In any case, he makes no attempt at normal courtesies, doesn't enquire who he is talking to.

"I'm a doctor like you, in the army. But in the capital."

"Ah, you're on your way to Brussels. Plenty of work there?" he asks ironically.

"I'm a venereologist. They're needed too, you know ... "

"Oh, I'm sorry. I didn't really take you for a shirker."

"And you're a surgeon, of course?"

"Yes. As you can imagine, there's nothing to be done there but cut them open, chop something out, sew them up again, when there's still some point to it."

The traveller no longer needs to push his opposite number to talk; the man does not even wait for the questions. As if he has long stored up the monologue in which his anger, his hatred are vented, unless it is simply sadness that carries him away. It is a strange elegy, rocked to the rhythm of the train.

The Ecstasy

"You really do want to know, don't you?" he asks, no longer with any aggressive intent.

Now he is just dejected, slightly bewildered, as he turns towards the window. His gaze wanders uncertainly. It is no longer Westphalia outside, but a bare, spongy, waterlogged plain blanketed by frosty mist. Later, chlorine gives it the yellow-green tinge of absinth.

He tells of waking at the bottom of a trench, as if in a mud coffin, of the sweat that cannot evaporate under the uniform cloth and congeals during the night. He tells of the smell of wet chalk and corruption that comes from the trench in summer. Only fatigue dulls the latent terror that crawls deep inside you like vermin. When all the men get up together, their sleep-walking bodies collide like those of blind people; that is the nearest they get to brotherhood.

"Then," says the man, "the waiting starts. The worst part of all, if you can understand this, and if I dare say it, is the empty time. The idleness makes you idiotic, and soon careless. It's a static war, you understand? You at the rear can never grasp the horror of it. Hardly any movement. Just the occupation of positions you have won. As if for eternity. A kind of obsessive expectancy. And torpor. Of course, the doctor has a different routine. In a sense he never lacks something to do. But he too sinks into the dream. You excise wounds. You tie blood vessels. You extract bullets and pieces of shrapnel. The flesh is lacerated with bone fragments. You amputate open fractures. You are cutting and tinkering without thinking about it. The wounded are no longer stupefied with alcohol or opium, they are anaesthetised. But you, as you work, are hypnotised. Not long ago they actually had to use horse serum against diphtheria – you must have heard about it in Brussels. The shears get slippery with blood and skid about in the wound. The saw trembles in your hand. In the end you would cut or not cut wherever you were told, like a machine, because that is why you are there. The only distraction is the campaign brothel. But that, if I may say so, my dear colleague, is where you come in ... You know why I asked for a few days' leave? Because I wasn't afraid any more, I'd got used to it. That's the worst of all. But try explaining that on a Saturday night in the bar at the Kneiphof, Königsberg!"

The man stops. He seems surprised, as if he'd jumped to the end of a speech before he had meant to and found himself with time he could not fill.

But the impression is misleading.

"There would be too much to say," the man goes on. "Can you imagine what it is like to fight an army you hardly ever meet? At Königsberg, in the *Norddeutsche Allgemeine Zeitung* and *Vorwärts*, I read lyrical accounts of hand-to-hand fighting in the sludge. If it was like that the butchery would at least have a few chivalrous aspects ... But look at our wounded: most of them never saw the hand that struck them. What the men are concentrating on all day is sounds ... Oh, you need a trained ear, you need to be a real music connoisseur to come out of there alive!"

The man tries to tell of the crashing of bombs, the drumfire of heavy artillery, the breathless bursts of machine-gun fire, the barking of the 75 mm guns, the hoarse yapping of the howitzers, the plaintive cooing of the flares, the whining of bullets, the treacherous song – that you sometimes catch just too late – of a stray bullet. And in the midst of this rhapsody you still hear the inane call of the bugle and the acid tones of the fife. The air around you is no more than a piece of material that is torn, ransacked, cut to shreds by the weapons. The earth itself starts to pitch and wallow. Suddenly all that stops. The silence maddens you. Every nerve is stretched to breaking point. You fear the worst. Often you are right: waves of chlorine, yperite, mustard gas roll from one trench to the other. You just have time to put on your mask, sweat clouds the lenses, you don't know where you are: blinded, the men of the same army totter to meet people they don't recognise, ready to rip them with their bayonets. Unable to stand it they pull off their ape-like cowls, and soon bubbles come from thcir eye-sockets and nostrils, and they cough up shreds of lung.

The traveller listens in silence, afraid that the slightest question would break the spell of this unspeakable litany, in which blood is finally indistinguishable from mud, in which corpses are eaten by the earth, sucked in by the slime. Sometimes the looters have to half exhume them before they can be stripped. Unless a new bombardment digs them up, turning over like a field the graveyard improvised the day before ...

"You get tired, talking about it," says the man, and it is true that he now seems to be rambling, losing himself in digressions. Everything runs together, nothing is more important than any other detail, since every detail is horrible. He will spare the listener the tetanised arms and legs of a corpse which suddenly unbend on their own, as if moved by a spring, against the sky. He will not dwell on the work of sappers digging tunnels to lay mines below the enemy trenches, pricking their ears for the sound of the enemy picks which may be digging beside them, or straight ahead, coming to meet them.

"You know all that, don't you, my dear colleague? You've already heard it a hundred times in the officers' mess. You haven't? That's probably because you eat well. None of that raw egg diluted with beer, or horse-bean soup. I'm sure you don't smoke dung cigarettes. I've seen men piss in their hands to quench their thirst. Well, I won't tell you about the way the foot-soldiers collide softly and work on each other with their bayonets or pig-stickers as if they were making love, or the corpses and dying men you find, after a charge, with their intestines hooked to the barbed wire. That might spoil your appetite. And that might be embarrassing in the mess or the casino? But excuse me, I'm losing my temper ... "

"Don't apologise," says the traveller. "I think I can detect that it's not really me that you're blaming ... "

The other says nothing. Neither confirms nor denies. But the traveller is fascinated and moved by the man's aggression, which keeps coming to the surface and receding again. It's the reaction of someone who knows a secret that he will never be able to share with those close to him, at Königsberg. He doesn't realise, thinks the traveller, that his attacks on me are also addressed to his wife, or his father. Really, he's having a domestic row with me. This war may have cut him off from his family for ever. It hasn't just isolated the troops from the home front, it has also dug a trench between the present and the past.

"You know," says the traveller, "even in Brussels it's permissible to take the view that this confrontation will change the very meaning of the word 'war'. War as it was celebrated until quite recently by the poets. I'm sure you know the fine, nostalgic song of love and death that Rilke dedicated to the exploits of one of his ancestors. That was yesterday ... It was the golden age!"

"Ah yes, the poets," the man grumbles. "What are German poets going to find to write about now?"

"I ask myself that too," says Gottfried Benn. "Perhaps they'll talk about something else?"

"Of course," says the man. "They will certainly talk about something else. They'll have to!"

"What I mean is," the traveller explains, "they'll *also* talk of something else. They might perhaps talk about the war through something else, do you think?"

"They'll have to," the man repeats with a sardonic laugh. "The subject isn't exactly 'picturesque' any more. Believe me, a rotting hero smells just as bad as a rotting deserter."

"I'm just as well placed to know that," the traveller remarks.

"The most extraordinary thing of all," says the man, "is that you can still have some good times, even there. Would you believe it?"

From one of his greatcoat pockets he extracts a bundle of photographs.

Good Lord! thinks the traveller. After that he's not going to show me his family holiday photographs?

"Of course, I haven't had time to sort them out: there's a bit of everything here. The war too."

The Ecstasy

In neat Gothic script the man has added explanatory captions to the snapshots: *Ruins of the Templars' tower at Nieuport; An English gunboat firing on Westende; Five metres from the French! Aeroplanes over Saint-Idesbald; Plantations of currant bushes on the Yperlée; Locks on the Dunkirk Canal; Fire at the engineering works at Forthem; Brickyard at Ramskapelle* . . .

"Look at these, rather," suggests the man.

One photo shows some soldiers in black underpants swimming in a river. Then, in another, they are naked.

"That was near Lille," says the man. "Now this one . . . "

It shows some men climbing a greasy pole. In another, what seem to be the same men are having their hair cut, laughing and smiling. And here is a photo of a bomb on which someone has written: "*Happy New Year!*"

"That was last January 1st," says the man. "Here, I've photographed the menu of our Christmas supper. We had Zeeland oysters. And we pinched some bottles of Graves and Château-Lagrange from the French. What do you say to that?"

In others, you see flat horizons, stagnant pools, a nurse with a pointed chin and an aquiline nose, a stretcher mounted on wheels, a corpse drifting among reeds, an open coffin, a dismembered village.

"No, don't look at that one. It's the others that matter."

Curious, thinks the traveller. The same man who was furious just now because he thought me unaware of the butchery in Flanders now wants to spare me the pictures which show it. The same man who could not find words strong enough to denounce the ferocity of the fighting has quite happily taken a picture of the "goodwill" bomb our troops dropped on the enemy one New Year's Day . . . But at the same time, isn't it modern history inscribing this logic in our microcephalic brains?

"The best things I've seen," says the man, "I wasn't able to take: some spahis galloping along the edge of the North Sea, frisking, festooned with ribbons. And then a girl walking along the road, shielding herself from the summer heat with a

sunshade. Imagine it: a sunshade in the middle of a war!
Sometimes, at Nieuport, we heard the sound of a piano
coming from an open window. It wasn't an hallucination.
There were some days when we hated our own people who
were not in the trenches to see what we were going through,
more than the enemy himself, who at least shared it, whose
dim silhouette we could make out through our periscopes ...
What are we trying to prove to ourselves with this war,
colleague? It's meant to prove something, isn't it? And more
than just the superiority of one army over another, am I not
right?"

"If it is intended to prove more than that," says the traveller,
"it's a terrible thing indeed."

"But now you're nearly at your destination," says the man,
"and I have been so talkative we haven't even spoken about
you ... "

As if we had talked about him, thinks the traveller. But he
really is right: in times like these any man is reduced to a single
experience. In any case, my travelling companion did not even
introduce himself, nor did it occur to me to reveal my identity
to him.

Has he been influenced by what he has heard at home about
the way the war is going? Misery seems to him to have gained
ground in the Belgian capital while he was away.

Coal is being distributed to the poor in the rue des Tanneurs.
(But we already know there'll be a shortage next winter.)
Elsewhere, soup and butcher's fat are being handed out.
Herring and rice. Even the middle-classes often seem content
with bean pudding embellished with croûtons. In the so-called
"hay boxes", lentils and dried vegetable are preserved, isolated
from the outside air by a wooden case with a double lining of
sawdust, wool, straw and clay.

Whether out of candour or cynicism, the military governor
has advised the population to replace potatoes by turnips and

sugar-beet. It won't be long before he recommends using artificial honey.

What has happened to the time when you could still get sturgeon, anthracite nuts, flannel at the markets near the Bourse?

The more the rationing, the more the fraud. Potatoes are sometimes hidden at the bottom of coffins ...

And as the shortages multiply, new substitutes are put into circulation every day. Starch is made with horse chestnuts. Soap with wood ash and ivy leaves. Oil is extracted from beechnuts and alcohol from potatoes. Malt is made by roasting grain. People don't yet smoke horse-dung cigarettes as they do on the Yser, but beech and chestnut leaves offer a substitute for tobacco. Soon we'll be entitled to carrion sausage, oil diluted with gum arabic, chocolate coloured with the blood of live-stock ...

And while this goes on the military doctor is not unaware that Imperial officers are inviting each other in the evenings, to knock back Madeira or coffee liqueur.

Only certain women are to be had for next to nothing. Happy when they can take away two or three tins of food or a bunch of asparagus.

In the slaughterhouses the tastiest morsels of old horsemeat are reserved to be requisitioned by the occupying forces.

One morning the officer passes the Anderlecht abattoir. It seems to him that an abscess of violence has formed here at the very heart of the world's violence. He recalls his impressions in a similar place in Berlin, when he was ten years younger. It's as if nothing had checked the expansion of horror in the interval. What you have here is no more than a metaphor of what must be happening at the front: an appalling anthropomorphism. He meets the empty gaze of a knacker, and thinks that anyone who lingers here, between these walls of meat and curtains of blood, must surely finish an idiot.

In the courtyard of the Hôpital Saint-Jean he comes across

some unemployed men who must have been repatriated from Germany and hospitalised. Emaciated bodies, shaven heads. As he passes they glower at him with what looks like anger. Then he realises that their hallucinated expressions come from some deep delirium or fever within them.

The military doctor recalls that from time to time you come across the corpse of a young soldier of the Imperial Army who could not bear to fulfil the mission for which he had been groomed.

Is all this meant to change his ideas? One afternoon the adjutant accepts an invitation from a Belgian colleague to visit the site for the Brugmann Hospital on which work was starting when the war broke out.

"You're not afraid to be seen in my company?" he asks the Belgian. "Couldn't it compromise you?"

"In war," Dr Lauwers replies, "the doctors of both sides are condemned to talk to each other, when it's still possible. Isn't that the privilege of those who tend wounds? Wounds can't be split up. The art of healing is indivisible."

The military doctor relishes the direction the conversation is taking. Standing in front of the dilapidated site where, by some miracle, the first buildings of the clinic have been erected between the edge of a forest and a row of gasometers, he is once more overcome by a feeling of timelessness, of a relative eternity. Does this not look more like the excavations of a city exhumed by archaeologists? Ruins attesting that a civilisation once existed here? And indeed, it did: not that of Byzantium, Argos or Tyre. The civilisation of medicine. And Dr Lauwers was scurrying about among the remnants of an empire.

"*Herr Doktor!* Have a look. Here is the tumour clinic. There we have the use of a radiation chamber . . ."

Dr Lauwers uses the present tense as he guides his visitor around the property. He does not say: "will be sited here", or "we shall have the use of". For him, it's an established fact. It would not take much for the military doctor, joining in the game, to ask to be shown round the dermato-syphiligraphic unit. Doesn't he catch himself looking round for the site, in spite of himself?

But this exhilaration cannot last for ever. As the shades of evening descend on these walls, they suddenly look irremediably derelict ... A veil of gloom enfolds them, perhaps a threat? Insidiously they begin to look like a forced-labour camp for invalids ... Unless it's a doctors' graveyard.

"Another time I'll take you to the urological department at Saint-Pierre," says Dr Lauwers, "or the institute for the war blind."

It would not occur to the German doctor to suspect his guide of mocking him, but he is no less uneasy for that. He suddenly asks himself whether he has the right to this man's friendship.

However, as he does each time a scruple troubles him, he brushes it roughly aside:

"I doubt if that is of much medical interest," he says.

More and more, the doctor in him is being doubled by a detective.

"I'm the VD sleuth," he quips to Carl Sternheim or Otto Flake. "Soon I'll be tracking down the pox with a magnifying glass, and writing my reports in invisible ink!"

But isn't his ultimate ally the vice squad, which is itself assisted by under-officers who unmask streetwalkers by accosting them? This "infiltration" turns out to be all the more necessary as "part-timers" proliferate: widows or solitary wives who, sometimes in order to survive, prostitute themselves to German soldiers, to the outrage of patriotic papers which call for them to be denounced to their husbands ...

Sometimes the military doctor asks himself whether he is still enjoying this game in which medical treatment is becoming repressive.

He studies the file of the woman Janssens, Augusta. "Said to have accompanied German non-commissioned officers to a hotel in the rue de la Violette with the intention of debauchery. Soon after, she was admitted to Saint-Pierre Hospital ... "

What must now be established is whether the woman Janssens, Augusta has contaminated a member of the German Red Cross. To this end the afore-mentioned officers have not hesitated to have her sent from her sickbed at Saint-Pierre, where she was under observation after an attack of *delirium tremens*. They have "liberated" her, they assure her, to have her examined by a trustworthy German doctor! This is not to the taste of the Belgian nurse who swears to God that the woman Janssens, Augusta is not syphilitic.

"Have you done the Wassermann test?" asks the military doctor.

"No," the nurse admits, "but you can see just by looking at her that she is not contaminated."

The doctor can't help smiling.

"Just by looking at her, you say? We are not in the Middle Ages, Mademoiselle ... "

What can the nurse be thinking? That to invite caution the woman Janssens, Augusta would have to present herself with her skin in shreds, covered in crinkled, greasy, bulbous scars? Riddled with scrofulae, pustules or papulous roseola?

But he is touched by the young nurse's retort that it's a question of principle: poxed or not, the woman Janssens, Augusta must be readmitted to Saint-Pierre without further ado.

An unruffled German interpreter keeps this dialogue of the deaf flowing.

"May I at least question the person concerned?" asks the military doctor courteously.

Yes, he may question her.

Soon the woman Janssens, Augusta admits to having "had relations with the said member of the German medical services, but vehemently denies having been infected".

"What are her means of support?"

The nurse intervenes to state that she is a "day-worker without employment from the rue des Pierres".

The German doctor wonders how this address might influence the woman's professional status, but does not doubt for a moment that the detail is of importance. He tries to imagine this rue des Pierres where, if he obeyed his own impulse, he would go straight away, to realise at once that the woman Janssens, Augusta could not have encountered the pathogenic agent of syphilis there.

"Actually, she happened to be caught in a state of vagrancy," the nurse concedes loyally.

"Very well, let's proceed ... "

It soon emerges that the woman Janssens, Augusta engages in regular clandestine prostitution. She even consents to undress, but refuses to be subjected to an "experiment" which, she says, would only be designed to confuse her.

The doctor asks more questions. He checks the kidneys and heart of this unknown, goose-pimpled woman. The interrogation clearly terrifies her as much as if it were being conducted by a police officer. The doctor feels overcome by lassitude. He knows that even if he managed to gain this creature's confidence, the anamnesis she would undergo would be of little help in the event of a latent, silent infection.

"At least you haven't any children?" he asks.

The interpreter translates:

"No, she hasn't any children."

"Can I get dressed, then?" asks the woman Janssens, Augusta.

"Just one moment," says the military doctor.

He would have liked, for some reason, to pursue the hopeless interview with this naked, hunted woman who is as defenceless as a child. He is struck yet again by the paradoxical chastity of these venal Venuses, as if to play at love, even for money, were still only playing, in a world which, alas, does not play. Lousy profession, thinks the military doctor. Dog's life:

what am I doing here, prodding bodies that war and male desire have cut adrift? Suddenly his gaze falls on the woman's thighs, as she sits astride a chair. These white thighs, a bit fat, already marbled with cellulitis and ocellated with varicose veins. His eye follows one of the veins which ramifies in ferny arabesques under the translucent skin. Seized by vertigo, he shuts his eyes for a moment. "Ochre sands of Africa, Grecian pallor, the sanguinous surface of southern seas . . . " he stammers. "Borneo, Polynesia. Polynesia, Eva . . . " He is shaken by a brief, hysterical sob. Later, he will tell himself: it was the absolute opposite of sarcasm.

"Pardon, Doctor?"

No one has noticed anything. He pulls himself together.

He won't even go on examining this body that he has had to snatch from the enemy like some ludicrous booty of war. It's beyond him. For once, he lets his arms hang. For once he is going to show a lack of professional conscience.

"All right, I'm handing her back to you," he tells the Belgian nurse. "But if I were in your place I'd give her a Wassermann test, just in case . . . "

"Really?" the young woman asks. "Because you haven't even offered a diagnosis?"

There's a glint of triumph in her eye.

Let her contaminate whoever she likes, thinks the doctor as he leaves the hospital, fleeing his surgery. Let her mark all those who, like me, take up with fallen women. After all, I myself, despite my job and because of it, and against my instinct – I run the risk of getting tattooed by one of them, sooner or later. Who knows if I don't even want it to happen?

Then, another day, the authorities of the Hôpital Saint-Jean are asked to supply notes relating to the illness of Liberski, Martha.

Another time, they have to delay the funeral and burial of Berghmans, Yvette to carry out an autopsy. It's never too late to pass the clinical sentence.

He contemplates his hands in the lamplight, hands that eczema has eroded in places down to the cutis. He whose skin is botched, compromised, touches the skin of others. With what right, he might wonder. Is he not at once both judge and defendant?

He looks at them more closely. These poor, learned, dreamy hands. They purport to meet the shadows of others in the dark, when one is blindfolded. They palpate, caress, knead, reconstruct a body that time is undoing, that eternity is frittering away. (In fact, they merely grope, these helpless hands ...)

No matter: you never track down or treat an illness except by friction, touch. You don't know human beings unless you rub against them, wear yourself out touching them: don't talk to me about any other humanism than that, thinks the military doctor. Anything that is not that humble touching between the infirm, that brushing against the carnal truth of men, is just a prattling, hollow Utopia, a sophism, a smarmy sin against the spirit.

Now he looks at the hand that writes. And he thinks: the hand that writes the fate of the hand that signs, the hand that relates all that, that traces the hesitant downstrokes, loops and upstrokes of the truth: that hand has burnt fingers.

His wife comes to see him: this time she is the one on leave ... As if she were falling back from a front opened at Berlin to join him at the rear.

"It's almost like that," she says. "The streets back there smell of corpses. And then, isn't it like being on holiday here together?"

It takes a good deal of obliviousness, of course, but Gottfried tries to make it like a belated honeymoon for her ...

Edith is astonished or amused at everything. She admires the Corinthian columns of the Gare du Midi no less than the Malibran Residence, which has a rotunda worthy of a casino at a health spa, or the glass roof of the Galeries Saint-Hubert, where he points out the motto to her: *Omnibus Omnia* ... He tells his companion that in Brussels the arcades, stations and prisons are conceived like cathedral naves.

Everything enchants the visitor, who nowhere notices the war. What in someone else might seem myopia or cynicism is in her no more than an artless blur softening time and things like breath on a mirror. Her husband trembles at the thought that she might be woken from this trance. She is filled with joy by the street-names she has marked in an old *Baedeker* bought in Dresden, from a second-hand bookseller close to the Opera.

"Many of those avenues may have been renamed," Gottfried remarks, "or have disappeared by now ... "

What does that matter? She repeats the names aloud, never tires of them. They make her pensive. Notre-Dame-aux-Neiges. Ferme des Boues. Quartier de la Putterie. Rue de la Vierge-Noire. Rue du Chien-Marin. Rue Montagne-des-Géants. Rue de la Grande-Ile. Rue Traversière. Rue des Clés. Rue du Regard ... She would like to know what the rue de Terre-Neuve looks like.

"I don't think the river runs there any more," says her husband.

She is intrigued by the Impasse de l'Enfer – Hell's dead-end.

"I don't expect the train will find it impassable," says Gottfried.

"So everything changes here," she says, almost nostalgically.

She would like to stroll on the Quai au Bois-à-Brûler, the Quai aux Barques, the Quai aux Pierres-de-Taille. On the Port des Juifs, the Port des Poissonniers.

"Those are strange quays," Gottfried objects. "Hardly anyone walks there. Brussels is a harbour in name only."

She does not understand:

"Do boats come here or don't they?" she asks.

She would like to go straight to the Tour Japonaise.

"Closed on account of military occupation," her husband informs her.

This time she seems disappointed. But they go to the Musée Colonial. The Kasai masks fill them with rapture.

"That's Expressionism before its time," Gottfried exclaims.

The next day, Edith wants to see all the places planted with trees. They visit in turn the Arboretum, the Winter Garden, and the large hothouse with palms at the Palais de Laeken in the botanical garden – where their gaze is transfixed by an interminable sequoia (*Wellingtonia gigantea*) and Rude's nymphs.

"Their Leopold II must have been a kind of Louis of Bavaria, just as dreamy but more brawny," Gottfried remarks. "He turned this town into a charming collection of Gothic bric-à-brac with tropicalist touches. He swept through it like a blast of föhn, sometimes veering towards the sirocco. It was never the same again. He despised his people, whom he considered blinkered and ungrateful, and he made life hard for his architects."

Edith now wants to buy a bag of whelks on the steps of the Bourse. At the city centre even the adverts amuse and intrigue her: "Vinegar of the Stars", "Palace of Toys", "Cristofle the Cutler", "Home Tailoring", "Byrrh: tonic aperitif and generous wine . . . "

She's right, her husband thinks. That too is a part of the city's discourse. Later, we'll remember it too.

When he no longer expects it, Edith asks him to tell her about the war, as he has experienced it here. He will have to tell her as little as possible. But he does not censor everything. He does not conceal the exodus of people in rattletrap charabancs for Sedan, Flushing or Folkestone. He reveals to her that the inhabitants go about armed with a passport inside their own country. That the only presents given to children at Christmas or the feast of St Nicholas are lead grenadiers and infantrymen and papier-mâché barracks.

He deliberately slips harmless, reassuring anecdotes into his account: that there had to be a round-up of stray dogs, that chestnuts had been shaken from the trees in the Avenue de Tervuren, that horses still ran at the race-courses, that game was hunted as if nothing had changed. That somewhere in Flanders you could meet a Mexican ex-empress who had gone soft in the head ...

For he is afraid this child who is older than he is and whom he has made his wife may suddenly emerge from her state of radiant somnambulism and ask for more details, more truth about what is going on ...

But having seen her worried face when he caught her unawares, he realises at last that it is not innocence or light-headedness that makes her ask no questions and seem not to notice the war around her. She is just pretending not to see. She is sparing, protecting him. She hopes to make him forget for a few days the futile struggle he is waging against an obscene epidemic in a besieged town. She has not been an actress for nothing, Edith Osterloh, alias Eva Brandt; she's only shamming the child ... He, in his turn, pretends not to notice.

There aren't enough hours to immerse themselves in all the museums she wants to visit, which occasionally open their doors in spite of the occupation. Out of panic, no doubt, she is excited about everything and nothing. The Egyptian Queen Tiyi (eighteenth dynasty) or a police helmet from the seventh hussars' regiment they come across in the Cinquantenaire. An Ethiopian *kissar* or a Burmese harp, at the Conservatoire. An incendiary bomb at the Naval Museum and a harquebus at the Porte de Hal. The sperm whale from the Scheldt and Bernis-sart's iguanodon, the Arlon ichthyosaurus and the great whale of Antwerp, at the Quartier Léopold. At the Musée d'Art Ancien they pass rapidly before Jordaens's *Suzanne and the Old Men* and Rubens's *Christ and the Woman Taken in Adultery*. They stop a moment in front of the *Dead Marat*.

"I didn't know that he died here," says Gottfried.

"Who, Marat?"

"No, David ... "

And now they are before the painting he wanted to show her more than any other. Together they immerse themselves in the winey sea of Brueghel's *Landscape with the Fall of Icarus*. The work of a man without illusions, thinks Gottfried, but a man who, before starting work, shut his eyes to capture the world's splendours beneath his lids, so that when he opened them the world emerged washed, pristine. How I admire this star we live on, the visitor reflects, although I only explore its hidden face. How I can resonate in sympathy with the Promethean pain that is nothing but nostalgia: the future and obverse of gaiety. I shall give vent only to the cries of a wounded Medusa ... In a poem born of the contemplation of this canvas, in which he vehemently protests against his incarceration in a body and a mind that have been foreclosed, he begs to be allowed

"an hour
of that good early light before the look began".

He desperately asks a caryatid also encountered in the museum to extricate herself from the stone she continues to support even at the gate of hell.

Impossible evasions, when the sun is burning our wings and everything pulls us down towards the sea.

Just a matter of tying a pretty bow around the magnanimous charade they have been playing throughout their reunion. Gottfried proposes going to a concert at the Vaux-Hall with a gang of German friends ... for all the world as if they were still back home in Berlin.

Sternheim and his wife Thea, Einstein, Flake and Wedder-kopp welcome Edith rather as if she were a ghost or a prodigal daughter. They take an aperitif together in the rue de la Madeleine. They judge it best to put the charming Frau Benn in the picture straight away.

"Has Gottfried told you," asks Otto Flake, "that this state is governed by a soldier-king, a flag-waving cardinal and seditious burgomasters? All this when Germany would be an ideal big brother for the country!"

"Did you know that the French and British don't know who

else to ask for help? Moroccan and Senegalese infantry, Zouaves singing the praises of Allah in Poperinghe and Dixmude, Cossacks and sepoys. Singhalese, Sikhs and Turcos – we've fought them all," observes the ironic Wedderkopp.

"All the same, my dear," Otto puts in, "life goes on. Read the clandestine news-sheets they pass round. Always plenty of lurid copy. There's just as much thieving, burglary and prostitution as before we arrived, you can be sure. Anyway, our beloved Gottfried knows a bit about that ... And look at the obituaries. People are still dying in bed ... "

Edith is overwhelmed. She turns this way and that trying to catch her husband's eye, discreetly imploring him. Thea Sternheim comes to her help:

"Don't listen to all that male gossip, my dear! These gentlemen aren't here as propaganda spokesmen for the pan-German ideal for nothing – are they, Carl? So they think with our Emperor that Germany didn't want the war. They like to peddle the idea that our losses at the front are light, and that there's nothing much to report from the Yser. And they're sure to approve our beloved governor when, on the very day some Belgian or British women spies had been executed at the national rifle range, he voiced his official displeasure at some local smugglers' barbaric custom of blinding finches!"

"You will observe, Edith," says Carl, "that Thea has remained true to herself: a hell-raiser from the days of the Commune!"

"More like an enemy agent," says Wedderkopp with a guffaw. "But suppose we talk about matters of the mind instead? What do you think of our good Carl Sternheim's noble gesture of some time back?"

"What was that?"

"He relinquished the money from the Fontane Prize, that he so richly deserved," explains Otto, "to a certain Franz Kafka who appears to be in need."

"It was Franz Blei's idea," Sternheim insists, somewhat irritated.

"How's that?"

"Well, it was really Blei who got me the prize, then urged me, considering the state of my fortune – isn't that right, my dear? – to bequeath it to Kafka. Incidentally, have you read him? You haven't? That's very remiss of you, he has much promise. Blei told me that this fellow, who is a German-speaking Czech Jew living in Prague, has fallen in love with a Berlin lady ... But he only visits her at rare intervals, when he gets time off. He stays with her at the Askanischer Hof for twenty-four hours, then goes back home."

"I don't see anything so unusual about that," says Edith. "I've had only a few days with my husband myself. And in forty-eight hours I'll be gone ... "

"Yes, but Edith, dear girl, the situation is hardly comparable ... "

"Let's talk about the dead rather than the absent," Einstein proposes. "Did you know that Verhaeren has just died?"

"A horrible accident," says Flake. "Falling under a train ... "

"It looks more like a suicide," Wedderkopp points out.

"That doesn't make it one," says Flake. "The man was a Germanophobe, very patriotic. That must help to keep you going ... "

"He was – incidentally – a great poet," says Gottfried Benn.

"For that matter," says Wedderkopp, "Trakl is supposed not to have died mad, but from an overdose of veronal."

"Cocaine," Gottfried corrects him. One at least who didn't leave the war to do its work, he thinks. He got there first.

"Someone who helped him a lot was Wittgenstein ... "

"Helped him to die?" asks Wedderkopp.

"No, to survive. For years he had been sending him an anonymous allowance. Drugs or no," says Otto Flake, "madness was lying in wait for him."

"He only went mad out of fear and despair," says Gottfried. "He was afraid of being executed, because he had already attempted suicide once. He preferred to die by his own hand.

Unless he just took an overdose. Cardiac arrest ... The absurd and splendid way to die."

"People say," Flake tells them, "that he was in the habit of visiting tarts, but that nothing happened with them ... "

"That's not true," Gottfried corrects him. "He talked to them. Listened to them. Drank wine with them ... "

"That's just what I mean," Wedderkopp insists.

"Well, it's not what you say," Gottfried cuts in. "Of all their clients he was undoubtedly the one who was closest to them ... "

"Well, if you think so ... "

"I think so."

"Of course, you've got some practical knowledge in that area that I don't have ... "

"Time to make our way to the concert," Sternheim announces, no doubt fearing the conversation may take an acrimonious turn.

"Don't be surprised, Frau Benn, if the hall is half empty. The Belgian citizens find it amusing to reserve seats which they do not turn up to occupy."

"What's on the programme?"

" *'Frauenliebe und-leben'*, the *'Wesendonk-Lieder'* and, alas, *'Das klagende Lied'* by that tedious Mahler ... "

"Don't listen to him, Edith," Carl Einstein whispers to her. "It'll probably be the best piece of all ... "

"Are those people your friends?" Edith asks her husband.

"You know, my dear," Gottfried replies, "friendship, like the wind, blows where it will ... That's its disconcerting virtue. Imagine someone asking you why you loved me. How would you answer? You'd probably list a lot of things no one would believe. That's just why you ought to be believed!"

"Never mind," says Edith, "But your friends frighten me. They remind me of Berlin. I didn't need to come here to meet them. It felt like already being back there."

The Ecstasy

The following night, Gottfried dreamed he met on the road some female midgets who were later to become streetwalkers. Later because, despite appearances to the contrary – they were wrinkled like over-ripe apples – they were hardly out of childhood. Edith, roused, reproached him wearily for frequenting such people. It's only pain, he said. Pain to be taken. Pain to be given.

The next day they go out walking again but their hearts are not in it. However, without having looked for them they come across traces left by Nele and Till Eulenspiegel. Here, meeting blind people at a post office. There, holding a cage in a church ...

"I should have been sad to leave without seeing them again," says Edith.

In the middle of a square Gottfried presents the statue of Vesalius – the greatest man from these parts, master of us all – the first to open the human body in order to understand it better. He himself died of cold, on an island where he had been cast up by a storm. When you have had so much to do with death, your own death sometimes tries not to resemble you ...

The last evening they are to spend together before Edith leaves, Gottfried gives his orderly time off, sending him to a hotel for the night.

"But why?" Edith asks nervously. "Isn't the house big enough? He'll think you're planning an orgy ... "

"That's what it shall be. A two-person, conjugal orgy. There mustn't be any witnesses."

"I'm sure he would have been discreet ... "

"It's not enough for him to be discreet: it must be far from everything ... "

"You're intriguing me ... " says Edith.

She is not far from being afraid. As if her husband were thinking of liquidating her, then committing suicide. Since the beginning of the war the *Düsseldorfer Tageblatt* and the *Berliner Morgenpost* have been full of such stories.

She recalled that the first night she had spent under his roof there had been no physical contact between them. He had sat on the edge of her bed asking her about life at Hellerau and Dresden and about how their daughter was growing. He seemed to listen to her with utmost attention, as if, beyond her replies, he were looking out for special information the importance of which she could not judge. News that might have fed his own thoughts on what he had experienced in Brussels since he had been there. He questioned her for a long time, much as you might interrogate someone suffering from amnesia.

He had not made love to her. He excused himself, declaring he was dog-tired. She saw then how fatigue was hollowing his features, turning his flesh to lead. As if, harbouring a secret too heavy to bear or share, he could not share love either. This was unexpected in such a sensual man so long deprived of his wife. You hear enough stories of soldiers famished for flesh, who throw themselves on their companions in the few hours they have together . . .

The next day, he took her. Gently, as one might a young mother hardly recovered from her confinement. Then, other times. Sometimes he went out in the middle of the night and did not return till dawn.

"Have you brought those laced ankle-boots I gave you the day before I was mobilised?"

"Of course I've brought them. I was surprised you haven't yet asked me to put them on."

"I'd like you to wear them tonight. To be naked, wearing those boots."

"I'd look like a tart," she said, laughing. "Is that what you want?"

"I don't want you just to look like an actress-tart, Eva Brandt, I want you to be one. A real tart. I want you to be the woman Brandt, Eva. The woman Osterloh, Edith. The woman Benn, Edith-Eva! Haven't we been play-acting this whole week, as if the war didn't touch us, didn't concern us? Tonight," he added, beginning to breathe hard, "I even want to pay you for your services!"

He was waving about some Belgian and German banknotes, crumpling them as if they were burning his fingers.

"I want you to understand," he said. "I need to do it."

She asked if that was a curiously indirect way of making her a present. Or if he had acquired a taste for prostitutes in the course of the war? If he couldn't do without them even when he had his own wife in his arms?

He said it was not like that. That he could not remember a time when he was not attracted by tarts, but that that had nothing to do with it. He said he wanted to pay her like a whore, but that should not cause her offence. That in his eyes it was more like a mark of respect, of deference.

Then he added:

"You were rich, Edith, when I got to know you. And I am going to be so poor ... "

She shivered. With humiliation? With fear? With pleasure?

She had tears in her eyes. Of shame? Of happiness?

Her lip trembled. She was laughing in her tears.

"I'll try to understand," she said. "I even think I do understand. You won't lose me, Gottfried? You'll come back to me after the war?"

"We'll stay together until the end," he told her.

Something had certainly happened here the previous spring that he did not talk about to his wife, or to any of his friends. In any case, wasn't the event itself an incognito?

It was over, he told himself. He already felt as if cast out by what had befallen him, and viewed it from such a distance that it seemed like something that had happened to someone else. Talking of his own adventure, he might have started his account like this: We have to imagine this man landing here, knowing hardly anyone, in an occupied country, losing himself in the maze of alien streets. We have to set our feet in his footprints.

Yet everything had started in such a banal fashion. The occupier, no sooner alighted in the city, had set out to be loved by it. The conqueror had really wanted to conquer. Walking with long, haughty strides in avenues that reminded him of the Middle Ages, climbing the steps to the parvis of Gothic chapels, casting fond, almost enamoured glances at the city's disorder, ready to revere anything, from the pilastered façades with scrollwork and gables that could be seen in the rue du Chêne to the seedy pub in the Marolles quarter into which he had ventured long enough to drink a glass of fresh water under the eye of a gypsy woman, leaving again, stopping under the grimacing gargoyles of a cathedral or coming across the inscription: *Abattoir* written above a house on the Boulevard de l'Abattoir, but not leading to any knacker's yard . . .

He pauses by chance before the tartan display of a rag merchant or an itinerant locksmith, or in front of a café "closed on account of invasion" . . . And he addresses a fervent supplication to the city which beleaguers him: "Dear city, please let me conquer you!" And he thinks: "Accept me into your community, make me your countryman!"

City of the south! he proclaims, for in his eyes this is a southern city: the heat of its stones seems to him feminine and sensual. Here, perhaps, a community exists; it must be permissible to win it over, to be clasped to its bosom, to be merged with it. Yes, he thinks, that must be more possible here than elsewhere, more than in other times. And he is ready to believe it is already an accomplished fact. He does not yet know that no one is more separate than the people here. On New Year's Eve, in the black cathedral that seemed white to him, the uniformed soldiers squeezed in among the faithful who seemed to welcome them. And he, the conqueror who does not believe in God – or at least believes he does not – believed at least in this: that the inhabitants and the occupiers were communicating together. It takes so little to nourish dreams of reconciliation.

And then spring came. And his eyes caught, took captive, so many signs, in the rue de l'Étuve or the rue des Alexiens, the Galerie du Prince or the Quai à la Chaux, that they thought themselves the owners of the city.

Yes, this occupier, this conqueror thinks he has appropriated the reality of the city. Whereas the opposite has happened: he has lost all of it, even its meaning. And with each hour of his peregrinations a little more of it escapes from him.

This is the time when we should not lose sight of this man, in case he vanishes over the city's horizon. There is a moment in every life when you meet, disarmed, your naked truth like a bayonet that has just burst from its sheath. You're not mistaken. You recognise it at once. All you can do is throw yourself upon it.

For Gottfried, this happened in Brussels, in the spring, during a dirty war in which he was not playing a particularly illustrious part. Usually, our man led an active life, dealing with wounds which were either above-board or hidden, silent, clandestine, conversing with them. It was not easy and it had no end. But he had chosen to live like this, among the cankers left behind on the flesh of men by their poor desires, among the pallid limbs of the women of pleasure, striated with their network of inky veins. One can take an interest in such things, as one can take an interest in him, and for somewhat the same reasons.

Now, however, he is unoccupied. He walks in civilian clothes along the rue Vilain XIIII or the rue de l'Aurore, the rue de la Vallée or the rue du Lac. Under a cloudless sky. They are just emerging from a winter that war has given the sting of humiliation. The conqueror thinks of Heine, who believed his move to Paris to be inscribed in the very logic of his destiny, and derived from that belief an exaltation that subsequent disappointment could not efface. He also remembers Rilke, asphyxiated in Paris by a surfeit of sadness. He thinks that he, Gottfried, is not going through anything comparable in Brussels. All the same, the faces he meets are blank, closed. Soon, they don't even seem hostile to him. No one speaks to him. No one takes any notice of him. He is forgotten. He takes some time to realise it, but this is what he has been hoping for. Now he is given up to his own autarchy. There are moments when you come up against the truth of your life. If that truth is glorious, so much the better. If it is one of abandonment, that too is all right. What matters is to embrace the truth of your life, whatever it has to be. To evade it no longer. He recalls the traveller in a foreign country who was delighted not to hear a single, treacherous word of his own language, nor to under-stand a word he heard around him. That – so he concluded, more or less – might make it possible to live in the company of men.

No doubt the conclusion was meant to be ironic. But it need not be. For this situation does not mean that people keep quiet at last, or become unintelligible. On the contrary, they no longer cover their traces, they forget their masks. You actually understand them better: they are no longer strangers in only the figurative sense.

Already, he is losing his way – we must see him losing it – in outlying quarters, anodyne roads, the rue des Sols, the rue du Lombard, the rue du Midi, the rue de Terre-Neuve, as if he were deep in the countryside, at the coast. He is no longer only a visitor. What he sees is more than a mere spectacle. As he turns into the boulevard du Midi, the stillness is shattered. He looks up, shading his eyes. He senses passing over him a gassy, tapering, sky-coloured monster. By the time he realises what it is, the airship is far away. But that is because, at the moment when he looked up, the sea moved under his feet. He has a feeling of walking above the bed of an ancient river. Perhaps it flowed here, or nearby, in former times. It might have been diverted. But people preferred to cover it in, build a vault over it, bury it alive. It was no more than a cesspit bordered by mouldering fields. Earlier, its oily, fungous water, in which drowned cats floated among the ordure covered in froth and grease, lapped against rotting quays. Its eddies and vapours hatched the eggs of an epidemic. Cholera raged where you might have had a presentiment of the sea. The city was dragged from its dream of being a port. Now there is only the spectre of a river wandering among roughcast façades, stalling against imaginary locks. But if a town has once been bathed by water, if it has almost linked its destiny to the ocean, it never forgets it. At any moment its drains awaken a phantom pain like an amputated limb. Someone walking on the buried course of a river does not know why his legs grow suddenly heavy, nor what poisons are drawing him into a reverie that is not his, restoring to him a memory not his own. Then he remembers that in former times the sea unfurled its waves upon this place, and that children playing at war still find fossilised shells and sharks' teeth in the sandpits that encircle the city.

We must imagine him, this man walking in a state bordering on intoxication. He is trembling like a convalescent taking his first walk after being pronounced incurable, which he may be. At least he has this unhoped-for respite.

In this state nostalgia knows no limits. To embrace the world more completely, it returns to its origins: in the blinking of an eye, history is effaced. You are no longer in Brussels, just somewhere between the Grande-Ile and the Rue du Chien, or between the Mont-des-Arts and the Galeries du Roi et de la Reine. *Omnibus Omnia*. You are at the confluence of the Tigris and the Euphrates, in the Garden of Eden, and already Adam's tree has grown up at the oasis, since Adam has been dead for some time: you are in cheerful mourning for him. From exile you have passed into ecstasy. You thought yourself lost in a foreign land: you have merely returned. The stroller, the conqueror, gives a start: he is rejoicing. Something weighs on his neck as if to break it, as heavy as the eye of God. Now consciousness is about to embrace the void itself, dancing joyously on the razor's edge that separates, liberates each thing from its identity: it is tottering like a child who has been given an alcoholic drink. Brussels: a fine town in which to lose your mind! A spongy city where you can ferment to your heart's desire! You can get tipsy on the risk of being engulfed, and confuse the tipsiness with the joy of being unburdened of reality. Henceforth to mime being a part of the world like a whore feigning pleasure! What economy! What good riddance! A little psychology and then, a moment later, no psychology at all! What peace! From now on, just an intermittent truth. What a windfall for a lyric poet! Others in his position gave way to this dizziness, savoured it, thereby assuring their errings of impunity.

He resists it.

It's still him we should see measuring out the city's streets, but he is already walking more slowly, going less far, just somewhere between the rue de la Croix-de-Fer and the rue Montagne-de-la-Cour, or between the Ixelles covered market and the rue Sans-Souci; and now he's no more than a quack taking a turn at the end of a consultation.

And incidentally a poet, in his lost moments. And he has those, too.

But from now on he goes about with a double, to whom he delegates his powers. This is the character who, in his stead, walks in Brussels, decides to leave for Antwerp, abandons the idea, starts pitching heavily in the midday light, dreams of linking this with that in his life, producing a synthesis, comes out in a palm grove, crosses an oasis that owes everything to the desert it negates, steps across a delta – for the sea is never far. And he too has access to "a kind of happiness".

The poet has made this character a doctor like himself, and a doctor of whores. He has not called him Blackwell, or Constantinescu, or Rosenblatt. He has called him Rönne, a brief, slightly harsh-sounding name. In fact, he has imagined as little as possible: he has used a character as close as possible to himself, not quite a double. Scarcely a reflection. But enough to stop him falling over the edge.

He wanted to conquer the reality of the city, and he failed.
From now on, Rönne will fail in his place.

Since Brussels is no more than a dream, and in this dream is Rönne.

To tell Rönne's Odyssey, it would doubtless have been appropriate to revisit the forgotten outskirts of language, set up house in the unavowable, renounce the words of the newspapers (those of the occupier, those of the occupied). It would have been necessary to sacrifice adjectives, as his friend Carl Sternheim recommended. But how could one do without ever saying "suave", or "gaping", or "blue"?

It was essential to cut down on dialogue.

Of course.

At this price, he would be able to use words in the way he intended: to tear himself on them. For only words can wash the wound they have themselves inflicted. Only they can weld together this debris of stars, people and flowers.

Later, the poet was to disown somewhat those early sketches, laugh at their imperfections, claiming he had rid himself of such states of the soul. No doubt they were merely pretentious effusions.

When he has forgotten much, he will notice that he has not changed in the meantime. You think you have plunged to the depths and surfaced somewhere quite different, facing another shore. You have not moved an iota. You have thrashed about at the centre of a canvas, you have been treading water . . .

It is exactly the same with the microbe that interests the military doctor. In just the same way, the Treponema he studies on the microscope slide in his laboratory on the avenue Molière, turns on its axis like a corkscrew, and while the spirilla surrounding it in the preparation swarm in all directions the syphilis Treponema, undulating frantically, produces no more than a kind of halo . . .

As for the poet, he will rely later, fanatically, on style alone to give form to life, that arrogant chaos. For better and for worse. He will put his faith only in that bellowing cry forced into the ear of a deaf God. You should not escape the form which scattered you, dispersed you, but restore it to intoxication! Therefore, let reality stay where it is, leave it to its murderous convulsions, its mountebank somersaults, its brutal displays, its imperialism, its aporia.

For him, everything ceased to be quotidian somewhere between the rue de l'Ermitage and the rue des Champs-Élysées, or from the rue des Sables to the rue des Fripiers, or between the morgue and the lunatic asylum. That was surely enough for a fancier of eccentricities. Beyond that line: excursions organised for a decomposing ego, the desertification of the mind, the cosmopolitan globe-trotting of the unhappy, idle consciousness! No salvation outside form! Don't spit in the air! God delivers to your door!

Why did Gottfried Benn believe that season spent in Brussels to be the best of his life, to be life itself, put forever into the imperfect tense?

Sumptuous solitude. Orgy of belonging to yourself. Sleepwalking at midday. Solar curfew. What a debauch! Compared to that negative trance was not all else mere biographical junk fit only to be thrown away?

We must imagine, one last time, the German poet a prey to fuliginous intuitions between the rue Nuit-et-Jour and the Ile des Mouches, on the Place Sainte-Catherine, or absorbed, on the rue Royale, in some ultimate hallucination, clinging precariously to an identity that is attacked as if by an acid ... There are so many dreamers, big talkers and armchair philosophers who will claim such intuitions as their own that one is tempted to leave the military doctor to his dishevelled wanderings, his step heavy, his breath short, his throat tight for a reason he does not know, along the streets of this city that reels along its own pavements ... Yes, one would gladly abandon him to his gloomy flashes, his amateur ruminations on eternity. So many more seductive poets have tramped the streets of this city, poets who did not come as enemies: why pick on this one, sweating blood and water in a precocious spring?

Because between two visits to whores, by turns physician and client, creditor and debtor, *Omnibus Omnia*, that man knew at once all that can be known about a city. We must see him, even under the open sky between the rue des Chapeliers and the rue des Petits-Carmes, burrowing like a mole. While the light drenches his stupefied, almost beatific face, he must have the feeling of raking the ground with words, to uncover some secret the world has buried there long ago and has since forgotten . . .

But even this light that buries him like an avalanche comes from below. He is no longer fooled by the mirages of streets that spread like esplanades over the desert of the city in spring, no longer lured by the whiteness enveloping him; he no longer even trusts the blue of the sky: things are moving beneath his feet. All that comes from below, not above. It's death, he understands. Even when we are happy, it is only because we understand. And the only thing we can learn is death. We can only attempt to know our dead, those whom our steps awaken and who pull us by the feet. Our dead, and the sea. Our dead mingled with the sea. *Thalassa. Omnibus Omnia. Omnibus. Omnia.*

Our dead, he thought. As if the dead belonged to us.

Undoubtedly, there is one death we harbour within us: the one we have inflicted.

And then, another again, thinks the military doctor, the one we have justified.

There is a day in the course of this war when he saw, at close quarters, death in the process of being inflicted. It was not, admittedly, an act of war. But war was invoked to justify this death.

He witnessed an execution.

It happened long before the spring in which one felt this delirious suspicion that the world did not exist. To begin with, it was not difficult to think about it. The memory of the death did not harry, did not persecute the witness. He even found himself chatting about it among friends, in the house Carl Sternheim occupied at La Hulpe, and that he had christened, in homage to the pacifist Tolstoy, "Clairecolline" – Bright Hill. And when the medical adjutant spoke of it, he did so with formidable coolness: if one admitted that war had broken out, no matter how frighteningly absurd it may be, one must also accept that "from the point of view of strict military logic" this execution was in line with the grain of history. It would be ridiculous, would it not, to consider it out of context. One would have had to start by not voting for the national defence budget ... When the young Hegel saw Napoleon passing on horseback in the avenues of Berlin, he commented: "There goes the World Spirit." Of course, the pacifists, no less than the nationalists, took him to task for an epitaph that had almost the ring of homage – was Hegel taking sides with a tyrant? He was merely bowing before the evidence.

Thea Sternheim, who was later to become one of the best friends of this man who could withhold his mercy with such coldness, thought at first: "With men of that sort any hope of communicating is doomed in advance."

There was not for a moment any question of remorse. He was not even tempted to forget, to repress what had happened. But one detail of the scene, then another – the awkward walk to the place of execution, since the site was on a slope and the rain that had fallen all the previous night had made the ground slippery; the wait for the condemned; the shortness of the wait; the acceleration of events when they arrived – all that comes back into his mind, and his memory itself begins to race to the rhythm of the action. So that he never thinks: How dreadful it was ... No, he thinks: How quickly it was done. How simple it is to kill a woman.

And, as often happens with this seemingly fearless man, the work of memory supplants remorse. In this way memory almost becomes compassion.

The war, therefore, has not left the medical adjutant to his own spiritual devices. It has not summoned him here for that. It hasn't even mobilised him solely to look after whores. One has at all times to deal with women, all kinds of women. So too one comes across martyrs. One could well have done without them.

The invader undoubtedly has every reason to beware of women. When they are not contaminating the flower of German soldiery, they are masterminding the information services with remarkable efficiency. Prostitutes or spies. Salome and Judith. And people claim that war is men's business! Every night the leading women, industrious, determined, smuggle young men of an age to fight across the Dutch frontier to the depots of the Entente. When there is an investigation to find out how this can happen, and how the Allies are always so perfectly informed about the movements of the German army, who does one find? Women, almost always women. If they are caught red-handed and tried, the worst that can happen to them is to be deported to Germany and subjected to forced labour. After the war they will return covered in laurels . . . So the occupying power decides enough is enough: if there is no longer a weaker sex, there will be no more pity either . . .

This time the most important spy network is brought to justice. The trial takes place in the Belgian Parliament, on the floor of the chamber in which the elected representatives of the nation once voted on measures for the protection of the public good, by standing up or remaining seated. Baize doors, in a decor where footsteps are deadened by woollen carpets, where panelling shines in the half-dark, where frescoes vainly unfold parables which the times have made obsolete.

At the head of the insurgents, a tall Englishwoman, slender, grave, absorbed in her role. She appears in a blue dress and a goffered straw boater with two feathers. A white collar, tight as a tourniquet. Her shoulders sag as if she were about to collapse at any moment. Extreme lassitude, pent-up energy. One might be surprised that she has renounced her uniform, her nurse's head-dress. But no matter what garment she wears, it must, as a matter of course, enclose her like a sheath, fall just as straight about her, with just as impeccable folds. Any collar must throttle her like this. She looks as if she has always been carved in the wood that leaders are made of. A warrior with bare hands. She used to be a kindergarten mistress. She must have talked to them in the same dull, colourless voice with which she addresses the judge. She is one of those who only hear their own voice, the voice of Antigone. Gentle, sober and unanswerable.

It seems she has been denounced by a servant herself subjected to blackmail: as if a little moral turpitude were needed to counterbalance her nobility. She does not deny the deeds with which she is charged: why should she disown them? She is not merely proud of them: she resembles them. When other prisoners around her start to accuse each other she does not waver, but looks at them with sadness. When the public prosecutor begins to get carried away, assaulting her with bludgeoning eloquence – when he invokes the hundreds of German women who have been made widows, their children orphans, through her fault – she seems, for a moment, surprised: you think she is on the point of contesting the figure, if not the charge. Then she refrains. You don't know whether it is because she has mentally estimated the number of victims attributed to her or whether she judges that any refutation would be futile. She just looks a little more weary.

She is called Miss Cavell. Edith Cavell. Hearing her first name announced, the medical adjutant gives a start. The coincidence seems to trouble him. As if women could not have the same name in opposite camps.

Of course she's called Edith ... he thinks. As if he also thought: Just my luck ... or: That only happens to me. For him, everything has to be double. The unity of his life is this doubling. This bifid reality. In one sense it's rousing, uplifting. In another fatal.

The hearing is adjourned. Soldiers hand the prisoners meagre bowls of soup in which ration bread soaks. If the lawyers have not the right to talk to their clients, the military doctor has this privilege. He is, in any case, the only German to whom the prisoners still speak. When they cannot make themselves understood with words, they can still stammer, exchange looks in which concern is tangled with distress. A Belgian princess who is also on trial will later recall the deference of the German doctor who put himself at their disposal. When many years have passed and she writes her memoirs, she will pay homage to this taciturn, modest but, in his way, brotherly man. However, she will not mention him by name. No doubt he has told it to her. Perhaps she would have been less surprised not to find only loafers and brutes policing the hearing if she had known that this name had appeared, and would appear again, on the cover of collections of poems ... But was it not better that it happened this way, that she knew nothing? That she had to do only with an ordinary, anonymous adjutant? Would not this very anonymity preserve the fragile truth of a dialogue that was hardly sketched, while the pale, tense prisoners feverishly ate their hunks of bread among the armchairs of the Belgian Senate?

The military doctor would have liked to exchange a few words with Edith. The *other* Edith. He was hardly able to talk to her of anything but the proceedings. Where she already was, no one could join her. Not that she forbade the attempt, but she was moving further and further away on the other side of things. What more could he have said to her? That they both had a pastor for a father? Far from bringing them closer, might not this new coincidence have made her still more distant?

He preferred to contemplate from afar this grey-haired woman who could not, however – he did a quick calculation – have been more than a few years older than the Dresden Edith ... The war must have marked, aged the Edith of Brussels in a few months. And now, the nearness of a death she knows to be inescapable ... So one could go grey in the space of a few days. As if, in a dizzy accounting, one were reckoning up the balance of a life one would not know, but to which one would have been entitled.

Greater than his regret at being unable to talk to Edith Cavell about something other than the timetable of the hearing, is the regret the officer feels that these two women, the Edith here, at the gates of death, and the far-off Edith who still seems so young, whom the war seems to leave unscathed, yes, he regrets that these two Ediths have not known each other.

This is a wayward, almost incongruous thought, to be sure. But the universal history of souls is marked out only by such digressions. Did his wife resemble an English nurse? Did not Miss Cavell have the same slightly awkward, patrician carriage as Edith Osterloh? Or did Gottfried already, prematurely, feel himself the widower of a woman of whom he could not, after all, know that she too had not very long to live?

Because this man Gottfried Benn had a predatory way of loving them, which did not make him a friend of women, let us not suppose that, as a doctor, he had already condemned his own wife in his heart! Perhaps he only loved her with a troubled nostalgia: as if he had already lost her, and as if the full extent of his love for her could only be revealed to him by the grief that would be caused him by her loss.

Did he have a premonition of all that while he waited for the sentence that was to strike another woman who was nothing to him? We can be sure he knew nothing of it, unless it was by that amorphous, drowsy knowledge of his.

But you can't answer for a death inflicted before your eyes without the whole world of the living around you being shaken to its foundations.

Five death sentences. Two of them to be enforced. For "high treason" – a paradoxical verdict when the accused has betrayed only the enemy ... But at least it's qualified by "high": that goes well with the accused. She will not have to lower herself to pick up the sentence passed on her. Only the British chaplain and the German padre still have access to her, to hear her say that she will die with courage, without hatred or malice towards anyone. Are they there to hear it, or to check whether she has said it?

Now everything speeds up, as if they were trying to forestall any intervention – who knows? perhaps by the Kaiser himself – that might risk commuting the sentence or pardoning the ex-lady-nurse.

No doubt the adjutant has little taste for witnessing the final ceremony: medicine in uniform includes such a mixture of genres! Yesterday, he was rubbing soft chancres; today he is to confirm the decease of two persons executed by firing squad, one a woman. But, even now, he does not call the law into question. His disgust dates from before the war, and its roots reach deep into history. It is not just disgust; nor is it a revolt, and his nausea has not dissuaded him from participating in the war, in his own way. He does not discuss the ramifications of it in detail.

As he climbs into the car beside the public prosecutor, who reached his verdict with a kind of icy passion, his helmet in full view beside the file which underpinned his malevolence, the medical adjutant still does not baulk. Without a word they pass along the avenues of a city on which dawn hesitates to rise. Miss Cavell had declared to her judge: "I have seen death so often that it no longer seems either strange or dreadful to me." The preposterous idea occurs to the doctor that in a different context he might himself have been the author of that sentence. Never again would death surprise him either. He had consorted with it too much. He was on familiar terms with the one that grabs hold of some, and now he was the spectator of the one that is done to others. Such were his vice and his virtue.

It is to be enacted at the national rifle-range, at the edge of the city. When they reach their destination, two squads, each of twelve men, are already lined up. The condemned are slow to emerge from their dark seclusion in the wings.

From a first carriage the chief accomplice of Miss Cavell alights, with the priest who is attending him. The condemned man plants himself in front of those who are about to cut him down, salutes them by raising his cap, and declares without warning: "Before death we are all comrades." The public prosecutor interrupts him at once, no doubt afraid the fellow might utter some historic words. Then Miss Cavell arrives and walks down the grassy slope, bareheaded, greyer still than during the trial, with an abnormally stiff step, as if all her muscles were tetanised by the imminence of the execution. She just has time to pass on to the German clergyman supporting her the words of a last farewell to those who are dear to her, to her country from which she is separated by the sea, as she will soon be by death, then she and her companion are blindfolded. Their hands are tied to the execution posts, as if they might still have tried to flee or make some gesture of self-defence. The next moment they are each riddled with twelve bullets: she has not collapsed, she seems nailed to the post, while her companion has fallen over backwards. Here the military doctor must intervene *in officio*. Free the woman of the rope, the bandage over her eyes, feel her pulse, record the impact of the bullets — thorax, heart, lungs — close her eyes.

She was, the doctor will certify in his official report, completely and absolutely dead, instantly. If he did not add that she had not suffered, it is because the military authority does not require such information, the subjectivity of which would always invite caution, and because the formula would have covered a remarkable recantation. To lay her in a little coffin, bury her in haste: it was all so quickly done, so smartly dispatched.

Was it this haste that moved the adjutant more than the event itself? Why does memory seek today to rehabilitate the event, at last to give it the time it needs? Because memory's turn has come; now it can set to work at its own rhythm. And it doesn't get carried away. Pity is rather a hustler. Memory goes jogging quietly along. It's fond of retracing its steps. And it likes the slowed-down sequence, the still.

The barracks at the national rifle-range, when they had emerged from the night, had an Oxford-style façade and some-thing Japanese about them. A building of gingerbread and nougat like a prop for *Hansel and Gretel*. A harmless decor. Then, in front of the marker's shelter, the two posts cut for the occasion: they had never been used before, and would be used only once.

And then, the almost dancing walk of Miss Cavell's accom-plice, the walk of a man who, drawing on the depths of his courage, could no longer hold back a secret joy.

And then, Edith. That hieratic gait that was explained only later: she was so afraid of collapsing in an indecent pose under the bullets that she had strapped herself up in her tailored skirt as in a corset, using safety pins like a baby's nurse ... an ex-lady-nurse.

Another time, it is the blindfold he thinks of ... How can the executioner fail to realise that it is his own eyes he is bandaging, that it is he who cannot look death in the face? Under the bandage blinding her, Edith could not see the light glinting on the twelve barrels trained on her, but she saw instead the sea that her thoughts had evoked a moment before. The sea, that no blindfold can censor.

Finally, that coffin, so small, for her who seemed so tall. For a moment you were afraid she would not fit into it.

Time would pass over all that. It would never, perhaps, be

painful to think of it. But as time passed you would realise with surprise that this death was losing none of its actuality, one might almost say: its freshness.

And once at least you would ask yourself: a doctor may, must, sometimes make such observations. But a poet – did he have the right? Would Hölderlin have done the same?

It's a question, not even a scruple. And you answer: Better you than someone else.

As happens whenever such a page of History is written, some people had to embellish or diminish it, amending it in one direction or the other.

Some claimed that the condemned woman had refused to be blindfolded. They said that her accomplice was executed before her, so that she had to endure this spectacle before dying herself. That she then fainted. That the soldiers immediately refused to take aim, and that a base creature had to slaughter her coldly, with a revolver shot point-blank behind the ear. That one of those who had refused to shoot was executed in his turn, and was buried beside the heroine in an anonymous grave.

According to a different rumour, Edith did not die at once; her maladroit executioners had to fire a second salvo, at the foot of the post, as if they were emptying their guns into a heap of rags. She finally died, her face sunk in the mud.

The military doctor insists all this is just a gross fiction. That a scenario is being wilfully remodelled. The temptation to reach for the make-up must be irresistible: they were playing at being embalmers. Curiously, the crueller the truth is, the less self-sufficient it seems. It has to be added to. Truth is always of less interest than the use that can be made of it. By its nature, it is never disinterested.

In a Berlin journal ten years later the former witness was to feel called upon to set the record straight regarding the circumstances of a death that a film appearing on London screens seemed once more to be turning into a legend. In it he paid a last homage to "the fearless representative of a great people", without, however, calling into question a verdict which had left her "her dignity as a combatant" ... In this way, he thought, she had stayed true to her cause. But he did not ask himself to what he, who had seen all that, had stayed true – or even if he had been true to anything.

In the meantime, he has seen a woman's blood flow without baulking. He has stood up to the sight. He notes that it did not even cost him any effort, which was as it should be. That is how such things should be done.

The sight of blood. To be of those who can stand it. To the point, perhaps, of having one's vision impaired? Is it clairvoyant to have blood, if not on your hands, at least in your eyes? Can you, without being a monster, endure a monstrous spectacle with impunity?

Everything is abnormal in times of war, he maintained. He envisaged war as one more disease. A disease among others. He has done his mourning, once and for all, for purity on earth. Then, like many men who have witnessed dreadful scenes, he comes away with that gaze that has not blinked, that has disowned its own confusion. A slightly haughty look, since it has stared down horror. A bit vague, as well, since it has seen a little too much, after all. A man's fatal look.

Fatal particularly to himself.

He believed it right to harden oneself. That that was how doctors, even poets, got through wars. He does not know it is a trap. That having stood up to it has, on the contrary, weakened him. An execution is not an autopsy. Had not he, who respected bodies, this time betrayed the body? Was not that like betraying oneself? It was indeed. But shying away would not have been less cowardly ... A traitor in being present, he would perhaps have been still more a traitor in staying away.

No doubt, he who allows such violence to be done before his eyes unwittingly sells to it, gives to it a part of himself.

Something of him, something of his very cells, is destroyed without his knowing. He who sees so much better, so much more than most, he the seer, has become, in a part of himself, day-blind.

If an emotion has been suppressed, does it not have to surface, to rush out somewhere else? The scene – the freshly-sawn post, the blindfold over the eyes of the woman one is looking at, the perforated lungs, the riddled heart, the little yellow coffin – all that has been implanted in him like a poison that will act, slowly.

He has made death invade him once too often. Is he really just slightly affected? Does he really know it so little?

He is, whether he wishes or not, for better or worse, someone who has witnessed that scene. He knows what he saw. Henceforth, he will be the poet of this knowledge. But perhaps such a poet is needed?

They had begun by overrunning a dead city. Had set the river alight. No tug in the harbour fairway. A poisoned python in the snake-house. They had marched down the Avenue Quentin-Metsys or the rue du Marché-aux-Souliers, in Antwerp, without having seen the enemy from close to. In Brussels, two thousand syphilitic bodies had passed through your hands since then, covered in mauve blotches or scales as rough as bark. You had sent them back to the front after a cure of scalding.

And finally, this putting to death of a grey-haired woman. The last stage of the sickness, the acme. The final incision. If, the following spring, everything in the streets of the city had been emptied of its reality – nightmare and trance, virulence and trivial death – was it not because of that crescendo of images from which you would have preferred to avert your eyes?

No bullet had been wasted: Being itself had absorbed its part of the salvo.

The military doctor remembered that in his textbooks on syphilis the sick people who had been photographed also had their eyes bandaged. That was to make them unidentifiable, of course. But at the execution ground at the national rifle-range, while the British nurse took on more identity than ever, it was the world around her that reeled blank and nameless.

Two years after the execution of Edith Cavell, almost to the day, Margaretha Zelle, better known as Mata Hari, was shot in similar circumstances in the opposite camp.

He was told that her body had been passed to some medical students to be peeled like an onion in an anatomy course. Some anatomist claimed to have constructed in plastic the abdomen, loins, diaphragm and buttocks, joined with stainless steel links. (The whole thing, mounted on pivoted boards with movable muscles and sectioned organs, could be supplied with explanatory labels.)

However, the age of the body thus moulded to the needs of the medical faculties does not seem to have exactly matched that of the former sacred dancer and pseudo-bayadère who finished up a secret agent, after becoming, little by little, a high-class striptease artist and *demi-mondaine*.

There is, therefore, nothing at present to prove that any anatomy students ever manipulated, in effigy, the torso and viscera of this fallen Salome. No matter. She had not with impunity played that role in the days of her ephemeral splendour. The head of Herodias's daughter for the head of John the Baptist ...

And the head of Mata Hari for that of Edith Cavell. All's fair in war, and this was merely applying the law of retaliation which reconciles the bloody history of man to his most suspect myths. The only difference, admittedly not trivial, being that, of these two women who were done to death, one, it seems, expired with veiled eyes, leaving behind the image of a heroine, while the other died bare-faced, stigmatised as a traitress.

How would it have appeared if Germany had been victorious?

The medical adjutant would have replied, no doubt: It wasn't so much her mercenary espionage that ruined the woman Zelle as the slur of prostitution. The loose women who decimated the troops of the Alliance and the Entente in their fashion in 1914 never received, as far as we know, the Iron Cross, First Class or the Légion d'honneur! Yet there is no international convention which defines the woman's body and its secret poisons as an illegal weapon. No, before death we are certainly not all comrades ... And all war is pornography.

October 1917: death of Mata Hari, revolution in Russia. The military doctor has reported sick and packed his bags. He has put the key under the doormat of 1, rue Saint-Bernard, Brussels. In a few days, he will open a dermato-venerological surgery at 12, Belle-Alliance-Strasse, Berlin.

He has not stayed in Belgium until the end of the performance.

The winter and spring of that year were among the coldest of the century. The seagulls fled the shore to escape being covered in frost as they flew, and took refuge in a glacial Brussels. There were victims: people not only die of wars, they also die during wars. The military governor recommended destroying dogs that could no longer be fed. The stigmatised members of the German army were parked in ever-increasing numbers in the dormitories of the Hôpital de Saint-Gilles. Once scalded, many of them found their way to a cell in the Forest prison for not having denounced themselves.

A battle of troglodytes still ground on, propped up against the sea. Those who came out of it returned with choked lungs, glazed eyes and grey skin. Then the English entered Baghdad. America, Cuba, Guatemala declared war on Germany. The whole world. Some countries you didn't even know existed. On the other side: the collapse of Bulgaria, Austria. In Brussels, the trams on regular routes grew ever sparser. More and more

English books were sold on the black market. Because of lack of forage, hay was made that year even in public gardens, on park lawns.

You would not stay long enough to witness the German defeat. To read the papers claiming that the rats were leaving, that they had already gone. And to see the Belgian and German socialists try out a fraternisation that was supposed to pass on the revolution that had broken out in Germany. The Americans distributed tin wheelbarrows and Negro masks to the sick children in the sanatoria. A concert was given at the Hôpital Saint-Pierre by an orchestra of infantrymen of the Australian army, conducted by a Major Armstrong of the Second Division. People out walking ate dried plaice and hard-boiled eggs washed down with sour beer in the cafés close to the Bourse.

The military doctor will not have read the notice signed by the director of the Opéra inviting artistes who were under contract in August 1914 to come forward in view of imminent reopening. For a time, Wagner and Strauss would be absent from the programme. Had not M. Claude Debussy decreed that they wrote boche music?

But in Berlin the demobilised doctor was to find his friend Carl Sternheim, expelled from Belgium where he had become an undesirable alien. And, one morning in 1919, he was to read in the *Berliner Tageblatt* that the remains of Edith Cavell had been reclaimed by her country of origin. Homage was to be paid to her when her ashes were moved, and the schoolchildren of Brussels would walk in procession along the Boulevard Botanique. Then Gottfried would see himself again in the garden bordering the boulevard, with his wife, admiring a giant sequoia. He would see the other Edith, the Norfolk Edith, upright with her back to the post. More upright than was natural. She was now going to rest beside kings and counsellors. He would feel himself suddenly grow ten years older, without the good and terrible reasons that were those of the English nurse.

Brussels, 1916

Long after, the children of Brussels would look in the sandpits and waste ground for Mauser casings, fragments of shrapnel, incendiary cartridges and sharks' teeth. He would remember one of those children who had pretended to point a gun at him, one day in a lane in the Bois de la Cambre.

Why, then, was this the most serious and the best time of your life? You do not choose your happiness.

A war that was supposed to last a few weeks had been prolonged for four years. An exile which ought to have seemed interminable to him had lasted, in his memory, no more than a season. That is the entire difference between war and the lives of men. While wars do not know how to kill the time of those who survive them, our ecstasies flash only for the batting of an eye.

No one, he thought, could have lived this war in such a senseless fashion. He had returned somewhat more uplifted and somewhat more despairing than he left.

When, at the time of the invasion, the uhlans, the *Feldwebel* or the dragoons had got what they wanted from a householder, they thanked him by chalking on his door: Spare this good man! He's already given everything! Don't set fire to this house!

On some days the new owner of 12, Belle–Alliance–Strasse would ask himself what they ought to have written on his: Lynch this man! Burn him! He's taken everything!

He has lost everything.

Berlin, 1926

Living Bodies

"Bloody hopeless!" the doctor mutters under his breath.

He has not yet turned on the age-reddened light that hangs from the ceiling like a spider on the end of its thread. Or rather, because of the strips of muslin and frosted glass that serve as a lampshade, it looks like a jellyfish suspended in murky depths. No doubt he likes the way the half-light softens the gilding of the Gothic chest and spreads a translucent drape over the green plush armchairs, the Pomeranian writing desk perched on dragon's feet, the little round table covered by a cloth with Tenerife-style embroidery. Over this ill-assorted furniture he runs the cold eye of the bailiff who might arrive any day to repossess it.

Through the half-open door he surveys the bookcase in the next room, with its glazed sliding doors, the sofa with broken springs that has taken on for all time the shape of a monstrous beast. The Wilhelmine porcelain stove. The Orchestrola gramophone. An alabaster lamp. A newspaper holder.

Then his gaze falls again on the consulting room, runs across the parabolic reflector, the telephone with its cranking handle, the ship's clock. Jolting against his own reflection in the wall-mirror mottled with age, it passes on at once. It makes a deliberate detour round the sloping steel examination table and the various metal implements which allow the master of the house, for the present, to practise his art. In only a few minutes the steel instruments, designed to probe the maladies of the human body, will continue to shine with a persistent, disturbing brilliance in the shadows. Nothing else will be seen, except perhaps the Christmas roses emerging from a flower-holder, their petals shining, strangely, like gas flames.

Nothing, except the girl sitting on the edge of the steel table, her back, for the moment, turned towards him.

A back stripped as if to be chastised. Motionless, almost to the onlooker's surprise. Yes, it seems improbable that these bare, humiliated shoulders are not shaken by sobs. Suddenly, wretchedness fills the room; only the girl's tears are lacking. And a doctor, powerless henceforth to console her for anything.

The doctor ought now to walk diagonally across the room, around the table, stop in front of the girl, take her chin in his hand and lift it as if to receive the image like a slap in the face: boyish haircut, thick, lurid make-up, false eyelashes heavy with mascara imprisoning a pair of eyes that burn with fever rather than life . . .

He will not perform this gesture. He won't abase still further the woman who, this evening, is almost a part of his furniture. He won't plant himself before her like a master. (This man is not, never will be, a master. Neither for good nor for ill.) He'll leave a doubt in the air. He'd rather see her slowly lace up her boots. He'd choose to contemplate the girl who, this New Year's Eve, is acting her part without furs or lambskin boots. Who can give nothing but her shoulder-blades, pointed like chicken wings, her protruding collar bones, her urchin haircut. She tries to stop a ladder in one of her net stockings with saliva . . . (She thinks he hasn't noticed, she thinks he doesn't care.) He is moved by the girl's scent, that he drinks in from a distance. This cheap scent she has just had time to spray on to her skin to mask the smell of the previous client, her afternoon's amours. You needn't have bothered, thinks the doctor, you could have sold your body to every man in the city and it would still have given me, unawares, something it has never sold, never tried to give. That's what I have come to find, beside it, tonight, under my own roof.

"Aren't we going to your place?" she had asked.

He at first took this to mean: "Aren't we going to our place?" Then he corrected himself.

"That's where we are – at my place. This *is* our place. There's nowhere else. I'm selling my flat on Passauerstrasse. Since my daughter has stopped living with me it's become too expensive."

"It's not because of memories of your wife?"

She's got feelings, this tart.

"No, it's not because of memories. It's because of the hard times."

"So you do everything here now?" says the girl in surprise.

She's in a good position to know. Didn't he receive her here some time ago now, to treat an attack of gonorrhoea?

He does not let on to her that, even while his wife was alive, he often liked to sleep in his consulting room. Or on the sofa in the next room. That he did not always switch off the light, so that he would wake more quickly in an emergency. He just shaded his eyes with a carnival mask. He does not tell her that on occasion he has kept a client here overnight, having confirmed her cure at the end of the afternoon. Nothing happens in Berlin at the end of the afternoon. The whole brick desert of the city, the expanse of neutral time around you, in which to think about the bodies that sell themselves without even knowing what they are giving, the souls you buy without even knowing the price of their corruption. He doesn't tell the tart: If I am glad to spend the night in the Belle-Alliance-Strasse, it's not just because I am now forced to. It's not just so that I can continue by night, with the bodies of women, the dialogue started during the day with the bodies of patients. It's because of the grain of childhood that time, war and suffering have chewed, ground small but never swallowed. So that I can taste it again between my teeth.

"I've heard from one of my colleagues," says the girl, "that you're not only a doctor. That you write poetry as well. That you're a member of the Academy ... "

"Oh no," says the doctor. "It's too early for that. Or too late ... "

But it's true, he reflects, that I'm in all the academies. This surgery is one of them. Even the bed we make love on. These are places of knowledge.

"Usually," he goes on, "you only get into the Academy you're talking about through a misunderstanding. When you join, what you haven't written matters as much, if not more, than the work you've actually produced. You don't want a drink? Light ale and schnapps? Bilberry liqueur, kirsch, cordial? We could even eat together here, you know. If you'd come last week, you'd only have been entitled to barley gruel and stewed plums. Next week: groats and noodles with finely-ground saveloy. On my birthday, or yours: one egg each, a slice of black bread, a glass of milk which, we hope, won't be as aqueous as diseased sperm. In a year's time, if we're still around: flour fried in rancid butter and horseradish, and pease pudding. The next day: potato soup with, as a special delicacy, the hock of a horse ineptly slaughtered off the Potsdamer Platz. However, for this gala evening we won't go to Kempinski's to eat supposedly Italian asparagus or artichokes purporting to come from Brittany. I suggest we stay here for a slice of marinaded roast meat washed down with German whisky. For dessert, poppy-seed cakes ... What do you say to that?"

The girl does not know how to react to this outburst of sombre glee.

"Well, it sounds as if what they told me is true: you're not rolling in money, are you, Doctor? Never mind, two jobs are better than one ... "

"The doctor can't feed the poet," he says. "Since we have been treating you and your little friends with bismuth when you need it, syphilis has been regressing. I hardly need say that the poet doesn't earn the quack enough to buy his cigarettes and toilet water! Did you know," he asks the girl seriously, "that each passing year less books are sold and read in this country?"

"Have you read *Mein Kampf*?" the girl asks.

He doesn't hear. He is thinking that, for a long time, he has hardly had a holiday apart from the ones he takes here, in the dead of night, after the last tram has clanked past from the direction of Belle-Alliance-Platz, when he links up the two or three lines of verse he has scribbled on the back of a beer mat at the Café Möhring or the Reichskanzler.

"You know, Doctor, you and I could come to an agreement ... "

"What agreement?"

"If you're short of money just now. After all, you gave me credit last time I had the clap. You never asked for your fee. So now the assignation will pay for the consultation. Tit for tat. With something else on account. If I give you a lot of pleasure tonight, you'll give me an egg or a packet of sugar as a bonus."

Funny, he thinks. When she came into the room just now I wanted to have her for nothing. Now she's proposing just that.

"It's true," he admits, "that I like to swap rather than buy. The job I do makes more sense that way."

"Mine too," she agrees.

She laughs.

"What's funny?"

"I'm imagining what my sisters in sin would say if I told them about this. They'd tell me I was no sort of business-woman. That I've got mixed up with a rogue who has taken me for a ride."

"I do feel as if I've struck a good bargain this evening," the doctor admits. "Who knows if I won't feel a lot less poor than usual?"

"I'll never talk about this to anyone," says the girl.

"Why? Would you be ashamed?"

"No, I think I'd be proud. But in any case, no one would believe me."

Suddenly amazed, the client realises that no money has changed hands. The wages of pleasure and the cost of the cure have cancelled each other out. Neither partner has skimped or calculated. A new equilibrium has been established, from which all usury is banished. Passing from hand to hand, the woman's body is soiled like a banknote, the stale smell of which clings to it. Whereas this woman's body is more likely to wash me. The client won't have engraved in his memory the unbearable image of the prostitute at the moment of receiving, wide-eyed, the gift she has asked for. In such a case she could not escape either the contempt she feels or that she inspires. She is lost in it.

"When I started walking the streets," she tells him, "it was during that time of high inflation. The client even had to pay for the hot water he used to wash himself before and after ... In the course of one day I sold myself for twenty million marks or for a cigarette."

"And you always found a taker?"

"The more people were ruined, the more they ran after pleasure. The same man who gave me champagne to drink was growing potatoes in his bath. A match cost more than the cigar it had lit three months before ... "

"And everyone started living beyond their means," says the doctor. "They have never stopped. People think that monetary reform has put everything back in order. They're wrong: people have simply embraced the poverty that threatened them."

"Today," she tells him, "one of my clients pays me for refusing him. And he isn't even impotent ... "

No, thinks the doctor, but he can at last weep for himself when no one else will. For that he could never pay enough.

"I knew an old prostitute," he says, "who came to my surgery for no other reason than to have her toenails cut. 'I've got no family,' she explained. 'Who would do it if you didn't, Doctor?'"

"One morning," the girl relates, "I went out before eating

anything to give blood for soldiers mutilated in the war. When they had taken it the nurses asked me some questions about myself, then shrugged their shoulders and without a word of explanation threw the test-tube and syringe into the dustbin. I walked off towards the Tiergarten, very crestfallen. It was stupid. I'd wanted to give my blood as a man parts with his sperm. And they'd refused me."

"You think you're giving your sperm," says the doctor, "even when you're forcing it on someone or having it torn from you ... It's only blood that can be given. And that can be refused." Sometimes, he thinks, to get your money's worth you can become your own tart or client, just as you can be your own patient or your own doctor. Those are the saddest days.

"You're probably waiting for me to finish undressing. We've already talked a lot ... You don't want to be whipped, do you, Doctor? Forgive me, but I don't yet know your tastes. I've brought my crocodile-skin whip anyway, just in case ... "

"No," says the client, "I don't want you to strip. It's a bit cold in this room. If you are not in a hurry, neither will I be. I don't want to be whipped, either," he adds wearily. "Not this evening – no desire to be beaten ... even by you. But I'm pleased to know you're capable of doing it if needed. That it's even your speciality. So you'll spare me the torments you've proposed, though I don't find the thought unpleasant. And if you are able ... not to be in a hurry. I know you'll think I'm taking advantage of you. But, anyway ... "

He had been sitting down. Now he has got up. He walks round the metal table and the girl. He goes to the window. With the thumb and forefinger of his right hand he parts two slats of the blind that shuts out the Belle-Alliance-Strasse. The pavement gleams in the gaslight. Far off you can hear the tram screeching round the corners of the square, probably empty. You can imagine the conductor with his leather pouch around his waist, swaying between the rows of benches and grabbing the metal handles that slide along nickel-plated tubes above his head, to keep his balance. The trolley-arm will light up the snow clinging to the wire as the car goes on its way towards the bridge in a shower of blue sparks ...

"Seriously, I doubt if you can leave here tonight," says the doctor. "There's black ice everywhere. Soon the elevated railway will be frozen solid! The snow is blinding those who go to meet it on the pavements. Do you see yourself leaving here in your high heels? You won't need a whip, but a white stick! Anyway, what time is it, and what day? It's New Year's Eve. Are we still in 1926, or have we already swung into 1927? You'll wait up for the fireworks with me, won't you? The firecrackers, the rockets? No, the flares you can see on the roof are different. A plumber working up to the last minute of the year with an arc-welder. Don't go away. It's not December 31, 1926 every day. Forty-eight hours ago a great Austrian poet died, and the newspaper says it was from the prick of a rose thorn. You can't invent something like that. He won't have seen that shower of sparks. He won't have held you in his arms to finish the year. I know: you were counting on pulling two or three clients tonight, over on the Grenadier-Strasse, and I myself had planned to go to bed early. It turns out differently. That's how things are. Nothing's certain any more, in Germany today ... "

The girl seems worried.

"Why do you talk about a white stick, Doctor?" she asks. "Before soliciting around Stettin Station I worked at the Sport-Palast, the nights when there was boxing. Between rounds I walked around the ring half undressed, to keep the public occupied with something to look at. I saw boxers going blind through taking too many punches. Some days I even thought I was going blind myself. The arc-lights dazzled me. When I left the Sport-Palast I found myself staggering. The snow I particularly hated. It burnt my eyes. I couldn't stop the tears flowing. Migraine pinched my temples like a tiara of barbed wire. I had to get away from all that whiteness as fast as I could. Don't talk to me about snow, Doctor, it brings back bad memories. Don't

talk to me about white sticks, it brings bad luck. For me, all
sticks are white, for ever. Lead me by the hand to your bed
instead, guide me towards your pleasure. You won't regret it.
But you're not going to keep that white coat on, are you?
Even if you don't ask me to undress, you don't plan to go on
wearing that butcher's apron? You look like a knacker from the
Alexanderplatz. Soon you'll take me for a lamb and cut my
throat. My blood will flow freely, glad to escape. You'll finish
me off with a mallet blow. You'll be on the front page of the
Berliner Tageblatt, like your Austrian colleague. But you will be
described as one of those pitiless murderers who go after
whores in times of unrest. Was it to butcher me that you lured
me here? In that case, don't let me languish any longer. And
what about that Christmas tree you've got adorning your
hallway? You surely don't intend to keep it until 1927? Don't
you know that a tree that's kept one day too long after the
Saviour's birth attracts lightning? When you looked out on to
the pavements of Belle-Alliance-Strasse, where no one passes
any longer – all the whores being at work – you must have
noticed the pine-trees thrown out with the rubbish on the
doorsteps and already decaying? Your flowers are a different
matter: I'm glad you have spread them all around us, for our
night of love. I can see you know them well, and love them.
You've chosen the bunches with a woman's care. Anyone
would think a woman had been at work here, but it's you who
have chosen them as if you were the mistress of the house. Am
I right? You've put them everywhere, yet it doesn't feel like a
graveyard. Perhaps that's what poetry is, Doctor?"

"That's what it is," he says, "so be blind if it appeals to you.
Don't lash me with your whip, but be blind for a night. It will
distract you. Relax you. Since you're good at feigning pleasure,
can't you feign blindness as well? You can grope around the
room looking for me. Your hands, to their incredulous delight,
will chance on springy flowers, drunk with freshness. Unlikely,
chimerical flowers, bought for how much, in what nursery, by
an impecunious doctor? You will be able to grasp them with

impunity: the thorns of the Christmas roses won't poison your blood as they did the Austrian poet's, who knew about death. He knew that you make your own death, you carry it like a child in your belly, suckle it, teach it to walk, to speak, until it is big enough to devour you. He himself chose a rose. Peace be with him. And pity on those poor prostitutes who have not found a sucker tonight. Pity and peace to the twenty-five desperate souls who, according to municipal statistics, will choose tonight to end their days. But you, whose origins and stage-name I do not know, I ask not to go: you'll meet no one on your way except the night-watchman, whom you'll frighten like a ghost, who'll hold up his dark lantern's flame to your face to see who you are. Peace on earth to fornicators of good will."

The girl starts singing softly:

> "In Hamburg's fair city
> In velvet so pretty
> My name I'll not tell for
> a harlot am I ... "

Just then the phone bell rang. It couldn't be an emergency. Not tonight. For tonight there could be nothing more urgent than to feel our bodies embrace, to thaw the pack-ice of the world. As if they alone still harboured the warmth of life. "Have you noticed, Fräulein, how I have muted the bell with a layer of felt? It's just loud enough to catch our attention if need be. Excuse me – it'll only take a moment. Good evening, dearest friend. I was just going to call you. I was quite touched by your invitation but I'm afraid I am unable to respond. I've heard that a large number of illustrious persons, none of whom are acquainted with me, will be flocking to your house tomorrow. I honour your friends, but they are not mine. You are, of course, at liberty not to understand, though it would be a pity. How can I explain why, in my present state of mind, any request affects me like an act of violence? I am more resolved than ever to belong to no community, of any kind. It's the resolution that is carrying me into the New Year. Hence, I repeat, I shall not be at your party. Think how little you lose thereby: I am hardly a society wit, and at least I'm sparing you the unseemly spectacle of my long face. Consider it a mark of respect: I can no longer presume to be heavy where you are counting on lightness to reign ... "

While he is talking thus into the receiver, mixing apologies with recriminations, claiming as a privilege the worm that gnaws him, the girl has sat down, legs crossed, in the misshapen armchair that faces the writing desk. She starts filing her mauve-lacquered nails.

A letter catches her eye. A letter that must have been broken off, abandoned there in the halo of lamplight.

"Darling, Thanks for your charming note, so admirably written, with a number of well-turned phrases. By contrast, in your last letter I came across the expression: 'the glory of the universe', which is quite calamitous and to be avoided at all costs. I say this because you insistently ask me to correct your style and a certain tendency to the portentous ... You show such kind concern for my welfare. I can say that my surgery serves me as refuge, asylum and poorhouse. Either the bell falls silent for long intervals and the doctor lapses into despair, or business goes better and the poet gets frantic, spending his days probing, consulting, pricking and massaging the sluts who darken his door. By evening he no longer has the energy to turn the day's emanations into poetry. All the same, please don't try to track the old bear to his den to comfort him. And don't take it amiss if I keep deferring our tête-à-tête. I can't see you for several days – that's how things are. All the same, no one ever sent me such lovely roses in winter: they'll help me to leap, feet together, over the threshold of the New Year. Rejoice, then: you won't have seen them fade. And, no, this time it's not even another woman. The actress only wanted to give a public recitation of some of my old poems from before the war ... I begged her to drop the idea. True, she had a pretty mouth ... But I can't agree to such a thing even for love."

Just as her client puts down the receiver the girl looks up from the letter and at once catches sight of the photo beside the lamp, in a little silver frame like a medallion.

"Is that your wife?" she asks.

"It's the woman who is bringing up my daughter. A long way from here. She's Danish. And a singer. One year, she sang a leading part at Bayreuth. Does that satisfy you?"

"You did love your wife a little, didn't you?"

"I loved her more than I could ever say now. Perhaps it's for the best that she is dead. There was too much life in her, it couldn't last ... When she was beside me, I didn't seem to see things as they were any more; Edith's shadow, her glowing shadow, hid the world's ferocity from me. It wouldn't have taken much for me to make a pact with the world, lapse into a kind of amnesia. Well, I didn't want to make peace with the world. That was out of the question early on, for me. I may deplore the fact, but what is the use of regretting one's own humiliation? It is a humiliation, isn't it? Yes, that's what it must be. All the same, if one's bent on telling the truth, one can't help sounding barbaric. Do you understand what I'm saying?"

He has come right up to her and taken her chin in his hand, as he had meant to do earlier. He looks rather frantic.

"Stop it, you're hurting me, Doctor ... "

"Ah, yes, of course. You understand that," he says. "It's even all you understand, what was I thinking of? But because of that ability Edith had to be astonished at everything, I may well have paid her less attention than any other woman, even the wretched creatures that presented themselves at my consulting-room door. My wife's light flooded my life, but I understood only wretchedness. That's a calamity. But it's also, I fear to say, a vocation. Edith masked my disease, but she didn't cure it. I sometimes reach a point where even grief's a luxury: I lack the leisure to feel it."

"But what do you spend your days doing?" the girl asks.

"Do I frighten you, perhaps?" he asks, probably hoping she'll agree. "How do I spend my time? You mean, the time I don't devote to my patients? Or to the women I lure here for the night, is that it? Do you realise that all women are beautiful? That they cascade into the desert of men like waterfalls? But sometimes I forget even that. I let them dry up overnight in my arms. All I'm left with is a blur of vapour. Then I remind myself that the only things that matter are the words that will save that at least. Words that will have no truck with the abominable fraud of History. That will mumble harmlessly in the margin ... Sometimes a friend – Carl Einstein, say, or Klabund – wants to meet me at a café. I always turn up early. You'd think I had too much time on my hands, or that I wanted to study the other party carefully as he comes towards me. When it's only to put on some sort of a face, I mean some general face to show the world. I'm so easily caught unawares. My own feelings leave me floundering. There was the war: my wife and a cohort of friends disappeared and now, far away, there's my daughter, who I didn't take the time to get to know, who I have neither the wish nor the courage to hold on to. Too many corpses have passed before my eyes – they've blunted my enthusiasm. Too many women rotted to the marrow have parted their legs before me for reasons other than love. Their vulvas and ovaries have become more familiar to me than the noses on their ashen faces, or the lost look in their eyes. I expect you're bemused to hear me talk like this. You must wonder what sort of a trap you've blundered into?

"You don't? You're not even a bit frightened? I can't plead having had too much schnapps or German whisky: I'm never drunk. But who do you expect a doctor to talk to about the ills of the body except another doctor? Who do you expect a soldier to reminisce with about war except another soldier? Who do you expect a poet to explain his poetry to except another poet? So when a man is all those things at once: doctor, poet and warrior ... Demobilised warrior, doctor to the poor, sterile poet ... Only a whore can listen, or at least pretend not to be deaf, since she's a daughter of war, a purveyor of scourges and takes off her clothes for love, just as the poet strips – and travesties – words in his poem, with the same unnatural mixture of raw truth and dissimulation. Yes, only a whore can understand ... This man, your very special client for just one night, the man nothing ever happens to any more, is in touch through his daily routine with life's most abject shipwrecks: the wars of men, the ailments of women, the sufferings of all and the poetry of a few. What more can one ask for? So I avoid social contact. Those still well-meaning enough to invite me on New Year's Eve meet with a harassed rebuttal. The only people I don't find overwhelming are those who deal with the body: we're of the same species, are we not? We who knead people's flesh, we know their real story and don't invent a different one. But your eyes are wandering ... What are you thinking about?"

"About travelling," she says. "Have you never been tempted to get away, Doctor?"

"Have you?" He turns the question back on her. "Are you a lady of no fixed abode? And how far can a sexual nomad roam? Walking out, don't you always walk into a trap?"

"You can also be wrong staying where you are," she remarks. He hasn't listened.

"My friends like to make fun of me for seeming never to leave this place," he tells her. "All the same, barely a month ago I visited the Balkans. For two days. Forty hours in a train. What's the point? Even so ... the woman whose portrait you admired just now, by the lamp, the one who lives in Denmark – I met her on a train ... She had just given a recital in Germany. After that, I went to see her in Copenhagen. She became my mistress. I left my daughter with her. One evening she sang a Schubert song for me, one she is very fond of, about those who have been disappointed in their expectations, a song overflowing with tears. It flashed through my mind at that moment that I could have snatched the Nordic woman from her homeland and fled with her to the south, to immemorial Greece, and renewed contact with the purity of a world arrested forever in its first morning. Reconciled Hamlet with Apollo. Brought the Orient to the Occident. Gone back to where man was not yet split from epic life. But that would still have been running away, and I did not see that I had any right to that .... I came back here ... Anyway ... "

He hoists himself from the armchair where he has been soothsaying in the dark. He takes a few steps across the room. Passing the girl, he puts his hand briefly on her bare shoulder. Then he goes to the window, parts two slats of the blind.

"Still snowing," he says.

But the snow that is falling is so fine that it only veils the scene, as if it were drawing a tulle curtain across it. It feels like having impaired vision, or living a bad dream. You think you can just catch the wailing of a siren, the sound of a child crying, the screech of a tram coming off the rails on Belle-Alliance Bridge ... You go from one catastrophe to another. At the corner of a street trapped in a net of frost, the fire alarm is gagged in its box by snow. This icing over of the city, this groaning of all its stones, did you just imagine it? The souls of men give out a lament like the cry of a starving seagull, no longer even knowing what it is that wrings it from them ...

This man who in a sense has not left the city since he came back here after the war, who has seldom even left the Kreuzberg quarter where he has set up his practice, and then has hardly left the surgery itself, begins to wonder why he has so resisted the call of the open spaces, the picturesque world far away ... I prefer being trapped here like a rat, he thinks, here in Berlin, where a battle was lost, where a revolution wasn't one, where the citizens proclaim each day how they identify themselves with the destiny of Germany, and where, each day, everyone thinks himself betrayed by everyone: those who went to war by those who did not fight, the war cripples by those who still have their arms and legs, those who wanted to win by the pacifists, the pacifists by those who have never accepted defeat or laid down their arms. Every day, in this city, someone finds someone else to detest. And if, by chance, he doesn't find anyone, he starts hating Europe for being responsible for his misfortunes. Even in the orgies of Sodom and Gomorrah, the whores of the Tauentzienstrasse have learned to solicit with a military step . . .

No matter. Not for anything in the world would he leave the little hell that had marked itself out beneath his eyes around a metal table and a wind-up telephone, a deformed armchair and a Pomeranian writing desk, an Empire-style lamp and a wall mirror, a gas street-light and a fire hydrant. And then, above all, he could not leave the women and men who had come here to confide their humiliation. What mattered was not to be distracted from those wretched bodies, come what may, as if you were in danger of forgetting them the moment you turned your back, and as if that forgetting would be worse than crime or war, worse even than death. The only geography that interested him passed through those bodies open or closed, those bodies whole or amputated, that venal flesh offered to him twice over. It would take more than a doctor's and a poet's life to cover all that. You can't do everything, be everywhere at once. Our time is measured out. He didn't claim to love human beings – but was interested only in them. And took no pride whatever in that. He had never been able to go into the country, even on a Sunday excursion, without a sense of unease, as the gusts of Saxon wind shook his heart, jostled him like a child, and the light that made the landscape vibrate nailed its rays to the back of his eyes. He did not refuse the beauties of the earth: it was more that they made too much impression on him, dragged him along in a sucking current . . .

"You know," he tells the girl, a distracted look in his eyes, "it's here . . . Everything. Landscapes. Even the landscapes. I have everything here . . . Under my hands."

"Doctor," she says, "I think I would have stayed with you tonight in any case, even if you hadn't obliged me to ... Even if you don't intend to make me any kind of gift. All the same, if you have a little sugar, or just sixty grammes of ground coffee, perhaps you could give them to me in the morning ... "

"Thank you, Fräulein," says Gottfried Benn, "for I'm really at my wits' end. I'm not writing any more. One shouldn't write today unless with a pen dipped in pus. A few poems still write themselves, in spite of me, across my prescription pads or on Belgian Defence Ministry letterhead, a souvenir of my time in a garrison. There's a shortage of paper; it costs so much nowadays ... I don't read any more. What ought I to read, anyway?"

"That book I mentioned to you just now – but you weren't listening – *Mein Kampf*: haven't you read it?" the girl insists. "They say that it's not a book like all the others. That even people who never read a book ought to read this one. The author was just a Sunday painter who did pictures for a post-office calendar. In the army he was only a corporal. The poison gas made him go blind for a time. Now he's written a book that has amazed everyone. They say you can't put it down, and when you've finished it you feel proud to be German ... Can you imagine it, Doctor? German! If only it were possible to be that again!"

"No, dear child, I haven't read the book. No more that one than the others. You say it's making a big impression? Believe me, the people who are impressed by it haven't read it either. They're happy if the author actually wrote it himself! In a letter my friend Carl Sternheim tells me the book's style is worthless; just for fun he rewrote some chapters correcting the syntax. The fact is, no one reads anything, no matter what, in Germany today. I'm not really a special case at all, which is a comfort. And you'll see that despite the fuss his book is causing, that Hitler of yours won't get three per cent of the votes at the next election. He's already tried one abortive coup in a Munich beer-hall, and he won't get any further. I must admit, I'm not

175

sure if that's something to rejoice about. We Germans are no
longer inside History, and perhaps your man was intending to
put us back there."

"You really won't read it?" she asks, disappointed.

"Well – are *you* going to read it? No answer? You see what I
mean! Nor shall I. The only books I manage to open now I
shut again immediately, banging them like doors. At the theatre
I try not to listen. In the propitious gloom of the auditorium I
think of something else. To escape those cannibal mouths
devouring everything that's on their lips. There's not a reply
they leave alive. No more words. No more readers ... But
notwithstanding that, everyone here claims to be a writer.
Sometimes, between two consultations, I receive some bright
young people who've come to talk to me about my work.
They are not to know that I may already be finished. It
sometimes happens that these new Hölderlins write verses in
which they have the misfortune to imitate mine. Can I be so
passé that I'm already being imitated, caricatured? No matter,
they address me as an equal. Aren't we all writers together?
They tell me of the indignation, the rage they feel at the state
of the world. Of course, they're likeable, in a way ... But why
call on me as a witness, as if I counted for something? It's the
only thing they can still express: the bombast of angry harus-
pices. It takes the place of talent. Or saves them the trouble of
acquiring it. They all want to purify the planet. Merely by
appearing so emphatically upon it, one supposes. By the
hygiene of their language. They think themselves quite immaculate, of course – my word, yes: diamond-pure. It's terrible.
As if the vital thing were to have a creed, to serve a cause, no
matter which. It gives me gooseflesh. What do they expect
from someone who has stopped taking any pleasure in himself?
Not a spiritual testament addressed to the rising generation! It
wouldn't take much for them to make me start having awful
doubts about the validity, the legitimacy of my work from
before the war ... Can't they leave me in peace? I wish I were
as worldly-wise as my friend Klabund, whose epic poem on

Cromwell was put on at the Lessing Theatre recently. A delightful friend, by the way. You can hear him at the Romanisches Café, churning out songs about soldiers' wenches all night long. One evening I saw him dance a Charleston arm in arm with Bertolt Brecht ... That forges brotherly bonds, even if one of us, as Péguy used to say, pulls the words from his own entrails, the other from his overcoat pocket. I'll let you guess which is which: you're not going to tell him. Well now, in his own way that man has given all of himself to literature. Alas, it has not always reciprocated his love. Now he is very ill. I'm his doctor, although nothing can be done to save him. If he died tomorrow, I should be very proud to be asked to compose his funeral oration – do you understand? In it I would describe only the little room where, on a worn-out sofa, by the miserly light of a narrow skylight, he composed like a madman a work that, despite everything, I know will not last. Yes, I envy that man, with good reason, I who don't write any more, as a protest against what I should have to say. When the war was over, we thought that nothing, ever, could be so dreadful. How are we to accept that, little by little, the worst is becoming possible again? And if you know that, how can you write anything else? That is how the temptation of silence can come upon you. Oh, not really a temptation – a weariness you can't admit. The weariness of Jonah in the Bible, falling asleep while the tempest rages and the whale shakes the waters around his ship. He doesn't doze off in spite of the fury of the elements, but because of it. It knocks him senseless. Another moment and he'll die of boredom. I'm at the same point. Jonah is my brother. But what Leviathan are we drifting towards? When Walter Rathenau was assassinated, someone said that what surprised him was not the man's death, but the fact that he was still alive the morning before. And even the killers didn't conceal the admiration they had for their victim – it was that admiration that they wanted to snuff out in themselves, since it was a final homage to the world they wanted to put to the sword and the torch. How do you like that reasoning?

Typically German, isn't it? Did you know that the German Revolution died very near here, even before it had seen the light of day? The insurgents had locked themselves in the *Vorwärts* offices on Belle-Alliance-Platz ... I could have practically seen the office stormed just by leaning out of the window ... I didn't look. All that just to make it clear to you that I won't read *Mein Kampf* either. All things considered, I think I'd rather read another book that came out this year, one whose author had the good taste to say, as he died, that it should be burnt, like all the other writings he left behind. A priori, that gives me confidence. One has to say that his isn't the usual attitude. If you wanted to indicate to posterity that the work – the one you had consigned to the flames – was out of the ordinary, you could not do better. Of course, you run a considerable risk of being taken seriously. Luckily, Franz Kafka must have chosen the right executor: he perjured himself, happily for us. Now we can read *The Trial* and *The Castle*. The author certainly isn't just anybody. That joke about Rathenau I just told you – well, it was his. I suspect that man must have known, before all of us, what times were in store for us. That frightens me as much as it attracts me. You'll tell me that your *putsch*-mongering corporal was doing the same thing in drawing up his little manifesto: predicting our future? So tomorrow we will know which of them was wrong, Kafka or Hitler – assuming, of course, they're not both right! But as for me, I'll read only Kafka. Solely for reasons of form. My friend Sternheim, who turned down a literary prize in Kafka's favour, didn't feel called upon to correct his style! And then, the words of revolutionaries, no matter what their party, don't interest me. They're of the wood that coffins are made of. They ought to burn better than others. However, it's often the revolutionaries who set poets' books alight, not the other way round. In a sense, Kafka behaved like a revolutionary in asking for his books to be reduced to ashes, to set a kind of example. Who knows if some agitator or other won't soon give him the satisfaction Max Brod denied him? At any rate, Kafka was right to tempt the Devil: the only books that are worth anything, apart from the ones you think you ought to burn, are those you have to save from the flames. To meet Kafka now, I shall have to read him. He's dead, and among the people I mourn for there is now this man I did not go out of my way to meet. It's like losing a brother you might have had. That just leaves his work. It's made to rectify that omission. I would even say that if it is not that, it is nothing. But if it is that, it's almost as if, in the end, its author didn't need to exist ... "

The girl chuckles, shrugs her shoulders.

"A moment ago, Doctor, with respect, you claimed this man might have been your brother. Like the one the whale was about to swallow, earlier on. Or the one who didn't write with his guts ... Could I just say in passing that you seem to have been finding brothers everywhere, this past hour. It must be the effect of that German whisky, or the schnapps, or the champagne you're deliberately not drinking, even though the old year is nearly at its end ... Never mind, it's going to your head all the same, isn't it! Now, that fellow who wanted people to burn his books, or who claimed he wanted them to – after all, if he'd really wanted them burnt he'd have done it himself, wouldn't he – anyway, you'd surely have wanted to know that man in the flesh, wouldn't you?"

"In the end, I think I should have liked to go and see him, yes ... " the doctor mumbles.

"You think, you think!" the girl interrupts him, suddenly upset. "Would you have needed him as a friend, yes or no? For Christ's sake, that's something you ought to know ... "

"I think I should have liked to meet him. But even more, I didn't want to. I was afraid that the man, with his way of being, his charm, his body, even his shadow, would have hidden the books he had written. Great books are always better than those who write them – did you know that? It's sad, but it is so. And then, the books I read, like the ones I write, are always my books, while I'm reading them ... "

"Really! Just now you were telling me that you don't read

or write anything any more ... Now here you are, all of a sudden, owning all the books in the world!"

The doctor blushes. He's been caught out contradicting himself. Or being frivolous. All the same, he isn't frivolous, this man: it's the last thing that could be said of him. He swears that he's going to make himself understood by this girl, this Elsa, this Helga, this Eva, or whatever she may be called. He has forgotten. He'll try to explain himself by drawing a somewhat precarious parallel between their two situations.

"The clients you pick up," he expounds, "one might say that between your thighs they're only deciphering the book they need to read? A flesh Bible ... "

"How you go on, Doctor!" says the girl, laughing harshly. "You are getting carried away. Don't you think you're laying it on a bit?"

She bursts out in an unpleasant, bitter laugh.

"Supposing I told you that most of my clients are illiterate? Didn't you tell me yourself that no one reads anything any more, in this day and age? So if anyone reads anything in me, it's never more a penny dreadful. Suppose I said, just to stop you dreaming, that one client nibbles the sanitary towel soaked in the last one's sperm, from the bottom of the bidet?"

"I'd answer that they both have a different thing in mind. The sperm a man gives, like a mother's milk, is never the same twice. Even if it is the milk of hell. The most cynical lout always believes in good faith, for the second his pleasure lasts, that he's giving more than the prostitute is letting him have. Even the body of a brute has such moments of naivety ... He thinks he's giving the best of himself. Alas, even the sadist thinks that. Even the rapist. Even the Tübingen Strangler. Such is the madness of desire. He'd need a different, heroic madness to resist it. His lawyer will never know anything of his frightening secret. And if he found out, he couldn't mention it in court ... The incommunicable suffering of someone who is only cast into the world in order not to understand what is happening to him ... Unhappy the man who climbs alone the Calvary of desire!"

"It's true," she admits thoughtfully, "that it never happens the same twice over. But it's not the whore's *savoir-faire* or the client's imagination that brings about the miracle!"

For an instant the doctor glimpses, as if for the first time, this creature whose function it is to milk men and who, once nourished with their juice, passes on.

"Tell me about them," says the doctor, stretching out as if absent-mindedly on the metal bench. "Tell me about your clients."

"What can I tell you, Doctor, that you don't know already? Don't they, too, fill your waiting room and tell you their secrets?"

"Not the same ones," says the doctor.

"You can be sure they don't tell you everything. Not that you're missing much ... I happened to meet one or two of them at your surgery. You have to pretend not to recognise them. The law of silence ... There's the one you ought to start by washing with black soap from head to foot, the way he stinks when he comes to your digs. I'm not talking of the ones who come because their wives are ill, depressed or frigid: that's the usual reason. I won't waste time on the one who comes in servant's livery to do the housework. If he only wanted to satisfy that need, which is actually useful, I'd have every reason to pass him over in silence. There's the one who asks you to dress up like a little girl, in a playsuit or sailor's suit, because he can't have an erection unless he imagines himself in the Tiergarten drooling over a little girl who has given her governess the slip. You give yourself to him and then you want to go straight to the police to denounce him, in case it's a real kid he has his fill of one day when the parks close. There's the one who asks you to pierce his navel with your stiletto heel, despite the yells he's sure to let out. Sometimes you'd like to finish him off by strangling him in earnest. But he pays well and he, at least, doesn't penetrate you – the ultimate favour. There's the priest who comes to treat himself to a tart on

Christmas night; if midnight strikes at the moment of coitus he crosses himself and starts praying. You don't forget that. Don't pull a trick like that on me for the New Year, Doctor. If I give you a lot of pleasure, please forget everything else, including the calendar! And then I must mention the kleptomaniac who can't leave you without taking your knickers, your candlestick or your alarm clock. The one who writes to you from prison and buries you in jailbird fantasies. The consumptive who gets a new lease of life. The syphilitic who ejaculates blood with his sperm. The one who can only rod you in time to a particular jazz tune. The one whose balls you have to pierce, and then sew up again after use with coarse thread, so that in a month's time he'll be able to have himself martyred again while bellowing with pleasure. The ones you have to give third-degree burns with a cigarette – they pay less if it isn't pale American tobacco ... Not to mention the heart case who expires in your arms, that you have to move out discreetly by the stage door: sooner or later every whore has some such beautiful death on her conscience. And every one has the right to a visit, one fine day, by the client who brings his wife, a radiant beauty, smelling like a walk under the limes on a Sunday afternoon ... You wonder what the man can want. Or his wife, depending ... Unless that is exactly what troubles them: they have everything to please and satisfy themselves. So they come to risk it all, challenge it all, in a prostitute's bed ... Then you come across the guy who seems to have no vices – they're the worst. Make sure you never turn your back on them, or you risk having your throat cut in your bath, before having time to call your mother. The usual sort are the ones who've drunk enough to accost a prostitute, but too much to press home the advantage ... You have to mount them like a nag or suckle them like a wet-nurse. But they don't give any more milk than a heifer. Anyway, I don't like sucking them; it seems you lose your teeth. Sperm is worse than sugar. (By the way, you will have some sugar for me, won't you?) The ones who don't make it finally have a crisis and get violent. You're lucky if you don't get a beating by way of compensation. They all want to show you, and prove to themselves, that in spite of being destitute and out of work they can still get it up, have intercourse, and pay. As time went on I got into the habit of keeping a notebook of the peculiarities of each of them ... Like that, when they come back I know what to expect. You see, Doctor, I also write ... "

"Because you might forget?"

"Sometimes I'm lucky enough to forget, yes. For a long time I thought the poor suckers liked it when I remembered their little routines. Actually they were disappointed. What they wanted was to tell them to me all over again. The last thing they wanted was to be interrupted."

"Do they often come back?"

"They always come back. The ones with the abnormal needs are the most faithful. If I don't see them after a certain time, it's because they're dead. Or someone else has pinched them."

"Widowed or jealous ... Just the same as an ordinary wife, in the end," says the doctor.

"Not jealous, no. I just tell myself I've learned someone's peculiarities for nothing. Wasted my time, that's all. If you were to die, Doctor, I'd know straight away. I'd have to find another quack. But I'd never find one quite like you!"

Funny, thinks the doctor, how they all talk about their clients in more or less the same way. They all tell roughly the same anecdotes. Whether they're talking to their pimps, their colleagues, or other clients, the language they use is never far from the way informers talk ... As if they couldn't forgive them for being unable to survive without them ...

Perhaps to stop him thinking badly of her, the girl adds: "Did you know, Doc, that most of the girls around here have recently got dogs? You probably think it's to protect themselves. It's true that in these times it's better to be on your guard against the Stuttgart Strangler, the Wiesbaden Vampire, the Frankfurt Satyr! But guard dogs have a different purpose: the client may ask us to fornicate with them ... "

"I know," says the doctor. "A friend of mine who is a vet told me the animals sometimes go mad because their mistress shows them too little affection ... "

"Your friend wasn't lying, either," says the girl. "But did he tell you that when the animal gets dangerous and starts biting the woman or her client, we have to call him to give it a jab?"

"You seem to think you're telling me things I don't know," grumbles the doctor. "But don't forget that I take your clients over when you've finished with them. I'm the one who gets to hear their final confidences. Herr Rudolf, for example, who thought himself a woman and had an artificial vagina cut into his perineum. He's just got a job as a kitchen maid at Kempinski's. And what about Otto who tried to cut his scrotum off with a slip-knot? Now he's an old woman who calls herself Ottla, dresses in black and never goes out without her imitation lizard-skin handbag. I'm sure you know Hansi Sturm who performs every evening at the Eldorado, where *she* sings arias from *Samson and Delilah* (Delilah's, of course, not Samson's) but is no less married and the father of two fine children for that. So much for the transsexuals. Did you know that they've opened an Institute of Sexual Science on the edge of the Tiergarten, where they treat paedophiles, care for transvestites and even chastise unhappy exhibitionists on demand? You must admit that you haven't yet seen everything. Not long ago I examined one of your colleagues who worked on the corner of Knesebeckstrasse. She wasn't ill. But for years she had not taken off the riding boots she specialised in. Inside them we found some banknotes that had had time to devalue ten times over."

"Doctor, why do you lump together those lunatics and the people like me who tend to their needs?" the girl asks. "Who even look after people who aren't crazy at all? People who just have some kind of taint. There are some who have never made it; they may be over thirty and they come for the first time because we've taken the necessary time, used a bit of guile ...

Afterwards they're all shaken up and start crying. We'd like to cry with them. You were a whore and you wake up a nurse: what do you say about that? Once or twice, three times perhaps, I've cured a man of the idea that he couldn't have pleasure with a woman. He sobbed in my arms, he was stupefied, but not so much as I was ... "

A nurse, indeed. One who always had only one remedy to administer. And invalids who all suffered appallingly from the same sickness.

For a few moments they are silent, as if getting their breath back after some obscure combat.

"Have you been with women anywhere else?" the girl asks at last. "I mean, the ones who walk the streets?"

"In Brussels," he answers, "during the war. They accosted the enemy with a kind of dogged violence. The city's hostility towards its occupiers had condensed into the bodies of these girls. Till you met them you didn't know how much you were hated ... "

We sank into that war, he thinks, like a bog. We were steeped in the bodies of women whose indictment rotted our dreams.

"But you know what can happen between warriors," he goes on. "There comes a time when, despite itself, without knowing it, the flesh fraternises. The reflex actions of the bodies are communicated to the souls. The moment when the soul can express only itself through the body."

The bought body and the buying body, he thinks, the slave and the slave trader, were tacitly reconciled, and soon felt more real joy than feigned pleasure. There's always a moment, when everything's supposed to be done by pretence, and truth suddenly shows through the make-up. It can be cruel. It has an unexpected, inexpressible purity. All the symbols vanish, the conventions melt away. It's something you can't admit. These states of consciousness do not last, of course. They're there just for the moment the universe is distracted from itself. Just long enough for a fine adultery.

"And now, in Berlin, is it very different?" the girl asks. "I mean, with me, for instance?"

"Here," he says, "all the war has left face to face, belly to belly, locked together like a couple of dogs, is the defeated, propped up on each other, clamped to each other, to save themselves, to be sucked down together ... "

I know no other city, he thinks, where prostitutes put such melancholy on show, where they offer themselves with doom all over their faces. They play on their misery like an extra attraction. It doesn't provoke the client, it offers him a living remorse. It's irresistible ... Tonight, he'd like to tell Elsa, or Helga, or Eva, one person's misery can find, if not a remedy, at least a mirror in the other's. We're living God's reprieve. But a reprieve can mean a special benevolence, or a momentary absence ... God showing us all His benignity, or going on strike – but even striking would give us relief, would take His weight off us ...

"One night," he tells her, "right here under my window, I heard a young man shout: 'Whore!' No doubt he was venting his disgust at someone who'd just broken off with him and was already walking off in the rain. That made me think. Any woman who leaves a man, or prefers another to him, lays herself open to being called a whore. And it's always been so. Without knowing it, that young gutter-snipe was expressing himself just like a Prussian bourgeois of the nineteenth century, or a rough foot-soldier of the fifteenth ... How absurd! If the woman he was berating actually was a courtesan, why should she mind being reminded of it? And if she didn't practise the world's oldest profession, the epithet didn't fit her any more than if he had called her 'God!' It would have been neither more nor less aberrant. Less, no doubt. And in any case, shouldn't we call 'God' anything that transcends us? Most likely, in shouting 'whore' he merely defined his own identity. Though he also usurped it ... 'Whore!' – that pathetic cry merely expressed his own inability to put any of his deepest passion into words. And what hopeless psychology. Did our bawler seriously hope to mortify someone he was giving the best reasons to leave him? There are some words you can't utter without their turning at once into boomerangs. No prostitute will be able to feel herself such as long as her status is turned into an insult. Yes, the more I think about it, the better it would have been for him to call the woman whose base betrayal he sought to denounce in the depths of the night: 'God!' His last chance to give an apt name to the cause of his pain, his anger, his feeling of abandonment. But who, in such a situation, would have thought of it?"

And you, Elsa, Helga, Eva or whoever, thinks the doctor, if you are God for a night beside me, won't it be for similar reasons? Couldn't I include you in that God who comes and goes, turns round, comes back, takes off again, re-opening and scarring the same stigmata to the heart's desire? I could have paid you for it, of course, as one burns a candle in church. And as you could have remunerated the quack for a similar service. As a doctor I was God to the tainted woman. As a prostitute you become God to your concupiscent client. A fair exchange. No one's fooled but each will depart cured for a time of his malady and of himself. But there's the embrace and the coitus. You invite her for an hour, or for a night. Those are brothel times. Elsa, Helga, Eva, grant me this dance, I pray. One more giddy round, my Lord, Sir Executioner, my tender nurse.

"Oh," he says, "by the way ... "

He keeps saying "by the way", just as he says "in any case", fearing there may be nothing by the way, throughout this night where all the channels are converging to form, when morning comes, a delta of silence and light.

"Since we're talking about God ... "

He says "we", but does he really think they've been expressing themselves together, through his mouth?

"Do you remember the Gospel story about a Pharisee who

invited Jesus to his table and was unable to shut his door on a sinful woman who came weeping to kiss the Messiah's feet? Well, this is how our host's reasoning went: if Jesus was the prophet he said he was, he would know what sort of creature he was touching. It did not occur to him that his visitor might have touched her for that very reason ... "

There was a time, he thinks, when the bodies of men moved more freely among the bodies of women than they do today ... Like vessels rubbing hull to hull at the entrance to an estuary. Then, the mutual knowledge of men and peoples passed through promiscuity. You brushed against each other, took the scent, like dogs sniffing at each other by way of dialogue. You didn't keep your distance, so that skins did not get rubbed threadbare and emotions exhausted when you finally did make contact ...

"You know what came next: that same Mary Magdalene was to discover later – not much later, it all went so quickly – the dark secret of the Resurrection! Was she the first to notice that the boulder sealing the sepulchre had moved, or did an angel or two appear to her asking why she was looking for the living among the dead? Or was there even an earthquake – the doctors of faith differ somewhat on this point ... But the essential thing, surely, was that she knew before all the others that Christ had risen. Just as it was she, not the Pharisee, who recognised the Son of God, and she again who knew that He had come back. It was the communication that happens between intuitive people. The couple of the year! He had forgiven her sins 'because she had loved much'. So who had she loved? Well, Him, for a start. I mean God. But men too, her clients ... And then, he'd had himself nailed to a cross to demonstrate a love of the same calibre ... You didn't stint yourself, in those days, when it came to showing your feelings!"

I'll be forgiven much, he thinks, because I shall have loved much tonight – loved Maria, Elsa, Helga, whoever. Unless, of course, there's nothing to be forgiven, just because of all that love for Elsa, Eva, Magdalena. For you can certainly love someone whose name you have forgotten ...

"Listen," he says.

In the next room he has left the radio on.

"It's Chaliapin," he says. "I know it's him because he doesn't sing, he weeps. Even in the *Barber of Seville*, he weeps as he sings. With all those tremolos. I personally find it stimulating ... "

"Doctor?"

"Yes?"

"Why do you go with street women?"

Maybe these biblical and musicological allusions have been too much for the poor child. Yes, child, he repeats in his mind, to save looking for other excuses. Maybe he's been pontificating, just a little. She might just as well have asked him: Doctor, why do you go with all those books? Including the Bible, with its cloak-and-dagger characters ... "Poor child" – you can talk!

"Could you change your job?"

"No," she stammers.

"Well then, that's why I go with street women!"

She doesn't quite see the connection, but she repeats:

"No, I couldn't. The life you lead is just too strong for you. When you've done it you're no good for anything else. I did once try to give up streetwalking, but life seemed quite false. I listened to people, and they talked like characters in books. With all due respect, Doctor, they sometimes sounded a bit like you ... "

She left the world of simulation, he muses, and found reality artificial ... And she may be right. Who could say the life of make-believe isn't the most real of all?

"It's like being in the war," he says. "If you've really been in it, if you've been a soldier too long, you have to stay a soldier. You've become one of death's whores. When you've noticed that peace is just a sham you can't help thinking that war is more – appallingly – honest. And you can't stop being a soldier. Or a doctor. That's why I've gone on being a doctor. For four years, I was a soldier's doctor, just as there are soldier's whores. A doctor of men, to console yourself for being one, even if you can't cure the disease. And when you come out, you think you've seen so much that the least emotion will overwhelm you. You think you've become hypersensitive. Whereas the opposite is the case. It turns out – and this can be devastating – that you have become addicted to strong sensations. You think you've put it behind you. You believe yourself out of danger – that's really the point. And you find you're still in the middle of a minefield. The trouble is that you've become your own mine. So don't talk to me about those ex-soldiers who proclaim their love of men while hiding their hands in their pockets. I've an instinctive mistrust of healers who are offended by the sight of wounds. You can only cure the person you know, and you only know the person you've rubbed against. You can't turn away from the scarlet mirror he holds up to you. If I went blind, I'd have to feel him, reconstruct him in the dark … "

Funny, thinks the girl. Just now I was the one who was afraid of going blind. Now he's doing it. It must be all this white paint around us.

"Do you realise that even if I were blind," he insists, "I'd still recognise my clients – and their ailments – by their smell?"

So would I, unfortunately, thinks the girl.

"Good blood and bad blood can't lie. I'm just the confessor of the body," he says. "In that capacity I'm in on the secret. You and I treat the same people, no doubt, but not the same illnesses. Often enough I have to cure them of the ones you've infected them with, you and your sisters. But the other sickness, the one that's driven them into your arms, is the first thing I diagnose when they walk into my surgery. It gives them that look of people drowning in the desert. It tears their faces like the rough draft of a letter they've given up trying to write."

"Is it a love letter, or a letter about lack of love?" asks the girl.

"A moment ago, if I recall, you asked me why I go with street-women."

"Yes. It struck me that you could have normal women, I mean, ones you don't need to pay. A handsome man like you must be able to have any woman he likes!"

"Oh, spare me the smooth talk, since you've avoided it up to now. Not between us . . . Yes, there are some women in my life, frequently actresses, as it happens . . . But I've already started breaking with Ellen, although she doesn't know it yet; I'll have to get it over and done with this year. With Ernestine that won't be necessary. She has so many lovers that some of them are bound to go missing from time to time. I'll be one of those. Five years ago I was close to Gertrud. Now we're much more distant."

"It's the same with us," the girl points out. "One minute we're close, the next distant."

He bursts out laughing.

"That's true," he exclaims, "but tonight we've telescoped a whole love story into a few hours."

And one that won't have a sad end, thinks the girl. The advantage of whores is that you don't need to break with them.

The women you don't buy, you have to seduce, he thinks. In the old days I used to find it exhilarating: the approach work, the laborious capture, the rituals of society mammals. Now, because I'm not attractive to myself, I find all that exhausting, and myself slightly disgusting. I don't want to waste the least rotten thing I have in me in a charade of that kind. So I prefer sleeping with tarts, since they're no more than abysses covered with skin. People are fond of denouncing the comic act the girls put on with their clients: the kiss-curls and faked pleasure, the loaded dice – but who knows if they don't tell less lies sometimes than deluded lovers, mistresses full of anguished hope, all those people living on misunderstandings that allow them for a time to escape the unbearable truth of life? Between the lines of the unequal contract which the client signs between the whore's thighs, there's all the talk about supply and demand, squalid transactions and bad debts. But at least he's only endorsing a lie that both the partners have agreed on in advance. This body of ours, the doctor would like to say, or indeed shout, to Eva, Elsa, Helga, is both the subject and the object of the terror that it feels and that it inspires, yet we'll both forget it in a moment when yours is naked before mine like a mute cry.

"Even with my wife," he assures the girl, as if he were completing an argument he had just conducted aloud, "there was a time when I had to pay her for making love to me ... It was during the war. I did it because of the solitude around us, between us. To show how disconnected everything was."

"She made you do that?" asks the girl, curling up with laughter.

"Of course not. You've not understood. I forced her. I felt I had to pay for her love, as if I suddenly had no right to it ... I'd gladly have given her all my wages. I should have enjoyed watching her count the money over and over, to make sure none was missing. I'd have liked to ruin myself for her in a single night. When almost everything has a price on it, why not put one on the conjugal game of legs-in-the-air? I've always had to buy everything, you know ... Nothing came to me free of charge."

"Except me," she objects.

"That's true," he agrees, astonished. "Except you, for a whole night."

For a whole monologue, she thinks.

Earlier, when I wrote poems, he muses, I felt like God's whore. But I too was a whore that God couldn't have paid.

"Except me," repeats the girl. "Except me, for a whole night. Just so that it's official."

And so that her verbose New Year's Eve client realises the magnitude of the gift, and is rendered speechless. But she can't help adding: "Next time I get the clap you'll treat me for nothing, won't you, Doctor? I'm bound to get it sooner or later . . . And that way, we'll meet again."

"Tonight," he says, "we're going to be poor together."

Tonight, it is the girl who is interceding for him. Interceding with whom he does not know. Tonight, his guest is going to tell him who he is. Even if it isn't only good news. Suddenly it seems to him that this girl and he are starting to understand everything together. That they have learned something about humanity as a whole that it does not yet know itself . . .

He thinks he can hear fireworks in the distance, and bells ringing. He does not look at his watch.

"Do you think our hour will come, Doctor?"

What an odd question. Is she talking about the hour when penniless doctors will at last cure incurable illnesses? When the good-time girls, called more poetically in French, girls or even daughters of joy, would finally deserve that name? Or did she mean the stroke of midnight on another New Year's Eve when the distinguished venereologist from the Belle-Alliance-Strasse would be seen entering the Café Adlon with a one-time courtesan on his arm, she now wearing a paste tiara and blue wings, like a Sphinx? A liveried waiter would place a portable telephone on their table, between their glasses of mellow cognac. The doctor would be brought the latest issue of the *Neuer Merkur* or the *Deutsche Allgemeine Zeitung*. In Germany, now an honorary member of the League of Nations, there's not the slightest *coup d'état*, political leaders have started dying in bed, the currency is stable and no one commits suicide that night: Expressionism is at large in the cabarets and poetry revues, but has deserted the streets.

"Forgive me, please. No sooner has someone taken the bait of my solemnities than I swallow it myself. You can rest assured that our hour will come, perhaps sooner than we suspect. But will it be the hour of the milkman, the almoner, or the performer of noble works? Who cares? In the meantime, we'll have lived vibrantly."

He had been walking around the room with big steps. Now he stopped in front of the swing-mirror.

Suddenly, he no longer knew what was mirror and what was window. As if he were seeing those pale thighs through a two-way mirror – legs that were parted and slightly bent on the metal bench. A third person coming into the room at that moment would have supposed the doctor was about to pull on his rubber gloves, pick up his needles and a suction extractor and proceed that very night to perform a clandestine abortion. How could the girl, who had thrown her head back, have been aware of her immodesty? Projecting towards him in the mirror, the legs looked enormous, out of proportion.

The doctor could not tear his eyes from this bluish, opalescent flesh. Brussels, he thinks; Africa, spring. Ink mingled with blood. How long ago was it? It was when the world was still able to draw inspiration from the commiseration that was its due.

His gaze moves to the belly, the throat, the eyes of the girl who has finally noticed she is being observed. She's not someone, thinks the doctor, she's a homeland, a season. The roots of my life join and intertwine in her. Birth's cradle and cemetery. The gaze that has met his might seem empty: it's merely wide-eyed with a nameless horror, fascinated by a catastrophe preceding birth.

He feels his gorge rise. It's not disgust. It's as if he had woken up to find blood on the sheets, without realising at first that it was his own.

It's not so much the nudity that tightens his throat, as all the digressions it sets in motion. You find infinity where you didn't expect it. He who hardly drinks feels a drunk's self-pity coming over him. He who does not touch drugs gives himself up to a delirious nostalgia.

It's fatigue, he thinks, gathering in the flesh of men even while they labour. My life has been nothing but an interminable sleepless night. He weeps without tears. Only his lip trembles.

"You know, Doctor," says the girl, "I'm not called Elsa or Eva. My name's Renate."

He feels dead-beat. He lies down again beside the girl, on the metal table. She snuggles against him as if she suddenly felt very cold. He's surprised at the weight of the cranium that seeks his shoulder. He recalls that the crania of corpses had the weight of cast iron. Is it this association of ideas that suggests another to him? It seems to him that this female with open legs is giving off the same scent as an autopsy. The sepulchral whiff of women that you could not have loved ... And yet ...

At one time he only wrote about prostitutes when death had already come to them, stranded in silt, steeped in a crazed naturalism of dark, flamboyant colours: sand in a drowned mouth. Or he would permit himself some disdainfully misogynistic quip: "A woman: something for a night. Something that carries a smell."

Didn't his dear enemy Bert Brecht say that you enjoyed a woman "like a half-smoked cigarette"?

What acid could have eaten away at the age to draw from writers such contorted raillery? And yet:

> "The copulating night
> gulps randomly among
> the starry hordes."

Why do you have to finish up alone, afterwards, wide-eyed, while the huntress-prey lies sated beside you, not even seeming to dream? Well, at least don't fall asleep in the curdled dawn, to avoid the tedium of waking together in the morning.

Why, the poet wonders, is woman disappearing from what little I still write, being only evoked in the form of a distant deity that might "approach and assemble the universe"?

On his lady friend in Copenhagen he writes arcanely

dissonant verses, but only to concede once more the shame that is drunk from desolation, and the ineluctable duality of man.

Furthermore, thinks the poet, you don't even mention death any more. But why should you call it back now? It's been everywhere. During the war, men's fraternity evaporated in the bubbles of their blood. And before women, you're seized by vertigo. If, to take them, you've got into a cannibal's skin, a squall sweeps you out to sea where you drown; in an instant you've lost yourself and the world. So you reach quickly for the crate of beer or the prescription pad, to note down, with the uncouthness of despair, those two or three mottoes that hold life together in you with the slender toughness of an angel's hair ... The only remedy to the drying up of all the springs. The last rampart against the flood of sand. Writing, to stifle the yawn that rises up from the days, fit to unhinge your heart.

Ah, you should remember the words of youth, when you still dreamt of women. Pleasure foamed on the crests of the waves, the sea was drunk. Even if

> "each wave casts you back in the dust
> pricking you with the thorn of the self" ...

Yes, let's renew the conviction that woman is a delirium propped against the void. A happy chaos. And the hetaera, a play of reflecting forms in which you forget the schism between yourself and the other. Her munificent mystery. Antiquity's greatest courtesan was called Psyche.

Isolde emerged, naked, from the winter night.

Now the poet is muttering, seeking the words of a poem not yet written, on the love that gives and denies itself, making life sob towards the abyss of eternity ...

"You're going to write about me in a poem?" asks Renate. He must have been dreaming out loud. He laughs.

"I'd write about you," he says, smiling, "if you had really gone blind ... "

He'd like to explain that a few rhyming couplets have never been more for him than a ruse against death. Silence would have been better, of course, but the silence of nobody is not the same as the silence of somebody. So the poem finds its surreptitious way into you like a scabies mite, lays its eggs, digs its tunnels and can't be got rid of. It's the pruritus of the soul. What more can you hope for? If a poem has not followed you around like an itch – or a remorse – it wasn't worth writing. If, for the present, I don't write – by now he's probably thinking aloud again – it's not because I'm tired or incapable. It's an act of continence. I'm waiting to be able to write the poem that would rekindle the thirst of the alcoholic who has just finished drying out, restore the withdrawal symptoms of the addict who has just kicked cocaine. I'm waiting for the words that will bring back to the brothel the reformed debauchee who's been cured of the pox, call the reformed felon back to his crimes. And the words that will push the man who has made his peace with men to declare war on God. If not those, I might as well keep my mouth shut.

"I have some clients who bed me, others who just look. And some who talk. They're not the same ones. Coming here, I knew you were going to talk. You're talkative like someone who's kept quiet too long. I didn't expect you to be a looker: as a medic you've seen enough already! I didn't know if we would fuck. I couldn't know in advance that I would want to. Normally, I don't like clients mixing their acts ... "

That's because I'm in the world and outside it at the same time, thinks the client. The unresting shuttle between people and things. You can't always be on the sidelines of life.

He contemplates the body whose tenant he is about to become. It's true that he has not looked at it properly up to now. He discovers the narrow shoulders, the fragile wrists, the wrinkled navel. Between the wiry hair and the Red Indian cheekbones, the predatory eyes made glassy by the client's expectancy.

Something induces him to reify this flesh, to see it solely as food for his covetous palate, to manipulate it like the movement of a clock. To take it only to learn from it. But if he really wanted that he would not succeed. He'd be unable to fend off a secret reverence for this ageless creature, for his own shipwrecked childhood. He'd give everything in the world if his body could have for a moment the rawness of this kid – for he fears that his own life has gone high from its constant heating up by the age, the city.

He looks at this body that has not been defeated by giving itself to so many of the vanquished. What science of shared solitude could equal the one this body knows? There is only one generosity: that which circulates from body to body. Prudery or affectation makes us talk of something else. But in the end, generosity is always of the body. Of that husk that each life bruises, lacerates, tears and wears out. Now and then, a few bodies, driven by urgency or panic, have done something for a few other bodies. And a few words, when they have made the journey from one body to another. And then, you have to desire them as much as the bodies themselves.

"To think that it's nearly daybreak, and I thought we weren't going to do it ... "

"You wouldn't have been pleased, would you? You'd have been angry with me."

"I should have been sad. I shouldn't have understood. I shouldn't have wanted to understand. I'd have been afraid, too."

"Afraid of me?"

"Afraid of a client who gives up what's due to him when all the words he says tremble with suppressed violence. Doctor, you're not really intending to use a sheath? You must know that I'm not dangerous any more ... "

She has gently straddled him. She puts her hand round his

scrotum and teases his anus with the tip of a fingernail. Bending over him, she brushes the man's breasts with the tips of her own. The nipples of each harden together. She takes the man's hands to guide his caresses: you'd think she wanted to paint herself all over with them. His palms are surprised by the smallness of her breasts, rest on her snowy thighs, brush the arousing, tepid cleft of her groin, grip her torrid flanks better to impale the girl on his upright member, driving it in like a nail, while she throws back her head and a long shudder shakes her haunches, and his hands close on buttocks of a childish freshness.

The girl's sex drinks his own like the lips of a wound.

"How you give yourself," he murmurs. Only this mark of gratitude escapes him, as his desire alone is now speaking in him. And yet none of this ought to be real. Nor the panting and moaning, that he has time to think she might have omitted ... Is she miming the feverish schoolgirl tremors as well? He will never know. There will always be a doubt, and all prostitutes know that even the most cynical partner will choose to be taken in. Then he opens himself to the wails that rock his enjoyment, so different to the grave and modest silence of the other women he has loved. He clasps more tightly to him this body that is shaken as if by sobs. He weeps in her: she weeps with him.

At the climax of his pleasure she seemed to him almost monkey-like and supremely beautiful. Was she still cheating as she placed a kiss on his mouth? He savoured the lips that tasted of nettle, iron, pencil-lead. The taste of a poor childhood. He discovered that she had used perfume indiscriminately all over her body. He smiled.

He congratulates himself on having deferred this tender formality till dawn. With the early daylight and the sounds of the city, the world was recovering its first simplicity.

And the man benefits from his temperance. He has forgotten that he was alone. For him, tonight, a woman has paid with her own person. He has forgotten that no one ever takes anything or is ever taken. He doesn't remind himself that he has merely been telling himself stories, since they rendered the pleasure still more extravagant. Doesn't the doctor know that any real situation prefers to play the double game, rather than be a straight lie; and that it is for each of us to draw from this very duplicity our reasons for survival? As we never entirely merge, in full transparency, with the one we cherish the most, how can we not be lifted up, for a spasm's length, by the journey we've made with a chance hostess? It might happen that after an hour with her we made an admission we'd have censored for all our lives had we spent them with another. And we might also receive a confidence of equal gravity.

At the end of that hour, we might have nothing more to say to each other, and separate perhaps for ever.

"Oh God, Edith," he had murmured as he spent himself.

Afterwards, he confessed his embarrassment over the slip. Renate smiled.

"A widower should never apologise," she says. "But Edith or no Edith, as you had a lot of pleasure you won't forget my little present?"

No, he hasn't forgotten.

Then, suddenly, the girl is delighted to hear her client say: "Yes, I remember: a bit of sugar and coffee. Wasn't that it?"

Her eyes and teeth shine in the early light.

"Doctor, would you believe that last night, even when you put the lights out and all I could see was medical instruments gleaming in the dark, I felt protected?"

Last night, he thinks, in 1926, I was wondering, ludicrously, where the party was to be that would warm my flesh on my bones? It was starting in this very room.

"Sometimes, in the night when in vain I'm trying to sleep, I think I can hear my neighbour singing. Sometimes I think he's making a woman's body sing. Unless she is the one whose caresses are drawing from him those feminine moans."

"And tonight it was you!" cries Renate clapping her hands. "Tonight it was your turn!"

"Yes," he admits, "tonight I was my own neighbour."

"I'd been warned," she says. "'Don't go to him, he doesn't like people. He frightens everybody. He's only a dead person's doctor. He hardly talks to the living.'"

I never say "happiness" to anyone, the doctor wants to reply. I say "dance". I seldom say "joy"; I say "song". Even corpses sing, sometimes. I hear them. Someone needs to, don't they? He'd like to tell her that he has found tatters of joy in the viscera of an unknown body. It didn't exist for anyone, had no one left to talk to, but I knew that it hadn't lived in vain. A god, whatever name you call him by, was showing his pride in having brought such a creature into the world. Yes, even beneath the jeers of despair, that song could be heard, the jubilation of a creature that had shown itself capable of such glee. And I caught myself singing with it.

"How funny," says the girl. "The only people I've met as a tart who I could enjoy being with were a few soldiers vaguely like deserters, some gangsters without too many regrets, some cops who were half gangsters themselves, or a doctor, a doctor of life and death, of whores and death. The others were so proper. They talked to say nothing. They did it for the sake of having done it. They lived for the sake of not living. When they happened to die, it wasn't their true illness that carried them off. They did not die of what they had lived."

"Most of those who deceive their wives," says the client, "would do better to cuckold the life they've made for themselves. Who would want to be faithful to the world as it is? It's only beautiful when betrayed."

New Year's Eve, he thinks. It wasn't an evening to analyse a canker or write a poem. Nor even to entertain a prostitute. That's what I liked about it. I said to myself: at least it will be an hour outside the world and the calendar. Off limits. As if the girl and I had been overtaken by winter and shut in together, as by a landslide or an earthquake. A natural catastrophe. Time has burst its banks and spread out into a delta of eternity. What we did – all that can happen between a girl like you, a blind tart,

201

and a man like me, a dermatologist covered in eczema, one New Year's night in Berlin in the twenties – we did against the world. And yet we were at the heart of the world – perhaps it started and will finish with us. *"Stille Nacht"* ...

"Nothing could have distracted us," he says, "not even an emergency call. We were our own only emergency. What is your phrase for accosting clients?" the doctor asks.

"Walking the line – *Auf den Strich gehen*," she says. "The whole night, we've been walking a high wire."

We were somnambulist funambulists, he thinks, that nothing could have woken, except the absence of love. This flesh must have been born far from here, in Wuppertal, Darmstadt or Tübingen, or even Linz or Klagenfurt – for didn't she have a trace of an Austrian accent – or even, who knows? in the Cameroons – didn't she have the crinkly hair and milky skin of a white negress? In any case, far from Berlin. This exotic flesh might even have been that of a transvestite. Tonight, the client would not have been unduly incensed by the fraud. He would not have loved this woman less if her flesh had been that of a man, for whatever her route, her journey had brought her to the Belle-Alliance-Strasse. Unhoped for, it was like a home-coming. A miraculous meeting of colliding molecules. A marvellous exception that confirmed the horrifying rule ...

> "In Hamburg's fair city
> In velvet so pretty
> My name I'll not tell for
> a harlot am I ... "

... the horrifying rule of that year of 1926, when two million unemployed and thousands of war invalids, amputees, cripples with leathery faces, had been put under the protection of four hundred and fifty thousand steel helmets. But what does that matter, since Frankfurt has staged its dance marathon and the capital has welcomed Josephine Baker and her negro revue? What does it matter, since Margo Lion, in her Christmas revue at the end of the year, has reminded us that we're in a state of levitation, suspended in mid-air? *Es liegt in der Luft* – it's in the air. What does it matter, since we can forget all that, this 1 January 1927, by going off on one of the picnic parties to Grunewald or Wannsee that nature-loving citizens are so partial to?

"All the same, you won't forget, will you, Doctor, that this same year Adolf Hitler, the writer whose book you have not read – perhaps you're a little bit jealous of his success after all? No, really? – well, he's not been content with writing. He has rallied German youth around him ... "

So he must have been thinking aloud once again, or at least revealing a part of what was in his mind. He will have to be more careful. Don't say too much of what you think, or not even enough.

When you said "I take you", he thinks – and this time does not say it – I understood it to mean rather: "I keep you ... "

"And now I'm going to lose you," he says. Here I am being formal again, as I don't know when I'm thinking and when I'm speaking. And because I'm always formal with someone I'm about to be separated from. I'm going to lose you, after possessing you for a brief moment, for a whole night. It's scandalous, of course, to own someone. But isn't it almost as unbearable to lose them afterwards? Perhaps we know nothing, Renate, of the immensity and the diversity of the scandals which we cause and suffer. When I say: 'I'm leaving you,' am I saying : 'I'm liberating you', or rather: 'I'm abandoning you'?"

Long after Renate had left, there was only her cheap, sweet scent floating in the four rooms of the doctor's apartment at 12, Belle-Alliance-Strasse. Far more noxious than the smell of the alcohol drunk there between 31 December 1926 and 1 January 1927. Little by little, the place began to smell of illness more than of love. It doesn't leave an aftertaste of ashes, thought the doctor pacing the deserted surgery, but of blood. And I know what I'm talking about, he soliloquised. He even added: It smells of a blood transfusion.

Then he remembered that the girl had wanted to give her blood for her country, and that her country had refused the gift, in consideration of her line of work.

She's had her revenge, he thought. She has given her blood; we have lived it together.

When she said goodbye, on 1 January 1927, the girl left behind a little handbag of embroidered taffeta: was it a wallet or a make-up case? It contained only a luminous lipstick, a nail-file with a handle of imitation mother-of-pearl, a nickel pessary, two latex condoms and three ten-mark notes rolled into a ball.

The woman Renate had not been content with not being paid for her services. She had left behind her takings, perhaps the income from a whole day of love. How shall I find her, he wondered, to return it to her?

Yes, how was he to make it up to her?

Hamburg, 1936

The Error

"We've each done half the journey," observes the father, as he invites Nele to sit down on the bench facing him.

Recalling the conversation later, she was to wonder if he had not been playing on words even then. Indeed, what multiple paths might he not have been alluding to?

And he himself had thought back to that day about ten years before when he had had the cruel and exhilarating feeling of having reached the summit of existence, so that there was now only the long descent on the shadow-side of things ... But it was only today that he had crossed the threshold of hell.

"All the same," she says, "it would have been simpler for you to ask me to come to Hanover."

"It was better that we met again in Hamburg," he replies.

Beside the sea she had only had to cross from Copenhagen to throw herself into his arms. As if only the sea separated them. He does not confess that, earlier, he would have been ashamed to receive her in his little furnished apartment in Hohenzollernstrasse, where he did his own housework. And that now that he is living in a *pension* in the Arnstwalderstrasse, he would still have been embarrassed.

As if she has guessed his thought, she insists:

"We could have gone to the Café Kröpke, I've heard it's very welcoming ... "

"An oasis in a desert!" he declares.

He is surprised to hear himself so cravenly disowning a city that has been hospitable to him, and that he still cherishes. That is how you treat a mistress whom you have in your blood but believe unworthy of you. As for the restaurant she mentioned, he doesn't tell her that he was there two days before and had borrowed a copy of the *Berliner Tageblatt* from a patient of his sitting at the next table, to keep abreast of things being hatched in the capital. In it he came across a tribute to himself on the occasion of his fiftieth birthday. The article underlined, without disagreement, the distinction drawn by the poet between the practical and spiritual worlds: which of them seemed finally more real? The writer showed a certain courage in insinuating, in May 1936 in Berlin, that it was still permitted to formulate such radical extravagances. For proof of his courage, it was enough to scan the reports published elsewhere in the paper on subjects such as the re-occupation of the Rhineland, the triumphant parade of the Panzer division on Unter den Linden, a final evaluation of the Winter Olympics at Garmisch-Partenkirchen, or the preparations for the summer Games in an almost Mycenaean setting. Not to mention those for the next rally of the National Socialist Party in Nuremberg ... Somehow, into the midst of this full programme, had been slipped the incongruous or anachronistic salute to a "fifty-year-old poet": what dissonance! But it had touched the heart of the poet in question, after the disapproving silence or discredit his last collection had earned him in journals more adept at saying what one was supposed to think or not think in Germany today. And he, usually so indifferent to what reviews said about his work, had asked the reader of the *Berliner Tageblatt* if he would let him keep the copy, had hastily left the leafy pavilion of the Café Kröpke and returned to his *pension*. There he had reread the article at his leisure and, unobserved by others, had carefully cut it out, thinking: I'll take it to Hamburg to show it to Nele, since she must have heard a lot of adverse comment about her father. Perhaps it will help to calm her ...

But, naturally, as he was leaving he had forgotten to put the article in his case.

In any case, Nele had not heard of the invective being launched against him.

"At any rate, not recently," she adds. "And then, it always

surprises me, but in Copenhagen no one knows I'm the daughter of a great poet!"

The poet thinks: No one in Denmark or elsewhere is going to risk trying to rectify that in the coming years ...

He looks at his daughter curiously, then with pride. He smiles. They had already spent two days together, but had not talked about anything, immersed in the quiet joy of being together. Gradually, however, the silence had become oppressive. For both of them, something was lurking out of sight, that both had decided not to mention.

Now it seemed to be coming out into the open. But unspoken thoughts still made their conversation strained.

"At any rate," he says, "you, at least, haven't changed."

"Not only that," she replies, "but I'm unlikely to have changed."

She said this without smiling. As if it was now her turn to play on words, and she was insinuating that as far as she was concerned she had not changed in any way.

"So, Hanover doesn't deserve its reputation?" she asks with concern.

It's just a charming city, thinks the poet, that can't get over grieving for past splendours. It must be almost pleasantly trite to die there, after Leibniz and the Charlotte dear to Goethe have started the trend.

"A city where even the soul is in barracks, where the soldiers get drunk with gloomy dedication. After a spell in the vomitory they immediately start drinking again. But you can see the *Bal masqué* at the Opera and Hans Albers in the role of Peer Gynt at the cinema. At the theatre, *Pygmalion*, with Gustav Gründgens and Jenny Juge."

He cuts his evocation short. He wonders in the name of what disappointed passion, what extinct ideal, a whole city could give itself up like this to a nostalgia without object. You are drawn into it despite yourself. Is it the echoes of bugles in the barracks' courtyards, the smell of graves in which you no longer know who is lying?

"They've little liking for Berliners there!" he declares, to break the silence. "Something that ought to be noted in the next edition of *Baedeker* ... "

"In my opinion," Nele remarks, "Berliners are not much liked anywhere nowadays. Do you miss Berlin?"

How seriously she asked that!

"I miss the swans and the crows bickering on the banks of the Lietzensee ... I'm even nostalgic for the smell of cold smoke that hangs around the railway stations."

These topographical references. This gravity in Nele. She seems on her guard like a woman watching for the first assault by an over-enterprising admirer.

"But what about you? How do you like Hamburg now?"

This time she does not reply. She is much too afraid of offending him. How can she explain to her father that as soon as she had set foot on land she had been afraid of the city with its canals and winding streets, its patrician dwellings and its domes covered in verdigris, that had seemed to her like a Copenhagen swollen out of all proportion, inhabited by giants? At once, she resented Copenhagen for being no more than a Hamburg for children, well-behaved as a picture, the capital of a Germany without Germany. Ah, it was Hamburg she feared, of course! When she blamed the whole of Germany for being the country of her so terribly German father.

"I was afraid we wouldn't be able to celebrate your birthday on the right day. A last-minute hitch. But I rushed here all the same ... "

"I too had some worries that almost prevented me from coming ... "

"Recent worries?"

"Nothing really serious, yet. And then a funeral ... The time it took for Spengler to be buried."

"A friend of yours? Is it serious?"

Charming little girl of hardly more than twenty: each time he tells her a piece of news, she starts by asking: Is it serious? She gives him a slightly contrite look.

"A friend, yes, in a sense. I was really a friend of his thought. He had seen, like me, that the fruit of civilisation was worm-eaten. That History was just a drifting. And progress a mental point of view. That the West needed to reconsider all its values in the dark glow of its death throes. He resisted better than I did, and earlier, the siren songs of the wearers of leather breeches. He even preferred to drown himself in the aristocratic comforts the vanity of which he had been the first to denounce. It's like this: we Germans are going to be separated from each other by the way we have marked out our territory in the realm of error. Oswald Spengler took his leave at the right moment: it is better, sometimes, not to have to verify the accuracy of one's predictions. You've a right to ditch the world once you have unmasked it. It's for us to survive with the memory of our errings, our groping in the dark. It's for us to witness to its end the tragedy whose dénouement others were better able to foresee, and left the theatre in the interval. Some didn't even take so long to bow out. Kurt Tucholsky, for example. A long time ago, he wrote: "I believe that all is error." Later he noted: "If I were to die, I should say: I didn't really understand." He left this country at a point when he had at least a presentiment of the scenes that were to be enacted. But he missed his native country. He came back once before taking his life. Had he stopped understanding in the meantime, or had he understood too well? I leave you to judge. It's sometimes the fate of those who understand too soon, before everyone else, to believe in the end that they ought not to have seen things so clearly. It would be too dreadful to have been right to that extent! 'The bourgeois age is departing,' he remarked fifteen years ago. 'No one knows what is coming. Where are we going? For a long time we have not been at the helm, we govern and control nothing.' At that time I did not read this writer. I only discovered him recently. I've had some leisure time since I've been living in Hanover. So on the quiet I read those I used to think – or assumed – were at the opposite pole to myself. That is sometimes quite a revelation. About myself, I mean. Among other things. Of course, I talk to no one about this. Who would have suspected me of reading such books? Certainly not those who will later be said to have known me best! But, my poor girl, you can't find my conversation very cheerful. I assure you not everyone is dead, and the living don't normally think as I do. Some didn't feel driven to suicide, and simply took the path of exile, as you know. By the way, do you still sometimes get news of Paul Hindemith?"

Nele does not reply at once. She wants to take her time.

So here we are, she thinks. He's going to talk about it. About Hindemith to start with and then all the rest. He won't be able to stop himself now. That's even the reason why he expressed the wish to celebrate his fiftieth birthday in a tête-à-tête with me, though he didn't realise it. He'll talk only about himself. From now on that's all that will interest him.

Revolt vies in her with weariness. Why me? she wonders. Why did he choose me to be his listener? After all, didn't he banish me from Germany after Mother's death, and hasn't he always kept me at a distance? Without intending to he has given me the chance to lead a non-German life; why should he recapture me so easily? Once again, he's going to try to make up for years of absence with two hours of excessive presence. Once again he's going to treat me *like* his daughter. Oh, that disarming nature of his that allows him to pick up with me each time as if he had left me the day before. Whereas I need some time to get used to my father again. Really, he has only sent for me so that he can talk to me about Hindemith, and then all the rest. He won't spare me a single detail. Hasn't he a woman in his life, to listen to him? He has always had women ... And I've sworn to myself never to be jealous. But he leaves his women, one after the other, and always comes back to me. He treats me like the only woman he could be faithful to. A terrible fidelity. So heavy to bear.

She is almost angry with herself for accepting him again so

easily, for acknowledging him, beyond all possible denial, as the author of her days and nights. She is face to face again with this man whose profound charm is acting on her once more. He's not a stranger to her, that is the least she can admit to herself. Everything except a stranger – alas. A moment ago, she was asking herself why she had come. Surely not to hear Dr Benn evoking Hanover, celebrating Hamburg, or expressing his regret for Berlin. Nor to listen to his impressions of reading Tucholsky . . .

And so, suddenly: Do you still get news from Paul Hindemith? It wouldn't have taken much for him to ask: Do you, at least, still get news from "my" friend Paul Hindemith?

What it must have cost him to ask the question! So much that she wonders if it would be right to reveal a truth that could only wound him. At the same time, she cannot arrogate the right to conceal it, making her father's show of courage futile. Because, of course, she still gets news from the composer – even more often than he did. She receives it from Turkey, where the most Germanic of German composers is residing until further notice, ostracised by his own country. He is hoping to go to Switzerland. He has been invited to settle in the United States. But wherever he went, he would never be able to prevent himself from being German. According to his wife, who also corresponds affectionately with Nele, wherever he is Paul believes he is in Germany. No one could resign himself less to exile! He carries in his baggage a country that now lives only in his memories, a Germany that no longer exists.

"Let's not talk about that," says the father, as if he already regretted having broached a delicate subject. "What would you like to eat, my dear. A cheese salad? Roast pork with cro-quettes? I advise you to avoid mincemeat: it could be half a harbour rat! Or what about some eel *au vert*?"

"In Hamburg," Nele decrees peremptorily, "I prefer fish."

"Halibut in remoulade sauce, then? Or braised salmon – yes?

Preceded by eel soup with apricot. We'll wash it down with a bottle of Trollinger."

"Wouldn't that be rather expensive?" she demurs.

"Nothing will be dear enough tonight, my child, as I'm the one being fêted! Make the most of it – we won't be eating sausages made of wood shavings, as in Berlin, or beer extracted from cow's urine ... "

"You know, Father, I mainly correspond with Gertrud. I was fifteen when we met Paul and his wife, and like all schoolgirls of that age I laughed too much, all the time, without reason. He impressed me a lot, but he must have taken me for what I still was: a very young girl, inclined to be mischievous and a little too noisy ... "

"He even thought you so immature," the father observes, "that at the end of our first visit to him in Charlottenburg he insisted on us accompanying him to the Staatbibliothek so that he could show you some original scores by Bach, Mozart and Beethoven which are normally inaccessible to the public ... He really must have thought you a silly goose!"

"But Father, it was you he most wanted to show them to! You were going to collaborate, he wanted to share his admirations, his strongest emotions with you. I was just the great poet's daughter, whom he had enough tact not to send back to her toys."

"Yet he offered to let you play with the electric train he was so proud of. Of the two of you, the child was Paul Hindemith. He was very disappointed that you didn't take it more seriously."

"It was a toy for grown-ups," Nele retorts sombrely. "There seem to be a lot of them in Germany these days. Goering too has his Märklin train-set. He plays the controls like a harmonium keyboard, to the astonishment of foreign visitors. The Danish papers talk of nothing else."

"You draw some odd comparisons," remarks her father. "Goering and Hindemith – I don't know which of them would be more horrified ... But you were telling me that

Gertrud had been writing to you often, for a long time? For her, too, you can only have been a child. Yet now you're exchanging letters from the Bosphorus to the Baltic ... "

"Gertrud was different. I wasn't only a child like the others, since she became in a sense my mother. My German mother, as I no longer had one, only a Danish mother ... "

They fall silent, giving themselves a respite. The father feels encircled. The image of Ellen Overgaard has risen up between his daughter and himself, just when he expected it least.

You just need to mention one woman with my father, thinks Nele, and soon they are coming from all sides. He loved the Danish woman just long enough to entrust his daughter's education to her. At the end, he asserted that he had not the right to threaten the Overgaards' conjugal harmony. A curious and belated scruple. You have to know how to end a liaison, he claimed. And in that art he was quite an expert!

"How is Ellen?" the father ventures, with slight apprehension.

"She is still just as kind to me. And just as strong."

And strong is what she had to be, thinks Nele. When she grapples with her memories. My God, Father, she thinks, I've been brought up by a woman who sang Wagner and admired only you! Sometimes I have seen her devastated by the passion you inspired in her ... That is what I am up against. It's no use living far away from you – will I never escape you?

"Let's come back to the 'German mother'," says the father. "Is she still that, now that she is in Istanbul and may tomorrow go to Geneva or Washington?"

"Because my German mother is also my half-Jewish mother," Nele replies, "one of those the Fatherland no longer wants on its soil ... You surely won't hold that against her? You know, not so long ago I must really have been no more than a baby to her. When she spoke to me, everything became 'little' in her mouth: Would you like a little soup, my little girl?

Have you a little headache? Perhaps you ought to take a little aspirin? I'm sure you would like us to go to see a little play together? 'Little, perhaps, I'm sure' – everything seemed tiny and uncertain to her. That must be the kind of person that Great Germany is rejecting now." After a silence she adds: "I don't mean to say that she was affected or fussy. She wasn't even very sentimental. But she was fond of me."

My God, thinks Nele, perhaps I've only denied that woman's romantic nature to defend her against my unromantic father ... No, it isn't even that. It was to hide my own romantic side ... I've crossed the sea to tell him my Danish love story, that ends so sadly ... I would have liked him to console the Little Mermaid drowning in her own despair. She fell in love with a married man. She had to break off ... But my father has only his own story in his head, his political story, which also ended badly ... I won't tell him.

How my little girl has grown up, thinks the father. How she has matured, far from me in a foreign country. I read the letters she sends me now as if they came from an unknown woman that I would like to meet.

"You know, father, I think Gertrud's still writing to me mainly to preserve the link between you and Paul Hindemith."

"Why?" the father asks rather brusquely. "Can't he write to me himself? Doesn't he know my address in Hanover?"

"Ah – you've every right to reproach him, haven't you? You resent everyone who left. As if they had the choice!"

She has almost shouted ... but not from anger. From sorrow. Someone at the next table has turned to look. For young women are brought up not to raise their voices in Germany now. Except, of course, when they are proclaiming their love for the new State being built before their eyes. On that occasion, they can give voice. It's only natural that such a spectacle should draw a cry from them ...

The father is angry with himself for having added this "little injustice" – as Gertrud Hindemith would have called it – to the great injustice that surrounds them: for pointing the finger of public accusation at a victim. He's ashamed of having resorted to a procedure that others, on a different scale, have turned into a system of government. But as his daughter's reaction stirs what is best in him, he only half regrets it. How could he suspect that she had shouted, almost shouted, against the injustice that had been done to her? The injustice of being unable to confide the secret that had haunted her cruise on the Baltic: Father, in my last letters I wrote that it was still cold in Copenhagen, but that I never tired of seeing the sea as it stretched away at Charlottenlund. I told you that the winter seemed interminable, and that only the terrible storms broke its monotony. I was trying to tell you about a quite different winter. It was the passing of love that I wanted to describe. I told you I was thinking about you all the time. It wasn't true. That I felt guilty about not writing to you more often. But what could I have told you? I assured you that sometimes I felt homesick, that I was afraid of forgetting my German, that I often found it difficult to picture you in Berlin or Hanover ... So many lies. I didn't imagine you anywhere. I was in love with a charming man whom I believed capable of passion. Had I confided in you, you would only have tried to dissuade me from loving love. I hate the pragmatic male turn of mind! How can I suffer so much from a malady that only seems to have brushed you occasionally? Was it that adorable mother who died much too soon, whom I hardly had time to get to know, who bequeathed me that?

"I recall," she says, "that the last phrase of the Ninth Symphony was locked away separately, in a metal casket. You could also read some extracts from Beethoven's diary at the Library – they were heartbreaking ... Shouldn't we fear that the new Minister of Propaganda will throw all that on the fire, or at least put it on the Index?"

"The diary is in some danger," her father replies. "It's a bit too sad not to appear slightly 'degenerate'? But not the *Ode to Joy* – certainly not. Isn't it on the programme to be conducted by the maestro Richard Strauss at the inauguration of the Olympics? Directly after the *Horst Wessel Song*. What a consecration! For Beethoven, I mean ... "

"What did you write about his music?" asks Nele.

"Beethoven's?"

"No, Hindemith's ... "

"He composed from my words. It's not easy to work with a musician. The poem precedes the music, but at the same time it has to anticipate it, presuppose it. I tried to hear in my mind the melodies the composer would articulate around my verse. I almost gave up several times. And then, just as I was about to throw in the towel, I thought of a lyric poem on the lines of what I was thinking at that time about the incessant flux of History, the perpetual, ineluctable meaninglessness of events, the hazardous instability of all terrestrial existence, the random, exaggerated nature of all greatness and fame ... A homage, if you like, to the eternal recurrence of human stupidity and divine cynicism! To my great surprise, Paul declared himself very satisfied.

> 'Farewell, early days that nestled
> filled with summer and contented
> peaceful landscape in the
> childish dreamy hand ...' etc.

I was still taking refuge in nostalgia ... I was doubtful about presenting my weightiest secrets through Paul's music. Anyway, he left out what I had expected to be most contentious:

> 'What say you of the rolling bilge of history
> first wine, then blood: the Nibelungen feast
> banquets and murders, orgies and judgements,
> roses and vines still wreathing the hall ... '

The Nazis would find that very 'out of date'! One can't

imagine verse like that being declaimed in a monumental decor designed by Albert Speer, by some actor with a nose and beard from the gladiators sculpted by Breker or Thorak, while the party officials appeal to the vigour of 'World Youth'! It would be downright provocation. But in 1932, under Otto Klemperer, you could still assert the tragic character of all destiny without causing a scandal ... Now that a tragedy on a global scale is being premeditated, it's that unhappy conscience that has to be outlawed!"

"There's something I don't understand," says Nele. "If the musician was felt to be a 'Cultural Bolshevik', how did the poet manage to stay? You're no less 'decadent' than Paul, I believe?"

"Oh, you can show me what's really on your mind and ask: You're no less decadent than Paul, I hope? Well, let me reassure you: the most decadent of German poets is still in Germany. Some of those who have fled or were banished – the Brechts, Bechers, Zweigs, Döblins, Werfels and Feuchtwangers, or the entire Mann family – couldn't match him, despite their talent, for philosophical degeneracy or moral putrefaction – not by a long chalk. That particular maggot has stayed in the apple! But have no fear, the censors are keeping watch! I didn't want to mention it, so as not to cast a shadow over your little stay in Hamburg, but the day before I got here a propitious wind brought me the news that any day now I'm going to be insulted in the official party journals. It seems I'll be called a swine, my works abject Jewish vermin ... I've seen it coming for some time. But I didn't know where the blow was to fall."

"And I thought you were grieving over the journals' silence about your jubilee ... "

"Well, as you see, they haven't forgotten it. They're going to celebrate it in their own way! The same magazines that never run out of soothing greetings to the foreigners who will visit 'a hospitable land that knows no hate' this summer, under the aegis of the Hitlerian eagles entwined with the Olympic rings, will castigate in my person the most innovatory current in poetry since Rilke and Stefan George. And talking about Stefan George, in 1934 I was expressly forbidden to give his eulogy."

Now it's his turn to shout. He is standing up. In the wall mirror above the bench on which his daughter is sitting he sees his own flushed face.

He's shouting, yelping with fear, she has time to think, caught in the trap he has set for himself.

However, he sits down and goes on in a hoarse voice:

"Before that, I was struck off the list of the Association of National Socialist Doctors. From 1933 I was forbidden to diagnose or write certificates or prescriptions. The quack disbarred. They claimed he had Jewish origins. For the same reason the writer was denied admission to the Union of Nationalist Writers. The poet nailed to the pillory! Caught between two fires! That left one way out: the army. Paradoxically. A way of being a doctor again, but in uniform, in the provinces. However, as you can observe, inclusion in the ranks of the Wehrmacht does not always protect you from insults and defamation! An officer to whom I unburdened myself about the threats hanging over me, that seemed to come from the SS mouthpiece, replied: "It would be worse if they praised you ... Insults coming from those people are better than any approval. A true accolade!" One day it will be necessary for historiographers to study the tributes and judgements that the various bodies representing the Third Reich passed on each other. When one is tempted to roll them all into one, it will be useful to remember those differences ... "

He stops for a moment, out of breath. He looks at his daughter, who is listening avidly. Her cheeks are crimson. There are tears in her eyes. They might be of anger, sadness, or humiliation. Could he suspect that she actually feels relief? Almost pride?

"Of course," says her father, "I didn't have too much trouble proving that I wasn't Jewish ... "

"How did you do it?" asks Nele.

The Error

"I reconstructed my whole family tree ... After that I was rehabilitated for a time, and even appointed president of an association that had wanted to exclude me the day before. But in it I was given tasks which amounted almost to policing. I had to purge the organisation of the 'corrupting elements' that were supposed to be making it gangrenous. Soon I proposed that the body be simply dissolved, and when I joined the *Wehrmacht* I tendered my resignation from it and from the Prussian Academy of Arts. I practised an aristocratic form of 'inner emigration'."

"In the end," says Nele, "you didn't gain anything by demonstrating your Aryan credentials ..."

A very relative kind of "aristocracy", she thinks, and in a moment feels herself drenched in sweat.

"Come on, Father, think a little. Almost all your friends – and even your editor – are Jews!"

"That too," he exclaims, "they – even you – are turning against me. I am the only friend Carl Einstein, to mention but one name, still has in Berlin."

But that didn't prevent my father, thinks Nele, from establishing an Aryan pedigree ... Where does anti-Semitism begin? It would have taken only one more step in that direction and, all unawares, he would have crossed the borderline of the intolerable.

"Father, why didn't you just let them say it?"

"The fact is that I really am not Jewish ... And rightly or wrongly I wanted to stay. I was afraid of losing my surgery. I lost it anyway ... But I didn't feel I had the right to leave. I thought I had to live out my destiny in Germany. I still think so."

Ah, that terrible, confusing Prussian naivety! thinks Nele. He justifies himself in such good faith. No opportunism. Not a trace of calculation. Will people find excuses for him later? And is it for me to decide?

"Was that the price you had to pay to stay in the Academy?" she asks. "Was the Academy so important?"

The poet does not reply. What could he say, anyway? That he sincerely believed the noble institution to be a citadel protecting what was left of the German soul? Or that in getting admitted the son of a Neumark pastor had simply realised a dream of his youth that he was incapable of renouncing?

"When Hitler came to power, by legal means, in January 1933, Heinrich Mann resigned. I thought he was playing politics ... That the decision concerned him alone."

"And you thought that by not resigning you weren't playing politics?"

"It was like that at first, yes," her father conceded.

For a moment Nele is almost sorry for him.

"Father," she asks, "what would have happened to you if the people in power hadn't chosen to inflict all this on you?"

"But, my darling, the question doesn't even arise. In view of my writings and simple logic, theirs and mine, the Nazis couldn't avoid inflicting all this on me!"

Nele thinks: this slope he's hurtling down, he must have climbed it first ... Why doesn't he say anything about that?

"Didn't you see what kind of regime you were cautioning, Father, or what pledges you were giving it? Do you remember what we said when I visited you in Berlin two years ago? Some brownshirts marched under your window in Belle-Alliance-Strasse. I told you how worried I was. You confessed that we ought to be far more worried than we were, living abroad. When we parted you confessed that you had committed a terrible error – and you didn't think fit to give me any explanations. I was still a child ... I was terrified. This evening you must tell me about it. I have never asked anything of you, but I ask you now. What you don't confide to me tonight you may not have a chance to tell me for a long time ... "

The quinquagenarian thinks: What I don't confide to you tonight I shall, no doubt, never confess to anyone.

"What I'm going to reveal to you," he tells her, "you might do well to forget, for a long time."

He is surprised by the solace he feels. So it was that, he thinks, that she had come seeking, that she came to give him, that May evening in 1936, in Hamburg.

It's really him I'm doing it for, she tells herself. For in another moment I should have done anything to get this weight off me. If he had any idea how it crushes me.

He had been professing for so long that the artist should withdraw himself from History, should not place himself in the service of "causes which exist only in the discourse of technicians and warriors" who are trying to mask their worst abuses with humanistic verbiage.

"Nele, look where that whole fine world, with its invigorating slogans and cheerful mottoes, has dragged us! Why didn't I remain suspicious, secure in my old positions! My real undoing was that I suddenly began to doubt them. Yes, I doubted the powers of intelligence. I'd had enough of being right against the world for so long. I wanted to take part in the world's error rather than not be wrong against it ... I who was sickened by the violence of the species at work, was tempted to join in. I picked, of course, the very worst moment.

"Oh, it wasn't one of those spectacular conversions! If I had been carried away by a fit of romantic enthusiasm, borne along in the tumult that passed over our nation, it would be easier to explain. But no one ought to have known better than I how to unmask the totalitarian lies that the events sprang from.

"It all happened when I was passing through a trough, a period of near somnolence. I lacked conviction. I was dying of boredom. It's a dangerous state. One should never be absent-minded. That kind of laziness is the mother of all abdications. You can trip yourself up in a way that decides your whole destiny. There are flashes of blindness as there are flashes of genius. They are the illumination of the imbecile. The word illumination has two senses: one refers to light, the other to darkness. And our way of seeing is such that it can, against all reason, mistake one for the other ... "

If you stumble once, he thinks, it's for ever. Really, we only appear to be awake. It's a mask. A sluggard's ruse. In fact, we are asleep on our feet. We've only got one eye open. Our most abominable crimes are often committed in a kind of torpor. And even our noblest and most generous acts are performed in haggard somnambulism.

"I was writing too little," he went on. "But I was working for the radio. Without realising it I was degrading, impoverishing my speech, spreading it too thin. The microphone is a cannibal mouth. You learn to talk about anything. So you say nothing. You never have more than one single thing to say, and you forget what it is. You merely formulate all the rest. You emit propaganda for the void. At one time Paul Hindemith helped me to fight against this wastage of energy, by getting me a commission for a libretto for an oratorio. I thought I no longer had it in me. I excused myself with this or that broadcast – about the creative genius, mind you! – to put off starting the project. Little by little I seemed to be getting a grip on myself again. I took care not to sound off on everything and nothing with the same aplomb. I wanted to find a subject to write about, a single one: mine. It was already too late. Unwittingly, I was ripe to conspire against myself. Instead of campaigning for the rule of imagination against the senselessness of History, as I had done earlier, I now rejoiced that there was only History left through which to think! It was an abdication, pure and simple. In the fight between me and Germany, I had felt called upon to support Germany! I sawed off the branch I was sitting on ... Incidentally, it was on the radio that I gave my listeners the good news. My voice didn't even tremble."

"But you must have been put under pressure," says Nele. "Weren't you forced to say what you did?"

"Not in the least! I surrendered to a regime that despised my kind, but didn't need to use any coercion to make me submit ... I was impressed by the youth that was rising up everywhere in a country that seemed to have had its future restored. Have I always been deluded like that? No, it was the only time I was to err. The murderous idea of a tragic clown, soon to be shared by a whole people, was swallowed by nothingness – but this time nothingness on a national scale. I thought I could see the Greece of the Doric age being reborn in Germany: art was no longer to be left in the margin of life, on the threshold of the house of mankind! What Faustian artist has not, in a moment of dizziness, thought of immolating his lucidity on the altar of a universe he imagines suddenly regressing towards its first dawn? He weeps in seeming rapture. His tears blur his view, hide the future charnel houses. He believes he is savouring the flesh of the cosmos. He does not know that he is already eating his own corpse."

"But why," asks Nele, "why this irony against – against yourself, or rather ... "

"This masochism, do you mean? Yes, let's say the word: masochism. The old illness of the melancholic intellectual. It has happened to others as well. It will happen again ... And then ... And then it was suddenly possible to believe that the most humiliated, the most dishonoured, the most demoralised of countries was experiencing its resurrection. Others might be troubled to see the German Lazarus rise up and walk, even if to a tune dedicated to Horst Wessel, that notorious pimp. But didn't the Jacobins, too, sometimes pick the wrong martyrs? Was not banal reality about to become human, superhuman? Had not I, as Zarathustra instructed, saved a possible chance in me so that a star might shine, a dancing star? I did not guess that it would be a *danse macabre*. That the regime was using the cloak of irrationalism to camouflage a homicidal logic."

"All the same," Nele objects, "you can't say that the Führer disguised himself as a gallant knight ... "

"It's true that the ventriloquist Superman has never quite

managed to hide the marionette squealing inside him. So he doesn't need to bother now. Once we have been told the production of the *Götterdämmerung* is sublime, we are less likely to notice that the bass who sings Wotan is a fraud. You wouldn't employ that troll with his blurred features, his greasy streak of hair, his gardener's trousers, as a night-watchman for a cesspit: in our exaltation we've given him the keys of the nation. But look at his drugged eyes: that man dreams, and his hollowest phrases put him in a trance. Paradoxically, that reassures people. The Swabian *petit-bourgeois*, the Westphalian horse knacker, the Heidelberg hotel porter, the revanchist shareholder in Tübingen and the Hamburg pimp – the one drinking his brown ale at the next table, for example – they all think that the bottomless thoughts of that tub-thumper who happens to look like them will tomorrow consume their debts beneath the ashes of their communist neighbour and that they'll be able to break their son's piggy bank over the heads of the Jewish democrats who lorded it over them yesterday. That's the whole of their metaphysics; like the canting ranter Adolf they don't ask for more. Apart from his way of gesticulating like a Bavarian baboon, isn't he magnificently trivial? Of an almost startling, almost grandiose insignificance?"

Why, Nele wonders, why didn't my father paint that portrait in the first place, since he can do it now? Three years ago I was an ignorant young girl, yet I could see it. Was it just that I was in Denmark?

"When Klaus Mann entreated you to distance yourself from those who were flouting all the values you had believed in, why did you not admit he was right? The letter he addressed to you from his exile was still so friendly, so deferential ... He begged you to open your eyes, but he didn't patronise you ... "

"But he wrote to me from down there in the Lavandou, and this was happening here. I thought he was a little too much at his ease, the son of a Goethean high bourgeois, honoured with a Nobel Prize, who had gone off to spread the word on the Côte d'Azur shortly after having approved the de-Judaicising of the legal system and the edict debarring Tucholsky from expressing himself while on German soil. So much for him. The father had little merit in quitting a country he had celebrated in accents of unbridled nationalism from his Munich mansion in 1914 to '18. Between the wars Thomas Mann was still calling Germany's enemies 'crocodiles' and stigmatising 'sticky pacifism' and the 'un-civic' Spartacists, when he was not rounding on the Jews ... The föhn sometimes numbed the wits of the patrician humanist whose exile will always be gilded."

"Klaus isn't Thomas," Nele retorts.

"Of course not," he agrees, "but Klaus was twenty-seven and I might have been his father instead of Thomas. It's not easy to accept the disappointment one arouses in a young man who once idolised you, who has congratulated you the day before on never having compromised, and who still appeals to what he calls your 'fanatical' purity ... You don't respond to attacks that come from too low – but neither can you rebut those that emanate from noble, irreproachable spirits, when they are really addressed to the worthier destiny those souls had dreamed of for you ... Who are we to cut ourselves off from the people? – that's all I asked Klaus in the reply I sent him. It was the SS who replied on his behalf: You are outlawed by the people with whom you claim solidarity. From one shore to the other I had invited Klaus Mann to bid me farewell. And it was the SS who gave me my marching orders. I still believe that those who are to judge Germany tomorrow ought to do it above all from here.

"It's curious, all the same, don't you think, Nele, that from where we are we can't hear even a whisper of the sea?"

Sometimes he believes I can understand everything, thinks Nele. Sometimes he must assume I understand nothing.

"It seems to me that even when you make an effort to put yourself in their place," she says, "you can't help being down on the exiles ... "

"I'm not talking about the ones who had no choice. But some who weren't obliged to leave might have tried to express themselves here, or to share in our silence. Were all the poets of this country supposed to abandon it to its fate? Despite appearances, it's not a simple problem. One might perhaps be glad that some at least have chosen to stay, to witness the end of the drama. Some others didn't have a ˙chance to get out ... There are some who wouldn't even have had the train fare. To regroup where in the world? There are some whom you would have killed by uprooting them. All are no more equal before exile than before terror."

Is it really for him to think that? she asks herself. The future will give the answer. There are moments when I understand him. There are others when I no longer understand him at all. It's a wound that is constantly being re-opened.

"I'm sure you know the painter Otto Dix," he says. "During the Great War he found himself, like me, in Belgium. He had even volunteered, as he was afraid of 'missing the action'. The idea of facing the enemy fired his enthusiasm. And then he brought back the most frightening canvases ever conceived. By comparison, some of Goya's paintings on *The Disasters of War* seem almost reassuring ... Doctor Goebbels threatened to set light to some of his works. (Goering, at the same time, was probably seizing others to hang them secretly in his private museum.) Nevertheless, Dix did not leave. 'In face of this country's landscapes,' he said, 'I stand transfixed like a cow.' We'll need some of those cows to attest that those landscapes once existed ... "

For some moments, his daughter has not been listening to the man who is speaking. Who is struggling, floundering ... A moment ago, she felt bitterness begin to rise up in her. Father, she thinks, you could have been a guide. I could have learned so much from you. That you removed me from your life, that you preserved your solitude – I could have accepted it in the end. But that you lapsed into error as soon as you were alone I find insupportable. I am alone now too. Maybe solitude is hereditary. Error is not.

Landscapes, the man is thinking. Sometimes one ought to attend to them more than to mental states ... While he walked in the spacious avenues of Hanover, past the old Renaissance houses or the statues in the park at Herrenhausen: fine-buttocked Dianas, full-breasted Neptunes, big-bellied Herculeses, or when he lost himself in the country that reminded him of the enchanted hours of childhood, he thought of the time when nothing had yet happened: neither the loss of his mother nor the hatred of his father, neither his passion for medicine nor the first line of a single poem, nor the meeting with a woman, then another, then another again – nor the error of a lifetime – the time when all was still possible. And he thought: beyond all that, yet closer as well, is the man whose eyes swept the Theatre Square or the town hall, the gardens of the Stadthalle, the façade of Wolf's wine-cellar or the yellow water of the Leine, one spring morning in 1936; those impressions are what is best and most intact in you, but no one will know them, and it will be as if no one had ever known you. Nevertheless, what mysterious joy, even if nothing of you were to remain but a glance cast at the staircase of the Opera or the glass roof of the station, in the heart of the old Guelph city! An image that caressed your heart for the length of a blink – you would have preserved it. A crumb of innocence that had escaped your carnivore teeth. Your only acquittal.

"I'm sure this will surprise you," he says, "but when I received Klaus Mann's letter the first thing that struck me was the address of the sender: Hôtel de la Tour, Sanary-sur-Mer (Var). A few years earlier I had myself made a short trip to the south of France. One of the rare escapades I permitted myself, as you know ... But Sanary did not ring a bell. And when we got the first news of the German emigrants in Provence – Schickele, Toller, Neumann, Ludwig Marcuse and others – and became familiar with the places where they were staying – Toulon, Cannes, Saint-Raphaël, Roquebrune, La Ciotat – I was surprised never to recognise any of the towns I had passed through in 1928 or 1929: Hendaye or Palavas-les-Flots, Arcachon or Biarritz ... I found it frustrating that I couldn't imagine them in places that had grown familiar to me. For the first time I took the full measure of their absence. Most of them had views very far from mine, and had become, by force of circumstance, my ideological adversaries. Now three-quarters of German literature had left; these men had made what from their point of view was the right choice, and I could not even picture them in a definite landscape. Their south of France was not mine; in that too we were apart ... And most of them had left in haste, thinking that Hitler would leave the stage one day and that everything would be back to normal after their brief excursion. Their way of being duped was doubtless more 'respectable' than mine, but it tends to prove that when they were caught out by events practically none of the poets of this country kept a clear head ... You know too that they have sometimes had a frosty welcome in fraternal, egalitarian France ... "

"They left without arms or luggage," says Nele hoarsely. "It was often dramatically painful for them to part from their books ... They say that Walter Benjamin copied out some of them in minuscule writing in notebooks, and sent others to Bertolt Brecht in Copenhagen. For I'm sure you are not unaware that Brecht has settled in Denmark?"

"I heard about it, yes," declares Gottfried Benn.

For a moment he imagines the author of *Mahagonny* sighting the Little Mermaid from the bridge of a ferry as dawn breaks.

Nothing is simple: this vision fills him with nostalgia.

"Father?"

"Yes."

"When did you understand?"

She's right, of course, to attach importance to chronology ...

She's less concerned to know when I understood than when I ought to have understood! When I had to, if I was not to be discredited in my own eyes.

"Sometimes I think I knew at once. But it was too late, the damage was done."

"*Le mal était fait,*" he repeats, the French phrase coming into his mind. He recalls a day of idleness in Hanover when, having opened a French-German dictionary, he had read the heading: *faire.* He had gone no further, but had memorised the whole entry. *Faire sa vie, faire son malheur, faire l'amour, faire le mort, faire nuit noire ... Savoir-faire ... C'est chose faite, le mal est fait, ce qui est fait est fait ...* He had been struck by the fact that you could say that *le mal est fait* but you could not *défaire le mal,* you could never undo the havoc you had wrought.

Yes, that's how it must have happened, thinks Nele. Doubt had gnawed at him right from the start, but little by little. But he must have striven to resist it with all his might. A desperate flight forwards, towards the abyss.

Germany, he thinks, is the land of impatience. The Germans are always in a hurry: to fight, to be defeated ... to be lost. It's only much more slowly that they then try to redeem them-selves. We are going to be judged by the date on which we chose to start being clear-sighted.

"There were those, of course, who knew in advance. Even before Hitler came on to the scene. Those who refused to acknowledge his rise to power. Not later than the burning of the "corrupting" books exactly three years ago, I ought to have come down from the clouds: what kind of writer accepts that books can be burned? Yet I accepted it. They weren't my books – yet. The Reichstag fire, three months earlier, ought to have made me see: I just affected wide-eyed surprise. But it should have been enough to read *Mein Kampf* to understand: poets are wrong not to read best-sellers. There is a disdain that can cost very dear. In the end, it was the assassins of Walter Rathenau who declared war on us, no matter what we may have thought of the victim."

"Instead of which," Nele puts in, "you waited for what to happen?"

"Like many others, I didn't start realising until the Night of the Long Knives: that was also the night of the slow learners! Suddenly, doubt was no longer permitted. We became citizens of a self-murdering country. Those who did not wake up that night surely missed the last station at which they might still have got off the runaway train. Like that SA man who died by firing squad crying: '*Heil Hitler!*', so deeply was the lie imprinted in his bones."

"But why didn't you proclaim your change of heart at the time?"

"My dear girl, when a poet has blundered as grossly as I had – so much more grossly than those who hate us maintain – he no longer has any choice as to the time or the place where he is to set the record straight. My poetry alone will reply on my behalf. It is my only truth. It knows which camp I belong to, and should I forget it again, it at least will continue to know. Would you like proof? I was blacklisted by the powers of darkness even before I had offended against them. I had given them pledges, yet suddenly I was no longer allowed to be a dermatologist in Berlin, or a poet anywhere in Germany! To tell the truth, these measures do honour to my censors. They prove them to be more discerning than I was. If I deluded myself at first about them, they did not for long have illusions about me ... If they in their turn have recanted and rehabilitated me, it was the result of a lamentable misunderstanding. The final outcome can hardly be in doubt!"

May they rather persecute you, up to a point! Just as much as it takes ... thinks Nele. She is not even shocked to think it. If they harass you, you are saved: your persecutors will have helped you. If they ever rehabilitate you, you are lost.

He falls silent. He has explained himself. For the first time and, he believes, the last. He won't say another word in his own defence. The only thing he might have added was this: I have never dreamed of belonging to a world where the blunder of an intellectual could pass unnoticed. We may suppose that by now the ex-rector of the University of Freiburg/Breisgau, Martin Heidegger, is savouring like me the bitter satisfaction, the ambiguous joy of finding out that an intellectual can never err without consequences ... Such is our formidable privilege. We cannot revoke it without annihilating ourselves. That said, what a windfall for imbeciles: if a great philosopher can make an ass of himself, how reassuring for them! They can talk about that instead of reading his books. Doesn't his *faux pas* relieve them of the obligation? I shall no more envy those who afterwards dismiss their errings as "peccadillos", he thinks, than those who have not compromised themselves at least once in the scandal of the universe ...

To his daughter he would have liked to say also: They have never touched a human body except for what they call love – and they judge. They have not touched one of those bodies corrupted or unravelled by illness – and they condemn. If I am to be judged one day, may it at least be by one whose hands have approached those fallen bodies, and who has listened to their disgrace. For then he will have recognised his own. If I am judged, let it be by one sunk in ignominy who judges another.

"There is a rumour," says Nele in a low voice, "that for the Olympics the Third Reich is going to try to show another face, that the state might be humanised ... "

"There's little hope of that," says her father. "Despite all their propaganda, I fear the Nazis do not love the human body ... The more they pretend to celebrate it, the more they victimise it, and when the time comes they will fall on it like predators. They've nothing but the body on their lips, but only to devour it. I'll wager the young Greek from Pirgos on whom falls the honour of lighting the Olympic flame will be as well built ... as a young German! Did you know that along the route the torch-bearers will take through Germany the peasants have been called upon to refurbish the fronts of their cottages, at their own expense? The 'Beauty of Labour'. Thanksgiving for the harvest. Ripe corn and flower-wreathed adolescent brows. A salute to the spade-holder standing to attention. 'Strength through Joy'. Soldiers watching over the peace of the nation. In a word, the stage-management has been perfected. Revivified antiquity, domes of light, seaside choreographies, tanned leanness, white heroines for mountain films, even the *Schupos* train stark naked on the parade ground of the Belle-Alliance-Platz. But every medal, even an Olympic one, has its reverse side. Those graceful ephebes, their pectorals crossed by a martial baldrick, brandishing resin torches in their cast-bronze fists, and those white-uniformed Gretchens, with their pleated skirts, fitted blouses and berets sideways on their heads, or those nude Amazons with alabaster faces – it seems they are taught to bridle their sexuality the better to shame the gamey generation, rotten with vice, that festered under the Weimar Republic! Well, from what I hear from some of my colleagues, these unprecedentedly abstemious athletes have strangled their instincts to such good effect that amenorrhoea is to be observed among the girls, and the boys exhibit sexual defects. That's where our leaders' hygienic programmes have got them.

> 'But man shall live in grief,
> the masses, muscle-bound,
> cowboys and centaurs,
> Nurmi as Joan of Arc
> the stadium sanctified
> with body spray ... '

"We should have seen it coming: the demagogue who parades these beautiful people under his whip only makes love to crowds because he cannot do it to girls; this hallucinating orator is celibate, this man-eater is a vegetarian! A give-away detail: his personal physician is one of my most obnoxious colleagues, Theo Morell, a dermatologist of breathtaking uncleanness. His dear client is obsessed by fear of the venereal peril ... We can only hope that one day this charlatan will infect his own patient! Don't laugh, it isn't funny ... "

But she is certainly not thinking of laughing. She knows that the sarcasms hide an incurable disarray. The drowning man's certainty that he will not reach the shore.

"Tomorrow," he goes on, "the gladiators who enter the arena will declare themselves ready to die for a master whose very appearance ought to affront their beauty. Who knows if the Olympics won't be simply a dress rehearsal? The participants will later be expected to pulverise records in competitions of a quite different sort. Even in ancient Greece, the Games preluded nothing but war. And I actually admired that. Tomorrow, the engaging Frau Riefenstahl, with her cap and her blue glasses, will need just one long panning shot to sweep the space that still separates the stadium from the battlefield. Then people may remember that the athletes' Olympic salute merely prefigured that of the warriors.

"Nele, we're so close to the sea, yet not even its smell reaches us ... "

The echo of breakers would be needed to cover the din of arms he has just suggested. The doctor is bathed in sweat. Not so much because he has mentioned the possibility of war, as because he has yet again evoked the human body and the treatment to which it is subjected. And because, as each time this happens, the emotion that invades him comes from far off, sent by the memory of the bodies of men you open, the bodies of women you take ...

He has stopped. Did I only ask her to come, he wonders, in order to tell her that? Yes, of course. How could he deny it? Why her? Because he could not have found anyone more devotedly on his side? But would that not be to get off too lightly?

"You do understand?" he asks, almost in despair. Not despair at being misunderstood. Despair, perhaps, at being understood too well. Who will judge us more pitilessly than someone who has acquitted us a priori, only to discover that her confidence was misplaced? And even if we were to plead successfully before someone who wishes to absolve us, would that not merely demonstrate the weakness of our case?

One last time, she would like to rebel. To summon up all her resistance and cry out: No, Father, all this is really too heavy for me to bear, it suffocates me! Haven't I the right to be only twenty-one? To have my own life, my own problems? Can't I be egoistic in my turn? I have never seen you after our parting without feeling all the weight of Germany descending on me. All the strength I have built up away from you, each time I come back I risk seeing it reduced to nothing! Why don't you ask your old friend in Bremen to arbitrate for you? He's always so distinguished, so well dressed, with his bird-of-prey profile. Herr Oelze, aesthete, lawyer and merchant of West Indian rum. Or have yourself judged by one of your mistresses, those perfumed theatrical ladies who take turns to embellish your bachelor flat? Why me? Because between 1933 and 1936 I have had the chance to mature? I have matured. One could have matured on less ... Why this evening? It's too late! It's much too early! It will always be too late, or too early! I'm not German any more! I've never been German! I don't know whether it is a good thing or a bad one. I don't want to become German again, even for an hour! You wanted it this way: I'm hardly your daughter ... Is it because you want to break off your scandalous liaison with the new Germany that you have decided to take up with me again? Or do you hope by confessing your fault to put right the wrongs you have done me? It would be unbearable for me to be sacrificed to the vocation of a father who lacked integrity ... Oh, I should like to be the most inclement of all your judges. I should like to let nothing pass, shut my eyes to none of your sins. Curiously, that may be just your opportunity: take it if you can ...

She would like to pour out all this. But she only manages to say: "No, Father, I haven't yet accepted it. I haven't agreed to a single word of your reply to Klaus Mann, or of your "Address to the Literary Emigrants", or of your "Homage to the New State", and perhaps I shall never resign myself to them completely ... But if you should have the absurd idea to beg mercy of me, who should I be to refuse it? Can you see yourself uttering a *Filia peccavi*? Of course not. You'd never ask anyone to forgive you. And, curiously, I think I'm beginning to accept that ... "

He would like to explain to his daughter once again that, no matter what you have done, you must respect the truth of your life – and that you never respect it entirely except in your innermost heart. No sooner have you handed it over to someone else than you have twisted it, revised it, touched it up. When you have once lost yourself, you should stay alone for a time, in the presence of your loss. There is a kind of blindness that you do not escape by confessing it: a trap – for the other, but above all for you – lurks in the contrition itself, that amounts to a sleight of hand. The least you can ask of yourself is to remain silent. You have to learn to live in a tête-à-tête with your error, as the invalid cohabits with his cancer. There may then come an hour when the defeat itself weighs less heavily than the manner in which you have coped with it. Just one more turn of the screw, and your soul will again be hitched to the body it almost betrayed. That, and only that, is why I intend to stay in Germany.

He would like to say all that to Nele, but he no longer feels he has the right to extract a moral from his story.

He manages only to say: "I have doubtless let myself in for ten years of purgatory ... "

Without knowing it, she muses, he has just entrusted a mission to me. To write a book on him. Later. When he is dead, if I survive him. Oh! not to whitewash him, rehabilitate him, cleanse him of any suspicion. In any case, who would trust a loving daughter to be objective?

She remembers the work she had read with deep emotion, in which Eugénie Schumann had done her utmost to prove that the musical genius who was her father had not succumbed to madness. As if that were a mark of ignominy. But it wasn't the memory of a madman that Nele Benn would have to defend – how much easier it would have been! – but the honour of a man who had verged on the criminal. She would not attempt that.

No doubt Klaus Mann had been right in writing of Dr Benn's "fanatical purity". And when she had thought a lot more about it, no doubt she would agree that "to be incorruptible" did not only mean to be someone who was not to be corrupted; it could also refer to the person who resisted his own corruption. That the finest and wisest mind she knew, which happened to be her father's, had failed dismally when so many cynics seemed to have conducted themselves better, was a mystery that the young woman from Charlottenlund would perhaps never unravel, which was simply beyond her: wasn't it even beyond her father? To do that might mean blaming the cynicism of life itself. No, she would not talk of that. She might, at most, allude to it obliquely. But she would set out all the rest. She would try to say who he had been. She was already thinking of him in the past tense. It would be a proper investigation. She began trying to scrape together the little she knew of him.

For, my father, she thought, all I knew about you for a long time was that you had sent me away, got rid of me . . .

She would have to learn everything from the beginning again.

Once upon a time there was a little peasant, his big daughter might have written – in the manner of a fairytale, though one would have to be wary of turning him into a legend – who had come to the big city to cut open dead bodies, tend bodies that were in pain. He had married a wife, and had a daughter. Then he had gone off to war. Already, he had played all life's games.

Had crossed a little ocean of History. When peace came he had returned to his island to find out what was left of the world, and check what remained of him. His wife had died almost at once. He had not known what to do with his daughter, and with his own weariness with living. He had cut himself off from his daughter, but kept his weariness. Nevertheless, he was as vigilant as a sentry. He tended poor people and wrote poems. His pen was a second scalpel, that sometimes sent out lightning flashes. Why was he not being more widely read, when he knew so much? Had he not sought loneliness in order to write? He sometimes spent the night with women intended for that purpose, taciturn, scented women, who revealed a secret. He was neither rebellious nor submissive. He had the bluntness of the timid, the brutality of the sensitive, the sensitivity of the brute. He thought he had never taken his eye off the target. One day, his vision grew dim. One might say, of course, that he lacked impetuosity. That he had too much heart, or too little. Yet he devoted all his time to the wretched-ness of life. He had not polished up his image. Expert in a science of man no longer in vogue, a bearer of obsolete knowl-edge. One day, no doubt, people would agree there was a lack of men of that kind.

Who would ever believe, Nele Benn of Charlottenlund wonders desperately, that my father's soul was more beautiful than his way of being?

"But you haven't told me anything about yourself!" says her father. "Now let's talk about you ... "

She bursts out laughing.

"What's so funny?"

"You don't think the transition might be a little abrupt?" she asks. "And then, as you know, nothing ever happens to me. Not everyone can afford the luxury of a biography. All the same, something is happening ... I want to leave Denmark."

"To come back to Germany?" he asks in alarm.

"Oh, no. Never."

On the contrary, leaving Denmark seems to her like leaving Germany a second time. A little Germany. But how can she explain that it is unbearable to her to stay in Copenhagen and its surroundings, that tiny village with its narrow streets in which everywhere she must bump into a man she has loved, whom she is fleeing?

"I've broken off with a fiancé!" she announces, in what she tries to make a playful tone.

"No doubt you were too talkative," he says.

"Really? Like this evening?" she asks ironically.

He blushes.

I know, Father, that you disapprove of the woes of the heart, thinks Nele, because art, in your eyes, is not in league with them ... But she sends out to him a silent prayer: I beg you, Father, do not heap sarcasm on love this evening. Do not tell me, tonight, that passion is nothing.

"It's too late to talk about me," she says. "Tell me about my mother."

Perhaps he thinks she is trying to steer the conversation away from a painful subject.

"No one, apart from you, can understand what I lost in your mother. But I don't harbour any illusions. A traitorous citizen, an absentee father, a bad husband ... They fit, you might say. They go well together, don't you agree?"

"Good heavens, Father, who's talking about that? Who's even asking about your feelings? Just tell me what my mother was like, that's all I ask ... "

"She was a radiant being ... The exact opposite of your father. And since you are talking about her ... I've brought this on her behalf. It's a bracelet that belonged to her. It came from her own parents."

Inside the golden band two dates are engraved: 1896 ... 1936. Neither her birth nor her death, thinks Nele. The original gift, and its rebirth. My God, she thinks, I understand why women grow attached to this man.

"Don't thank me," he says. "It's not a gift from me. It's from her. Since her death I've only been a receiver ... Nele, never marry," he adds bizarrely. (Is he implying: if you're like me? Or: because you're like me?) "Marriage is not for you ... Travel around the world instead. Read Aristotle, Nietzsche and Tolstoy. You never know how much innocence you destroy in the other. (Or had he meant to say: Betray? Was he trying to talk about betrayal yet again?) And your Danish mother, the woman who brought you up, I really loved her as well ... "

I know that.

Beside her, he muses, "magnolias fell silent". But the schizophrenic in me would not bow down. He merely inclined his "desolate brow". Who is drenched today in such torrents of light?

"I was quite small," Nele remembers. "We were still living in Berlin, in the flat on Passauerstrasse. We, that is, Mother and I. You were just an occasional visitor that Mother no longer really expected, even if I still hoped for you each evening. And if you came nevertheless, Mother always seemed so happy to welcome you. Happy, and slightly astonished ... If you didn't come home, she would sometimes get up in the middle of the night, go to the kitchen and cook a tomato, some onion and a piece of bacon in a saucepan. Meticulously. With patience and gentleness. I would tiptoe to join her, to share in her nocturnal feast. "Your father hasn't come home," she would say. It was a piece of information, not something to dramatise. Then she would start talking to me about you, in a low voice. She told me you were a kind of scholar in your own way. A man of the new times ... I've forgotten the rest. Those are the only memories I still have of Berlin."

"There was worse ... " he says.

She starts, as if he had lit up her secret thoughts.

"Worse than who?" she asks. "Worse than my mother, or worse than my 'Danish mother'?"

"No, of course not. Worse than the wrong I did them ... There have been many other women ... "

"I'm not unaware," she says with an impudent, almost conniving look in her eye – probably because his answer has reassured her – "that my father has many successes . . . "

"And therefore many failures," he says. "That's how one should sometimes look at things. There was worse. That is to say, I behaved worse to others."

He talks as if he were dealing with crimes committed by a strangler or vampire straight out of the Sunday edition of the *Berliner Tageblatt*. For a moment Nele pictures time-bombs placed here and there beneath the feet of various unknown women, right across Germany . . .

> "Loved so many lies,
> Sought so many lips,
> And always more questions . . . "

> "Break-up, and your face, alas
> Glistening with tears . . .
> Debris, all the ruins
> So naked in the morning . . . "

There was Lili, he remembers, who almost managed to escape me when she went to Vienna. Lili who thought she was running away from me . . . Then she was back in my life and, sadly for her, I was back in hers, though I could do nothing for her: I see her now, disfigured by a suffering without bounds and almost without an object, a name – though she gave it mine . . . There's an image of pain that makes you mad with helplessness, and soon fills you with hate. It's an abyss. All that is left is for you to die together. If one survives, he's an assassin. You lived side by side. Then no more. Then you tried it again. And nothing of all that was really possible. Yet we must have looked like an ordinary couple. There are no ordinary couples: it's a miracle, an injustice. It can become a curse. Lili was attached to me like a child, like an animal. She expected everything of me. Everything is always too much. She warned me of her suicidal intentions on the telephone. She could no longer articulate her words. She was sobbing. I rushed to her. She had thrown herself from the window. The firemen were already carrying away her broken body. Of course, it had nothing to do with me. Of course, it had everything to do with me. How can someone who has shared in the life of a suicide victim make us believe he did everything possible to prevent it, that he was just unlucky, that he is not the beginning of a murderer? Henceforth a lake of blood separates us from the life we had imagined for ourselves. I told myself that if I got over this grief I would be a new man, of a species never before seen on earth. I got over the grief. I did not become a new man ... Sometimes tears come into my eyes "without reason". The tears of someone who for an eternity has denied himself the right and the time to weep. Tears which come from very far off, and which no mirror would catch ... Even Lili's tears I lack. They were, even then, the salt of the earth. I am bereaved even of her despair.

For a moment he believes that he has just told this story, that was floating about inside him, to his daughter. Nele is watching him. She is waiting. He has said nothing. Something held him back at the last moment. Was it the idea that his daughter might reproach him more strongly for this death which he failed to prevent than for his brief adherence to a shameful regime? Good heavens! Such things cannot be compared, he sermonises himself.

"Some years ago," he says, "a woman killed herself for me, 'because of me', as people say. People also said that I left her because she was poor ... Can you imagine that? As if poverty were ever a problem in my eyes. When it is sometimes a person's lack of poverty that troubles me ... "

Lack of poverty, he said. He didn't say: wealth. The word "wealth" is banished from his vocabulary, Nele notes. It would burn his tongue. But why is he inflicting this on me as well? And in my book, she wonders anxiously, should I talk about it? No: about all the rest. The life of this man, not his deaths.

There was worse, he declared. Let remorse spring up at last. She must be an expensive dancing-girl that can dance like that on your heart. Is it not strange that he has chosen tonight to divulge all these confidences – he who is usually so secretive, almost taciturn? And how does he imagine that anything could be worse for me than my mother's death? Because Edith Osterloh died a natural death? How many times has he not evoked the cancer that killed his mother as the ultimate horror? It does not help to be a doctor; illness and suffering go on having no purpose or justification for you. That's even why you became a doctor: out of desperation.

"And now, of course, other women have come into your life?"

In what a tone she asked that, his twenty-one-year-old daughter! It almost puts a smile on his face.

"I have some lady-friends, yes," he agrees. "Especially some women I like writing letters to; their replies brighten my solitude ... They are often women who write, or could have written. I like the way women use words. Even when the words seem futile or neurotic, they crisp them in the pan!"

"And do you still like women who repeat the words of others? Actresses, I mean. Are you still seeing Wedekind's widow?"

The father realises why his "seeing" them irritates his daughter. That her mother was originally an actress and the woman who brought her up a singer, must make her resent these doubly disloyal rivals ...

"Tilly Wedekind sometimes comes to visit me, if her tours bring her near Hanover ... And then Elinor Büler, who was so sympathetic towards me at the funeral of the one I just spoke to you about, who took her life ... "

Nele shivers.

"Are you cold, darling?"

Not at all. She is just thinking that it was on his way back from the funeral of Edith Osterloh, on the train from Jena to Berlin, that her father met the "next woman", the Danish one ... He doesn't lose a day, she thinks darkly. Hardly is one in the ground than another opens her arms to him. Thus is the baton passed ... And thus is this so solitary man never alone.

"And then, above all," he says, "there is my great, my best lady-friend, Nele Benn, who lives in the kingdom of Denmark ... "

She has held out her right hand to him over the table as a token of assent, as a woman being courted might do with her admirer, and he has seized it. Their neighbour has again turned round, frowning. He must be thinking: These fifty-year-olds can afford some nice young flesh in Germany these days, even if they hold some pretty subversive opinions, from what one can hear ...

"Who knows?" asks the father. "Perhaps the future will say that I did well in removing you from my life ... "

She snatches back her hand, as if she had burnt it on her father's.

She is furious. You won't get out of it like that, she thinks. Was Germany going to be a country where one was in danger of seeing all the women die because of you?

"I wasn't thinking of myself, Nele. I was only speaking of Germany – what it might think."

"You know, Father," she says, bristling, "it has sometimes been hard for me to give up Germany entirely. In my way, I too am an emigrant. But in my case it wasn't National Socialism that drove me out, but my own father, who always thought me capable of following his reasoning. And who sent me books that kept me attached to my original culture, so that I remained uprooted ... You see, if I like replying to the letters that I still get from Gertrud and Paul Hindemith, it's because they represent my Germany! I'll never forget the holiday I spent with you five years ago, near Bad Tölz, while you were both working on your oratorio. You should have seen yourselves doing physical training exercises before starting work! We crossed the whole of Germany in an open tourer. In Frankfurt we climbed the tower the city had put at the composer's disposal. His grand piano had had to be hoisted up the outside with a pulley ... We visited Colmar, where the altarpiece by Matthias Grünewald that so fascinated Paul is kept. After that I had to go back to Copenhagen as if nothing had happened, as if it had been just a parenthesis. I was devastated. You must imagine it: for a whole summer you had given me Paul Hindemith, and Paul Hindemith had made me a present of Beethoven and Matthias Grünewald, of his cordiality, his passacaglias and his basso ostinato – in short, all of Germany!"

"A different Germany," says her father. "The last years of peace in the Weimar Republic. But we didn't know it."

"You said enough bad things about it! And now Paul Hindemith has had to leave, perhaps for ever, who knows? It's here that something is rotten, not in the state of Denmark! And I shall only come back here at rare intervals, to meet you in one town or another, as your mistresses do ... To listen to your monologues. To hear you advancing, in such a soft, gentle voice, such abominable ideas ... As you did in the obituary to your friend Klabund that you read to me one day so unemphatically. Almost jubilantly. It sounded like a lullaby written by a poet to protect the sleep of another ...

"Sometimes I tell myself that I needed a father to show me the saddest, most dreadful aspects of life. But he did so with such tenderness, such strange generosity, that there was, perhaps, nothing better he could offer me ... "

One evening, she recalls, one of those rare evenings when you had come home to the flat on Passauerstrasse – perhaps it was just for Christmas? – Mother sat down at the piano and played for you. You suddenly looked so much at peace. Then

Mother asked me to recite a poem of yours that I had learned by heart ... I was terrified. It was "Cancer Ward" ... Everywhere corpses dissolving ... I said the poem as if I didn't understand a word. Mother and you were very amused by my choice and my naivety. In fact, I was so well aware of the horror your poems gave off that for a long time poetry was nothing but that: a refuge of all terror, a den of nightmares. But one of the first things I read when I knew Danish was Andersen's *The Improvisatore*. Why did I love that book so much? Because the hero of the story was a poet who was in league with joy, festivities, wine. Women fell in love with him, and didn't suffer for it afterwards. Laughing, he climbed the wall of a volcano ... So the life of a poet could be like that as well? Why was my father so unlike him? It was a revelation. Father, I wondered, you who take dusk with you everywhere, why did you not tell me that life could be so ... dancing? Your immense shadow eclipsed the sun, hid the horizon from me. I won't write that either, especially not that, in my book. I shall tell about Christmas, the piano, my recital. I shall not quote Andersen, nor the wine or the volcano. All the rest. I shall talk only of the rest. And what I have heard this evening I shall try to forget first of all. I shall remember only the banks of the Alster, the braised salmon and the bracelet that belonged to my mother. The bracelet twice engraved. I shall, for a time, go back to being the sentimental young girl who has just passed two carefree days in Hamburg with her father. Then one memory will rise to the surface, then another. And one day when my son, if I have one, has asked me some questions – or a stranger who might have been my son – I shall remember everything at once.

"I'm going back to Denmark all the same," she added. "Don't worry about me. The country that is so modest you would never suspect it had a bloody past. The country which makes itself as small as possible, as if trying not to be noticed by History, and where you are careful not to talk too loudly about metaphysical anguish or affairs of the heart. But I'll probably end up falling in love there again. I'll have children that I bring

up in Danish, and who will never set foot in Germany except
to visit their grandfather. I'll go back to Charlottenlund
tomorrow."

"I thought we were staying another day, and going to see
the snow leopard at Stellingen Zoo. It's one of the most
important in Europe, it seems."

"They say the same about the one in Copenhagen," she
replied. "Everywhere in the world the zoological gardens claim
to be the finest on earth."

"But none," he said, "will ever equal the one in Berlin, that
I took you to once when you were very small."

He has remembered the big cats. What memory, instinct and
reflexes they had left could discharge themselves only in the
muscles rippling under their coats: the most archaic and noblest
form of captive consciousness that did not yet admit itself
vanquished. It seemed as if, from one moment to the next, a
thought was going to arise from them in its elemental purity.
Waiting for it, you felt only the keenness of their suffering, and
you were almost surprised that the earth did not tremble, that a
crater did not open at the back of their cages. Who will ever
release the Creator from the pain of His creatures?

"You can be sure that in these troubled times the Berlin zoo
has become a rendezvous of conspirators, spies and revolutionaries ... What state secrets don't those animals hear, locked up
in a country which is itself in a cage?"

Apple blossom on the banks of the Elbe, the bright gleam of
girls on the shores of the Alster: you think you could remake
your life straight away with any of them, that you need only to
decide. Reflections of patrician façades in the water's mirror.
The opaline globes of street-lamps. Frogs gossiping among the
water-lilies. More bridges than in Venice. Gothic Venice.
Venice without Venice. Labyrinth of canals. When the fog
descends, you think you can see all the bridges breaking and
the wooden gables tottering. The whole city begins to tremble.

"And what are you going to do with your life, my darling,"
he asked again.

"I'll become a writer, of course!"

"My sad example has not dissuaded you, then? Who knows? Perhaps you will become in your turn an eminent representative of 'German literature in exile'? Like the best of us, is that not so?"

Mingled scents of coal, coffee and rubber. Oily canals. Tepid mist. Soft shower of rain. Emphatic emblem of the Hapag company, purveyor of voyages. Stocks in exile. *Mein Feld ist die Welt*. The world is my field – but the sea is a door, and you are locked in. The heavy step of a man of fifty on the glistening cobbles. His daughter has just noticed a white hair on his coat collar. She takes it between thumb and forefinger.

"And you, what will you do now?" she asked.

"Oh, I'll go on writing decadent poems, a little more clandestinely than in the past ... I haven't yet exhausted my censors. No doubt I'll be expurgated. No matter who governs Germany tomorrow, I'm sure they'll reduce me to silence.

> 'For us is to keep silent,
> Knowing this world will fade,
> and when its last hour passes,
> Not to let drop your blade.'

"I've cut myself off from everybody at once. And I didn't even mean to!"

For a time, he also thought, I shan't even be a contemporary. I'll be as alone as in Brussels, in my youth, during the war. A war which may have merely prefigured another. Who knows what one can write in a situation like that? If I'm not careful it might even be interesting!

"You'll be careful, won't you?" she asked anxiously.

"If I have to," he answered with a laugh, "I'll bury my poems as I write them, in the country, in some corner of the Weser or Solling."

"Will you keep a diary?"

"Up to now I've never kept a record of anything except my income and expenses. Very few of each. When you lead a double life, it's difficult to keep a diary that does not turn into a mere memorandum of your schizophrenia . . . "

The sarcasms of gulls with rancid wings. Spray sticky with salt. Exhausted surf. Panting shore. Grey coal, tobacco dust, adulterated rum. In a cellar in the Sankt Pauli quarter a tart is smoking a cigarette between the lips of her second mouth: she's paid one mark for each smoke-ring. At the end of the Helgoländerallee a transatlantic liner passes as if it were gliding along the harbour-front cobbles. Rusted hull. Wheezy packet boat. Husky siren. The boat one is not going to board. No embarkation for Cythera. The city that will remain your prison. No open sea, no more horizon. Bulging waves. The sweat of History.

"We'll have heard the murmur of the sea after all," he said. "It may be that we won't see each other for some time. I'll write to you. Even though I know a poet's words prick and stab those they are meant to caress."

It's true, she thought, that I'm going to receive letters from him as dense and sharp as steel. She feels exhausted, as after long weeping. Far off in the estuary a ship calls for the assistance of a tug with a blast of its siren. A pale, distant appeal that for a moment seems destined to go unanswered.

Berlin, 1946

The Stones

It's curious, says the survivor, you'd think nothing was happening any more. No more events: as if the air had been
overloaded with them. No more time, nothing but space. But a
razed space. One could follow the guide, from what is left of
the Anhalter Bahnhof to Tegel, passing through the Tiergarten
and Wedding, then turn across what remains of Grunewald,
Charlottenburg, Wilmersdorf and Dahlem with a loop around
the Wannsee lake – a pilgrimage to the site of Heinrich von
Kleist's suicide, and the place where later, quite recently,
Heydrich, Eichmann and Goering decreed the so-called final
solution to the Jewish problem; from there one would cross via
Mariendorf towards Steglitz and Tempelhof – what's left of
Steglitz and Tempelhof, that is – and come back to Schöneberg, 20, Bozener Strasse, with a glance at the Bayerischer Platz
in passing, where the underground station was bombed: five
hundred deaths, we were told, or even more; such figures are
only decided long afterwards, when they have only abstract
importance. Why should we not imagine a tourism of the
ruins, or follow a signposted route that would allow us to go
on excursions among the dead stones.

"You will not recognise Germany!" the Führer had warned
us. We should have done better to take him at his word. But
we didn't hear. Instead, we listened to an Austrian commercial
traveller in riding breeches, his skinny torso hung with a
shining baldrick, who dreamed of being a great architect. Ah,
that love of monumental buildings! Wasn't Kuppelberg going
to contain St Peter's, Rome, seventeen times over? While now
only ten per cent of Nuremberg is still standing? Wasn't the

stadium of this defunct city supposed to leave the Circus Maximus far behind? And was it not the Zentralbahnhof's vocation to swallow New York Central Station in one mouthful? While there is not a single platform here that could receive a train that had strayed from another time and place. Hamburg's Grosse Brücke was going to overstep the Golden Gate in San Francisco. And the mausoleum to the dead of the First World War was to do the same to the Arc de Triomphe in Paris. The Reichstag was to be preserved, but as if to bear witness to the mediocre ambitions of the Weimar Republic ... To show the scale of the former world! Yet the Soviets have surmounted it, the summit of the city, with the victor's flag. Hitler's architectural fantasies are balanced only by the annihilation of three-quarters of Frankfurt, the forty-three million cubic metres of rubble in Hamburg. The ninety per cent of Darmstadt blown away in less than half an hour. In the whole country, a total of five million houses demolished, one billion seven hundred million bricks recovered for re-use. Not a bad score, is it? And for the Father of the Nation, as good a way as any to have his wish granted. Thus his love of gigantism and mass, his craze for size, have been materialised, once and for all, but inversely, by the destruction, the obliteration of the cities over which he ruled. Let him whose ambition was to raze London and Paris be consoled by the thought that at least he annihilated, among others, some German cities ... As if he had for once got his aim slightly wrong. Hadn't he turned his master builder, Albert Speer, into a Minister for Armaments and this as early as 1942? All he had had to do, really, was shift his rifle from one shoulder to the other. Just one regret: that having gone to earth in his underground bunker, of modest proportions, he was unable to gauge except by hearsay – of which he didn't believe a word – the immensity of the damage. But why should he hang about at the scene of the crime? Wasn't it enough for him to have incited it? At least he was spared being told about the devastation of Nagasaki and Hiroshima: the poor man would have gone green with envy. A pity, all the same, that in the end the parsimonious tyrant even denied us his remains, as a last cippus erected to his earthly glory!

The blackened façades of Reinickendorf, gaping windows, the charred beams of the villas of Moabit. In the Tiergarten the houses have slid into their own cellars, vanished into themselves. The jagged gables of Grunewald, fragments of wall, torn, ragged, crumpled, rolled into balls like tissue paper. How fragile we were, how at the mercy of the first leather trousers to be spewed from a posthumous nightmare of Bismarck. Brutalised by poverty, blinded by misfortune, drunk with humiliation, depraved by the arrogance of a different age. We're fingering the wages of all that: collapsed ceilings, gutted floors, carbonised shells, shattered concrete, mountains of debris in the streets of Kreuzberg. All that flows along the Landwehrkanal is a river of gravel, a torrent of brickbats on to which venture, tottering like drunks, women in search of a garment reduced to rags, a scrap of furniture that will remind them of ordinary existence, meaning pre-history; yes, women, and children playing at war when war has hardly finished; only the children and the women are familiar with the debris of the cities broken by the bombardments of men, they have learned to walk on them as on black ice, an unsteady ground; they seek no matter what, any fragment of anything that might help them to survive, to remind them how they lived before, and it is as if they were skating on a cascade of blood-soaked nothingness, like the knight who rode across Lake Constance and fainted only when he arrived at the shore on hearing that he had been supported on a thin film of ice. Women and children scour avenues which are no more than tracks of frozen lava, moraines that have swept away everything in their path; women and children form chains passing back and forth buckets with handles that cut the palms of the hands stretching from one to the other, buckets filled to the brim with debris: what else is there to find, except at rare intervals a dented bowl, a boot without a sole, a gas-mask with its snout torn off? Don't they have to exhume at random these useless objects, functionless tools, and transport debris from one spot to another, to persuade themselves that it has been worth it, has made sense to survive? Always women and children, more apt than men to believe in miracles. One woman, fleeing before the Soviet army in the direction of Königsberg, had noticed the corset of a pregnant woman beside the snowbound road and put it on, and still wept now with laughter and gratitude at the idea that she may have owed her survival to that unique circumstance, that unhoped-for find ... *Ich hatte Schwein* – I had the Devil's luck! She did not realise that the Russian soldiers sometimes even raped women about to give birth, as the writer Ilya Ehrenburg had actually incited them to do: "Crush the Fascist beast once and for all! Use your strength to break the pride of the German women! Take them as your legitimate spoils! Kill even the Germans still unborn, valiant Soviet soldier." A member of the Red Army may have torn that corset from its owner before violating her ... But in the bomb craters or between the swaying walls of a house that you expected to collapse, even noiselessly, at any moment, among the twisted rails that no longer led to any station, what could one hope to find, except some filleted waggon, some overturned carriage like a pachyderm at the end of an iron safari? Over there you could see some scraps of cloth caught in the branches of a tree in the Hubertusallee, cloth discoloured by the snow and ice, flesh-coloured shreds ... unless? Here your eyes could follow the whorls of a spiral staircase that corkscrewed into the sky, still standing upright like a dream. Why was it, the escaped stroller wondered, that not one of these unlikely images surprised him, that he had expected them, that they imposed themselves like something self-evident, so that he had the disquieting suspicion that he had always carried them inside himself? As if everything that was supposed to take place outside us had run its course in us already, even long ago? What the survivor means is that long before he first saw the city submerged by a tide of fire, of molten metal, then saw it again as if still stupefied, dumbfounded by the vociferations of a hysterical god, yes, long before he had visited, explored it in all the nooks and crannies of its disaster – for he has not been able to complete this tour of the scorched city, torn from its own skeleton, in one, two or even three excursions, for though you may have survived you are not exempt from decrepitude, and fatigue drags at each of your steps, a fatigue that has nothing to do with age, a fatigue born of the events like one of those maladies that sin engenders and of which you cannot be cured; nevertheless you did not grow tired of pacing the boulevards, or rather the passages, the grey arteries of this city buried up to its cornices in its own foundations, entombed beneath the avalanche of itself, and dying of asphyxia like those fallen cetaceans that are crushed by their own weight; yes, if the old escapee has not yet given up measuring out this desert of shale encumbered with men who, like insects, refuse to abandon the beleaguered anthill, it is not to find out more about the state of these fractured and blackened stones, it is not to draw in with astonishment this smell of smoke and cold ash that will never be dispersed again, no, it is rather to verify the cruel correctness of a diagnosis made long ago, long before all this happened. But registering this does not bring resignation. Berlin ... Berlin ... mumbles the man, the former inhabitant of this city, and he could say nothing better: all is contained in those two syllables which, in other times, expressed the very tremor of life, its shimmer, its halo, and now spell only an epitaph. Berlin ... , as if the old survivor, the former citizen of this place, wanted also to promise that he would never leave it, that he would never again let it out of his sight. He would be too afraid that someone would really finish it off in his absence, and that he would not find it on his return. That he would not find even this spectre, this architectural palimpsest. For as you wander the corridors of this maze, where no crossroads are intact, do not twist into a cul-de-sac, where the exhausted avenues no longer reach their own ends, where each way is blocked, each view opens on a dead end, you are assailed by echoes, the trembling reflection of what has been. For an instant you no longer know which of you, the city or yourself, haunts, and which is haunted. Shutting your eyes, you retain no image of this mirage; all that remains is a bitter after-taste on your tongue.

They tell you that the districts are divided into "zones" and claim that these zones are "occupied", but that's pure irony: in reality these zones exist nowhere, and the men occupy nothing. No doubt what we have here is not an end but a beginning, that ushers in a new conception of space. In that case Berlin would merely proclaim the fiction of a future world, though the world does not yet know about it ... Each graveyard in this city would be only the graveyard of a graveyard: the city itself. The ruins would feed on each other, reproducing themselves continuously. We should witness the negative of a miracle: the multiplication of stones.

This is what it had to come to. Perambulating among the façades licked by tongues of soot, walls in strident mourning for the city, or wandering among back-yards that shut themselves into a truculent widowhood, one concedes the implacable logic presiding over this. Only the eyes of the Teutonic corporal had not registered it. "I've finished with politics. It disgusts me ... ", he may have muttered, during the night of the twentieth to the twenty-first of April, nineteen hundred and forty-five, still navigating below ground in his concrete bathysphere. But he remained to the end the only resident of the city who did not have to watch as it was brought to a state of incandescence, as it boiled in a cauldron of hell. Nero, at least, admired the burning of Rome that he had set in train. Right to the end, the Führer was spared the sight of the ruins he had so relentlessly engendered. "What Have You Done to Save Berlin?" he asked on posters and placards on walls that promptly crumbled, so hard had he laboured for Berlin's annihilation.

At Stalingrad, already, incessant bulletins announced the victory of an army of corpses. So many troops were reported dead by starvation that the general staff grew suspicious and sent out forensic pathologists to confirm that they had not committed suicide. But there was no possibility of error: when opened up the bodies proved so atrophied, eroded, internally ossified that they could easily have been twice their age. The entire heart devoured by one of its ventricles, the intestines as smooth as carnival streamers. Here, at any rate, were men who should not be defamed, called insubordinate or posthumous deserters. There had been suicides at Stalingrad, as elsewhere on the front, men who put an end to themselves with a single blow or, if too weak, struck again and again, mutilating themselves until death intervened. Many, however, drugged by the snow, were spared the trouble; they just lay down on the ground that the snow had veiled in dazzling, fearsome insignificance, while their eyes were burned by the whiteness of things. However, it was reported that even at Stalingrad a soldier had been saved from certain death by the love of his wife: a bullet that ought to have pierced his heart had buried itself in the enormous wad of letters from her that he always carried under his greatcoat. Was this plausible? If it was a legend, one could understand its being invented! At all events, the Führer would not have heard of it. He no more appreciated good news of this kind than the bad news he refused to listen to. But still, thinks the survivor, one would have liked to read those letters. Herta ... , he muses aloud, Herta, my wife ... , thinks the widower, his voice growing loud. And he reflects, incongruously: I ought to have written to her more often. For miracles were rare, they went against the grain of things. For example, those few villas that had been spared in the residential quarter of the Tiergarten: why them? The Italian Consulate, the Danish Embassy, among others. And above all, those other houses that were neither the embassies nor the consulates of any power, but which, cut off from the urban context in which they were inscribed, seemed to glide on the edge of emptiness. They were the surprising thing, not the ruins. You had to stop describing the dead as if they were stupefied at dying. You could not even say: Let the dead bury their dead! There were too many of them. And they were no longer anyone's dead. One should be glad if the dead did not bury the living themselves.

You must, thinks the survivor, the reprieved man, carry out an autopsy on what is fallen, and take a census of what still stands.

A winter Sunday, in Spandau. A landscape struck to death. That will not rise up again: it has seen too much. The survivor, the old soldier, recalls the time he spent in the garrison here, just before another war. Involuntarily, his eyes seek the window of the bicycle shop, the stall selling cuir-bouilli cases and colonial trunks in the market square. He listens, despite himself, for the distant, melancholy call of a bugle. A lock gate has run aground in the middle of the Spree. Dead leaves rustle on the pavement. A dog howls, seemingly at random, as if not mourning any particular master. The stroller, the demobbed soldier, deciphers on the signs at street corners names in Gothic letters which still vainly proclaim the status of some venerable place: Juliusturm, Zeppelinstrasse, Reformationsplatz . . .

Another time, you come across a roundabout spinning aimlessly, squeaking amid the waste ground of the Lustgarten. Only the wind now drives the frozen cabins. How long has this fair been here, surprised now by the frost? You could imagine that it had been half-assembled the day before war broke out, and that no one has had time to dismantle it since the capitulation. Snow-drifts the size of icebergs have formed along the roadside. Surprised, the stroller raises his head: stalactites have closed like ice jaws on the cornices and gutters. *Achtung! Dachlawine!* – Danger, falling ice – croak the starlings, exasperated by the cold. Icy squalls draw out roofs of snow like canopies between the street and yourself.

The walker is passing a courtyard on the Fasanenstrasse when a jumble of gaudy objects catches his eye. An oilcloth pushchair full of soft hats. An accordion with mother-of-pearl flanks. A wicker trunk for homing pigeons. A coffee mill. A copper boiler. A *Wehrmacht* helmet. A portrait of Lord Wolseley. A storm lamp. A ski. A Butagaz bottle. Half a clock. An aquarium with a carpet of mossy weed and gravel at the bottom. A moth-eaten muff. An Iron Cross, Second Class. A banjo dribbling snow. A name plate of the Pariser Platz ... All this put on show ... he thinks. And suddenly he realises that it really is a display. You are so used to the scattering of things that you might have thought all these objects had accumulated of their own accord beside the pavement. No, a bric-à-brac dealer has patiently gathered them to put them on sale at the same time as the photos of soldiers in uniform which are the star-turn of the collection. Unthinkingly, the old soldier is surprised that no parent has kept the portrait of this alert lieutenant with his fine moustache, or of this youthful sergeant-major already mentioned three times in dispatches. Then he understands that there is probably no living heir to receive these souvenirs of fallen soldiers ... At first sight, you'd say they were all alike, regardless of age, rank or uniform. Then, looking more closely, you discover that there are not two among them who have waged the same war. That if this captain, paying no attention to the fiancée at his side who is feasting her eyes on him, fixes his gaze imperiously on the horizon, that urchin in the *Volkssturm* is so petrified with fear that his face has taken on an ecstatic expression, dazzled by the destiny awaiting him. In one you discern perplexity, in another you divine apprehension. This one believes himself virile, that other is only melancholy. This other again must have died before he knew what Gehenna he was being flung into. And that last one, who had understood, vanished before he had attained resignation. What candour in this old man, what maturity in the yes of that child ...

While one is about it, some genius of a scrap merchant might get the idea of selling the city itself, what is left of it, in bulk, like a morbid curiosity, to an eccentric millionaire. Or put it up for auction one Sunday morning on the Hermann-platz, at the exit of a public concert of the "Voice of America", the profits going to the war cripples or the children not yet born here. God, thinks the stroller, how biting the wind is suddenly ... Herta, he thinks. My wife. My child. He does not know what to do with his black mood, he has too much sadness. Herta who was my second wife, for the length of a second war, as I lost another after a first defeat ...

What is most terrible is not the loss of everything, but the unfathomable innocence of things that have survived the catastrophes. That bathroom suspended between heaven and earth, with its pink tiles, flowered basin and a standing mirror that, as far as one can see, was not even cracked while every-thing around those few walls collapsed. The bath, its feet uprooted, has capsized like a skiff in a raging sea. What has become of the woman who powdered herself there before going to a gala soirée at the Schiller-Theater or the Kammer-spiele? Did her husband have time to flee, plunging into the furnace still in his dinner jacket? And in what makeshift orphanage does the child now sleep, bathed in bitter tears, if he escaped from the nursery with wallpaper showing scenes from the story of Baron Munchhausen? On what domestic felicity did that unhinged door once open? What could be seen from that window blinded by boarding nailed up in haste? Would no one come to collect that girl's bicycle innocently leaning against a street-lamp, its spidery wheels turned into rosettes by the snow? Who would lift the lid of that piano deposited undamaged in the street, to find the keyboard intact? There are prodigalities even more unnerving than misfortunes. And superstition, no doubt, will protect that umbrella with a horn handle, planted in the ground like a rapier, from pilfering hands.

Some façades have sprouted galvanised pipes that smoke like cigarette butts. Sometimes a trap-door lifts in the pavement, and you have time to meet the eyes of a face puffed with cold, eyes drowning in hate.

One evening, as he is going back home to Schöneberg but has lingered to one side of the Westfälische Strasse to savour an unaccustomed sweetness of the air, he hears voices quite close to him in the ruins. He stops for a moment. A man and a woman are discussing *mezza voce* a domestic problem: how one uses his time and the other the housekeeping money, the education they ought to give their child. The eavesdropper would like to move on, away from the couple whose intimacy he has surprised. But he is held back by something that disconcerts him. The fact that to overhear this conversation he has not had to force or even open a door ... that it is happening under the open sky. He raises his head.

On the first floor of a building whose façade has been blown away, a man and a woman are sitting facing each other. As if nothing were the matter. They are alone in the world. They haven't yet noticed that the wall that separated them from the street has disappeared. Or they have long since finished grieving for it. This might have happened in Sicily, one day when the volcano threatened to erupt: people would have been forced to continue the quarrels started in the shade of their homes in the open air, in the noisy *piazzetta* ...

For the rest, the stroller notes, summer will return even here. But now he begins to panic: what summer will it be, in what year? Dizziness comes over him. Memories and seasons change places or mingle, since all are henceforth inscribed in this same decor of immovable ruins that no longer winds forward before your eyes, or in your memory.

But the summer light makes the immobile landscape tremble. In this same street the goose-stepping soldiers marched, danced. And not far from here the bodies of those being executed jumped, danced under the impact of the bullets. For some time everything in this landscape has been dancing. The very reality of things. Or their unreality. The houses started moving. The boulevards were shaken by convulsions. It's enough for the light of an imminent summer to lick and caress these decapitated churches, these mutilated statues, these gaping doorways, this porridge of stones, this purée of concrete, and you doubt the evidence of your eyes. That the sun should rise again on such a panorama is an event in itself, thinks the man saved by a miracle.

You're wandering in a *trompe l'oeil* universe. What is door, and what is window? Furniture in the street, heaps of excrement under the roofs. The outside is within, the interior outside. The city has been turned inside out like a glove. It's gone arse over tip. It's had its guts pulled out. It's been laid out at everyone's feet. Now it's as much horizontal as vertical. It's been melted down. It's been remodelled. You'd think a housebreaking giant had turned everything upside down in his rage at not finding what he came for. The optical illusions assailing the stroller fill him with black hilarity. He keeps getting farcical ideas. This field of rubble ploughed and sown by death, where death has laid its iron eggs, may be no more than the expensive backdrop to some ultimate theatrical performance put on for the armies by God Himself, with enormous resources, just to poke fun at Richard Wagner. The Creator has turned Fra Diavolo, manipulating the residences of incendiary adults like doll's houses, balancing the roof ridge of one on the frame of another. Here, a ceiling hangs seemingly in mid-air. There, a chimney stack sets off in search of a roof. You can see what is happening on all the floors of a building at once, as in an avant-garde stage-set. No one's activities escape you, from cellar to attic. Everything now unfolds in complete transparency. No one has secrets for anyone. History has undressed human beings and will not cover them up again for some time. On the black market you can swap emptiness for overcrowding. What the poet hardly dared dream, war has accomplished, stitching together the murderer's revolver and the survivor's umbrella on the sewing-machine of time. You'd think that blind people had been killing each other here. For once, the nightmare is outlasting the night.

We look at the ruins, thinks the ruins' pedestrian. But more than that, the ruins look at us. The anthropomorphism of the stones. Each ruin is a wide-eyed, demolished face. Each ruin holds out a mirror to us. We recognise ourselves in it so much better than when there was a construction there – when a construction usurped the place of a future ruin. We discover at last that we are our own ruin.

Goethe, the perambulating poet recalls, said that "to build a house, to plant a tree, to bring a child into the world, is to act as a man". In the last weeks of the war, at Landsberg, the poet could not read anything except that: the intimate writings of Goethe, his letters to Bettina and other privileged correspondents. Strange how we Germans, whatever side we come from, whatever our vision of the world, whatever our sympathies and detestations, are almost always reconciled by the name of the "Aulic Chancellor". Why read him in Landsberg in 1944? In search of what key to the events of that time? Hoping for what consolation? At that time, what was one to think of a formulation like: "To build a house, to plant a tree – Goethe's tree, no doubt, Goethe's majestic oak at Buchenwald! – to bring a child into the world ... "? I who contributed only accidentally to bringing a girl into the world, and have hardly concerned myself with her since; I who in this base world have not planted even a sprig of sweet pea, what lesson or balm was I expecting from the Aulic Chancellor? As for his invitation that we should build our own abode, I wonder what he would think about what has happened to the German cities. And whether he would repeat his enthusiasm for Valmy?

Again the poet raises his eyes to the first floor of the building in Westfälische Strasse, on the threshold of which he stopped just now, then his gaze climbs the other floors to the top. There it steps over a half-dismantled balcony and climbs down floor by floor to the ground floor of the building next door. No disrespect to Herr von Goethe, he thinks, but we can't go on telling the story of these people as in his day, as if nothing had happened. Of course, we can try to do so, as many surely will; nor do we doubt that they will have millions of readers. Sometimes, even, they will write fine books, on subjects like a professor infatuated, unhappily for himself, with a cabaret singer, or a tuberculosis patient in love with the X-ray photo of his beloved, or a chronicle of low life, of pimps and petty criminals from the Alexanderplatz quarter, or even, looking on the bright side, about the sufferings of a young man in the grip of an impossible love, or the torments of that colleague of mine who was not afraid to exchange his soul for a few moments of real living ... These days you only swap your soul for a cigarette end, and if you lose your shadow, it's because your body has got tired of dragging it along in all the havoc, and cut it adrift, fleeing wildly along some blazing road! Now that all the fictions have been burnt in one *auto-da-fé* or another, or have gone up in flames with the towns that inspired them, it must be all over with fine German writing. Since the appalling fiction of History had turned itself into reality, it won't be decent to imagine any other for quite some time to come!

There won't be words, either, to talk about the disaster. Language will be too poor to express even this gaping hole. Of course, here as elsewhere, you can bet that the traffickers will do good business. In the very heart of chaos they will effort-lessly unroll their neo–Weimarian style ...

The poet dreams of a language that would put itself at half-mast and which, to rise from its ashes, would first draw up a balance-sheet of its own bankruptcy.

The newspapers told us that at the Nuremberg trials new terms had to be created to describe retrospectively the crimes that had been committed. How could one not also forge a new writing to evoke the ruins? To echo this bareness, sentences pared to the bone? The peace of graveyards calls for a language disinterred alive. Against those who, lamenting the fate of stones, made their heart one more supernumerary stone.

Night is falling. Before moving off again, the man shuts his eyes. He listens. Lately, he has often thought he could hear the muffled rumble of an avalanche. A distant falling of stones.

Back home at 20, Bozener Strasse, he examines aerial photos of the bombed city in the glow of his writing-desk lamp. From that height, all you can make out are the cells of a sacked beehive, as delicate as lacework.

And then, the litany of children fleeing on the highways, cripples collapsing in public squares, prostitutes opening their overcoats to show they have nothing on underneath. Here, an organ grinder fraternises with two Soviet sentries. There, a preacher urges his listeners to put their trust, at last, in the mercy of Christ. On a platform in a railway station a liberated soldier does not even glance at the photo held out by the mother of another. A female tramp doubles up over a piece of bread as if it were a newborn baby. A one-legged angel that has fallen from the roof of a cathedral dances in front of the building. However, the examiner prefers to pore over other pictures: those showing squares black with delirious crowds in Paris, London, Brussels, New York; roofs covered with humans like bunches of grapes; young women riding down boulevards on armoured cars, their arms loaded with flowers. Why does he dwell above all on these young people wild with delight, these radiant girls, these ecstatic old men, these policemen wreathed in smiles? Because, he thinks, it's this unbridled joy, still more than the horror of war, that condemns us. They may forget their sufferings but they'll always remember that joy. And it will be even less forgiving than pain itself.

But now he comes back to the other photos. Any man who has seen these images, he thinks, is in a sense guilty. Perhaps the world will not regain its innocence until all the witnesses of these scenes are dead. That is the greatest scandal. He remembers those harem photos that mercenary voyeurs had taken clandestinely to satisfy colonial concupiscence ... Those por-

traits of mousmees and belly-dancers were intentionally porno-
graphic. But the looker's naivety was as profound as the
indignity of those looked upon. And those photos were only
involuntarily cruel.

That, he thinks, is how one ought to photograph Berlin.
With the same inane perversity. With that obliviously pitiless
gaze.

The following night he dreams he is crawling among the
rubble after an earthquake; with bleeding hands he desperately
tries to dig out someone who must be close to him – but who
can it be? Aren't most of his loved ones dead? If they are
buried, isn't it in his past? He wakes with a start, smeared in
sweat, with racing heart.

At least my dream was about a natural catastrophe, he
thinks . . .

The truth is, the Berliner discovers, that a year after the end
of the war they have not yet started rebuilding the city. The
year zero is being eternalised. No doubt they could have rebuilt
some quarters in a few months. But they hesitate to start. Why?
Perhaps they are seriously wondering whether to stay here. Are
they planning to abandon the unlucky place? Tomorrow the
population may learn without surprise that they are invited to
emigrate, to fulfil their destiny elsewhere. It's worse than that.
Not only is the city not being rebuilt, it is being destroyed
twice over. So bent are they on starting everything from zero
that they repudiate not only the war but the entire past. Were
the bombardments just a beginning? Is the intention to leave
no trace at all of a story that some call shameful, others tragic: as
if it had been neither?

That's why the images of 1946 confirm the memories of
1945! The seasons unroll against an unchanging backdrop. The
ruining of the city was an event: it is turning into a way of life.

After each air raid, those who were unhoused by the final

assault scribbled on the bombed façades a last message or
appeal: "Richter and Bloch families all alive – Günter where
are you?" Thus men signed the stones before leaving them to
seek a new shelter elsewhere.

There might, of course, be another reason for preserving the
ruins. For turning them into a natural museum.

They would act like this, thinks the observer, if they
intended us never to think of anything else. Henceforth our
ruins would not merely surround and beleaguer us, they would
define us entirely. They would state our identity. They would
tell us, once and for all, who we are. Who we have to deal
with.

If that were the case, what ambiguities would beset us! For
when we say: our ruins, the thinker wonders, do we refer to
ruins we have made, or ruin we have undergone? Do we think
of the crime or the punishment? At Landsberg, during the last
two years of the war, apart from Goethe, the intimate writings
of the Aulic Chancellor, his correspondence with Bettina
Brentano – which really means Bettina's letters to Goethe
rather than his replies to his "dear Bettina" – apart from that
the poet-doctor had managed to read only the thick, pithy
novel of an epileptic Russian genius devoted to this thorny
question: does grace sometimes take tortuous byways to reach
its goal? So that a crime might come back to its sender like a
boomerang, but to enlighten the target? The poet was not able
to accept this metaphysical sleight of hand without some
reservations, some scepticism ... What, then, do our ruins
commemorate? A bitter defeat or an expiation?

He thought of Kaiser Wilhelm's "Memorial Church". A
memorial to what? To Wilhelm. But now, without needing to
rename the building, we can give the memory a different
trajectory ... The votive church is henceforth dedicated to
war. Without raising the awkward question whether it is a
reminder of aggression or of martyrdom. Or both together.
The more so since it has been decided in high places not to

rebuild the church. Or rather, to half-restore it, without resharpening its fire-ravaged steeple like a pencil point. Decapitated it was, and truncated it will remain. Like memory itself. A monument consecrated to partial amnesia ...

For, how many of the survivors would heed this lesson petrified at the centre of Berlin's star? We might remember a thousand times that we were guilty. And a thousand times we would forget it. We might be tossed for eternity between the inexpiable and its repression. There is a time for all things, says Ecclesiastes. It might be so for our ruins: a time to excavate them, and a time to bury them again ... And even when we remember, we shall wear a forgetful look.

Let us also consider this: we have made ourselves so guilty in the eyes of the world that no one notices that we are also our own victims. It is a strange situation. It would certainly have fascinated the epileptic of St Petersburg. It would have given him food for thought, to the point of making him cry out in pain, pushing him to the brink of madness. With good reason.

But I'm getting carried away, thinks the thinker, I'm running ahead of myself ... Let's not be precipitate. For the inhabitants of this city will need a lot more time just to take the measure of the crime they have committed against the world. And by that token it will take even more time for the world to start thinking about the wrong that has been done to us. We have done such wrong to the world that for a long time we shall not be entitled to think of wrong done to us. For a long time it will seem scandalous to think of us otherwise than as the worst assassins. For a long time we shall be simply unthinkable as victims. Of course, thinks the old man, I shall not see that time. No doubt as much time will pass between this spring day of 1946 and the one when this city will no longer be merely accursed and engulfed in its shame, as has already passed between this spring day and the day when a St Petersburg epileptic wrote a book in the form of a detective novel, that I read at Landsberg during the last two years of the war ...

The Stones

Contrary to the wish of the Aulic Chancellor, I only made a child in order to disown it immediately, I have planted no tree nor built any house, but had I my child beside me I do not know how I should explain to her the story of this city. Perhaps never twice in quite the same way. For this city has lived as many stories as it numbered inhabitants at the time when we forfeited the right to weep for our city.

The observer runs his eye over a tourist's guide to the beauties and curiosities of the city of Dresden. The Brühl Terrace. The nymph fountain at the Zwinger. The hunting lodge at Moritzburg. The citadel at Pillnitz ...

He flips the pages nervously. The splendours of Baroque Germany. The majestic course of the river. The delicate armature of the bridges. White pleasure boats. Tourists sitting at the balustrades. Lovers walking the paths. Children naked in the fountains. Diners seated beneath parasols. Charabancs and river-boats. Nothing but images of peace, summer serenity. No squadrons of Lancasters or Flying Fortresses. No Altstadt carpeted with flames. No Frauenkirche transmuted into a mountain of sandstone. No headless towers, rivers of blood or fleeing refugees. The guide dates from before the war; the observer has read it mechanically, seeking by a reflex action the debris and disasters it could not yet contain. But when would the next edition be? Only after one had exhausted the new guides to Kiev, Warsaw and Coventry?

While the poet is leaving his apartment on one of his "Kantian" walks, as he likes to call them — for he finds more wisdom in this habit of the philosopher's than in all his writings — he notices the porter sitting on a stair to polish the varnished bannister. The porter is going to repeat this position on each of the ninety-three steps making up the staircase. That he should show such concern after what has happened — is it ludicrous or admirable? Or even repugnant, wonders the poet, whose preoccupations never leave him. It's simply human, he interjects ironically, knowing that when you have said that you have, alas, said nothing at all.

Evening falls on the city like soot.

When the sky clouds over in Berlin, the light itself seems to be incinerated. The walker feels his throat constricted. He tells himself: It's the smoke choking the atmosphere ... The smoke that comes from tile stoves fed with charcoal. But it is emotion that is strangling him. It's the city itself that has him by the throat.

The murderous city, or the vanquished, tortured city? Could it be that the city has injected some of the suffering it has caused into these stones which now exude it without being able to rid themselves of it? Could it be that the stones are impregnated with the blood of victims the city sacrificed, before bathing in that of its inhabitants? Yes, it is possible. And that too, would be part of the punishment.

If I had that child still with me, the child that Herr von Goethe wished for all of us, that is what I should try to explain to her. Better than I was able to do when she came to see me at the beginning of this spring.

Above his head the rotor of a helicopter hacks the thick air, chops it into slices. Then silence falls again, suddenly pierced by the twittering of a bird lost in the Berliner Strasse, outside all seasons, outside all reason. A bird from another world ... thinks the walker, or only back from Africa? Else ... mumbles Gottfried Benn.

> "Waters stand behind my eyes
> and I must weep them all.
> Always I wish I could fly
> Away with the migrant birds ... "

Else Lasker-Schüler. She had celebrated the winged voyagers. She did not wait, for the worst to happen here before migrating – she took wing to Palestine, that sacred place, where she died in 1945, an odd year to choose ... She never did anything by halves. She who had affectionately baptised him "the Cyclops, her non-Jewish friend, the Nibelung, the Barbarian"! As if to dilute the femininity which the young poet – seventeen years her junior though no one would have guessed, least of all the poet – troubled in her, she made him call her "The Prince of Thebes" ... How had the Prince judged the Barbarian, the Nibelung, her half-blind Aryan friend, from afar, after 1937? What was her verdict? No doubt we should never know.

> "There is weeping in the world
> As if the Good Lord had died.
> And the leaden night that falls
> Is heavy as the tomb ...
> Oh, let us deeply embrace.
> On the world's door knocks a longing
> of which we shall have to die."

And now she was really dead. The Prince of Thebes always kept her word. She had indeed died of longing, a few weeks before the end of the war. And before the start of the year zero. For the history of this country was to start again not just from a dead city, but by paying the posthumous homage due to those who had vanished.

Else to whom, the old poet remembers, his first poems had seemed as if wrought in blood. What she feared above all was that he might show her commiseration. She was wrong in this. Pity should be left to God. Lord, look down on the disarray of strong spirits, who are always misjudged. There are majestic gods and paltry ones, thinks the poet. Else believed only in a God who was haughty, generous and full of gentleness; it was for Him that she wrote. May He not have proved ungrateful.

The young poet had left her as soon as possible. Have pity also, Lord, on tardy regrets and vain nostalgias.

> "Happy the dead who return to peace
> And stretch their pallid hands

Towards the shadowy, grandiose angels that walk
with beating wings in the tall house."

Else Lasker-Schüler. Auschwitz. Palestine. Berlin. Knot of
intertwined blood. Even when we remember, we shall wear a
forgetful look. But still, forgetfulness will avail us nothing.
Remorse is a faithful mistress who is never late for a rendezvous.

In Fehrbelliner Platz the stroller has stopped. He is eyeing
from far off a man in a shop window who seems to be making
a sign to him. A sign, really? It isn't a sign. It's a voice the man
is addressing to him. From a big square mouth comes a mute
cry. A cry that at this distance you cannot make out. A man?
It's not a man. It's an angel. Two immense wings rooted in the
shoulders frame the vociferating face.

The walker goes towards him.

Leaning on his counter between two sides of beef hanging
from hooks, the butcher is addressing him.

Not surprising that the walker could not hear him from that
distance. The meat-merchant is hawking his wares from the
other side of the window separating his display from the street.
Perhaps, too, the stroller is becoming a little hard of hearing.

Not surprising that at that distance the stroller could not
recognise a butcher. The moment before he would not have
believed that anyone could have offered such quarters of
pendulous meat in Berlin! All in all, an angel would have been
more likely. Perhaps, too, the stroller's sight is growing somewhat dim ...

Looking more closely, indeed from very close, since the
stroller is not afraid to squash his nose against the pane, he sees
only a mass of bones, tendons and ligaments, and very little
meat. The two carcasses hanging providentially from the sky
must have been stripped by eagles before landing! All you have
to admire are two bare ivory hulks spattered with black clots.
The butcher with the almost inaudible voice, in this square in

the annihilated city, may look like an archangel with ever-lastingly folded wings, but an impure archangel not so much fallen as soiled with blood.

The stroller backs away, fearing to recognise himself not in the reflection sent back by the glass, but in what he sees through it, and he retreats from a slaughter-house that seems erected in memory of him.

Life may pretend to go on, and it even goes in reality. The men grow tobacco on their balconies and the women plant tomatoes under their bedroom floors. Everyone tends his hanging kitchen garden. Seamstresses gather up scraps of cloth to create evening dresses and ballroom slippers: one must suppose that society women will soon make use of them, and therefore that society still exists. The Reichstag lawns are ploughed, the shrubs of Grunewald transplanted. The Russian soldiers acquire Mickey Mouse wrist-watches at any price. Berliners exchange washing coppers, pianos and women's underwear for coffee, chocolate, oranges, flour, eggs and soap. It is still so cold: all the trees of the city, the bannisters and steps of the staircases, and even the crutches of cripples, have already passed through the stoves. Is there any other market than the black one? Life itself is a black market.

Sometimes, when you look up, the sky seems almost un-inhabited, now that the aeroplanes have gone and the sirens no longer invite the population to bury itself alive ... Little girls are allowed to give their dolls' tea-parties in the remnants of bunkers, and boys turn machine-guns into merry-go-rounds.

Thus German humanity comes back to itself ... Is it only a new humanity? Who could be sure? The old men regain possession of the cities, wearing knapsacks and armed with a cane or an ice-pick, as if they were climbing a mountain. Arriving at the rubble's summit, will these new explorers, these urban Alpinists, plant a flag as a sign of conquest?

And the children, born the day before, will they know anything except this floe of frozen ballast, or will they remain children of the stones, as there were women of the ruins, themselves reverting to childhood, busy moles burrowing with their buckets and spades?

Over there a marriage is being celebrated in a church whose roof has flown away; here, avid readers are consulting books in the open air in libraries without walls.

Have we become indestructible troglodytes? The city seethes with life.

One ought at least to keep a souvenir, mumbles the stroller, bending to pick up a piece of clinker, a little block of concrete with a captive flower of rusty metal. I'll put it on the mantlepiece, he thinks, in the Wintergarten.

The Alexandrov troupe is playing "Kalinka" at the Femina, between two acts by contortionists and jugglers. Marlene Dietrich is parading in an American army officer's uniform on the ruins of Hamburg, and Ingrid Bergman, fully dressed and radiant, is posing, in a bathtub cut in two by a shell, to charm a photographer from the Magnum agency.

We shall remember another city, criss-crossed by horse-drawn tramcars, cabs and double-decker buses, barges dancing on the foaming waters of the Havel, aeroplanes passing under the arches of the bridges. You met at the Café Schön. Amazons patrolled the central avenue of Unter den Linden. The porters in the apartment blocks accompanied you to the lift to show you to the upper floors.

The roads that no longer exist will be rebuilt without changing their names. That will be a mistake. It will be like parents who have lost a child and give its name to the one born after . . .

Later, the film newsreels will show us what happened. The children of those who still had the heart to beget them will laugh at Goering's paunch, Goebbels's limp, the Führer's tantrums . . . It's not so much the horror of what happened that will make us anachronistic. It is ridicule. The laughter of those who follow will be enough to cast us back to the Palaeolithic age. As for us, we'll hardly muster a smile for those elegant creatures, upright as caryatids, with their hair formed like a shell, and those little men wearing boaters and dressed in black, looking serious and inoffensive as they watch the first Zeppelin pass overhead from the white esplanade of the Brandenburg Gate: ourselves, in another time. For we know where we stand with regard to them, and their future.

Year zero plus one. Germany has been condemned in the persons of the administrators of the massacre and a few sabre-rattlers. All the others, it seems, will be denazified. Germany is now divided, but neither the crimes nor the suffering can be cut in half. She will be lucky if they are not doubled.

Some women have survived. We shall remember that their generosity sometimes made good the men's abjectness. The men will notice that the women are still beautiful, and desirable. They will find each other again in shady arbours. They will have idylls again. We can be sure: they will learn to dance again.

> "Debris, all the ruins
> so bare in the morning –
> only one thing is true
> you and the unlimited."

"I see we are neighbours, young lady," declares the doctor, glancing into the courtyard where a withered maple stands.

"Yes, we are, Doctor. We live in the same street; from our windows we have practically the same view ... And then, we've been neighbours for longer than you think ... "

"What do you mean?" asks the doctor somewhat wearily, hardly intrigued by this information.

"I was born at Fürstenfelde," she persists, "a few kilometres from Sellin, where you spent your childhood ... "

"My childhood ... ," he repeats distractedly, as if the word had little meaning for him.

> "A land a sombre sea
> and then a realm that ends
> so far away no light
> ever returns from there,"

she quotes.

"That land is not the country of my childhood," he points out. "Nor of yours," he adds, purely out of politeness. "Our land," he says, almost regretfully, "isn't washed by any sea."

"What does that matter?" she asks, unabashed. "Will you come one last time," she goes on,

> "for we were so alone
> we plunged ourselves in a cup
> full of images and dreams.
> Yet that was only today
> and our sea was the night,
> we were each other's prey,
> the white cargo."

Damnation, a poetess! thinks the doctor. He just recognises his own poem, though it might have been the fumblings of a beginner. He supposes she's starting by obsequiously quoting his own work before slipping in her own. Young people often do that, he recalls. They used to come before the war, to the Romanisches Café or Möhring's, with a sheaf of lousy rhymes under their arms. They thought I hadn't noticed the formidable gift they were about to make me, ill-concealed as it was in their armpit, and always started by reciting poems by me, out of either politeness or tactics, depending. They were very downcast when, most of the time, I failed to recognise the poems they were gabbling, but that was just a last reprieve. Sooner or later the young person would produce his rubbish, or more usually hers, and I was asked to respond to it at once, to pass judgment there and then on the author's genius, assess their chances of success, lavish encouragement and draw up a letter recommending them to an editor in vogue ... Now the war is hardly finished and it's all starting again! He is tempted to tell his visitor: "All right, no need to pretend ... Put them on my writing desk: I'll get in touch ... "

"So you haven't come for a vaccination, Fräulein Kaul?" Dr Benn asks prudently.

"Oh yes, of course I have! Isn't it compulsory?"

"Yes, Fräulein, you're right, the law requires it – since the occupying powers have imposed laws on us, for our own good. So you came for that after all?"

"Yes, I made an appointment for that reason," says Ilse Kaul smiling. "It was so convenient, you see. I had only to take a few steps to reach your surgery ... But you are right to wonder ... For it's true that I didn't want to be vaccinated by just any doctor!"

"Really, Fräulein! I'm sure my reputation isn't such that you have no choice!"

"Let's say that I haven't come only for that."

"Why? Are you unwell?"

"I've the constitution of an ox. One needs it, as you know, in times like these ... "

"I understand. But do you or don't you need the vaccination?"

"Since I have to ... "

"You don't believe in immunisation?"

"Of course. My belief in it is unshakeable, although I'm sure you'll agree that these days you can't immunise yourself against anything."

"Not against misfortune, undoubtedly," the doctor observes sententiously.

"You can't even immunise yourself against joy, Doctor," his client replies with a smile. Almost with effrontery. (With a magnificent impudence, the doctor will think later, re-running the scene in his mind.)

"You can't immunise yourself against anything, Fräulein," the doctor repeats, though without ironic intent. Perhaps he is trying to gain time. "Now, if we had been able to vaccinate ourselves against events ... "

"We should have done so," she agrees.

"Have you noticed that in cases like that the legislator does not interfere?" he asks. "He respects the free choice of the conscious, responsible citizen."

"Who are you thinking of? The legislator before the war, or the one who declared it? There's no more prolific law-maker than the tyrant, doctor. Far from doing without laws, he secretes more of them than any democrat."

"There has never been a dictator who did not want to prove, contrary to all appearances, that he wasn't one. Take the law he adopted to protect German blood ... "

"He protected it to such good effect that in no time he was spilling it on every battlefield in Europe. But we're starting to philosophise ... "

It's true that the conversation is languishing somewhat. There is an unresolved tension in it. They both know that at any moment it could tilt over into emotion – or ridicule.

"Is it true that disease is rife in the city, Doctor?" the visitor asks.

Good God! She's talking about Berlin like a fashionable salon.

"How does it manifest itself?"

"How does what?"

"Why – the typhoid ... "

My word! Doesn't he sound interested!

"Oh, in a feeling of stupor," he says. "Headaches, shivering, giddiness. Facial oedema. Nasal bleeding. Aching limbs. Digestive disorders. High temperature, of course ... But why are you smiling?"

"Oh, nothing," she says. "the professional language. The clinical description ... "

"What do you expect of me? That I compose a lyric poem about it?"

She is making him nervous, even irritable. He wonders what she is after, this client who is not like the others. What is there to add?

"The eyes become fixed, glazed. The stomach is distended. Then it starts to void, and that only ends in death. You'd think the whole body wanted to put an end to itself. Which is what happens. You void yourself, lose yourself on the way ... At the same time you ramble, even start singing! You are assailed by memories from the past ... You visit foreign cities where you have never set foot. That's how you make your exit. Shitting out everything you've got in you. Reverting to infancy. Exploring time and space ... "

"A truly local illness!" she exclaims. "Some people around here must enjoy that: regressing, getting back to primal innocence. As if nothing had happened ... "

"To do that, young lady, most of them wouldn't even need to fall ill!"

They laugh in unison. For the first time. They can't know, yet, that there will be others. But they are quietly beginning to feel at ease.

"But have no fear, the vaccine itself has only good effects. A slight temperature for forty-eight hours at the most. Perhaps a little delirium ... but no complications."

"Not even a slight hallucination? I'm going to be disappointed!"

"You must comfort yourself with the thought that I may have forestalled an illness that was lying in wait for you."

"I'll think: Dr Benn was my shield ... "

"Oh, I've never yet helped anyone to survive, you know ... I might well have done the opposite. I've never been anyone's shield. More like a lance ... I've been a lance more often than duty called."

"And which end did you hold it by?"

"Good question," he concedes. "Sometimes by the handle, sometimes the point."

He wonders why he is being drawn into this unusual patient's games, that no longer really disconcert him. For her part, she notices that the doctor is getting gloomier joke by joke. There is an awkward pause.

Herta ... , he thinks. Herta, my second wife, for whom I was neither shield nor rampart. Herta whom I didn't vaccinate against any calamity. The grave I dug ... And even thinking of myself – have I been able to ward off the curse that has ravaged my life? It's true that doctors as a rule do not vaccinate themselves ...

"I never thought about it until this morning," he says, as if he had voiced his thoughts aloud. "I thought about it thanks to you ... "

"About what, Doctor?"

"Oh, I don't know – the real meaning of vaccination. What do you do in life, Fräulein, if I'm not being indiscreet?"

"I'm a dentist," she replies.

"Oh, you're a dentist too? I'm hardly surprised."

"You guessed?"

"No, I just had a slight hunch."

"Because you heard me prattling naively about the virtues of the medical art?"

"No, it was more the way you felt obliged, out of pure kindness, to quote some of your poor colleague's poems ... "

She laughs. He likes this laugh. As in another time, he thinks. A time you thought was over. Yet which is so young. The laugh of youth from another time. He's ready to back that laugh. He's surprised at still being willing to bet on anything.

"You look dreamy, Dr Benn," says Ilse Kaul.

"Don't you believe it, Dr Kaul," he says. "Don't trust appearances. Strictly speaking, I never dream. I'm just flattered that you should know some of my poems. I'm honoured that anyone should have learned, remembered poems by me, after all this time, after what happened."

"That surprises you?"

"Yes, it bowls me over – although I've learned never to be surprised by anything."

"Not even by something better than expected?" she asks, smiling. "So you're not just surprised, are you? You're happy."

"Well, yes, I am actually happy."

What a curious word, all the same, he thinks. He did not realise it could still have a meaning. He repeats it, as if to convince himself, to test it. "Happy ... "

"That a woman reads you?"

"That a woman like you should think fit to read me, in 1946 ... Why should I deny it? I'm thunderstruck. A woman I'm going to see again. Often. As often as possible. What would you think about tomorrow morning, for breakfast?"

He thinks: a woman with whom I'm going to spend the rest of my life. He wonders if he hasn't said it out loud.

Then, for the first time, he really looks at her. He finds her better than beautiful. He notices her youth. Someone of whom you could guess why they survived, if such reasons were possible. Someone who deserved to survive – which ought, of course, to have been the case with the majority of the victims of this hecatomb. But who would have found arguments to convince God Himself that she so deserved. When you think that you have yourself had all too many opportunities and even reasons to die, and have certainly survived only by accident, you have an eye for such things.

You have reason to be stupefied, all the same. But in face of Dr Kaul, you don't want to be surprised by anything. Not even by something falling to your lot that you have long believed you had no right to.

"That's not all," he says. "I still have to vaccinate you."

"Against you?"

"No, it's already too late for that! I can't change anything there: it's beyond my competence. Would you prefer the right buttock or the left?"

Thinking back on the scene, how he will relish that first time the woman of his life burst into it and he was able to ask her, with impunity, to offer him her rump! He could, at least for appearances' sake, have suggested the arm or the shoulder ...

"There," he says, "you can get dressed."

And he thinks: provisionally ... Is it from frequenting death, or from being supposed to combat it, that doctors are authorised to take liberties and talk smut without vulgarity, because the implications are mysteriously altered? If he put his hand on this woman's backside, he can't help himself thinking, it would be a curious way of saying: Look, we're still alive ... In the jubilation this recent meeting has inspired in him, he knows that the pleasure of being seduced by a person of the opposite sex is heightened because a doctor is involved. He remembers that in the barracks in Brussels in 1916, in Hanover in 1937, at Landsberg in 1943, in the midst of stifling and bloody triviality, there would always come a time when the only men he could still talk to had something to do with medicine.

Has the patient begun to follow the interior movement of the man who has just become her doctor?

"What you have just injected — is it bacilli, dead strains of virus, toxins?"

"Oh, a cocktail of assassinated bacteria ... One person's sorrow is another's joy — you're safe at any rate! Did you know that at the front thousands of soldiers inoculated themselves with real illnesses to escape the horrors of war, though they risked dying as a result?"

"To escape being ordered to fight?"

"To escape the world altogether. Sometimes, to save their skins, or what mattered of them, they injected themselves with thallium or salicylic acid, at the risk of killing themselves with an overdose. There were also those who were willing to mutilate themselves, sacrificing the fingers of their right hand with a blow of an axe, or shooting themselves point-blank in the foot. Others gave leeches the pleasant task of consuming one of their eyes. Others ingurgitated anything they could get their hands on: excrement bought from sick comrades in the infirmary ... Or soft soap, gunpowder, tobacco soaked in water, dye, or just screws, nails, thread, greatcoat buttons, pebbles, aluminium foil, hair, pubic hair."

"What did they hope to achieve?"

"To render themselves useless. But those were the ones who hoped to get out. They wanted to live! Most were exposed, and shot like deserters. They were not the strangest cases. I'll let you into the secret about the suicides."

"What interest has the army in carrying out a post-mortem on itself?"

"There are reparations to the families of the deceased at stake. Only in some cases was it possible to ascertain a precise cause: fear of punishment for a crime committed, unhappy love, a shameful disease. Usually it was an unpremeditated act, done under an irresistible compulsion after consuming large quantities of alcohol. Especially when spring came round ... You should have seen how the army turned it into a moral issue! Ignominious flight, as against a heroic death facing the enemy, a death that 'served some purpose'. They could not foresee that the Führer himself ... If only he had done it earlier! For years he used it as a means of blackmailing his own people. After working through piles of case documents and psychiatric records that explained nothing, I finished up by reversing the assumptions and regarding suicide as much more logical than survival. Suicide under the flag was a testimony to common sense. But I'm getting carried away, I could go on for ever. Stop me, Fräulein, interrupt the old dotard I've become. I've so little chance to talk. I had almost forgotten all these things, though that's no excuse, of course ... "

"It might really be better not to repeat what you have just

told me ... You'd be accused of giving in to cynicism. Just as you were exactly thirty years ago, when you brought out your poems on 'corpses washed like benches' ... "

"Ah," he said, starting to pace up and down the room, "you know about that as well? I can see you've heard about the poet who went picking over corpses, fed his fantasies on filth, lost his faith in human progress and wallowed in nihilism! You've been warned about the intellectual dandy, the gourmet of strong emotions, dreaming about a highly aesthetic annihilation of the planet. A professional *agent provocateur* ... Professional indeed? Half-time, perhaps, the other half being devoted to healing the bodies I was supposed to want annihilated. The marvellous Walter Benjamin was accused, just before his suicide, of intending to write an essay on 'medical nihilism'; I was to have featured in it, in the excellent company of Jung and Céline among others. And while we're listing doctors who have wielded the pen, why not include Brecht and Döblin? Because they happened to believe in 'human progress'? There's more to be said about all this. Humanism can be very devious at times. Even the charming son of Thomas Mann, who kindly warned me about my error – rightly, as I soon found out – later put me into one of his novels in the guise of a salon Cassandra whose esoteric prophecies put him into a state of trance and who rejoiced to see civilisation sliding pathetically towards the abyss ... On one point this portrait coincided with the truth: the unflattering description of my physical attractions. My short stature, my corpulence, my gentle, cold blue eyes, even my sagging cheeks and thick, 'cruelly sensual' lips. I am as ugly, aren't I, as the author of *Mephisto* obligingly reminded us? For heaven's sake! I know well enough that I haven't the mug or the figure of a poet! But isn't it better so? My poetry, too, sometimes has a hangdog look about it, don't you think? But what is more important is that while Klaus Mann was denouncing my aberration, the Nazis were driving nails through some of my books ... By then our country had fallen prey to the casters of spells. And since then I have published, clandestinely

and at my own expense, a number of anti-Hitler poems. All
the same, no later than yesterday, I had to be expurgated.
Having become undesirable in the eyes of the future vanquished, I remain unwanted by the recent victors. The matter
is closed; I've merely been moved from a black-list to a grey
one ... To become white, I should at least have emigrated,
should I not? What do you think?"

She says nothing. Perhaps she has no opinion (if only that
were possible).

He doesn't give up.

"For example, Furtwängler," he says, "who conducted
Mathis der Maler in 1934 – that piece by my friend Hindemith
of the Goebbels-like nose and beard – then resigned all his
posts and refused others: should he have contemplated leaving
when everything in him rebelled against it? He would have
been received in other countries with open arms, he would
have been lionised as a symbol of resistance to oppression. He
preferred to stay here in a precarious position, so that he could
exert the weight of his disapproval where it actually mattered.
Does that make him a scoundrel? The whole question has been
avoided for the last ten years. The artist in exile existed as a
kind of phantom or remorse, and that was something, of
course ... But the one who had to be gagged because he was
still here, who was buried alive, whose mouth emerged from
the sand to utter a mute cry – didn't his dumbness make as
much noise as a good many far-off speeches? Apart from that,
one is beginning to realise that there were as many kinds of
emigration as there were emigrants. Döblin had every reason to
envy the luxurious retreat of his colleague Thomas Mann, and
Lion Feuchtwanger, who thought so highly of the Soviet
Union, nevertheless preferred to take refuge in the United
States. Was it better, in the end, to resist out there or hibernate
here?"

"I don't know," declares Dr Benn's patient. "Perhaps we
should leave it to tyrants to generalise?"

"What is to be feared is that those who decided one way or

the other, no matter what they chose, will never be able to speak to each other again. That would be the Führer's ultimate victory! Make no mistake, dear colleague, I'm not at all blasé; I've not got over all that. And like almost all those who were involved in it, victors and vanquished, I have not yet fully come back from the war ... Who knows, in any case, if it isn't going to flare up again in other forms still unknown? We doctors have a sense for such things, have we not?"

"For the things of peace and war?" she asks.

"For what finishes, and what never stops finishing."

"Well, as for me, I'm not much of a palm reader ... "

"No, but you have placed your hands on the bodies of men. They've been soiled – or cleansed – by the contact. There always comes a time when what separates people or draws them together are not their convictions, their professions of faith, or their differences of opinion; often these things don't even decide whether they hold the same opinion at the same moment. At another time they might have agreed. No, what unites them are the upheavals of History that they have passed through, sometimes even on opposite sides, the disorders that have deflected them from their lives, or at least from the idea they first had of them, the kind of weaknesses that have been exposed in them, that have compromised them in their own eyes. What unites them is the tree they chose to climb in the forest of all the possible courages, that hid all the others; but above all it's the eyes of the dead that they have had to close. There are, literally, corpses among us. It is our dead who weld us one to another, or chain us, or interpose themselves, reconcile us or set us apart ... You're a doctor, haven't you read the same message in your corpses?"

"I only read what's in their mouths," she rejoins, bursting out laughing.

"It's true your patients present themselves agape. Really, you're just anticipating the forensic pathologist!"

"Sometimes I manage to extract the malady with its root ... But when I came here I didn't realise I would be drawn into a discussion of the way of all flesh ... Can I ask you a question?"

"Please do ... "

"Those suicide cases whose files you studied: did you only meet them on paper, after they had 'succeeded', if I can put it like that? Did you meet any in the flesh, when they had failed in their attempt?"

"Of course. But no one was supposed to know. Any suicide attempt was sanctioned, absurdly, by ... capital punishment!"

"What did you say to them? What could a great German poet say to those people?"

"'A great German poet', as you so kindly put it, has no more words than anyone else for such occasions ... He probably has less, since his weigh more heavily. Restoring someone's faith in life when they have tried to lose it and bombs could fall at any moment is not so easily done ... They were astonished to have survived the war, and themselves. They found themselves reluctantly invincible ... They drew little pride from it. They couldn't help addressing me as if they owed their survival partly to me. Either to thank me, or to blame me. Out of that curious misunderstanding could come a dialogue on the reasons one might find to live again ... Would you believe it, Fräulein? One soon gets a reputation as an expert in such matters. I still get letters from desperate men today. Or from men condemned to death ... When they find out I'm a poet as well, they seem mainly afraid that I might write their story one day ... "

"Public scribe for people at death's door! You must still have a rich future, Doctor. If you really were the cynic you are called, you would surely espouse the world's barbarism more readily? One last question: do you like flowers?"

He has sat down in the Wintergarten. Through the window he looks at the rabbit cages in the courtyard, the hydrangeas. Do I like flowers ... he murmurs. Surely. He is suddenly so cold. What an idea, to switch off the electric heater as soon as his visitor had left! He gets up to put on an overcoat. He even puts a hat on his head, as if to elicit a gesture of intimate amusement. The consultation is finished for today. The medical or the legal one? My God, he thinks, I almost started pleading my own cause. Lucky I got cut short. But now I'm as shaken as if I had really tried to do that. The idea of justifying yourself in the eyes of someone who is nothing to you, who must be surprised to find your conscience bad, as another might find you looking unwell . . .

A metal band constricts his brow. In his head a cat that was meant to drown in a sack starts to wake up. Sadness, asleep for a moment, struggles and snarls, with all its claws out.

Why has he tumbled from so high? He has decidedly lost the knack, the habit of being happy. And even that tragic mirth, so close to euphoria, he had felt just now in his attempted self-rehabilitation. A flirt, he thinks, I've flirted with the soul of this beautiful stranger. And all because, before presenting her rump, she had the grace to quote some lines by me that I hardly recognised, they came from so far back, like the body weighted with stones that comes to the surface when the crime is long forgotten, the case closed . . . Let's hope I won't be called to account. I've been shooting a line to Dr Kaul. I've made advances, courted her wildly, resorting to schoolboy stratagems. As if, by heaven, before I could seduce her I had to turn myself back into a virgin in my own eyes. I'm going to make an appointment with her. Not to besiege her even more. To have all my teeth pulled out. And especially my tongue – that above all.

Having missed the opportunity to despair completely without having grasped the chance of rejoicing either, he lapses into a kind of vacantness. There's no one now to observe him. He has taken off his hat and placed it beside him on the sofa. He has unbuttoned his coat, but not yet taken it off, just letting the sleeves slip down his arms. As if he had neither the strength nor the will to do any more. All his energy is straining towards a single goal: to find the meaning of what has happened. How, he wonders, could I pick up the conversation again, giving it a different slant?

I should tell her, thinks the doctor, that in Cologne a bomb exposed an archaeological site the existence of which had been unknown. Mosaics from a temple dedicated to Dionysus ... And that a disciple of Ferruccio Busoni, finding his master's tomb open after one of the bombardments of the capital, grabbed the urn containing his ashes and carried it through the burning city to a place of safety ... Why talk of that first? You have to start with something ... Something comforting. Then quickly pass on to the question of the cold. During the last weeks, it wasn't just bullets that were killing, you had to outwit the frost as well. Meet the icy blast obliquely rather than head-on. Use your elbows amid the universal cold. Cold is the twin of death. At the end of the war it made the earth as inhospitable, uninhabitable, as the other planets. You blew up your gloves like balloons before putting them on, for they would retain the warmth of your breath for several minutes. The fighters' hands froze to their rifle butts. The cold tore your nails off. What happened to your blood? The cold drank it like a vampire. You feared you would find yourself bloodless, unawares ... You wondered if your heart would be the first part to freeze. I knew people who were hoping for bombs to land so that they could warm themselves at the fires. From 1937 on, the Führer collected the "People's Penny" against the winter. We did not know that the winter would last so long, or that the Führer would make it perpetual. We drank nothing but melted snow that had been boiled. Some people washed in mustard. After that he set in train the "Blood and Soil" programme. And indeed, the soil was steeped in blood. We should have listened better to his promises. In a sense, he never lied to us. Blood and cold. In Berlin in the last days, pools of frozen blood. We had first to unfreeze, awaken from our numbness in the tepid medium of defeat, to grasp the full scale of the disaster.

I would have to tell her about the hunger of even the well-fed, the relatively privileged group to which I belonged, of the exceptional hand-out, at Christmas, of an extra ration of smoked saveloy and powdered sardines. But still, I was not to be pitied. Tell her, too, that in barracks far from the front it was boredom that finished you off, little by little, even if you read Goethe and Dostoevsky. You found out that inaction did not make you more innocent of war than fighting did, and that the ineffable monotony of this life was more brutalising than danger. You were only dragged from your torpor by the approach of the enemy; then you had to destroy your papers and books, bury them or set them alight.

Yes, tell her about that first – set the scene. But to "tell her about that" is to tell it to her, Dr Ilse Kaul, as an invalid eagerly describes his illness in all its details, not leaving out the smallest of them, in the hope of helping the diagnosis and being cured. And then, you really only want to answer the question: Do you like flowers? Yes, I think so ... especially asters. And more generally, autumn flowers and ornamental plants: lunaria, stellaria, valerian, chrysanthemums ... I'm sure that landed gentleman, that warlord that I hardly got to know, Ernst Jünger, Ernst *Junker*, such a devotee of botany, would second me in this.

Then explain to that unknown woman – who already isn't unknown – to that qualified listener, what I wrote there, in the Landsberg barracks, while we waited for the outcome of the war, that is to say, for defeat: my conception of a phenotype whose nature would embody the characteristics of our time amid the chaos of History. Would she be offended to hear that despite all that happened, and even because of it, I had not abandoned the idea of a de-secularised prose whose author would be governed by a god, an absolute, by whatever name it was called? At Landsberg, in the depths of melancholy, I saw more clearly than ever that what would survive us were those forms devoid of faith, hope or any real recipient – yet charged with a meaning, a tragic substance, that was deepened by the mystery which concealed it ... Our only biography! I was sure to be accused once again of rabid nihilism – whereas I am really just a "de-moraliser", one in whose eye new worlds would emerge, before I immersed and lost myself in order to find myself anew. For even in the depths of desolation we are allowed to see floating past us such wonders, visions charged with female seduction. We are not redeemed by them – on the contrary. But they exist. The ecstasy does not last, but the images that words transmit are inexhaustible – words, those crutches of imagination, those false limbs of reality . . . Careful now! Should I tell that woman that the joy of saving those forms is not exactly love but uncannily like it, that it makes you think of love? How can one not connect the two? It is all so . . . erotic! The prostitute, the rat, the poet, all under the same roof: "To each is given the sky, love and the tomb." Will I have to go back to that, believe in it again, even publish the results I arrive at? I could call it: "Expressionism Phase II". There would be only an appearance of continuity. But to proclaim the transcendence of style, only an internal act of style would be needed. We live in a void of values. All contents but one have collapsed: form itself as content. And let me not be told that in this I am trying to "escape meaning". Even if I have nothing to tell but my journey towards "a lotus land where nothing changes, all stands still". The country where we would be allowed to forget winter. That second homeland on which others will be eager to assert that I have been shipwrecked . . . To come out of the war with such ideas in my head – I dare say it will give a bad impression. I'm used to such misunderstandings by now. Each of us projects his humanism where he can. For my part, I tend to believe that it would be still more repugnant to emerge from our recent history without professing such ideas . . . As one of my distinguished colleagues put it: "To scandalise while remaining decent – that's art."

But doubt once again engulfs his mind. Fatigue crushes him. I'm as drained, he thinks, as if she were really there in front of me, this new woman, this stranger already so known . . .

In reality, what exhausts him is having to say all this without her being present. What makes him breathless is this dress rehearsal before an empty chair, in the deserted flat, on the ground floor of 20, Bozener Strasse, as the shadows gather and night begins to fall. He feels as weary as a tennis player acrobatically and unfailingly returning to the other side of an invisible net, to an absent partner, a ball that exists only for him.

Am I fond of flowers, Miss Kaul? And how I am fond of them! But I haven't yet told you which. The fact is that despite appearances I have easily climbed the slope of getting to know people . . . I prize chrysanthemums above all. Just look into the courtyard: you can see the flowers most precious to me. For I haven't yet told you about the people I have loved. If I haven't done so, it's because they are almost all dead. I'm their widower. I'm not sure whether, before I became that, they had the leisure or the magnanimity to think of themselves as those who were living for me. I seem to have reserved them for later . . . I haven't yet scaled the mountain of my dead for you, for fear that an avalanche of mourning slide over me.

> "All these graves I have dug
> on hills and beside lakes
> the mounds from which I saw
> the open earth . . . "

For my mother, first of all, thinks the son.

His mother, with the illness she bore in herself like another child, a younger brother for Gottfried, delivered up to the obscurantism of his father – who worshipped a narrow God, thin as a razor-blade. I was too young to relieve her suffering, thinks the son. The son's ineffable aversion to his father was matched only by his immoderate love of medicine. So that he fought henceforth, a corpse between his teeth, against the race of killer-fathers. He could not have known then how many

opportunities he would have to practise his art, in how many
ways and in what historic circumstances! It seems one now has
only the choice of being a pimp, a monk or a soldier.

For a long time I was too young, he thinks, and then,
suddenly, too old.

> "The open earth
> that I carried and carry still –
> as seaweed and shells in my hair,
> that I questioned and question still:
> How is it, the bed of the sea?"

Then there was Else, Fräulein Ilse . . .

A second mother, though she did not know it and he did
not suspect. A Jewess into the bargain, before that word took
on such gravity in Germany. She has just expired in the land of
her origins, of a death born fully grown at the same time as she.

"She who entwines you steals away my horror," she wrote
to the young poet. But he did not seem to believe it either true
or important. She was really defenceless, even against him.

> "All those graves, those hills
> in which I was and am,
> sometimes a white wing
> now brushes across them."

Edith. His first wife, wedded at the same time as a first war.
Of course, it will be said that he did not love her, that he was
incapable of loving. A son she had from another marriage lost
no time in dying. Just as a child of Else Lasker-Schüler's, stuffed
with poetry to the point of seeming arrogant or insane, also
vanished "prematurely". A lot of sons were beginning to die
before their mothers. The times were like that. They would be
for a long time.

To survive was becoming a paradox.

Then, war again. And again a wife. (Did you have a right to
a wife for each world war?) Herta von Wedemeyer, daughter
of an officer from Hanover. A secretary. That was useful –

hadn't the writer just fallen into disgrace? She typed his texts. For a long time, she was to be his only "editor". Almost his only reader ... She was tall, slender. Twenty years younger than he. She had recognised him. He was grateful to her. So it was a story of recognition between a man and a woman, in those times! She had only him. He had only her. It was probably not love. It was an obscure yet fanatical comradeship. After all, it might have lasted for ever.

Ensconced in the army, he looked into suicide cases. Once again, death was drawing close to him.

Now it comes back to him: he had talked about the soldiers' suicides to Miss Kaul, Dr Ilse Kaul. But perhaps he had only mentioned them so that he would not have to recall a suicide that touched him more closely.

He had not told her that Herta von Wedemeyer, from Hanover, had also taken her own life. And that he, the suicide expert, had been unable to prevent her.

Capitulation was imminent. The major had done what he thought right: to save her from the final assault on Berlin, he had sent his ill wife to the country, on the banks of the Elbe. The village where she took refuge was hemmed in by the English, the Americans and the Russians. She was seized by panic, the doctor explains. To himself, for the hundredth time. As if he were preparing himself to explain it, too, to Dr Kaul.

She injected herself with a double dose of morphine that we had kept for us both, in case we were pursued together by the enemy, he explains, tries to explain, to become accustomed to the unthinkable. When we parted she took the poison with her without saying anything, and used the double dose on herself. Did she think me already dead? It was in July 1945, the war had finished for practically everyone, even on the banks of the Elbe. I was responsible only for her, that creature who was so much more modest than the terror that seized her, that devastated her.

The Stones

"She can no longer lift the blooms
nor waken reflections in the roses
that I have set down –
yet she is herself a metamorphosis."

For we ought to see Herta here, coming home to Bozener Strasse, as she did after a long ramble, with her stick, her big bag and her red hat, still confident in me, in my power to protect her.

Women have killed themselves for me, Miss Kaul; or in spite of me, but doesn't that come to the same thing? The Führer wanted everyone to die for him: his country, his people, finally his wife. And his dog. As for me, there are some corpses that I could not prevent. Despite myself, I found myself the Bluebeard of my own story, the Führer of my private life. My own war has had its victims. Did I even know of all my "murders"?

This world did not merely designate its victims, it also chose and fashioned those who were to execute them. Sometimes, as is known, they reversed their roles. As for me, I've always been essentially a survivor. A fugitive animal – sentimental, perhaps, but wild. Those who escaped don't have an easy life: they have bad dreams. But still more pale and curdled were the dawns of those who died, in a sense, in my place. Those, Miss Kaul, are the things we shall talk about only by the obliquest hints.

When I think of all the men – and women – I knew who put an end to their own lives, and when I consider that at the end the Führer claimed to resemble them, that seems to me his supreme recantation: for he did not die alone – that is the least one can say. He took a few million dead with him. He even usurped his place among them.

But now I am really in spate ... Have you noticed, Fräulein, that whenever it is convenient for us to lose sight of our own actions or responsibilities, we have only to mention Hitler?

How comic, and lamentable, it suddenly seemed to him to

speak of the deaths of those close to him, as if it were his duty. Wasn't this just another way of appropriating them a little more?

Did it belong to him then, the death of the father he had so detested, and had then just been slightly ashamed of? And finally, in spite of all, he had loved the man who no longer exasperated him, whom he took to drink a hot chocolate at Möhring's, the old man who lost none of his dignity even when treated like a child. (The retired pastor cut a very provincial figure in Berlin when he visited his son, expressing himself so loudly in public places that everyone turned to look.)

The doctor could only just avoid feeling resentment when he died in October 1939, on the eve of the war, as if the old man had done it on purpose, by some piece of peasant malice or trickery . . .

Was there any reason to mourn the loss of someone he had spent his life fleeing?

Then it was his younger brother's turn. And after him another brother fell, then a third, on the field of honour, as the army likes to express it, to exonerate itself before those it makes widows or orphans, and a fourth was twice grievously wounded. The others became invalids and were ruined. A first cousin, also a writer, died in the summer, his only son the following winter: "The typical hecatomb of a German family of moderate importance at the end of the first half of the twentieth century . . . "

Mechanically, the doctor performs the gesture of taking off his hat, as if he were still wearing it, as if he were baring his head before all these assembled dead.

Such, Fräulein, is my *curriculum mortis*.

There would surely be time to talk about the living as well!
But that sounds like a plural noun. I have only my daughter left.

She visited me in the spring, for the first time since the start of the war. She was just passing through Berlin as a reporter, in Allied uniform ... She stayed at the Hotel am Zoo, occupied by the Americans. She had married and taken Danish nationality, and viewed the city reduced to its stumps with the eye of a foreigner, an adversary.

I have been told that Erika Mann, the eldest daughter of Thomas, also became a war correspondent for an American newspaper. It is, in my eyes, a part of our punishment that our children return to Germany only in transit, carrying a press card that legitimises them in the name of a distant country responsible for our defeat ... It has been said that our children would be the first to judge the history of our generation.

"Miss Kaul, I shall have to introduce you to my daughter Nele," murmured the doctor. As if he were rehearsing his lines.

He could still see her on the step, that April day when he had opened the door to her. The slightly tearful look she gave him, the amazement – then pity – that she could not disguise, while she held out three packets of Philip Morris, as if she wanted to get rid of them at once: they were burning her fingers. In his daughter's eyes he could read the impression he made on her. She had left a father in his opulent prime. She found him now whittled, pared. How could she have dissembled? How could he not have seen what she saw, in the doorway of 20, Bozener Strasse, in which he was framed, definitively, as in a painting? He must have looked like a ghost spewed by events she thought she knew all about, but of which this unknown man she suddenly felt so close to seemed to reveal a new aspect, since she was, after all, made of the flesh of this loser. "Ah, not to grow so old as to contemplate your own mortal remains, and mock them ... "

We talked of something else.

Of her husband, a man much older than she. Strange, aren't they, Fräulein, these age disparities between husbands and wives today? No doubt she was seeking in him the father who had cut himself off from her. For must we not always find explanations of that kind? Then I asked her about the twins that heaven had sent her. About how they had lived under the occupation. She had had to make up clothes from scraps of material and old rags. But when Denmark was liberated Gertrud Hindemith had sent her magnificent garments for her kids ... I understood that that was what my visitor had been leading up to. It was time for the rift between me and Paul Hindemith to be healed. And then, she thought, I ought also to be reconciled with Klaus Mann. She declared herself ready to take the first step in my name ... To prove to him that I never really compromised myself completely with the regime. And that the best proof of this was the way the regime had treated me. I was reluctant to give an answer to this. I told her I would think about it ... She looked distressed. Really, I was discouraging her initiatives. I was far more touched than I could show her that she should still be concerned for her father's reputation, for his posterity. Hindemith, I thought, I should have liked to see again; I missed him. But perhaps it was enough, in the end, that my little girl, my big daughter, now Danish and respectable, had kept her love and respect for me? I asked her what she ate. "Fruit and cereals," she said. Isn't that a bit austere?

Now she has gone back to Denmark, my tender-hearted mermaid. I promised to go to see her one of these days. It's amusing in a way: she lives in a town called Charlottenlund, whereas she might have been living here in Charlottenburg ...

This coincidence filled the doctor with joy. He found a kind of consolation in it. Charlottenburg ... Charlottenlund ... He put his hat back on, got up and set about making the introductions, there in the middle of the drawing room.

Miss Kaul, I don't think I have yet told you about my Danish daughter: here she is ... He took off his hat and bowed.

Nele, my darling, I haven't yet had a chance to talk to you

about my neighbour, Miss Ilse Kaul, who is also my patient ...

Miss Ilse Kaul, of Charlottenburg, or Schöneberg, doesn't it come to the same thing? This is Mrs Nele Soerensen, née Benn, from Charlottenlund, whom I have the great pleasure of introducing to you ...

With the precision of a discus thrower, he threw his hat across the room. It landed in an armchair. Good gracious! Who would have thought old Benn could be so frivolous at his age, when the mood takes him? Certainly not he!

There he stood in the middle of the Wintergarten, contemplating the washing in the courtyard, which for an instant reverberated in the sun.

The old man hesitated briefly between distress and euphoria.

Mirth was upon him.

Of course, it doesn't happen at all in the way he has planned. For example, Gottfried says to Ilse — as if it has just occurred to him:

"I really ought to tell you about my daughter."

"She must be grown up by now," says Ilse, musing.

As if she had known Nele in the old days.

"But," says the doctor, "she is married, she has two children. I should even tell you ... "

"That she's older than I am?"

"Well, as far as I can judge you must be about the same age."

"So much the better," says Ilse.

"Why is that?"

"I'm glad to be her contemporary. We'll get on well."

"You haven't lived the same history ... "

"More than those who will follow us, anyway ... "

"You think they'll understand what happened even less than we do?"

"Oh, much less or much more, depending. But the result will be the same in both cases: we'll find it very difficult to talk about it."

And, another time:

"As I stand before you," he says, "I lost a wife no later than last year ... "

She laughs nervously.

"It makes you laugh?"

"You talk about it as if she were a dog you had lost in a public place ... At the same time, it's dreadful."

"We were more like two dogs," he says. "Who had lost each other."

"You know," she says, "we ought to make a pact. A truce."

"What do you mean?"

"Do you remember how you behaved when we met for the first time?"

"When you came to my surgery?"

"Yes ... I know you now as such a quiet person, but within ten minutes, that day, you were presenting yourself before the tribunal of History. You wouldn't stop ... I had asked nothing of you. I was just an ordinary patient who had come for a vaccination from her local doctor ... Apart from the fact that I remembered having read some poems by that man as a student, read them with enthusiasm ... "

"You should have stopped me ... "

"That's what I did. But I'd like to settle all this: I'm not a Denazification Commission, Dr Benn. Do you want to set me up as a public prosecutor again? Find a real lawyer! For the present, I don't want it to start again at a different level. I don't want details of your past: as widower, cannibal lover, absentee father. What do you expect me to do with all that now? I might as well answer at once: No, Doctor, not today. What do you hope for from me? That I come to the conclusion, all things considered, that you're a bad lot? Later, Doctor, later! Another time, if we're given time ... Do you know what you would turn into if you insisted on speaking now?"

"No – I really don't ... "

She laughs.

"A boor. And a bore."

Was it the same day, or a little later, that he asked:

"Don't you think that together we ought to draw some conclusions from all this?"

"Do you think," she asks with a mischievous smile, "that we deserve to?"

"Now it's you who are talking of deserving! Do you think this country has deserved to survive? Yet it is going to survive. To survive what it has done, and what has been done to it. That day you came to my surgery, since you remember it so well, do you know what you said to me?"

"I can't have said much. You talked all the time!"

"You said: Doctor, I didn't come here to philosophise on the way of all flesh ... "

"So?"

"You were quite right. You had come to ask for my hand."

"Your hand! How you go about it!"

"Yes, my hand. In these times of want, I've nothing better to offer you. This hand that has done everything. For better and for worse ... "

"I am, in principle, resolutely opposed to marriage ... "

"That's good, so am I! One more point in common between us ... So let's set aside our principles together, that will be easier. I'll withdraw everything I've written on the subject ... "

"You know what Knut Hamsun said: 'There's only one love – stolen love.'"

"But by getting married we'll form a gang. We'll steal our love from our respective biographies ... "

"Take care, Doctor. Karl Kraus tells us that 'When a lover of women falls in love, he's like a doctor who infects himself from his patient.'"

"Clearly, you've read everything there is on the subject. So you will know that Kraus adds: 'Those are the risks of the job.' So let's live dangerously! In any case, if it's risky to get married, how much more risky would it be not to? Didn't you ask me if I liked flowers? Yes, I do. Very much: roses, asphodels, resedas, lilies, lilac and asters. Especially asters."

Sometimes they went for walks in the avenues of the zoological garden. That took the place of their honeymoon. Most
of the enclosures were empty. Because it was winter. Because
the last battle for Berlin had been fought here. A wall of fire
had risen up around the garden. Hundreds of animals had died
with the soldiers. Sometimes the men themselves had finished
them off with cold steel. A soldier had killed the gorilla Pongo
in his cage with a bayonet. A panic-stricken elephant had
escaped, trumpeting on the pavements of the Ku–Damm ...
Some hippopotami had survived by staying under water.
Others had tried to dig trenches. A tapir had frozen to death.

"After the capitulation," says the husband, "some people got
hold of a wild boar, a donkey and some baboons that had
survived to skin them and sell their meat on the black market,
on the bank of the Landwehrkanal. Others butchered a dro-
medary. The one who inherited the hump was surprised to find
nothing but water in his tureen ... Buffalo were harnessed to
clear the ruins. All the trees spared by the bombs later finished
up in the braziers. Potatoes were planted in their place."

"It seems," says his wife, "that about a hundred animals were
saved: a cassowary, a Japanese stork, a sea-horse, a giraffe, a
Chinese alligator, a male Siamese elephant calf: they were
picked up in other gardens, scattered all over the city."

"Is it an illusion?" asks the husband. "What has survived is
the scent. The tenacious smell of the big cats. Dead or alive? In
the old days I used to like walking here. I admired above all a
jaguar, or rather a panther. Set free, it would have leapt over
the world in one bound!"

> "Its gaze is from the passing bars
> so wearied that it nothing holds.
> It seems there are a thousand bars
> and out beyond the bars, no world."

"Who is that by?" asks the husband.
"Rilke," says his wife.

"I didn't remember ... Lately I've had hardly any time to re-read the poets. And then, I was afraid of repeating them."

"In the psittacism now prevalent in German poetry there is little danger of that," she says.

"Do you remember," he asks, "Hans Albers singing *'Mein Gorilla hat' ne villa im Zoo'*? That was in '32 or '33. It didn't live there for long."

"I was a bit young," she says.

His wife had taken his arm. He looked at her profile for a moment, before she noticed and turned towards him with a questioning look ... He liked observing her clandestinely. Looking for what? The light of love? The aura of happiness? The stigmata of suffering? No, what he liked to check was the confidence her expression showed. Confidence in the world. In the world's future. And even in him, her old husband.

To live again. Was it possible? Was it necessary? Was it desirable? Was it decent? Was it permitted?

Only a man and a woman walking together in a field of ruins. Nothing had predestined them to live this melodrama. Nothing – except everything. Nothing now required them to live something else. Nothing – except everything, again.

The old man was gripped by a slight intoxication. His blood was leaping within him like alcohol. It seemed that something like the exact opposite of what had transpired here for the last five years was happening inside him, and even around him. If he had had to explain it, he would have said: It's as if we were being given more time than space once more. After being scattered across the space of death, we are going to have a little time ahead of us again. All this swept down into him and caused great uproar. He was shaken by a squall of eternity. He had to lean on his young wife's arm. This dull joy, this blind and muffled joy, this sickly euphoria jostled him, dragged him willy-nilly, made him choke.

These ruins, all around them, represented the human beings

the ruins had betrayed, had been insufficient to shelter. Yet despite them, it was human beings that you met among them.

How many times, thought the old man, have we believed all was lost – through our fault, or even without our doing – only to find that our time was not yet up. This time, again, you've got away with it, and this is the strangest, the most "undeserved" time. And it was time, the old man mumbled. For unhappiness can become a bad habit which finally makes you stupid.

We ought to meet here, he wanted to say to Ilse, as if the meeting had still to happen, here, amid the ruins, because everything meets here. And if it happens, it's because we are certainly entitled to it. People will be scandalised that we have brought it off. They ought to be still more scandalised if we didn't. But human beings have made their destiny such that nothing equals the scandal of guilt, except that of innocence.

A woman pushing a pram was venturing on to the ice of a frozen lake. A pram in which was a living baby. During the exodus prams and pushchairs had been used enough to transport dead children rather than living babies, or else the little that people possessed: chickens, a ham, family jewels, a savings book, a knife ... You'd think that was the use they were first intended for.

Soon more and more women would be seen walking like this on the frozen waters of the Halensee, the Leitzensee, the Wannsee. Kids would have snowball fights in the Wilmersdorf woods. Time would pass, and when the first fine days came, on these rubble-strewn staircases of the Elephant Pavilion, you would see young women of Berlin sit down to offer their faces, eyes closed, to the sun. A little more time, and you'd be able to admire, in a cage, a Sumatra tiger, a Japanese stork, golden pheasants, a helmeted cassowary.

To enliven the ruins the high wire of the Barclay acrobatic troupe, the most daring in the world, or the trapeze of the

Sarrazani Brothers, would be stretched from a church steeple to a bell-tower.

> "Living is throwing bridges
> over the transient river,"

Ilse Kaul quotes.

I, thinks the old man, I'm the pebble the river rolls, drags, wears and polishes. You, my wife, are the river.

"Does the pebble love the river that drags it along?" asks his wife.

"If this is not love, what is love?" asks her husband. "You can't live any other way than this, yielding to the current, clutching at shafts of light. Under the water the stone still cries out its ovation to life. This is no doubt what my biographers will call a marriage of convenience."

"And they won't be entirely wrong ... ," says his wife.

"Come," says the man. "Let's go home. Perhaps even the witnesses of this criminal world have earned some rest?"

Berlin, 1956

The Last Words

His neck propped awkwardly on three pillows pushed under him against the head of the bed, he feigned interest in the photos that had been taken at the Hotel am Steinplatz on his seventieth birthday. Salt-free diet. No beer or cigarettes. Each day, nothing but a glass of the red wine he had never liked. But he should not be disobliging to the visitors who had brought him the images of the recent event "that was still engraved in the memories of all".

He slapped them down like cards on the duvet from which he emerged like a seal on an ice-floe. Soon, however, details began to capture his attention. What did these snaps reveal that he had not noticed at the time the event took place? There's Oelze, his conversation partner since time immemorial, with the face of an ascetic Spaniard. Walter Lennig. Franz Tumler, who does not put on satyr's airs for nothing. Max Nieder-meyer, the handsome, mysterious and fatal editor who seems cut out to play golf champions and lady-killers in Hollywood movies. His wife and his secretary-mistress are not far off, sending him uneasy glances ... Hans-Egon Holthusen, who doesn't look bad either, with a hint of the visiting Bavarian about him ... And who's that? Don't know him. During cocktails some people turned up who hadn't been invited. But that had been expected. It was only at dinner that they had been twelve. Ilse, with her imperial white hairpiece; it's the fashion, but she submits to it with elegance. Then Nele, who never returns to Berlin without apprehension, to see her old father. Is it he who makes her apprehensive, or Germany? Thilo Koch. Which of these shady characters, since they are all going to survive me, is thinking of writing my biography? the poet wonders. All of them, perhaps. Such a fine subject, is it not? And one which admits so many diverse interpretations ... To each his version of the facts, and the Devil take the hindmost. To each his own Gottfried Benn.

How impressive they all looked. You would have thought they were rehearsing a play under the guidance of an invisible director. Unless it were the septuagenarian himself, passing in front of the buffet and beneath the chandeliers with elephantine grace. Well, he'd certainly played a close hand. For it was around him that this generation had regrouped, and even the following one. This world that had done so much to annihilate itself still had a few handsome remnants. In some pictures Ilse wore a forced smile, of one who kept her own counsel. Like a wife who was afraid of soon being left. She was only half wrong. But there is leaving and leaving.

There are only two or three portraits where I have a kindly look, he thinks. Probably, I've not often been kinder than I needed to be.

More than by any other, he is suddenly struck by this picture of the table before anyone was sitting at it, unless everyone had already got up. But no, the table is laid, the plates are empty. The candles lit. You'd think none of the guests had turned up. Perhaps they've all been victims of a catastrophe. Or have they decided at the last minute to fête someone else, at the same hour, in another place? No doubt those candles will burn down in vain, in honour of a poet as yet unknown.

It is nevertheless clear that the hero of this ghostly banquet will be dead within the year.

Don't forget the flowers ... Above all, don't forget the flowers!

All this was so unlike him ... So much so that when he decided to receive his friends in a Charlottenburg hotel on 2 May 1956, he took the trouble to add: "This is a real

invitation. Lounge suits desired." You might have thought it a
joke. But he was so little inclined to jest that he openly pitied
in advance everyone who was to surround him that day:
"You'll see: it will be a terrible day, a painful hour to be got
through together ... "

It was so unlike him to be the centre of this first and last
celebration.

Don't forget the flowers on the table ...

A party, then, for him who never threw parties: how could
he have done, when he had actually lived in his surgery for a
time, and even now occupied two or three ground-floor
rooms encumbered with books and manuscripts, where he
moved without the agility befitting a host? So let it be an
hotel, on the corner of Uhlandstrasse, and in it, a feast lasting
three days, from the first to the third of May, the first with Ilse,
the second shared between his wife and his daughter, the third
in the company of his wife, his daughter and his friends, in a
neutral place, a hotel in his own city, the one where he had
spent most of his years, and had lived the worst rather than the
best, yet a place without references or memory, so that the past
would not interfere, would not come back to disrupt the
ceremony. Nevertheless, the poet would not banish these
fraternal shades, but would welcome them only within himself,
in the nest of memory, while all around the guests did not
even suspect their presence as they gave free rein to their
moods, speculating on the future of Germany, the shocks of
History, the disorder of the world, and confessing their surprise
at finding themselves together again to celebrate the man who,
in their eyes, had best expressed and even incarnated all that at
once.

"One day when I visited him at his house, it was so cold: it
was during the blockade ... "

"All I can see is a bar on the corner of Bozener Strasse – you
know, the 'Dramburg' ... "

"Ah! That's where I met him last time ... He talked to me
about *Under the Volcano* – you know, that masterpiece about an

Englishman getting drunk in Mexico, unless it's the other way round."

The last time ... The last time he ... You don't realise how apt your comments are, he was thinking, my dear and admirable friends: this may be the last time you will say "the last time" with regard to me. You are wonderful in your generosity, displacing yourselves to embellish the old hack's reunion, and wonderful in your simplicity, never suspecting that he's busy snuffing it under your gullible eyes. It's the end of the safari. I could hardly invite you to my flat, since neither the doctor nor the poet have managed, in their common and double life, to scrape together enough to receive you in a mansion with garden, outside staircase, porticos and balustrades. It's over. I'm never going to be seen in one of those photos of the writer who has become a legend in his own lifetime, in the running for a Nobel Prize if not already sporting one, leaning with studied negligence against a column at the top of a marble staircase as he welcomes his guests in one of those quasi mythical properties you find reproduced in school anthologies: Goethe at Weimar, Tolstoy at Yasnaya Polyana, Maeterlinck at Horlamonde, Gide at Cuverville, Thomas Mann at Munich, Kussnacht or Pacific Palisades, Mauriac at Malagar, Axel Munthe and d'Annunzio who knows where ... All those places where genius had breathed. To him were left the places sacred to neither God nor man. His only dwelling place: a few poems open to the sky, with banging doors. (He organises a reception, his wife had thought, he who never owned even a purse!) So he would only receive them here, in a hotel on the corner of Steinplatz and Uhlandstrasse, in a lounge suit, slightly strained, intimidated even, almost apologetic: "So you felt obliged to come? What a drag, isn't it? You won't hold it against me? You're going to endure the most mortally tedious evening of your life ... " I hope to God they haven't forgotten the flowers.

Images persisting beneath lids that grow ever heavier. He called it a seventieth birthday celebration. If it were only that!

Who suspected that in reality he was celebrating seventy years of survival, ten of which, at the lowest estimate, were also years of resurrection, in this land whose destiny he had espoused at the worst moment, in the heart of this city whose downfall he shared and loved?

As far back as he can remember, he has always been dead-beat. Everything good he has done was done in spite of his exhaustion. All his errors issued from this bottomless weariness; all his faults fed on it. How could he have lasted so long, dragging with him this load of meat worn out in advance, this body that had flipped from childhood straight into age, his energy gone with the baby's bath-water. If he had only been able to feel for a single day unspent, unfaded. It's terrible, he thinks, but we have the wrong idea about suffering: in the end, it does not arouse emotions but brutalises us as surely as wine, numbs us like solitude and cold. All his life: this mixture of incessant labour and paradoxical indolence. Fatigue is never anything other than the beginning of death, its first twinges.

Just look at him. Consider once more that head of a Pomeranian pork-butcher, or vendor of *Delikatessen*. A cranium closed on accumulated pain. Why do you sometimes come across him, as his wife has just told the guests at table, to the great amusement of the whole gathering, reading a book in his office without having bothered to take off his hat?

Probably not because most of the books you can read today – to hear him talk – are not worth raising your hat to. He is more or less bald. The hairs of melancholy sprout low on his skull, and he combs them far from any mirror. He only tries to keep himself, as he puts it, "a clean little old man". He is stout, as if pregnant with the failed saint he carries within him. He is ugly. His beauty is not of this world. Who is hiding behind this aged seraph? A cruel, gentle, patient artisan with words, the conqueror of a new prattle.

Berlin ... , he stammered, and it was as if someone were pacifying hell on earth with tender words. He wore on himself the marks of the city's sins.

Berlin, 1956

A combine harvester of memories, a mill of oblivion. A machine for being alive.

He looks again at the reception photos.

Those three days of festivities took more out of him than you would believe. The official homage at the American Library. An actor read his poems. He also had to listen to a hyperbolic address by a city official. Then he offered his thanks. Briefly. He thought the blood was draining from his veins. He felt himself going white as a sheet. He said to himself: If only they don't notice. Ilse, of course, he couldn't keep in the dark, deceiving the vigilance of wife and doctor.

The flowers? A diversion. A camouflage. To mask to some extent that body, that mass of meat: fat, muscle, tendons, viscera, humours, secretly corrupt, sick. A sac of hidden grief. Fated flesh.

He plants himself solemnly in the middle of the drawing room, glass in hand. So that he could grab an arm if he collapsed. Did they suspect that the man they were paying homage to – who was, almost by accident and slightly para-doxically, one of the century's poets who would last – did they guess that he was no more than a corpulent spectre? A Parsifal gone mouldy on the hoof. And then his genius, still referred to in official speeches though not always, he feels, to his credit, more as an aggravating circumstance . . .

How many of those around him knew that this was a corrida at the end of which was to die, still standing up if he was able to, a bull heartbroken with emotion, fuddled with sometimes self-inflicted wounds? Who would see that blood had been spilled? Everywhere the insipid smell of congealed blood. Lucky the scent of the flowers covers everything. But it's also a certain sense of infinity that discomfits him, pierces him, splits him like a gourd.

No, they don't know. They don't want to see. They're benignly myopic. So much clairvoyant childhood has been squandered in each of them. German history has tossed them about like starlings in a storm. All they have left is the rough draft of a soul. They're what is called a generation.

Where's that smell of vomit coming from? From nowhere and everywhere. God has puked on us. Lucky the scent of the flowers covers everything.

All around, the city is being rebuilt. But it seems that to be rebuilt it has first to complete its own destruction. The old man covertly eyeing his daughter thinks that he would like to snatch her from the reunion and tour the streets of Berlin with her on his arm. He still nourishes the unreasonable hope that he might make her love the city. He'd like to tell her its story. Even the episodes he has already narrated to her ten times, in letters, or on a visit he made to her in Denmark. What is the strange identification that makes him unstoppable on this subject? He'd like to show his daughter how little mountains had been created just by heaping up the ruins, how grass had grown on them, then birches and wild roses. He'd like to tell her about the blockade, as if it were not already ancient history, for everything that happens here seems to date from only yesterday.

Do you realise, he would say to her, they were sometimes the same planes that came back, or ones like them, but instead of unleashing bombs on us the Dakotas, Lancasters and Yorks bombarded us with provisions. A deluge of meat. Dehydrated milk, powdered egg, dried grapes. And to mark his solidarity with the besieged city even Paul Hindemith came, after fifteen years of absence, to conduct a concert ... We ought, Nele, to ride along the Ku-Damm on the top deck of a bus. The branches of the trees would caress the windows as we passed ...

Do you know, Nele, that the Café Möhring, that was forbidden to trade for a long time, has been allowed to re-open at last? Would you like to try *Apfelstrudel* with custard there? He forgets that the child he is addressing in the secrecy of his heart is now a woman of forty.

It's not such facts that this woman needs to know; she has not become a reporter for nothing and is completely up to date with German developments. She'd like him to tell her about his recent trips to Switzerland and Belgium – has Brussels changed since it inspired my name? – and the cure he tried at Merano. And about the success that has crowned his life's work when he no longer hoped for it. The Büchner Prize. Büchner, a poet and doctor like him. Expressionism a century before its time ...

"Did you know," Oelze asks no one in particular, "that Gottfried's poetry is being analysed in theses in universities as far-flung as Flanders, Vaud, Minnesota and Wisconsin?"

"That's normal," says the poet apologetically. "There are only two sorts of writers: those who write vast amounts and attract few commentaries, and those who write little and are glossed unendingly. Bizarrely, I'm one of the latter ... When I re-read my own poems that are the subject of learned exegeses, then these exegeses themselves, I sometimes feel there's been a mistake. They're beyond me."

Such is the gentle revenge, thinks Ilse, of the man I knew when he was crushed and broken – as if under a curse. Yet none of those present here ever doubted the change of fortune would come. Not even he ...

All the same, he cannot understand how it has come about. Lazarus is the worst informed about the circumstances of the miracle. That's why, when he tries to explain his comeback, he mixes everything up: the destiny of Germany, the fate of the old capital, and accidents affecting him in the most intimate way ...

"I was very impressed," Hans-Egon Holthusen tells him, "by the way you explained your repudiation of the simile in lyric poetry ... "

"Yes," replies the poet, taking up the point, "I don't like to see the colour announced in advance, so to speak ... Either one is in the metaphor, or it isn't one. The poet who says 'like' is necessarily looking at reality from the outside. He remains a voyeur."

And suddenly he thinks: Whereas in life I've condemned myself to a perpetual 'like' and 'as'. I've never been more than a half-interested, mournful spectator of the world's metaphor ... Altogether, I was *as if* in the world, and *as if* in life. But appearances were deceptive.

You'd think he had only been put in this world as phenomenon and instrument of knowledge. Earthquake and seismograph. Wound and scalpel. Melody and violin. Blood-darkness and spear of light.

Now he spreads the photographs carefully on the white sheet like patience or Tarot cards. Their enigma is that they do not refer to the high points of the ceremony – the speeches at the end of the meal, the arrival of the birthday cake, the final congratulations – but to rests, mute bars. But it was during these blanks that the fate of the soirée was played out, the truth was imprinted on the guests' faces. He is stupefied to see so much yearning in his wife's gaze, and such grave tenderness in the eyes of his daughter. How oblivious he was! He had himself been surprised, recently, at how little his moods and emotions related to his surroundings. Now he effusively embraced a person who was nothing to him, now he seemed hardly to recognise someone close to him ... Did this show indifference? In two or three photos taken in May he could make out only a look of dim compassion, directed at all the people present. To whom, or what, was it really addressed? He looked like a captain thanking his crew before going down with his ship.

He realised that he should fix on the events of these last ten years the same gaze as the photographer at the Hotel am Steinplatz on 2 May 1956: a look more indiscreet than conniving.

He has taken refuge in the dimness of the office, the windows of which give on to the yard where hens cackle.

They don't disturb him, even if at times they drown the melodies sung by Richard Tauber on the Rias-Berlin radio. It is the only message coming to him this summer that he is spending alone. He has let Ilse go to Greece. A country to which he has devoted so many pages and where he has never set foot. Now he has sent his wife in his place. Because she is still young, and avid to discover the beauties of the earth. As a pledge she has left him a little dog which he finds now exasperating, now touching. This woman could make him love anything that lived. Today, no doubt, she is walking on the shore at Epidavros. Or else at Aegina, unless she is visiting the citadel of Corinth ... She understands that he does not want to leave the Bayerischer Platz. He lives on his memories of the Gigantomachia he saw long ago in the Berlin Museum, that cynegetic frieze in which colossal figures convulsed in an exuberant jungle. He was amused by the declamatory excesses of a monument indignant at being imprisoned within the walls of a museum. It had not given him a desire to go and see for himself. Far from Greece he had written the homage to Sparta which established a risky rapport between power and creation ... That was where, for a time, his fascination with ancient art had led him. It was better to listen to *Plaisir d'amour* sung by Richard Tauber at 20, Bozener Strasse on a summer afternoon. In any case, he too was in Greece: far from that country he was reading a *Life of Alcibiades*.

He has raised his head for a moment. Through the pierced curtains that show a floral motif, his gaze fastens on the washing strung across the courtyard, flapping in the wind like a banner. What use is such reading to me, he wonders? And he is not afraid to add: a few words away from my end? Was it merely an offering to cultural hygiene? What lesson can one draw from the misadventures of Alcibiades, ten years after the city where one lives has been half razed to the ground? You would have to be of a rather dreamy nature to come picking here for information of any value to the world of today, after Auschwitz, Nagasaki and Yalta. It is none the less true that Dr Benn reads this kind of work as others listen to the one o'clock radio bulletin: to hear the "latest news" . . .

However, Alcibiades . . . No tyrant of modern times resembles this young man, indolent and coquettish as a girl, full of promise but unsteady, vindictive like a jilted lover. Once he saw fit to turn the head of his master Plato, though his politics were a stinging rebuke to the sage's doctrine. A fine occasion to meditate on the precariousness of thought, if not its powerlessness to govern the behaviour of a man of action! Who could have described Alcibiades, still adolescent, weeping in the philosopher's arms over his own limits, his weaknesses and the felonies he was premeditating? If Alcibiades prefigures neither Napoleon, nor Hitler, nor Stalin, let him resemble History itself: a little bastard mad about his body, a megalomaniac rentboy . . .

No matter, what use is it to prove all that, while the laments sung by Richard Tauber on the airwaves of Rias-Berlin unwind their sobbing convolutions? You'd be quite surprised at Dr Benn's musical tastes, preferring Puccini and Sibelius to the "Well-Tempered Klavier", and enraptured by the sentimental songs you could sometimes hear a barrel organ grinding out from the back of a courtyard.

"It was too bad for Nietzsche, wasn't it, that Gottfried wasn't his contemporary. The poet would have cured the philosopher."

The speaker of these last words, his old friend Oelze, has always been fascinated by medicine. But as if medicine were only the art of curing . . .

"The poet, perhaps," Walter Lennig observes, "but the venereologist?"

Everyone laughs.

"The venereologist would have taken good care not to," says the doctor. "Nietzsche may never even have had syphilis. His madness came from deeper. And as for the poet, he couldn't have administered more than a homoeopathic treatment to the author of *Zarathustra* ... Imagine if we started treating, even vaccinating, the great geniuses for what was sometimes the cause of their inspiration: we'd deserve to be called charlatans. All the same, we do lack a biological history of the great artists. Information on Hölderlin's height, Goethe's blood pressure, the allergies of the Romantics – that would replace a good many literary theses!"

"Don't you miss your surgery, Doctor?" asks Max Niedermeyer's secretary.

At least one question with its fair share of humanity ...

"Let's just say that medicine doesn't miss me! And the arrangement suits my wife: it seems I used to frighten her patients. We only had one waiting room between us, you see."

"Towards the end," says Ilse, "some of his pseudo-patients only came to see him for the charm of his conversation. Isn't that so, Herr Lennig?"

"Whereas when I sit down in my wife's chair, I actually want a tooth pulled out," says the doctor. "Her business has always done better than mine. The discovery of antibiotics has been calamitous for specialists in my field."

"The same applies to false teeth," Ilse retorts. "The ones fitted after the war can withstand anything, alas! We weren't very far-sighted ... "

Do they realise, thinks Gottfried Benn, that once a doctor you never stop being one?

"The strangest things," he says, to oblige his listeners, "did not happen in the daytime in the consulting room. They happened on night duty, on the GP's visits to remote quarters, bombed, sometimes without electricity. To treat the person who called you, you had first to reach him, with a pocket torch ... It was an adventure in itself." Where did I read, he wonders, that the wandering Jew made love while walking?

Ilse, he thinks. Avoid talking of her, or with her, in front of the others – hide behind wisecracks. Compose a sort of epithalamium. Tell her, as I thought yesterday, then forgot, that she has been the last "Belle Alliance" of my life. Avoid the tremolo. Don't make it too affecting. Talk to her about her hands, their gentleness, their agility. Hands which point the direction, open the way.

He goes back with her to the zoological garden. You find extraordinary specimens there. A jealous, neurotic serval. A South African suricate with strip-tease poses. An exhausted panda, so expensive to maintain that there is a collection to cover the cost. A petrified bison that gives an impression of energy forever turned against itself. And then a couple of Siberian tigers.

The Javan leopard. "Intact", the poet would like to think, as if it were the same one as in the old days.

"You see," he tells his companion, "they've come back."

He listens to a Hindemith concert on the wireless. Post-war Hindemith. Concertante works and the *Harmonie der Welt*. Not without emotion does the poet plunge again into the forest of sounds that his friend's genius opened to him in other times. He finds it still as it was. The strings rustle and the brass flashes as of old. It is a forest never menaced by any bomb … The war has passed round the periphery of the work. Not to the point of cutting off the ecstasy towards which the polyphony strains. You just feel that in the old days more light would have drenched it, lifting the music to a Baroque euphoria. It seems unable to attain elevation, as if the turbulence of History, though nowhere perceptible, had grounded it, pinned it down to rhetoric. It no longer vibrates. You detect the assumptions of a solid, old-fashioned *Weltanschauung* such as Reger might have answered to. Has Goebbels's censorship reached him after all, even in America in 1950?

Once more, images of that summer passed in solitude in the Wintergarten at 20, Bozener Strasse, while Ilse Benn crosses the Peloponnese, admiring for two, and promising herself to tell it all to him when she returns, as if he had mandated her, sent her as an emissary into that Doric world where his spirit has roamed so often ... Why does he never go to confirm his intuitions on the spot? Because he has only one life.

Images of that summer, or rather sounds of it. The popular tunes sung by Richard Tauber. Why did they move him so much? They spoke so little of the man he was, his own life. They weren't addressed to him. They were like a telephone call from a child who briefly mistook him for his grandfather. Or a wave from a beautiful stranger on a station platform, her tear-blurred eyes having confused his face with her lover's as the carriage windows began to move ...

Often what moved him most was not meant for him, came to him as if by oversight. What matter? It was the misunderstanding itself which overwhelmed him.

He listens to the "Blue Danube". That hymn to a river any colour but blue. But people need to tell themselves stories. Ah, those gentle, incorrigible dreamers! More incorrigible than dreamers, more dreamers than gentle. Happy if they manage to dream at all, even if it's not about what is best in them, or for the noblest causes. Sibelius's "Valse triste". Tchaikovsky's "Pathétique". Why does he enjoy pathos and melodrama so much in others, and forbid them so strictly in himself? It is because he, the poet, who puts art above everything, can only talk of the life which is beyond life. That's the poet's speciality, as the doctor specialises in venereology. It does not make him enjoy the stories of others less, the stories that fall short of life. That only resemble life: like Ilse Benn's dog, "they lack only words" ... He sincerely loves those legends that don't really draw from life, since if they expressed it as it was they would be unbearable. But such stories are needed, and Dr Benn is a good audience: he's happy that others take it upon themselves to make up the stories that lull him, make his throat go tight, draw from him more than one tear, whereas the most terrible events he has witnessed, which have nourished the marrow of his work, have left him dry-eyed. Addinsell's Warsaw Concerto. Gounod's "Ave Maria". "Two Little Blue Satin Shoes", music by Charlie Chaplin. He wouldn't switch off the radio for anything in the world. With regard to the things that touch him most, the doctor's been on the verge of tears for more than half a century. Only on the verge. Hence the reputation he has had, and will have, for being emotionally arid. And for having poor musical taste ... "Curiously, he was not musical. He was partial to sentimental kitsch ... " He reserves his tears for trivial matters, seems only to be moved when listening to fables or ballads drunk on their own mawkishness. He has shed more tears over the death of Mimi in *La Bohème* than over the sufferings of his clients or the deaths of his comrades. Each time he has been bereaved, his pain has only mumbled seven or eight syllables of a poem abandoned deep within him, parched in the desert of his life, as sperm is said in certain people to rise to the brain during the act of love. He was accused of insensitivity, and believed it himself. To touch the world's core, he seemed to have made a detour around the world. He wept only beyond tears. Such weeping belongs to literary history. It sometimes appears, inadvertently, even in anthologies, where you hardly expected to find it.

In the heart of the Berlin summer, the poet was finding it difficult to breathe. He wondered why he had to put out his tentacles in all directions – Alcibiades and Richard Tauber, the "Blue Danube", Athens and Chaplin – to give himself some chance of understanding *in extremis* the disposition, the chaos of the world. To bring in something other than dross with his nets. The game made him breathless, but that had always been his method. Some people said of him: Did you know, he hardly reads anything? And others: Would you believe it, he's informed about everything? In fact, the poet did not relish having to criss-cross the globe like a special envoy. He wasn't a reporter. He was just trying to pick out a note of eternity in the din of a pot-pourri. It had always been so. He had to play on all the keyboards at once: Alcibiades, Sibelius, Epidavros ... if he was at last, by combining them, to understand anything, and so escape for a moment from dread. People had been right to think him a Jack-of-all-trades: he was merely an amateur of the universal.

He only wondered why it took so much effort to maintain the rhythm of this waking dream. Why each hour of his life, even the most passive and torpid, tested him like this. Why existence, for him, had become so – tauromachian. He feared relaxing his vigilance. There is a knowledge which gradually crushes the man who is its depositary. It's such a frightening little miracle, sometimes, to survive for one more hour. But the stones of Berlin, the beautiful blue Danube, the memory of Warsaw, the dust sticking to the soles on the road to Argos: there was enough in the mixture of all that – rubble, splendours and mud – to make you feel enclosed, engrossed in the task of putting together two ideas.

"And tomorrow, Doctor, what are you going to entertain us with?" asks Thilo Koch.

It's true that the next day they are to meet on each side of a microphone, under the eye of a camera, in a studio of the Sender Freies Berlin in Grunewald. The main thing, as today, thinks the doctor, will be not to wear death on your face. To avoid saying: "in fact", "fundamentally" and "I mean" too often. That will be the most difficult part. As for the rest ...

"I assume that you, at least, are not going to ask me if poetry can change the world, or if it improves our lives?"

Thilo Koch laughs:

"No, Doctor, I know you've no taste for that kind of cliché, and I know in advance the answer I'd get ... "

"Nor will you ask me to abandon the monologue and solemnly address the nation?"

"Good heavens, Doctor," says Thilo Koch, "will you go on insisting that you've never been asked any good questions?

Have no fear about me, I'll not lay hands on your insular attitudes ... "

It's my "insularity" that improves my life, thinks the doctor, to the extent that it can be improved. And it's my solipsism that communicates with the German nation, to the extent, of course, that anything in me still communicates with it ...

"Nor," Thilo Koch goes on, "shall I engage yet again in the eternal debate on Form and 'art for art's sake' ... "

That may be a pity, thinks the poet; one can never talk enough about that, and on that subject I've always something to say ...

"By the way," Thilo Koch asks the company in general, "did you know that even Bert Brecht once declared that the attacks on formalism reminded him of an ugly shrew calling any pretty girl a tart?"

"You see?" says the doctor. "On all the essentials Bert Brecht and I have always agreed."

Everyone bursts out laughing. The poet doesn't know whether it is for reasons they would acknowledge. He had hardly meant his remark as a joke ...

"By dint of decrying art for art's sake," he adds, "they'll finish by discrediting art itself."

For a moment his weariness gives way to anger. Ah, form, how it bothers them! How it's been vilified! To believe them, our love for it is suspect, something that sooner or later leads to ideological perversion. When, in a moment of giddiness, I was fascinated by National Socialism, it certainly wasn't for love of form! It was rather my love of form which later opened my eyes. How can they fail to see that apart from our aesthetic joys – that we ought to stop being ashamed of – the only question is whether or not life is worth living? No more nor less.

My God, he thinks in a moment of panic, why did I accept the idea of this televised interview? Though I think I turn everything down, I still say 'yes' too often ... Three months ago I tendered my resignation to the Academy of Fine Arts. "I shall not be fêted." I begged Max not to publish a "homage". I didn't want any press conferences. "Neither speeches nor potted plants. Let's leave the ceremonies to the field-marshals, the professors and the film producers." I promised myself to spend my seventieth birthday in a country where the mimosas would be blooming ... For a last time, I fiercely defended the monomaniac, almost lethargic and frankly "bionegative" character of my activity. My illness itself gave me the energy. And I was rewarded by a remission. The Academy made me withdraw my resignation – my abdication of a king without lands ... Here I am again, apparently having got off scot-free, and even drinking hard, for one evening, amid my loved ones and my generous friends. I, who would have so relished keeping quiet, am starting to hold forth again, using up words that can't go to the poem as the bull goes to the heifer ... It makes no sense. "I'd rather speak of ... Berlin," he says out loud.

"Pardon, Doctor?"

"Berlin," he repeats. "Tomorrow I'd like to talk about Berlin. Of the dead season, as the old capital of the Reich finishes going to rack and ruin. Dividing itself up more and more, as the mirages of reunification recede before our eyes. The library I'd like to borrow books from is in the East, no longer accessible ... "

There's a kind of wall, he thinks, dividing this city. How could I leave this place? When my whole work postulates this division, which is the split in being itself.

"Make me talk about that, dear friend. I can still talk of it without betraying my ideas or distorting the facts ... I'm like this city. What happened to it befell me also."

And then, again, images of that summer he spent alone in his apartment at Schöneberg. You'd think the situation kept being repeated, and that in these last ten years his wife had been in the habit of dumping the doctor to wander alone in exotic decors and enchanted landscapes ... Poor Ilse! She'd have some reason to see ingratitude in these recollections of a man she had so cosseted. Memory is little concerned with fairness ...

He peels an onion, cuts it into slices that he heats gently in a frying pan with a piece of butter. The maid is on holiday, and he has learned to do a little cooking. The peace he finds in it. The dreams he has watching an egg dance in boiling water. Or an omelette crackling in a pan.

He lifts his fingers to his nostrils and notes with amusement that his hands reek of onion. Then he looks at them. These mercenary hands that have been turned to every task ... These pianist's hands that have spanned the whole keyboard of human activities. What is more, they have recently become twisted by rheumatism. He looks at them with respect.

He lunches in the kitchen. He sees trembling on the sunny wall the green shadow of the bottle and the purplish one of the wine it still contains. Then the shadow of a hand flitting gracefully about the bottle's neck, filling the glass. Soon he is playing with these silhouettes, composing elaborate choreographies. His hand seems to open to receive a dove, gathering in its message ... Then he lets it fall on the table. Mottled here and there with patches of age. It seems to draw into itself all the world's age, and all the youth that still survives in him. Now he turns his chair towards the wall. Still life with chair and bottle ... he thinks. Which will both soon be empty: first the bottle and then, one day soon, the chair.

Some quarters of apple are discolouring in the fruit dish. Then the light changes. The ceiling lamp sheds an illumination so pale that he prefers to switch it off and finish his meal in the half-light. But now it's a different meal, eaten a different day. A winter day. A sooty sky clings to the cornices on the other side of the yard. His gaze slides along the walls, the windows, getting used to their volumes and colours. They're black and bluish and yellow. They come and go, swirl around. They're beautiful. The eye has just decided: they are beautiful, undoubtedly. Because they are still alive. In a room on the other side of the courtyard children are dancing together. No doubt they've invited each other. A Saturday or Sunday afternoon in winter. It must be the winter of 1945, for this time Ilse is not absent: she simply has not yet entered the life of the man who watches. She's only preparing to do so. If only one could live a few more days like that, he thinks, winter Saturdays or Sundays which rend your heart. And even the summer which followed. In summer it would be red and ochre, and the children would still be dancing. It would be beautiful. Beautiful, undoubtedly, because it was summer. Summer spread out on all that. On everything. On Berlin. And he who watches thinks already that he may no longer be there to watch ... But what does that matter? It would have happened in him first. And then survived itself a little thanks to him, outside him?

The same winter, again; the winter before Ilse Kaul. Sometimes when dusk fell he did not light the writing-desk lamp at once. He wrote in the milky glow of snow from the windows. He wrote on the backs of letters he had received by the morning post. Not out of miserliness. But in the interests of concentration. It was words, it seemed to him, that one would have to economise with in future.

And, suddenly, chandeliers are blazing over his head. Not only on 2 May 1956, in the Hotel am Steinplatz, but in Wiesbaden, Geneva, Knokke-Le-Zoute. The critics no longer disparage only him. He is invited to contribute to a review. Then to another. He is asked to empty his drawers. He is published in Switzerland, re-issued in Germany. It's true the texts are already there. Some, written during the war, anticipated the present with surprising accuracy. Berlin recognises itself in this Berliner who has shared its effervescence, its fall, its rebirth. All this starts at the very moment when the blockade is strangling the barely resuscitated city ... It is invaded by the steppes. Intermittent lighting. Inoperative heating. Ailing post. Closed shops. People fight for lard, coffee. It's a Thermopylae, thinks the poet. Once more what is happening around him resembles what is in his heart of hearts. As if by contagion, the blockade of all reproduces that of the no longer published poet, who persists in writing by the light of a paraffin lamp. "Static Poems". "Three Old Men". "The Voice behind the Curtain". "Postlude". The readers are captivated by the introverted texts of an old man, texts they no longer expected but which pose all the questions they have been waiting for – even if they offer neither an answer, nor a message, nor a solution. Soon, thousands of people are recognising themselves – heaven knows why – in this account of a man's tenacious, invincible excursion in search of his own expression. They feel solidarity with someone who offers them only the gropings of a feigned blindness. Yet no one was more unreasonable. No one realised what had been missing in literature until they read his work. The man who thought he spoke only for himself finds himself at the centre of public attention. He is not in the least surprised. A major literary prize. A national decoration. Critical studies abroad. Those who disowned him yesterday at best hold their peace. Those of his generation who, willingly or not, recognise themselves in him, as he identifies with them: "Men of first hand. Mourning and brightness." And then, above all, those who are beginning to write today. He is one of the few men of yesterday that the Germany of tomorrow is curious to meet. He is amazed: so his words have not been withdrawn from circulation for ever like counterfeit money? This veteran sitting astride the year zero, one foot in the past – that is, the Flood – one foot in the future. Half antediluvian, half prophet.

He looks at the people assembled here this evening. For the first time. Some only knew each other by name before today. Without them, he thinks, I would not be here. Each of them must have done something for me, at one moment or another, something that has supported my life.

He also thinks: the next time they gather, it will be at my grave.

Max, who published me while my name was still on excommunication lists.

Walter, whom I always meet at the Café Dramburg, and to whom, for some time past, I've been talking about my father – the fundamentalist pastor whom I've been learning to love again since his death. I feel it may be time to be reconciled with him. I forget that he did not help my mother to die. I forget that God did not seem very pleasant when He spoke through his mouth. I re-read the Bible, that great book written for children and old men, and I understand better why the reader of the Psalms and the Book of Ezekiel did not take the detour of Heine or Schopenhauer. Finally, I accept, even approve that he did not hang a reproduction of Friedrich or Gainsborough on the walls of the family home ... Why did I fall out with him over that, even feel humiliated, whereas now it moves me? Whereas now it makes me ashamed of having despised him? Do you have to age, to take possession of your own acts, your blunders, in order to learn to love the poor mistakes, the dear ignorance of your father? The man you had known as a child endowed with a beard and an eloquence borrowed from Moses, had given way in later life to a little old man with a sweet tooth ... First too big, at the end too small: are fathers never the right size? The most difficult thing in life is to draw up a synthesis of yourself.

One day when I was attending the harvest festival at church, and the farmers were bringing in their offerings of grapes, pumpkins and leeks, their jugs of milk, their bouquets of asters that the light inflamed, I saw my father following a tomcat with his eye and heard him mumble: One should become like him ... Why didn't I share more moments like that with him?

So, Walter, I must have bored you stiff more than once with these family stories in front of a tall beer in the "Dramburg". I always arrived at the rendezvous first: to make peace with your father, even posthumously and by proxy, you can never arrive too early.

I believe too, Walter, that we met to talk Berlin dialect together. We reminisced about the bitter winter of '47, the blockade of '48, the monetary reform, the creation of the new

Republic, the end of rationing, the economic miracle and the spiritual bankruptcy ... And what else? – The death of Stalin, some scandal or other reverberating at the Dutch court ... They were real pub conversations. I speak of them in the past tense: who can say how many more we shall have?

Sometimes, Walter thinks, he would go to sit alone at another table, to write one or two lines of poetry, correct a third. Ilse came to fetch him at the end of the evening, when he forgot the time and his fatigue. She drank a beer with us. Often she said nothing.

Ilse looks furtively at her husband. She says to herself: I've chosen that old man for life. Soon he's going to ditch me: death is the worst adulterer. But after his death, what a burden and a tyrant he will be! And she thinks: let him only be burden and tyrant enough.

Friedrich Wilhelm Oelze watches the doctor talking to Walter Lennig. Thinking about his father. And Ilse observing her husband. He's on the point of feeling jealous. For no reason. They've been writing to each other for a quarter of a century: Gottfried's three wives and his many lady friends do not seem to have received so many letters from him ... But perhaps we could only write? thinks Herr Oelze, with a twinge of melancholy. One day I took the train from Bremen and came to Berlin to meet him, without telling him in advance. I went as far as Bozener Strasse but I did not dare ring his doorbell ... I took the train back to Bremen in a state of great confusion. Nevertheless, each time one of his wives died it's to me that he turned, it's to me that he appealed at the outrage of her death – but he also became more tender, more attentive to me at those times ... As one might be with a legitimate wife one had long left, and to whom one came to confide the end of an affair. I should not have let that man abandon me, lose me, for anything in the world.

It's Friedrich Wilhelm Oelze that the doctor is thinking about now, though without turning towards him. For he feels the other's gaze resting on him and, heaven knows why, making him uneasy. He does not want their eyes to meet. Thinking about Friedrich Wilhelm Oelze, the doctor fixes his eye on Ilse Kaul's white hairpiece, the crest which gleams under the chandeliers like an attribute of her sovereignty. That man has come here this evening to honour me; he has always been my companion on solemn occasions, the celebrations as well as the hours of greatest difficulty. When he knew I was living in penury, at the end of the war or during the blockade, he supplied me with coffee, rum and cigarettes. He has never let my birthday pass without sending me flowers – tulips or white carnations – as to a woman.

Have they remembered the flowers, I wondered this evening. He always remembered them. But in daily life our friendship wilted, wasted away. One day I took a train to Bremen with an intense desire to see him; arrived there, I thought myself idiotic and turned on my heels without even phoning him ... I admit that's an emotional way to behave. But I had been conducting a monologue for so long and had got so used to my autarchy, that when this man rose up in my path, wrote to me begging, then demanding, a reply, I was almost afraid. He was as prosperous as I was penniless. As far removed from the social pantomime as I was myself. Except that he supported the Nazi party ... I always acknowledged that his intelligence was superior to mine. But he did not write. I think that what impressed me at once about him was that his misanthropy even exceeded mine. Now this man was addressing me, and his words unleashed, liberated mine, relayed them so well that they soon became indispensable to me. Before I knew him, I did not realise how barren and isolated I was, how far I lacked an echo. When you have given yourself up long and fetishistically to solitude, you cannot know that doubt is in you like the worm in the fruit, gnawing ... No more reference points. Criteria all gone. You no longer know who you are. You've sold your shadow. Then you need someone to cross your path, cure your monomania, carry you – without your even knowing you are carried. The poem's soil is irrigated, grows fertile again. I was to be the poet, he the one who talks to the poet, challenges him, keeps him up to scratch, pushes him on ... I don't know why the roles were allocated like that – for there are some works of mine that he could almost have co-signed. They owe him everything ... Ah, all the letters in which we exchanged views on the structure of a poem, talked "technique", how much they went beyond their apparent concerns, how they made me strong. They not only reassured me about my talent, they offered me a future. Our missives went out from two strategists who had formed an alliance against the same adversary: a certain indolence of thought. One can imagine how such relations can become strained at times ... The life of the mind allows little compromise. Those who have chosen to lead it do not spare themselves, permit themselves neither weakness nor slackness, forgive themselves nothing. The mind expects, and gives, no indulgence. How many times did we nearly fall out! I think it's because we inspired fear in each other. We took turns at asking too much of each other. In such cases brotherhood is never far from resembling that of Cain and Abel.

I know nothing of Friedrich Wilhelm Oelze's private life; I have never set foot in his patrician residence. We communicated only the essential.

Twelve at table. Couldn't it have been a larger circle? Bluebeard shows such loyalty in friendship. Is there anything more gracious than the friendship of women?

To Thea Sternheim, whom he had lost track of for a long time, he has written again, summarising the intervening chapters of the serial story of his life. Is the sequence of days nothing more than a collection amassed by a maniac obsessed with the passage of time?

To Gertrud Zenzes he can start by saying that, for him, nothing has been easy and nothing has turned out really well. He can congratulate her on her move to New York. She is one of those who are perpetually resurfacing. On the eve of the war he received a parcel from her containing Nescafé, a pineapple, cigarettes and a tie from Broadway. In his penurious state this gift seemed endowed with both magic and an almost unbearable violence ... He had to entreat the sender never to send anything again! He remembers the day in Hanover in 1935 when they parted; they didn't know that it would not be for always, nor that it would be for so long. How much waste, perhaps, in our lives. But also, all had not been lost after all.

There are so many others to whom he could write: Lotte, Tilly, Elinor, Ernestine, Erna, Astrid, Ursula ... , talking portentously of the course of the world, the absence of any key that would free us from enigma, confused feelings, random separations and the need for reunions ... That which has replaced love − is it not steeped in a bottomless melancholy welling up from existence itself?

This is when he also remembers Else Lasker-Schüler. He knew her forty years ago. She has been dead for more than ten. But not long ago he gave an address in her memory at the British Centre. Everything came back at once, in disorder. He could never foresee when he was going to think of her, and he never thought about her twice in the same way. Tiny as she was, she ate nothing. Indigent, she impoverished herself further, with a kind of exaltation. She took majestic liberties, which saved her and sucked her down at the same time. To cross the Kurfürstendamm at night with her on your arm was an adventure from which you were surprised to emerge alive. The world stopped: it was it or her! But her eccentricities, her gypsy adornments, her caliph's jewellery, her poor, childish ruses, could not protect her. One day, some time after the First War, she had begged him to meet her in Switzerland to spend even just two hours with her beside a lake (she had written: "the sea"). She added that she often wept with fatigue, a fatigue that went beyond all sadness.

He had not answered; he had not gone with her to see the camellias in flower in the heart of Ticino. He had crossed no lake with her. Those two hours he had not spared her, the gouty old poet was now to devote to someone else, in memory of her.

In homage to Else, who had been the first to listen to his poetry and had loved him for lyrics so charmless and so strong, he now receives young German poets, by appointment, from two until four on Friday afternoons.

She is the reason why he does not turn away these amiable time-wasters with courteous firmness. Why he never refuses such interviews. Perhaps, too, because they never take the same course twice. So that he can go on hoping to reveal to one of these visitors a secret he would never have confided to others?

He might have been glad of this juvenile attention. He is merely surprised that his work has survived the events, and his own quarantine, so well. He is amazed that young people born not so long before the war could find in it an object for study . . .

"I'm not here, Sir, to submit my novice's poems to you," says the young man with a slight tremor in his voice. "I've come to ask why you acquiesced in the advent of the worst in this country?"

Is his voice trembling with fear or anger, hatred or sadness? How long has this stranger with the fine, aristocratic features been meditating his approach? And how long has he been holding that sentence he has just spoken in readiness?

Of course, thinks the poet, one of the pack was bound to ask me that question in the end. You can't always choose those by whom you are called to account.

He feels torn between tiredness – Will it never end? Will there never be a last time? – and a feeling of relief that surprises him: So here is someone who does not take things at face value . . .

Yes, this asker of awkward questions, this young judge made up for all those who thought they only had to pick up from where German poetry had left off in 1933 . . .

But fatigue crushes him: is there a chance in a thousand that he will at last be able to say something convincing? The fact is that his task is less to convince than to discover – like this young man, and with him – the truth . . .

"I don't know," he stammers. "We believed in a real revolution. It was one, alas, and you know where all revolutions lead . . . "

His interlocutor does not react. He has achieved his main purpose: he is being listened to. The slightly curly hair . . . The girlish features . . . Klaus Mann! thinks the poet. The purity. The same ardent life. Too much purity to accept the war. Too much impatience to resign himself to the kind of peace that followed when it failed to keep its promises. And to think that it has not even occurred to the old man to show this graceful, fragile commander the door. Because he was Klaus Mann to the life? He won't even ask him his name. What would be the use?

"I should tell you, Doctor, that I have not come here out of bravado, to examine a case. Other inquisitors – perhaps less well-intentioned – are taking care of that. But I belong to a generation which has had no right to any truth except the ruins. No one will explain anything to us. Whereas it is clear that you know – whatever your interpretation may be. But you will soon be gone. We have to know in what country we are going to succeed you. Whether it gratifies you or not, you are one of us. We have the feeling that you lived at the dawn of Nazism like a drug-user about to take his first trip. We just ask you to tell us what it was like . . .

Doesn't seem so interested in the withdrawal side, this young man. He's right. I've not been sparing with commentaries on that aspect . . .

"You realise," says the doctor, "that whoever you are it could happen to you too … "

"Exactly, Doctor. It's because I understood that that I'm here."

The poet blushes. He impresses him, this young man, dazzles him, this child so preoccupied with regaining an innocence he has not yet had the time or opportunity to lose. The old man feels like a tsar who has to tell his son that he, the son, is not besmirched with the blood of a regicide … I'd like to help the young man, thinks the doctor, prove to him not so much my innocence as his own … But to do that, do I need to exculpate myself a little?

"You know I've explained myself on all that in a book. You've read it, at least?"

"Of course, I've read *Double Life*. One can't say that you subjected yourself to self-criticism of the usual sort … "

"Don't you think that the usual sort of self-criticism is often not much more than a manoeuvre by those who indulge in it to disarm criticism and get off lightly? They stay in charge of the game."

"And that 'game', if it is one, is not one you want to play?"

"When one has been called, as I have, a pig by the Nazis, an imbecile by the Communists, a spiritual whore by the democrats, a renegade by the emigrants, a pathological Antichrist by the devout, do you think one is tempted to add an epilogue of one's own?"

All the same, thinks the doctor, I can't tell my visitor outright that because what I did was irreparable, I can't even pretend to repair it. This young man must be the same age as my daughter was, one evening in Hamburg, when I told her that in different words, and since then the same number of years has passed. He must have been born the same year as I talked about it to Nele … For the last time, as I thought. He must be about twenty … he could be my grandson. And I'm still at the same point.

"Do you know the story of Kurt Gerstein?" the old man

asks. "You don't? It doesn't ring a bell? Gerstein, after studying theology at Marburg – as I did, incidentally – joined the SA in 1933. He was a fervent Lutheran. He was soon horrified by the language used by the Nazi officials about the Old Testament. After clashing with them he first thought of studying medicine, then took a decision that had been ripening slowly in him: he joined the SS with the sole aim of infiltrating it and exposing its misdeeds to the Allies ... "

"The Trojan Horse strategy ... "

"More like the lion's mouth. He found himself involved in carrying out the so-called final solution to the Jewish problem ... "

"He found no way to extricate himself?"

"Not at once. Don't forget that he wanted to be as effective as possible. In for a penny, in for a pound – to unmask the whole system ... "

"The allied authorities didn't want to receive him?"

"On the contrary! They listened to him. Only they didn't want to believe what they heard. They feared a trap ... Unless they just pretended not to believe. Some thought they had better things to do than destroy gas chambers."

"What then?"

"He gave himself up to the enemy. He committed suicide in prison, in Paris in 1945. But he was branded all the same, posthumously, by a denazification commission ... "

"All those crimes for nothing," says the young man. Then, after a moment, he adds: "What an example of 'German seriousness' taken to the extreme, to the absurd! But why do you tell me this, Doctor? You surely don't equate this man's attitude with yours?"

"In *Wehrmacht* uniform I never worked as anything other than a doctor ... "

"Which means? Surely you don't see in Kurt Gerstein's strange 'martyrdom' an inspiring example for us?"

"I would only say that Lieutenant Gerstein was guided to his choice by a supreme realism. He even found a way of reconciling his religious ideal with his utilitarian concern, his unbelievable pragmatism ... He only wanted to 'limit the damage', to use that phrase."

"At the cost of a human 'fire-break'?"

"Yes, and no one can count the victims to whose fate he contributed by staying at his post. History does not tell us ... His error was to assume that the fate of millions of Jews really mattered to the allied representatives he spoke to. Their 'realism' did not mesh with his own. Gerstein wanted – with utter futility – to be a double agent working at the same time for the Nazis and Eternity ... "

"Perhaps God might not accept being served at the price of such arrangements."

"It wasn't God who made Gerstein's plan fail, it was men ... I didn't tell you this story to kill time, you know, or to evade questions directed at me personally. I just wanted to make you see one thing: that whatever the German guilt in this war, there are perhaps no two Germans who incurred it in an identical way."

"So that I can't ask you about the collective guilt, Dr Benn, but only about your own."

"My conviction – perhaps it's a fatal error – was that the life of the mind draws on what is best in man and is lived out somewhere above the mêlée ... "

"Isn't that still your credo today, doctor?"

"Yes it is. I shall not let go of it now. When a powerful idea has decided the whole shape of your actions, it's too late to change it ... "

"So you might commit the same error again?"

"What I say is that I should be judged on the totality of my actions, and the links holding them together. I do not, think, of course, that I should commit the same error again. But I might well commit a different one: I might despair of the race in some other way ... That's what is called my nihilism, you know? Have you heard about it? Ezra Pound once said that he had got to know sorrow too late in life. For sixty years he had

been mde of stone, like youth ... Sixty years! Imagine that.
Lucky man. My sadness came on me at once, and never left
me ... "

The young man is tempted to object: That's no excuse ...
But he gives up the argument. He despairs of shaking the old
man's conviction. He doesn't even want to. As if the doctor's
sadness had invaded him too, and now filled him completely.
The doctor, however, is unwilling to take advantage of his
young interlocutor's generosity of spirit – or passing weakness:
will he never clear his name?

"One day, shortly after the end of the war, I visited the
historian Margret Boveri, who devoted thousands of pages to
the question of betrayal. My case interested her. She believed
there are situations when you cannot help betraying something,
whether it be your country, the government, humanity, God,
or yourself ... Only the hero can avoid the wrong betrayal.
She also thought my aberration of '33 was dictated by my
rebellion against the ideals of the Enlightenment, and the
hypocrisy of an epoch that refused to acknowledge the dread-
fulness of life ... It was all intensely interesting, but I didn't
stay long ... "

"Why? Were you disappointed?"

"Oh no. But without intending to she was cornering me.
How could life have failed to terrorise me? It seemed that only
one thing could give me impunity ... "

"What was that?"

"Madness ... I may have only just escaped it, you know.
During the First War ... If I'd let myself go a little more ... I
was close to the abyss. It was the doctor in me that saved the
poet. Have you ever wondered what would have become of
Hölderlin if he had not gone out of his mind? And remember
that if I'd gone mad I might well have met the fate the Hitler
regime reserved for lunatics ... "

The young man is not really listening. He is deeply shocked
that anyone could imagine a different destiny for Hölderlin

than the one he actually had. But more than that, he can't help imagining that if Dr Benn had actually succumbed to psychosis at the beginning of the thirties, he could have met the fate the Third Reich held in store for the mentally ill. His head spins.

"No doubt you've read my twenty-two poems against Hitler?"

"'The rat presents itself as pestilence's cure'? Yes, I know them. I've read your whole *oeuvre*, Doctor. Several times."

"What do you think of those poems?"

"That you display a heroic spirit – rather belatedly."

"Would you agree that they are very far from being the best I have written?"

"My God, you're not going to disown them?"

"You don't quite understand me. What I mean is that poetry is ill suited to a subject as trivial as Chancellor Hitler. Do you know what is the best statement literature ever produced on that subject? *Arturo Ui*? Obviously not ... A sentence – just once sentence by Karl Kraus: 'On Hitler I find nothing to say.' That's all. It's final. Some dismal minds have actually mis-construed it, finding the remark 'ambiguous'. Could anything be clearer? But still, we were talking of Kraus ... Have you heard any recordings of his voice? It's the shrill, almost hysteri-cal voice of a dictator of thought! Kraus's insults and indict-ments were more than a match for his unfortunate detractors. You needed the range of Freud or Hofmannsthal to stand up to them! Luckily, Kraus was at least even-handed in his tyranny ... But we were lucky not to come under it!"

The visitor's good sense bridles and chafes under the para-doxical hypotheses the doctor is putting forward, as if trying to lull his vigilance. "If Hölderlin had not gone out of his mind, and as for me ... " "If Karl Kraus hadn't been an enlightened despot ... "

"It isn't the oratorical tone or the bawling that matters, it's the message," he declares. "Anger sounds the same in the mouth of the dictator and the just man. But the words are not the same ... And no matter what you say, Doctor, other writers have, fortunately, had something to say about Hitler after Kraus ... We who were born a short time before the war are going to find it so hard to find out what happened ... Our embarrassing questions will be answered with such bad grace ... As if all we needed were a joke by Karl Kraus to enlighten us! And if it comes to jokes, I prefer Karl Valentin's riposte to the Führer when he came to congratulate him in his box after a performance. Hitler assured Valentin that his act has always made him laugh. "That's strange," the actor replied, "yours has never amused me at all." However, a few witty repartees will not be enough for us, nor authorial comments: 'A little too brief, young man'. Under other circumstances, perhaps. Not this time ... But you look tired, Doctor. Perhaps you think I'm taking liberties."

"No, of course not. Really, we haven't said anything yet. Just touched on the subject ... You know, I agree entirely that it would have been better to be one of those who opened their eyes from the first ... But when that has not happened, you have to look for other solutions – do you understand? To envy the lucidity Klaus Mann showed when it was needed, or his uncle's discernment, or Tucholsky's intellectual panache – it would be ludicrous, almost indecent to do that now, wouldn't you agree? And then, I'm only talking about the good people. There are others I respect less who were also not wrong. You know, people who are always in the right, adopt unassailable positions at just the right time – I don't know why, but those people who are professionally incapable of error have always made me uneasy, profoundly suspicious ... I may be wrong again, and there are certainly saints ... But I've too much scepticism in me ever to have been 'admirable'. I don't even regret it: it wasn't within my reach. At least it's saved me from being a giver of lessons ... Today the pontiffs have taken over from the butchers, and there are those among them who only make us forget the mistakes they made yesterday ... by the ones they make today! They can do and say anything, permit themselves everything: they take advantage of a general amnesia

which is propitious to them ... Must I recall for you what
Thomas Mann wrote and proclaimed between 1920 and 1933,
until people close to him made him aware of the enormity of
his successive blunders. Yet it's his BBC speeches that History
will remember ... "

"It's not your scepticism that is at issue, Doctor. It's your lack
of it in '33."

" 'To be wrong and to continue to believe your conscience –
that is being a man.' I wrote that in a text on the way artists
have to come to terms with the unsteady, cracked image that
life has inscribed in their mirror. Sometimes I tell myself that
the single error that hounds me – my name will never be
mentioned without evoking it – is something I should claim
positively. Only through it can I achieve such humanity as I am
capable of, and through the disaster it let loose in my life. I
must stand by it – can you understand that? But in silence ... "

The old man seems worn out. The visitor says nothing.

It's dreadful, he thinks. He won't take a step to meet us.
He'll prefer to wall himself up in the terrible solitude of the
redeemer who lost his way. At the same time, he's right: who
could be more human than the sage whom wisdom deserted,
or the saint who, for only one moment, slipped from grace?
What he calls his "unsteady image" is his own kind of
transparency. The limpidity he regained on the other side of
the mirror he broke to reach it. Such is he, soiled and
respectable. Disarmingly pure, and himself disarmed ... I only
hoped he would say a certain word, just one – I don't know
which – and he has not done so.

No matter, Doctor. I came here to say it, but I will be
content with thinking it: what you did leaves us for ever at a
loss. We shall never be consoled for what happened to you. We
shall never quite recover from what happened to *us* through
you.

What they can't explain to themselves, thinks the old man, is that I'm not defeated. My life has not got the better of me. I admit, it's inexplicable.

That young man, thinks the old man on the evening of 2 May 1956, surveying his daughter and his friends around the banquet table and feeling as weary again as the day he received him, I should have invited that young man here. Would he have come? I'm not sure. He would have felt so ill at ease, alone, desperate. Nele, you would have looked on him with surprise, tenderness. Klaus Mann ..., you'd have said. See how like him the young man is. And I should have felt alone in my turn. You're angry with me, I know, for not making any attempt to make up with Klaus immediately after the war. I thought it was for him to make a gesture ... But underneath, I knew that we should never see or talk to each other again. Then he committed suicide. I'll not tell you of the strange respect that act inspires in me: you'd only interpret it as rancour.

And I see you again so care-worn, my little girl. Do you remember that other birthday dinner we had together in Hamburg, just the two of us, before the war? You had nothing but love – or rather the sorrows of love – on your mind. And today, twenty years later, I find you a prey to the same pangs. Only just divorced from your wholesale merchant ... and already tempted by another adventure. Still just as young, therefore. Still my little girl, with a heart so big you don't know where to put it ... Where did you get it from? From your mother, without question. If it had been up to me, I'd have advised you against affairs of the heart. If need be I'd have forbidden you love – in vain, of course. Do not believe I don't take your dear torments seriously! Could the melancholy they arouse in me absolve me from thinking of the childhood you spent away from your father? Could I be so inept at repentance and the examination of conscience, as people are inclined to believe I am, that I should have found such a convenient means of showing you, in spite of all, how much I cared?

Some while ago I intended to write you a letter in which I would yet again have decried passion, that perpetual alibi of idlers it excuses for not creating ... But what good would it have done? It would not have consoled you for the failure of your marriage.

However, as if to preserve the mood, I went to my library and took up Bettina's Letters to Goethe, the *Marienbad Elegy*, the *Correspondence* of Caroline von Günderrode ... Normally, I've no taste for these so-called intimate writings, in which the writer poses so carefully for posterity, and which are punctuated by cries, lamentations and domestic jeremiads.

But at that time this debauch of feelings, this orgy of sensibility filled me with a fascinated disgust.

Bettina Brentano's string-pulling intrigues as she besieged the old Goethe, inducing him to say and write far more than he really felt for her. Charlotte's exaltation. Christiane's abnegation. Mme de Stein's wounded *amour-propre*. The senile seduction manoeuvres of the great Goethe himself. The slow waltz hesitating endlessly between inclination and duty. Garrotted sincerities. Such was the lot of the Aulic Chancellor and his female admirers.

As for La Günderrode, her odyssey was still more heart-rending. Savigny's fatuous coquetries. Clemens Brentano's emotional inveiglements. Caroline's disappointed love, grandiose renunciation and final suicide. Arnim's tardy remorse ... My God, what novelettes! A Rhenish ragout ...

I confess to preferring lachrymose music-hall songs that tell about the same misadventures – minus the Romantic histrionics. It's very unfair of me, I know. But it only applies to downright kitsch ... What troubles me more is the growing success of a certain kind of bookshop-window paraliterature. Don't put this down to petty jealousy, Nele. Just think: we've been through the Germanic trauma, or perhaps the universal human one, for all I know. There's nothing to put out the flags for. And all we can find is Romantic trash to console ourselves with for the massacres, and to reconcile ourselves with the

species. Two conflagrations "Made in Germany" have passed
break-neck over these pampered sensibilities, and now we see
again in the bookshop windows, as if nothing had happened,
the same sickly love stories, the phthises of half-talented
poetesses, the ostentatious suicides of delicate souls! Kleist, by
contrast, seems to me to have committed suicide only to escape
the next chapter of this catechism of mawkishness. And Hölderlin took refuge in insanity to avoid lapsing into the platitudi-
nous melancholy in vogue ...

Thirty million men have died on the battlefield, but the
spectres coming back to haunt us, the graves again being
decked with flowers, date from the dawn of the nineteenth
century ... Perhaps we ought to rejoice, all the same, that
these pleasant trifles have survived the abominations in the
human memory?

Yet I recall a satire by a political cabaret singer directly after
the war, in which he took Goethe and Schiller to task for being
born too early, for having in a certain sense deserted at
Stalingrad and Dresden, fled the last page of German history ...
But he did them the honour of assuming that in our time one
of them would have been gassed at Birkenau and the other
hanged at Plötzensee. He did not say which would have ended
where.

What was it, my darling girl, that set my teeth on edge in
that catalogue of palpitations, old-maidish vapourings, cardiac
arrhythmias, bloodless bleedings? I concede that one ought to
have found there the highest expression of the spirit, carried to
incandescent levels! But I sensed imposture ...

What struck me was the arbitrariness of those aristocratic
sufferings, their dilapidation ... They were certainly no more
elevated than the most trivial of ours. The noble souls paddled
in a thick broth of over-ripe sentimentality ... Examined more
closely, all the gallantry, the protestations of magnanimity, the
edifying homilies, turned into a masked ball and soon a dance
of death! But how correctly those people went to work! Ah,
the velvet massacre of fine sensibilities, the half-tones, the

carnage dressed in lace, in a decor by Watteau. The homicidal minuet. The *mezza voce* wrecking of hearts! Admire the artistry!

Should I not have been more in sympathy with that expression of life's disasters? No, it proved all the more alien to my nature for seeming so close ... I could even explain why. On this planet shared between bulimia and anorexia of the heart, every contact with another was turning into violation. You lacerated with the lightest touch. Ah! I should have preferred a sausage-maker's sensuality to these rustlings of gossamer wings, these frolics of bats, these vampire somersaults! You should have seen those cripples and amputees turning as murderous as scorpions – both to each other and to themselves. Killing themselves ruthlessly even in others. A few inspired flashes did not justify this worldly deliquescence. I had no stomach for a cough syrup that exacerbated the fits instead of soothing them.

By comparison, what virility you found in Schumann, or Chopin.

> "Quiet death,
> how much unlike the death
> in paroxysms of pain
> or the artillery barrage."

Did you know that at the end of his life Goethe – since we always come back to him – pretended to envy the fate of Werther? Addressing the character whose dying had "brought him luck", he did not hesitate to assure him: "What you lost was little enough ... " One more pose? No doubt. Goethe never stinted them. Why, this time, do I want to believe it?

It will be thought that I was arid, cold. And the people who think it will be those who are unable to see how barren and frozen the world is. They find illness terrible, war abominable, debauchery sordid, earthly death dreadful. Isn't that a partial, selective, metonymical judgement? Whereas the whole world horrifies me, globally. But, that being granted, I fight it toe to toe; I negotiate with it, tame it. Sometimes, when I see a man chatting to another, smiling to a woman, making a child laugh,

I can't get over it, I'm stupefied. How do they manage it, I ask myself. Why don't they relate to each other like animals? Since that's what they are. And sometimes, of course, that man is no other than myself.

But we live in countries in which, too often, feeling finds only a sticky, mawkish expression. It's a matter of organs. And I know about organs, how small and insubstantial they are.

As for me, I did not appear to have any passion to tame. Oh, I don't deceive myself, detachment is seldom thought heroic . . . It does not claim to be. It just presupposes a little courage. I've no other contract to make with reality. In life, you never choose more than the rope with which to hang yourself. I wonder if consenting to grow old was not, in my case, the worst risk I could have run. Mission accomplished.

The old man has noticed that in the course of this spring radiant young girls have been coming to ask him about the "meaning of his work". Good heavens, does it speak to women as well? Is it not merely a male fantasy?

He does not pretend that he is not charmed by these encounters. These feminine attentions. It's not the midday – or midnight? – demon that's got into him. To do him justice, he has avoided the absurdity of awaiting great age before taking an interest in young women. In truth, that interest – that preoccupation – has never left him. No, it's something else. When a man has lost all hope, he has no reason for preference between the sexes. And if he has kept a little, it is usually women who have inspired it.

All the same, he is surprised: why now? That's to say: why so late? Why all women at once? It's like the notoriety, the fame even, that has descended on him like an avalanche when he no longer expected it. One might, of course, pose the two questions together: between the belated arrival of celebrity and that of certain young women, might there not be a relation of cause and effect?

A pity he has passed through so many disasters – even if they are what really interests him. A pity that illness, senescence, have gained a foothold on his robust carcass. He would have liked to prolong this period of pacification, of sweetness. A vain regret: even his lady visitors must have sensed that he had not long to go. That's why they came running. What they "saw in him" was the singular charm of something soon to be extinguished for ever. In him they scented the father at the end of his tether, plucking a last endearment from a magus about to vanish. Wrenching it from him like an avowal. He knows it's the *requiem* being softly intoned in him that lures them. He does not hold that against them. Nor does he blame himself for responding to their expectation. He prefers to be lulled, even if the lullaby is already a dirge.

Some of them wondered if they would have to contend with a dried-up, didactic, eccentric dotard. The man they found was gentle, amusing, touching – just slightly broken.

Could it be love they are offering him? No doubt. And it would need only the slightest incitement for the flesh to claim its due. As he sometimes verifies ... Often, too, he guesses they have not come to declare themselves but to say goodbye. That they already regret his loss. He no longer really tries to seduce. He has learned to suspect the emotional cannibalism that so many patriarchal ogres indulge in to make themselves feel alive ... And he does not really need this succession of erect silhouettes in his former waiting room on Friday afternoons, whose perfume lingers after they have gone, leaving their host to dream ...

This is how one should spend one's time, he thinks, listening to a student with a peachy complexion ask him if "woman, in his work, can be anything other than concubine or madonna?"

"But of course, Fräulein. Woman has the gift to cover every field ... ," he says, watching Ilse Kaul through the half-open door as she arranges narcissi and daffodils in an alabaster vase.

Sometimes, the presence of women is so violent for him that he would like to hide his head in his hands to reconstitute in secret the image of almond eyes, the defenceless whiteness of a throat, the tumble of auburn locks, the open wound of a mouth, the liquid flash of teeth, the childish curl of an ear ... He would like all these images to run in his veins like alcohol, to warm him for as long as he can keep them captive: the reflection of her who in a moment will have vanished as she came. He has turned towards the window, bowed his head. The visitor might misunderstand, think she is tiring him.

It's the opposite. He is more alert than ever: piercing the pearly shadow that scintillates beneath his lids in a phosphorescent swirl ...

This way, he will not have to say to her: Don't go so soon ... She'll never leave. He keeps her his unwitting prisoner. Almost as if he were abusing her in his sleep.

All these beauties who think he is half asleep do not realise that the doctor has hypnotised them. Now they can leave if they like, it makes no difference. They have lost their shadows, as one loses one's virginity. He has possessed them no less than if they had departed bearing his child.

My poems, thinks the poet mischievously, were sometimes the fruit of a conception no less immaculate and just as clandestine. Thrown into the world's arms, in my panic I gave that octopus a child.

Saying goodbye to one of his visitors, he struggles to keep her features in his mind. Sometimes he fails to recall them. If, in a sudden flash, they reappear, it is like a conquest each time. Busily he whets in his mind the singularity of certain carmine lips, the fine down revealed by a tan, or the impertinence of a lock of hair. If he forgets a detail he feels as if he has lost everything. He is bereaved.

Sometimes I obliterate even my own face, he acknowledges. I forget proper names. Am I becoming absent-minded? But might not what we call "absent-mindedness" be some small part of death?

He never confuses one face with another, nor does he shuffle them like cards to make one from all – like this or that friend of his who called himself a ladies' man but excelled only in amalgamating them, reducing their plurality to an anonymous singular . . .

It must be love they are offering, since it is love he receives.

But that is not really the point. What matters more than anything is that women have granted him absolution, when one has died because of him, he has been powerless to save another and has failed to protect a third from a distress that resembled madness; who knows how many other defenceless beings who happened to be women he has accounted for? So these emancipated Berlin girls he receives so graciously are not so much potential mistresses as messengers bringing glad news. Women are a nation, and nations like kings are entitled to show clemency.

In front of a café on the Kurfürstendamm in the late afternoon, facing a glass of white wine and a red-headed girl. He is not talking. It is enough for the old man to let the spirit of the city pass to him through the young woman. A shower drives them inside the café. Copper pans, zinc table-tops, varnished panelling shine all around them. They can admire in silence the dexterity of the black barman, the vivacity of the half-caste waitress. The diners' heads are scalped in the lamplight. Newspapers hang like washing on wooden frames. At a nearby table sit some slightly grim lovers. The red-headed girl has a face over which no shadow has ever passed. Life has not yet had time to molest her. The old man is not going to ask for her address or telephone number. Nor even her surname. He'll be content with a first name – Inge – for now. He'll go back home head bowed, throat a little tight. I've known as much solitude as days in my life, he thinks. I never fled howling from loneliness.

Sitting in front of a café on the Ku-Damm, another time.

Today he is not to meet anyone. It's enough for young women of the city to pass before his eyes, as in a film which is soon to end. Gentle apparitions whose features can only be guessed at against the light – but where do they get that gait, almost awkward in its urgency? That fervour to live. The old man marvels. He wonders to what he owes this beatitude that caresses his heart as softly as cygnet down. In other times it would have been the blade of a knife, that only by some miracle did not cut into the flesh! Blessed be this wordless, illiterate message.

If he closes his eyes now it is not to create the dark room in which are developed cherished negatives, but to hear better the splashing of a public fountain on the corner of Olivaer Platz. He thinks that at certain hours he would have liked to take a little of the benison shed on him now to a person dear to him. He thinks that some at least of his poems ought to have flowed like that water into its basin. More often, his poems had scorched like acid.

To read his poems, you would hardly suspect that he could have ascended to this heavy euphoria. His work had never taken the time to speak of such things. In wretchedness as in joy, it had borne arms.

One evening, he is dining in a *Gasthaus* on the Fasanen-strasse. Opposite him, a poetess besotted with white magic. Before meeting her he did not even know that white magic existed. For good reasons, he knew only black.

While she tells him about her experiences of possession, he watches her face form itself, decompose, reconstitute itself again, in the light of the candles placed between them on the table. The face matures and ages, is rejuvenated and dies, resuscitates itself several times a minute, passing and passing again through all the ages of life. Now Raphael, now Klimt, now Schiele. In the space of an hour, the old man has fallen in and out of love with the poetess several times. Being in doubt, he renounces conquest once more. At most he pays her token court. In order not to appear discourteous. Almost relieved that she has not responded to his limp advances.

He prefers to return home on foot along the avenues of this city that is re-making itself without recovering its composure. No matter! One more day on which he has not died of boredom, which is no small thing in times like these. He recalls that at one point the poetess said to him: "Doctor, you are asking me a question that might change the nature of our relations." Was it she who had said that, and what was the question? He no longer knows.

He stops where the pavement is being repaired on the Berliner Strasse. The storm-lanterns cast an immense, grotesque shadow of him which lurches on the screen of a façade. He cannot recall the subject of this exchange. That's it, the end ..., he thinks. You talk about a possible mutation in the relations between a man and a woman, and a moment later you don't even know what it was that might have been transformed!

At any rate, his partner had soon changed the subject. Their relations had not been modified at all. It was better so.

"Do you believe in God?" enquires the graduate in German literature who is writing her thesis about him.

"Why, does it show?" he asks, taken aback.

"That you might have faith? Yes, a little ... "

"No," says the poet, "not that I believe ... That I think about God, that's all ... "

For he was thinking about God that very moment. A God who, like the Sphinx, had received no answers to the riddles it had posed but had spared those who had proved incapable of answering, thus submitting them needlessly to cruel trials.

He also thought of the dead. His own dead who, at that moment, must have been pressing closely around them in the room, to warm themselves from the contact with the young graduate, and to prevent themselves from dying still more.

"No, Anna, I'm not sure I believe in God. But if I were God, I'd believe in you ... "

Then he falls silent. More and more often he lapses into silences quite unlike those of earlier times: the muteness of the drowned. This afternoon, his silence is steeped in a secret gaiety.

"You've stopped talking, Doctor," says Anna. "Aren't you listening to me? I'm a chatterbox, I know. You wouldn't believe it, but I've only been like this since meeting you!"

"Oh, I can believe you. I move ravishing women to speech ... And in their company I can at last be silent. Joyously silent."

Might not the end of life, he wonders, be in the image of life itself: always and immediately a prey to death? His eye drinks the sparkling light of a last Berlin spring. He tastes a moment of pure virtuosity.

One last time the old man knows the agitation of love. He is stupefied. People will say: It was because Anna was so pretty, and it was almost summer. He had always been susceptible to young flesh ... They will forget that it was his last spring on earth, and that he certainly knew it. They'll say: She might have been his grand-daughter, or very nearly. For his love to have been less ridiculous and obscene, she ought to have been old and ugly – the woman to whom he hardly declared himself, did not take time to infect with his own agitation. They will not see that he simply wanted to converse with someone who knew only by hearsay of the disasters that had blighted the world. He wanted to listen to a girl who had been born a short time before the catastrophe, and had no memory of it. He wanted to talk to a creature not burdened with a memory stained with blood, ingenuous enough to believe the world better than the one she had been told about. The final hope that Germany would not suffocate tomorrow under the ash of braziers lit by another Germany. He utters the silent wish that, for this hour, the sun's rays would warm only him. Egoistically. That Anna would make him happy for one more hour, then leave him without hope.

The graceful child talks to him of his poetry, quotes it. Of course, this flatters his vanity. But above all he is surprised to reflect that his poetry has been fed on everything that in others would have negated it. It has been organised, harmonised thanks to a latent, internal rhythm that made the words stay unsteadily upright, advancing with the sureness of a tightrope walker on a wire stretched above a precipice ...

He watches the girl whom the light seems to illuminate from within like a lamp, intercepting the gaze, so grave yet playful, that rests on him. He listens to her laugh. For he could not tire of hearing this laugh which is the world's childhood. He is proud to have provoked it. Remember, he notes, that I have again made Anna laugh ... Remember that she read my poetry as if it were in the process of being composed. It's the words that did the work, words from before the war. Words equal, in a sense, to any test, that he rediscovers as she restores them to him ... What sweet revenge on those who had declared the lugubrious rhetorician mummified in his mannerism!

Then he thinks of God. Who knows? Perhaps it would please him if God – or the Sphinx – were mixed up slightly in this affair.

"Did you doze off, Doctor?"

"No, my child, as always I was asleep with one eye open."

But, now that he is for once submerged in the purity that irradiates a human face, he is surely not going to interrupt the visitation with an ill-judged remark?

"We should organise a celebration," he mumbles.

"A celebration?" asks Anna.

"Yes, that's what I said: a celebration."

Nevertheless, Anna is not invited to the Hotel am Steinplatz on the evening of 2 May 1956. It would have been difficult to explain her presence. Such are the incongruities of his life. And yet, if he were not afraid of being misunderstood, of putting a damper on the evening, it's to those now present, his wife, his daughter, his friends, that he would like to confide his intention to stop writing. For some time past it has seemed that he only had to pick up his pen to secrete impeccable verses. As if he couldn't stop himself. Glittering objects that only interested him while they were being produced. Smooth poetry, without asperities. Without surprises – at least for their author. He reverts to strict forms, that enchant and lull the reader. At the same time, without intending to, he has returned to the vocabulary of his beginnings: "poor ... eye ... dark ... flesh ... skin ... clear ... come ... lie down". His commentators have noted the fact. Wasn't that an irrefutable sign that the circle had closed, and that he had no more to do?

Some depart with elegance. Some even collapse with a certain distinction. But when you have been an Expressionist, you cannot finish up in the cosy guise of a man of letters.

Why, on an evening like this when homage is being paid to you, must you also think of the damage you have done, the mess you've made? Because you are surrounded by your friends and family, that is to say, those you have considered least. He leaves them only the dross of his solicitude. I've stopped creating, he thinks. Soon I shall have stopped harming.

He runs his eye once more over the photos he has laid out on the edge of his duvet. It's not even worth propping himself up higher on the pillows to get a better view: they won't tell him anything more. The table is deserted. The chandeliers extinguished. The serviettes crumpled ... It was very soon after leaving that table that he slipped from fatigue into illness. Hypertension, intestinal haemorrhage – according to the official bulletins. The doctor knows well that the true diagnosis is formulated elsewhere. He is not one of those doctors who cannot read in themselves the evidence they would decipher in any of their patients.

At all events, he thinks, the important episodes of my life, starting with my birth, have always happened in a year ending in 6 ... I merely have to complete the series.

"Six is the Devil's number," he explains to Ilse, "because that envious digit never reaches seven, which is the number of perfection. So it can only be six, six again, always six ... "

One night, he dreams of Ilse, Nele, Anna, Herta, other women, tied to pillories, blindfold. He is struck by the fact that they all have grey hair.

He reads a biography of Chekhov. Perhaps because the Russian was – doubly – his colleague. In 1885, when his reader was about to come into the world, the Russian doctor undertook autopsies on suicides. Almost twenty years later, he came to Germany to die. He had not much liked the capital, finding the women there singularly lacking in grace. He then went to take the waters at Badenweiler. That's where he croaked. He had himself used such a term; then, at the moment of passing away, had said more politely in German: "I'm dying" – *Ich sterbe*. You recognise the exquisite politeness of a man at pains to be understood by those crowding around his bed.

Why do we read the lives of famous men? To find out how they managed their exits. Why do we re-read the Bible? For a crash course in the language spoken on the other side, just in case ...

"Do you remember that book, Ilse, which described the events surrounding the death of La Duse? She died in America. She was entitled to a first funeral in New York. Then she was transported by ship to Naples, and the ceremony was repeated. When her body passed through the straits of Gibraltar, all the ships which passed hers lowered their flags to half-mast. But I like Chekhov's death even better ... "

"Why's that?"

"Because it's more like … "

"More like what?"

"Like what death really is. No red velvet curtains. No steamship sirens. Just an oyster cart with the coffin wedged into it. I wonder if Chekhov knew what he was dying of. If he'd made a correct diagnosis. If he was a competent doctor."

But, he understands, it's not Dr Chekhov's death that one should ultimately envy him, but his life.

Twenty-three stringed instruments vibrate in unison from the little wireless set that Ilse has put on his bedside table. The symphonic *Metamorphoses* composed by Richard Strauss as an epitaph for a bombed city, a demolished theatre, a vanished world … But what will our heirs think, the invalid wonders, listening tomorrow to this music in which the composer takes his leave of all he has revered? Swansong at the end of a long farewell encompassing all his work. As if this music, prostrate in its bed of nostalgia, had been written entirely in the past conditional. The *Metamorphoses* carried the number Opus 85: the same as the number of years the musician had spent on this earth. But did the catalogue record the melody respectfully dedicated to Goebbels in 1933, or the "Olympic Hymn" of 1936? One was not sure. So when people listened to Strauss later, what would they hear? The man accused in 1945 of having become a "war profiteer" – while the inventor of the V2 was invited to move to America with all the honours due to his rank? Or the composer who sided with his librettist Stefan Zweig when the latter fell foul of the anti-Semitic Reich? How would they listen to the highly civilised music of one who was, for a time, the accomplice of barbarism?

These ambiguities struck a chord in the Expressionist poet on his bed of pain, who received no answers to his questions … Yet the last sounds died away in a seraphic, funereal song written on the eve of his death by a stout bourgeois who was known to be fond of playing cards in a bar between volleys of invective from his shrewish wife.

You might have known everything: war and peace and the
absence of peace; love and hate and the absence of love. You
might have approached everything: women, poverty and death.
You might have heard everything: been deluged with insults,
then heaped with praise. You might have lived all that, yet still
found yourself at the end as if without a biography. Virgin of
all you enjoyed reading in the biographies of others. Tiresome
postures and bad reputations. Contradictory rumours: He disliked improvisation and paper serviettes, and public transport,
and taxis, and Rilke, and Trakl, and music ... Trakl, really, are
you sure? He said so! He also insinuated the opposite. What
does it matter? And his poems on Schumann and Chopin –
music-lover's poems. No political understanding or sense of
humour. As far as political understanding goes, I won't argue –
but as for sense of humour! What an idea! Sometimes he'd have
to step aside to deal with a fit of laughter. He never made the
first move. Towards the end he put on the airs of a busi-
nessman. He couldn't be ruined as he was never rich. As a child
he went barefoot. He admired fine English cars. He knew
nothing about Chinese porcelain. How much hatred he stirred
up! How much fame he was consecrated by! A macabre fame.
How much incomprehensible joy, too! In the end, he played
himself like a gambler. He was his own only outlay. Cards on
the table. How many secrets! Always expectant. But no hope.
Never indifferent. How much movement! How much inertia!
Tragedies without causes, excessive felicities. As if fate had got
the roles mixed up and made a Professor Unrat into a Doctor
Faustus despite himself. "We have lived something other than
what we were, written something other than what we thought,
thought something other than what we expected, and what
remains is something other than what we planned." A life
without a story, in sum?

If he had been donjuanesque, it was towards Creation rather
than its creatures. He had trawled the unacknowledged regions

of humanity, and their hidden beauty. Just long enough to ascertain, like Don Juan, that you don't always understand what you seduce.

He would be read with surprise and some uneasiness, as his relative immortality itself confirmed. The blithe distress. The gloomy patience. What would age in his work would not be its horrors: history would vindicate them. But his rare illuminations would be less easily explained. His occasional wonderment at being here, even in horror. I ought to be just an end, he thinks, and not the beginning of anything else. But still, those poets of tomorrow who visit me today, what do they take away when they go home? My word: that spasm transmitted from the hanged man's body to the rope from which he hangs.

> "You've saved yourself, all right,
> but *who* is it you saved?"

At the beginning of June the pain becomes so intense that it even expels the terror of seeing it interrupted for good. Oedema binds your legs. Rheumatism brings you to your knees, lays you out, stands you up again, stiffens you, bows you down once more. The muscles are exhausted. The blood pressure collapses. You drown in yourself, but without hope of going straight to the bottom. And every part of the body that is not tetanised is afflicted by intolerable itching.

He is turned away from the Schlangenbad sanatorium because, they explain, his admission would be premature: if his blood pressure went up a bit, if he had injections to reabsorb his rheumatism, they might be able to examine him ... Has he, without showing anything, picked up the unstated message whose code he knows too well? Does he think: They don't know what I know? Or: They know, but are not saying. They think I don't know. Or again: They know, and know that I know. Or is he to enjoy what is known by that gentle word with almost maternal resonances: a remission?

This year, had he lived, his father would have been ninety-nine. So the son was not to live to the pastor's centenary? Poor father.

No more walks on the arm of Ilse Kaul, along the Kufsteiner Strasse, or in the park at Schöneberg. He urges his wife to read Faulkner's *Light in August*. Curious how a writer who talks about something quite different, even opposite to us, can still be close to us.

"Read quickly," he says to Ilse, "so that you have time to tell me your impressions."

However, he who has expatiated so much on death does not say much about it now, as if by accident. He just makes arrangements. He has never earned much of a living, but he is making sure his dying will not cost his dependents a penny. He has sometimes weighed heavily on the living while alive: he would like his death only to lighten their load. If it can be done, he should ask the Writers' Association to meet his hospital expenses. He also learns that the state of North Rhine-Westphalia intends to award him its annual prize. He could ignore these alms. But his final destitution inclines him to consider them. Ah well, if the provincial reward did come his way ... That is: if Ilse and Nele could receive it ... To hang on until then. It's a race between pain and honours: what a farce, yet again.

He has other worries, too. Check the scansion and tension of some of your own verses that you recite to yourself. Put in a word to help a new poet's career. Glimpse the face of a young woman that in another life you might have seduced, if only for a moment. Quickly learn something, anything, about the south seas, Easter Island, the death of Athens. As if that might be of use to the soul where it is going, might help it sail more ballasted, armed, pregnant, towards the void. Quickly give and receive, exchange, barter a scrap of immortality for a titbit of knowledge: he'd like to stop playing Doctor Faust, and content himself with being Dr Benn!

A drop of water swells on the petal of a rose Ilse has put in a vase on his night table. It grows, starts to roll, is about to fall … Is there no cliché you are to be spared?

Supposing, for the sake of argument, you did not know death in Venice, or that of Socrates, or those of Virgil or Ivan Ilych, or death in the afternoon. That still leaves death in Berlin.

On the grave of Eleonora Duse, Olga Signorelli had had the words engraved: "Pardoned, desperate, confident". Don't forget to say that no epitaph should be inscribed on yours. No statute, motto or sentiment. Let only the figures talk: 1886–1956.

Above all, don't go past the summer.

> "The worst:
> Not to die in summer
> When all is bright
> and the earth light to the spade."

Don't wait for autumn. "Never more lonely than in August," he had written in 1936, "the hour when all is accomplished." And twenty years passed. Only yesterday, he was asking:

> "Is it end or beginning?
> Then the hours will carry him
> to June, perhaps, with the roses."

And now June is over.

Ten years of shared life, Ilse, my wife. Hardly more time than two world wars chained end to end.

You are going to lose not only life but words, that you thought you owned. You're afraid they'll never pass through anyone else. It's not just death we're talking about, but censorship.

The Last Words

He once wrote on a scrap of paper – where? when? – *The Aesthetics of . . .* , and did not get any further. As if death had struck him down at that moment. But no, the paper has had time to yellow, the ink to fade. Did doubt beset him? Too much choice? Or did he simply give up believing in the "aesthetics" of anything at all?

A last letter to Oelze, your friend of long standing, the man who gave your work a ladder to climb. Considerately – for you know the idea of the end terrifies the addressee – you slip in the words: "One does not fall. One ascends." For what it's worth. Never does any harm ... But you don't hide the fact that to escape the pain you would gladly throw yourself under a bus.

Later, readers were to note that this text contained a gap. As if the recipient of the message, before passing it to the public domain, had covered up or scratched out a sentence. What did it say? That God existed? That He did not exist? Or that the poet was going to abridge his suffering, was using all his medical means to that end? More probably that.

The hands of the man and the woman never meet, he has written, over the unbridgeable abyss. His hand seeks the hand of Ilse Kaul. Finds it. In a will of a kind that can be opened before death, he has stipulated that he wishes to die in his wife's hands. As if he needed special authorisation from the Medical Faculty. So they joined hands at the moment when he was to pass through the door at whose threshold she would stay behind. One hand will close, clench, stiffen and go cold around another, warm and living hand. Presently this hand will have to free itself from the other as from a steel manacle. We are not quite there yet.

He thinks back to that holiday in Helgoland where he seems one night to have sought his companion's hand in this way. Unless, yet again, he had allowed or even encouraged her to go alone to Helgoland, since she was so fond of travel while he preferred to stay in Berlin-Schöneberg? Did he ever go to Helgoland, or Travemünde, or Wilhelmshaven, or Lake Constance, with or without her? No, it was at Knokke-Le Zoute that his hand once stretched out over the void in this way, and that time he had gone without her: he had been honoured, had made a speech about the haughty legitimacy, the desperate grandeur of words, their solitude, and then no hand had closed over his, as it did here, at Helgoland, Schlangenbad, Berlin, to ease his way. He remembers the literary prize that might still be his, and would solve many things: a jury favourable to him has promised to phone as soon as it has finished its deliberations. Meanwhile, he remembers Chopin, that is, his poem about Chopin:

> "Each finger was to play
> with a force consonant with its structure,
> the fourth being the weakest ... "

Chopin saying:

> "My attempts are completed in that measure
> which it was given to me to accomplish."

And I, wonders the man who has just quoted himself, what have I really finished, accomplished? Five or six adamantine lines that I've managed to nail into poems rotten with literature, that will survive in the memories of a handful of aesthetes who despise vulgar minds. He thinks: you fall, despite what I said. His hand fastens around his wife's. For now, you will fall no more. I've also, he thinks, handled a few hundred tarts riddled with pox to the roots of their hair, that not even an Alexanderplatz horse-knacker could have stomached. But at the end of the tunnel the only certain thing is the fragile wrist of a woman you've known since the day before, or so it seems: you've smoked the years like cigarette butts, in two or three puffs of oblivion ... All the same, you can have been wrong about practically everything, and at the end ring as true as the middle finger of Chopin's left hand on G sharp. The piano of our time has been tuned *in extremis*. It seems, thinks the doctor, that I have fine hands, of the kind one likes to join when they have not had time to compose themselves naturally, in the haste of departure.

"The rules of the prize," says a voice in the telephone receiver three steps from him, "stipulate that only a living artist can receive it. We are frightfully sorry ... "

Splashes of light from the crests of waves. No one will know that I've had to pass though everything to be nothing at the end. I've gone simply because I've exhausted everything. "More light!" said the Boss. How naive people are: stunned by the obviousness, the banality of it – though without reason. So let's be without imagination. Grounded Icaruses with cast-iron shoes. Well, now I've said my piece: no more jeremiads from me. Yet how could someone clinically dead not see more light – those who come back will confirm it ...

When the president of the jury for the prize of the state of North Rhine-Westphalia emerged from the room where they had been conferring, Berlin radio was already announcing the poet's death, so that he had to phone the Minister of Culture in person to raise a delicate point of procedure. The minister urged him to antedate the decision: "See that he gets it anyway, dammit!"

But in the end, all that remained was this woman's hand, her hand and her wrist, only this fine link to hold back the world: the hand of a woman who has loved you. *Te spectem suprema cum mihi venerit hora, te teneam moriens deficiente manu*, this woman's wrist for a man who would not let it go, frail sceptre of a king dispossessed of all except, for another moment, words, three or four words that will survive him for a fraction of a second, just long enough to breathe them out like a mist: Ilse, my darling, the proud poverty of words, why did I, tell me, no, tell me nothing, already I'm no longer speaking to you, why did I have to betray that pride for a moment, long ago, I think, but no, it was yesterday, yet I knew her well, knew only her, she knew only me, and again I recognise her: she was proud like love.